Mary Brock Jones lives in New Zealand but loves nothing more than to escape into the other worlds in her head, to write science fiction and historical romances. For many years, she was a sedate office worker by day and a frantic scribbler by night.

Her parents introduced her to libraries and gave her a farm to play on, where trees became rocket ships and rocky outcrops were ancient fortresses. She grew up writing, filling pages of notebooks and filling her head with stories but took a number of detours on the pathway to her dream job. After raising four sons, a career as a government veterinarian and more than one house renovated, her wish came true.

To keep up to date with her latest news and releases, sign up to her newsletter here:
www.marybrockjones.com/

Or find Mary here:
http://www.marybrockjones.com/
https://www.facebook.com/MaryBrockJonesAuthor
https://twitter.com/MaryBrockJones

By Mary Brock Jones:

NZ Historical Romances

A Heart Divided
Swift Runs the Heart

Hathe Series

Resistance: Hathe Book One
Pay the Piper: Hathe Book Two
Toil and Strife: Hathe Book One and Two
Aftermath: Hathe Book Three

Arcadia Series

Torn
Taken

TAKEN

Arcadia Book Two

Mary Brock Jones

Mary Brock Jones

Auckland, New Zealand

Author: Mary Brock Jones
Published by Mary Brock Jones
RD 1,
Warkworth, New Zealand 0981
www.marybrockjones.com

Book Layout © 2017 BookDesignTemplates.com

Cover design by Amygdala Design. www.amygdaladesign.net

Taken/ Mary Brock Jones
ISBN: 978-0-473-56962-4

Dedication

With thanks to all those who believed in me. Most importantly, to my husband Jeff.

CONTENTS

CHARACTER LIST AND GUIDE TO PRONUNCIATION i

CHAPTER ONE 11

CHAPTER TWO 33

CHAPTER THREE 57

CHAPTER FOUR 77

CHAPTER FIVE 101

CHAPTER SIX 117

CHAPTER SEVEN 135

CHAPTER EIGHT 155

CHAPTER NINE 175

CHAPTER TEN 189

CHAPTER ELEVEN 217

CHAPTER TWELVE 245

CHAPTER THIRTEEN 261

CHAPTER FOURTEEN 281

CHAPTER FIFTEEN 309

CHAPTER SIXTEEN 327

CHAPTER SEVENTEEN 343

CHAPTER EIGHTEEN 359

CHAPTER NINETEEN 379

CHAPTER TWENTY 409

CHAPTER TWENTY-ONE 427

CHAPTER TWENTY-TWO 439

CHAPTER TWENTY-THREE 465
CHAPTER TWENTY-FOUR 481
CHAPTER TWENTY-FIVE 497
CHAPTER TWENTY-SIX 521
CHAPTER TWENTY-SEVEN 537
CHAPTER TWENTY-EIGHT 559

CHARACTER LIST AND GUIDE TO PRONUNCIATION

GUIDE TO PRONUNCIATION

Plains names are pronounced similarly to their English sounds. Mountain region names describe a person's closest family connections. The emphasis is usually on the first syllable, but this can vary.

Mountain Language Sounds:
- 'ch at the end of a word - like the Scottish ch.
- 'h in the pronunciation guide indicates a degree of aspiration in the sound.
- a further, slight aspiration is shown by an apostrophe just before the letter in the pronunciation version (italicized - stress syllable shown in bold)

CHARACTER LIST

BEREN FAMILY

Sarwenna Beren (Sar): Eldest daughter. Union Representative for the Sulwith solar field workers.

Rhyn Beren: Sar's father. Workshop supervisor, Sulwith solar field.

Catra Beren: Sar's mother. Previously the Sulwith solar field union representative. Now the regional Councillor for the Sulwith region of the plains in the lower house of the Arcadian Council. A seat she had previously held when Sar was a young child.

Arionna Beren (Ari): Sar's younger sister. Thirteen standard years.

Daffin Beren (Daff): Sar's brother, aged ten standard years.

Finneas Beren (Finn): Sar's brother. Aged eight standard years.

WINTER FAMILY

Sol Winter: father and head of Winter Solaris

Helena Bascombe Winter: mother.

Caleb Winter: Eco-engineer with the Survey.

Ethan Winter: middle brother. Deputy head of Solaris

Silas Winter (Si): youngest brother. Systems programming genius.

Winter Solaris: - the solar energy company owned by the Winter family, usually shortened to Solaris. The dominant supplier of energy to the central zone of Protos and owner of the Sulwith solar field.

Den Coille family

Bram mar Gliocas duine Scathach den Coille: Father and head of den Coille

Bram mar **Glee**-o-cas d'win **'Skar**-thar'kh den Coyle

Bram, son of Gliocas, husband to Scathach, of the family Coyle.

Scathach ingh Coibhneas bean Bram den Coille: Mother and doctor.

'Ska-thar'k ine **Coy'**-nee-ars bee-**arn** Bram den Coyle.

Scathach, daughter of Coibhneas, wife of Bram, of the family Coille

Cumchdach mar Bram an Scathach den Coille: Eldest brother and heir to head of Den Coille.

Coo-'var'kh mar Bram an **'Ska**-thar'kh den Coyle

Cumchdach son of Bram (father) and Scathach (mother), of the family Coille.

Samhchair ingh Bram an Scathach den Coille: Eldest sister.

Sarm-**'hair** ine Bram an **'Ska**-thar'ch den Coyle

Samhchair, daughter of Bram (father) and Scathach (mother), of the family Coille.

Seolta mar Bram an Scathach den Coille: Second brother, generally held to be the cleverest (or most cunning) of the den Coille's.

See-**ole**-tar mar Bram an **'Ska**-thar'ch den Coyle.

Ceart mar Bram an Scathach den Coille. Third, largest and quietest brother.

Kee-'airt mar Bram arn **'Ska**-thar'ch den Coyle

Fioruisghe ingh Coille beann Caleb den Winter: younger den Coille daughter. An ecoengineer with the Survey and head of the Mountain zone survey team.

Fee-or-**'hrish**-gay ine Coyle bee-**arn Kay**-leb den Winter

Fioruisghe, daughter of the family Coille, wife of Caleb, of the family Winter.

Aigherach mar Bram an Scathach den Coille. The youngest den Coille. Around eighteen standard years in age.

Aye-ger-ar'kh mar Bram an **'Ska**-thar'kh den Coyle

Den Coille: name of the festia pollen company owned by the den Coille family. Wealthy food company in the central continental zone, Protos.

SULWITH TOWNSFOLK

Geordie Mactavie: autistic boy who can read the solar and air patterns to adjust solar sheet placement for maximum energy production.

Marget: town information clerk and receptionist for the union office

Gabrallie: Mayor's assistant (woman).

Old Rab (Rab Koor): one time head of the Solaris repair shop, now self-appointed custodian and doorman in the Solaris admin office.

Tom Crabster: Sulwith solar array manager – but Rhyn does most of the day to day organising.

Brill Devaney: chemical engineer. Search and Rescue squad member.

Tai Meynard: head of the Sulwith search and rescue squad and town.

Moline Granth: Solaris Sulwith safety office and acts as town forensic specialist.

Min Walters: chief nurse in the Sulwith emergency triage clinic.

Emilia: house matron of an in-an-outer hostel.

Doc Kaybee: the Sulwith clinic doctor. She has known Sar all her life.

Jarek, Phinnea and Marshea Drocash: Maxell Drocash's daughters. Phinnea is in Ari Beren's school class.

Maxell Drocash: A metallurgy technician at the Sulwith solar field.

Mairi: girl repairing roof after sandstorm.

Gered Burgaldor: Sulwith mayor.

Maddie: talented clothes designer in Sulwith

Faridtha Carmal: owner of a lodging house in the Beren's street. Takes Sar in when her family re-locates to Urbis.

SOLARIS EMPLOYEES

Joff: head of Solaris security.

Dan: the 'nice young man' heading the Solaris security team guarding Sar.

Doc Marsten: the Winter family doctor.

Graffin: Ethan's chief assistant

James: the Winter homestead factotum/butler

Wilmena: protocol department assistant, Solaris Dridust.

OTHERS

Anna ingh Eolas an Sumhneas den Falasch: fiancée of Cumchdach den Coille.

Ann ah ine **Ee** oh lars n **Soov** nee ars den **Far** lash

Marshal Marco an Fallon: Supreme Field Commander of the Federal Police of Arcadia (the marshals).

Deputy Malgrave: deputy to the Alliance representative on Arcadia.

Keownmar den Rith: head of a small company located on a northern mid-oceanic island. A distant cousin of den Coilles.

Hilmar a Kevand3: representative of the off-world company Kevand3 from the planetoid Surned

OTHER TERMS

Upper House. The upper house of the planetary government. Members are titled Representatives (eg Representative Joe Gibb)

Lower House: The Federal Assembly (eg Councillor Catra Beren).

Regional House: Local government body, governing a particular region eg Protos Central, which includes the plains, mountains and deadlands zone of TAKEN.

Moons: Jacopus is the dominant and most functional moon. The other small asteroid like moons are only visible in certain geographic locations to the naked eye, depending on coordinates and a clear sky eg the deadlands beyond Sulwith.

Protos: main (eastern) continent

Deuteron: second (western) continent

Feldwesten: third (southern) continent

Deadlands: the desert region of the eastern part of Protos central.

Nieten: native grazing animal farmed for meat & hides.

Wernet: - small bloodsucking animal (like hornet equivalent)

Dridust – largest town on the plains. Site of the Solaris head office and the main hospital for the plains region

Manascraoch - home city of the den Coilles. A fabled western mountain city, built entirely in the branches of enormous baullnia trees.

Festia – a swamp loving tree and source of the edible pollen sold by the Den Coille company

Brakka: derogatory slang word, equivalent to bastard. (means a small, ground dwelling pest animal)

Glitchit – small bug (like an ant). Stores water in an underground communal nest.

Falk – flying predator of the plains.

Salk – smaller cousin of the Falk, found only in the deadlands now, but just as lethal.

Foxllar – plains ground predator. Hunts nieten.

Chapper - ground dwelling animal used for food.

Smak – teenage slang for awesome, great, good.

Dask – equivalent of coffee. Main stimulant drink used on Arcadia.

Fratter – small desert predator, like a fox and a very persistent hunter.

Nanoglit – very small amount.

Natheen – browsing animal, cousin to the domesticated nietens of the open plains.

Ganda – a small, ground dwelling animal of the plains. Hides in burrows when Jack Robber avian hunting.

Farantee plant – web like plant living in desert margins where there is a trace of deep water.

Rakter – vicious desert ground predator. Cunning and devious. A smile of a rakter bite means untrustworthy and dangerous.

Berings Cooperative – a small trading company based on one of the transcontinental islands off the second continent.

MEASUREMENTS

Arcadia uses decimal based, Standard Galactic units for distance, time, mass etc. They have been expressed here in current day terms i.e. second, hour, day etc. However, that is only a current day translation. The Standard Galactic units used throughout the Alliance, irrespective of planetary or deep space location, are based on Natural Units of measurement i.e. on universal physical constants independent of planet or spatial location. On Arcadia, they are roughly equivalent to the following current Earth measurements.

DISTANCE

1 Standard galactic metre is roughly equivalent to 1.5 metres or 5 feet.

Standard galactic kilometre (generally referred to as Kays) = 1000 SG metres.

Time

Standard second is equivalent to 5 metric seconds.

Standard minute = 10 standard seconds.

Standard hour = 100 standard minutes, and is equivalent in usage to an hour, but in time is almost 1.5 hours

CHAPTER ONE

Mountains and valleys erupted from the floor in front of him, sharp-edged peaks slashing through the clouds and slopes mantled by an unbroken quilt of trees. A posse of storm fronts from the ocean roared up the steep faces, only to smash headlong into the wall of hot air rising up from the plains on the eastern side. A violent clash of opposing currents that fractured the clouds and released a torrent of water onto the greedy trees below. Water, dirt, saplings and bushes all swirled together in a nightmare slurry that barrelled down the hillside in a river of mud and debris thundering straight for the city woven through the forest of the lower slopes.

Ethan Winter watched his brother's mouth snap shut in a grim line. This was memory for Caleb, not forecasting.

A bare few tendrils of cloud survived the cataclysm to escape over the dividing range and drop their pitiful remnant of water onto the eastern slopes before disappearing into nothingness over the parched grasslands coming into focus on the far side of the ranges. A vast tapestry of ever moving grasses with the occasional town or tell-tale flash of a solar field the only signs of habitation. The image grew, spreading east to the searing heat of the deadlands where the last strands of the underground aquifers reaching under the plains failed and vast fields of solar panels cloaked the sands to soak up the energy that drove the world's industry. Empty sands devoid of life.

Still the holo-image grew. Ethan stepped back as the greedy sands lapped at his feet. "There's a point to this?"

His brother zoomed the field's controls back and down onto a large homestead in the middle of the grasslands. An archaic, very non-Arcadian house sitting in an oasis of trees and flowers and framed by a rim of native plantings. Ethan could recite the name of every plant and shrub, thanks to his mother and grandmother.

Ethan scowled. "I know what our home looks like."

"That's what it looks like today." Caleb's fingers played over the com patch on his wrist. "This is what it looked like after grandmother planted the Earth parts of the garden."

Ethan had seen the images before; he didn't need to see them again: the grass a rich green, flowers that would never survive today's long drys, a host of flying, crawling and zipping creatures playing in and around his grandmother's beloved trees, filling the air with song.

Then Caleb played on his com again and the image abruptly shifted. Death pervaded the scene. Dry, dusty grasses and dying trees with the song all but vanished. "This is what it will look like when our sons and daughters are grown."

Too obvious a line, brother. Caleb had only recently married his volatile mountain bride and they'd been too busy saving the planet to think of planning a family. Ethan resisted the impulse to take another step back from the encroaching sands. "I do know all of this. You've been shoving stories of impending disaster for Arcadia at me ever since I got out of prison."

A stab of pain twisted Caleb's mouth, but Ethan refused to let it silence him. He'd been pandering to his brothers' sensibilities over the prison thing for too long. "You think I don't know what will happen to our home, to the planet, if we don't change? What faces Solaris?"

Caleb lifted an eyebrow. "That's your main concern? The business?"

"If Solaris doesn't adapt, we'll be out of business, and that will hurt your shares as badly as mine, brother."

A growl from his brother. "I don't work for Solaris."

"How could I forget?" Ethan stabbed a finger against the hated Survey logo on his brother's chest. The same logo had cursed the tunics of the guards in his prison.

"Those scum weren't Survey. Not real Survey."

Maybe, but their boots had felt real enough. Suddenly, Ethan was tired of it all. "Thanks for the advice, brother. When you come up with a way to put it all to the Old Man, we can talk again. For now, I've work to do. Someone has to make the credits that pay for that lake of yours." And someone had to try to save Solaris, the company Ethan had loved ever since he'd been old enough to learn figures and listen to his father's talk at the evening table. The words had left him spell bound by the company that seemed to that young boy like a giant, intermeshing wonder to be endlessly savoured. A fascination he'd never lost.

Caleb flung out an arm and a nearby chair crashed to the ground. Another swipe of his hand and the holo-image flashed out of existence. "One day, brother..."

Ethan didn't want to know what came next. These days, he and Caleb could rile each other up so quickly that Ethan sometimes despaired of ever finding his way back to the big brother of his childhood.

He walked over to his desk and sat behind it, seeking refuge in the familiar façade of his office. The smooth walls, the desk from a named designer up in the capital city of Urbis, the expensive rug on the floor and the interactive artwork dancing in the corner. The office reeked of wealth, power and ambition, a useful tool against those who came in expecting a coddled and toothless second son of Sol Winter.

Caleb had never been one of those. Picking up the downed chair, he placed it very precisely in front of Ethan's desk then sat down, raising one eyebrow in that irritating way of his. Ethan had never managed to learn the trick of it. "Work?" said Caleb with a dry look and a snarl in his voice.

"Not all of us get to swing a shovel or stomp about in mud. If you want someone to change Solaris, then someone has to figure out how. I'm heading off on a work trip this afternoon and have to finish these prep notes before I leave."

Caleb looked about to explode. He stared at Ethan with storm-dark eyes and a clenched jaw. Ethan stared right back, in no mood to apologise. He waited, beyond caring whether this ended in a childish brawl. Maybe he needed it, needed to feel he could still make his big brother treat him like normal, or what used to be normal.

Caleb knew him too well. A twitch of that stern mouth and a narrowing of eyes at Ethan's hands laid flat on the desk, he drew in a breath, settled his shoulders and raised his hands, palm out. "Pax, little brother," he said in that cool voice of his. "You're good at what you do, and Si and I both know it, including what you did to repair the mess those parasites left of Solaris after they stole it from us."

"It's not over yet."

A flush. Caleb hated reminders of his head office's double dealing as much as he hated reminders of what his family had suffered. "You'll fix what's left and the company's in good enough heart to support the changes."

Tell that to the Old Man, Ethan wanted to say. But there was no point. Their father was a law unto himself.

"So where are you off to?" said Caleb, shoving those long legs of his out in front of him and too obviously trying to be polite.

"The den Coille brothers, then up north to the Sulwith field."

Caleb shot up, all signs of good will vanished. "You don't need me then." A glare, a quickly hidden shaft of pain in those clear blue eyes, and he swung around and marched out the door.

Ethan should have known better than to mention the brothers, but Caleb had rattled him. The den Coilles might be related to Caleb, thanks to his marriage to their sister, but it changed nothing. Both Caleb and their youngest brother Si took Ethan's friendship with their one-time business rivals as a personal insult, and there was little he could do to change it. Ethan's brothers had managed to stay free in those dark days when the den Coille and Winter wealth was grabbed by their enemies, for which Ethan was eternally grateful. Yet because of that, they could never understand what those months in captivity were like for Ethan and the den Coille brothers, wondering each day whether it was their last. He sighed and fingered his com, bringing up the records he needed.

A few hours later, he hissed a curse and slapped away the files. Thanks to Caleb and his nagging, all he could see was that holo-field instead of the tables and figures in front of him. Why Caleb imagined he had to bludgeon Ethan with the situation on Arcadia was beyond him. Ethan saw enough in the reports coming across his desk every day to give the proof to his brother's lectures, and after nearly dying thanks to the short-sighted greed of others, he wasn't about to fall victim to it himself.

"Winter Two signing out," he said to his com system. The all secure code came back and he rose from his desk in relief. A quick trip to grab his gear from his quarters above the company offices and he headed off to the landing field. Moments later, he'd buckled into his flyer and lifted into the air above the sprawl of the Solaris head office complex. He needed better company than dry data and sibling niggles.

The inn stood four-square on the edge of the Junction City landing field, as it had for hundreds of years, and looked little different now than in the original images. Stone walls latticed with wooden beams, windows shining in the stray beams of sunshine, and a mix of native plants and settler flowers gathered in cheerful consort around the front entrance. Nestled into a last fold of the great ranges splitting the continent north to south, Junction City sat at the convergence of all the routes from the continent's central zone up through the one valley lying between the western and northern ranges. It was the easiest pathway through to the fertile down lands and delta country of the continent's northern zones. As a natural meeting place for travellers, the landing field inn had long been considered neutral ground for mountain and plains folk alike. A last finger of mountain forests beckoned from the bar windows while below, the grand sweep of the plains rolled out into the far distance. When Ethan walked into the bar, the room held patrons wearing both the dun of the plains and the forest green of the mountains, filling the air with a comfortable mix of standard, mountain and plains speech.

The doorman cleared his ID without checking it and he made his way to his usual table. The den Coille brothers had already arrived, taking the seats with the best view of the covering trees as if needing proof they could always reach them.

Sometimes, he thought none of the den Coilles would ever willingly leave the sanctuary of the forest again.

"Ethan. About time." The eldest brother stood. Dark like all the den Coilles and with the compact build of the mountains, Cumchdach den Coille was a man Ethan had come to trust in those bleak prison days. His booted foot shoved a chair toward Ethan. It was the one Ethan always sat in, set against the wall and looking out to the bar. The inn was safe enough, but he still kept a watchful eye on the rest of the room as they talked.

Then he stiffened. The brothers stopped talking and twisted round to look.

"What in all the bogs is the Alliance doing here?" said Cumchdach, glaring at the precisely dressed official walking in the door. Ethan had met the woman too many times for comfort, but this bar was the last place he'd expect to see Deputy Malgrave, second in charge of the Alliance office on Arcadia. Officers of the all powerful organisation that was final arbiter for the human-settled planets rarely ventured out of Urbis, preferring to keep their publicly visible actions confined to the government chambers of the capital. More worrying, the woman made straight for the brothers and Ethan. The Alliance made no secret of keeping tabs on the den Coille and Winter families since the recent troubles, but they were usually more discreet.

She stopped at their table. "Ser Winter, Sers den Coille."

Ethan had to work hard to dredge up his usual façade of courtesy. "Sera Malgrave. You're a long way from home."

The Deputy gave no sign of discomfort, standing square and solid from the severe cut of her grey hair to the off-world boots on her feet. "I had a function at the university here and was told that you had all gathered at the inn. It seemed a useful opportunity to confirm that your families remain aware of the Alliance's concerns for this world."

The Alliance's threat to close down Arcadia and forcibly remove all settlers from this world unless they stopped destroying its environment, she meant. Ethan smiled at her with all his teeth. "Fully aware, thank you, Deputy. Solaris has nothing to hide and is cooperating with all Federal directions."

"As is Den Coille," said Cumchdach beside him, one hand firmly clamped on his youngest brother's arm."

"Excellent," said the woman. "I look forward to viewing the results of that cooperation in the near future. I will be reviewing the financials for both your companies in the next quarter." A last stare at all of them and she turned around and walked out, back rigid and head high as if unaware of the five pairs of eyes following each footfall.

Cumchdach glared after her. "Did that woman just threaten to seize our companies?"

"She can try," said Ethan. "Won't do her any good."

Regardless, none of them relaxed their vigil. Cumchdach activated his com and ran a scan of the bar and exterior. "She's gone," he said after a moment. "Her flyer lifted off and I can't see any official Alliance staff registering on scan."

"Just the unofficial ones," growled Seolta, the brother next in age.

"Don't forget the Feds. They're bound to be prowling around too."

"As always," said Ethan. He leaned back and let his gaze travel around the room. Too many refused to meet his eye.

"I need a drink," he said and reached for the bar slot to dial up the strongest brew on offer. The den Coille brothers copied him, and all of them sat in silence, slowly drinking as they watched the doors. Only when the first drinks had been downed did any of them begin to drop their guard.

Not that they relaxed, but then, they never did outside their home territories these days. Slowly, talk resumed.

"Where to next, Ethan," asked Cumchdach, passing him another drink.

"Out east. Our biggest solar array, right on the edge of the deadlands."

A grimace twisted that strong face. "Rather you than me."

Ethan grinned. No, he couldn't see the mountain man going there. The den Coilles appeared to think a drought had hit if they had to pass more than a day without rain or the shade of trees.

"You'd go if there was money in it," he said.

"Desert and blazing hot skies?" A belly-deep laugh. "Nah. I'd send Seolta."

"And he'd do it," said Aigherach, who was too young to be here, but no one was going to say that to a boy who'd lived through hell. He still had his limp, but the bright colour on his cheeks was back.

Seolta's mouth spread into a smooth smile, hands rubbing together. "For a healthy fee, brother, from your personal account."

Cumchdach shoved a mug of frothing liquid at him, stabbing a credit mark at the slot.

"And that's the only fee you'll be getting today, Seolta," laughed Ethan. He ignored the hand-flip back. He and Seolta had never been fully at ease with each other. "Nor would I let any of you near one of Solaris's solar plants. You den Coilles are making quite enough money on your side of the mountain. The plains are Winter lands, even if the cursed Survey is trying to turn our beautiful desert into a tragging marshland like your hillsides."

A roar of laughter greeted the old joke. Once it would have been a call to corporate battle, but that was before he and the den Coilles had been captured and threatened with execution by government officials gone rogue. The Ecological Survey was the arm of government charged with protecting the environment of the planet Arcadia, and most of its staff gave their lives willingly in that service, until head office hijacked the department and turned it into a corporate raider. His elder brother Caleb and his wife Fee fought back, hiding out for months until in one swift move they and the Federal police reminded the Survey bosses who really ran Arcadia and freed Ethan and the den Coille brothers from prison. He shifted in his seat as an old twinge in his side bit back and thrust the memory down. He was free now and would remain so.

Seolta crashed his mug on the table, sloshing drink too near Ethan. "How's your brother's lake coming on."

"My brother and your sister," Ethan reminded him and watched in satisfaction Seolta's hand clamp down on the mug handle. "When I saw them yesterday, Fee told me they're making good progress."

"Fioruisghe," growled Ceart, the fourth and most silent of the brothers.

"Give it up, brother," said Aigherach, laughing. "Ethan's a plainsman."

"And they know nothing of manners," shoved in Seolta.

Ethan nearly rose to the bait, then saw the suspect tilt of the mountain man's mouth. Fortunately, Cumchdach decided to intervene before it got serious, jabbing Seolta in the ribs and raising a shoulder in apology. Not for the first time, and Ethan doubted it would be the last. He raised a hand in thanks. Seolta's biting wit had been tough enough to stomach before prison, but it had hardened into something dark since their release.

"So this power plant," said the eldest den Coille. "Is it profitable?"

Ethan grunted a yes. "The most profitable field we have. That's the problem."

"It uses those old sheets your brother complains about? Cheap and profitable but kill everything under them?" guessed Cumchdach.

Caleb was an ecological engineer, one of the Survey's best, but he was also a Winter. He knew solar power generation inside out and had been nagging his father for years to change the solar array types they used. "Yes," was all Ethan said now.

"And the ground under them?"

"Marginal desert land, becoming drier every day. Cut the field down in size, and the Survey can revegetate to push the desert back."

His big brother loved their land in the same way Ethan loved the business. Yes, the plains were home to Ethan, the dry endless expanse as much a part of him as the tables of figures and projections he revelled in. His real delight, though, lay in the endless challenges that came with a company the size of Solaris. While his father lived and breathed, Ethan had no hope of taking control of it but, one day, Ethan would put into action all those dreams he'd had since boyhood.

"So you going to downsize or close it?"

"Depends on what I find when I get there. I'm hoping that a change in array types and downsizing will do the job. Standard redundancies and retraining options for all redundant workers, with relocation assistance. The normal package. It should save enough jobs to keep the Assembly off our backs."

"The Feds will make you close it," growled Seolta. "Just to show they can."

"We'll see." Ethan picked up his drink. "They have to deal with Solaris first, and then there's the locals. That's the other problem."

Seolta's dark eyes flashed in glee. "You have union problems," he crowed.

Flying over the deadland plains a few hours later, Ethan couldn't get Seolta's words out of his head. No one had ever accused the second den Coille brother of stupidity, and this time he'd been right on the money. Ethan had learned long ago to never make decisions without going to a site in person, to feel the land and sky, meet the locals and match figures with reality. To see if some of his other ideas might work there. After that, it should be a simple matter of finalising the staff figures and agreeing to a plan for those losing their jobs. A routine business change. Except the ground below gave the lie to it being so simple and, for the first time, he knew doubt. Anyone who lived on the edge of the deadlands had to be tough.

His flyer began to track over the solar field.

The Sulwith Solar Array was a jewel in the Solaris empire, a truly enormous expanse of solar collection sheets covering the land as far as the eye could see and more. A layer of sheets that smothered the life out of anything beneath them, leaving barely a gap open to the sky. When he'd first read through the field data, he'd mused that the workers running Sulwith were born with magic sensors in their veins, fine tuning the alignment of the panels to soak up the strongest rays of the sun in a way unmatched by any other Solaris plant. Now he saw the proof of it as the intensity readings from his scanner showed little change from one end of the field to the other.

That changed nothing, according to the Survey. The holo-image Caleb had shown him had been no flight of fancy. Thanks to Solaris covering much of the plains in their solar panels and the den Coille's planting of the mountain slopes to the west with the swamp-loving festia trees, source of a highly nutritious pollen, the climate in this part of their world had become dangerously unstable. Too much rain drowned the western slopes of the mountains, undermined the soil structures causing lethal landslides like the one that had nearly destroyed the den Coille's home city a few months ago; too little fell here, turning grass and scrub lands into ever expanding desert. Caleb's holo-vid had not exaggerated. The two opposing climate zones clashed in an escalating war right over the jagged peaks of the western ranges, worsening the effects on both sides.

He flew low over the last of the sheets, heading for the line of dusty hills at the end of the solar array. Sheltered in a fold of the hills, the town of Sulwith was home to the plant's workers, and not much else. He pulled up the plant file as he skimmed over the endless array but didn't need the precise voice of his com program to tell him facts he already knew too well: profit high, worker skill high. Other options for workers in Sulwith—nil. Not that it should be a problem. Any worker would surely jump at a chance at escaping this forbidding place.

"Union representative bio," he ordered his com.

"Recently changed," said the voice. He knew that. Catra Beren had been a thorn in his father's side for years, and he'd made no secret of his glee when she won back the seat of Representative to the Council for this region. Let Urbis cope with the fiery trade unionist. Anything to keep her away from Solaris' boardrooms.

"Has her replacement been elected yet?" It wasn't in the file he'd drawn from company records when he left Dridust.

"Her daughter, previously her principal assistant. Image on screen now."

A crowd scene, blown up to zoom in on the woman standing beside the instantly recognisable figure of Sera Catra Beren. The mother was in full warrior mode, haranguing the crowd and stirring up the workers, but the woman behind her stood silent, face closed and body rigid. She had her mother's dark hair but cut short and wore a plain tunic, soft trousers and tidy shoes, looking like any one of the women working in admin in offices here and up in Urbis. A woman content to merge into the backdrop of her mother's energy.

But this woman had taken over the union at a time when all the workers had to know change was coming, and there was something about that closed face. "Tell me about her."

A millipause of silence, then the cool voice said, "The company records are still being updated."

"We must have a bio at least."

"Nothing yet recorded in the company files. The appointment is still being processed."

"Then search other places," said Ethan caustically, vowing to chew someone out when he got back home. It wasn't only Solaris technology that was past its use-by date. Thankfully, a file soon popped up. The com intoned the readout. Bare data only, telling him little of the woman behind the figures.

Education, good. The Plains Higher School in Junction City may not be as prestigious as the elite business school in Urbis he'd attended, but the college was known for a liberal bent and had a reputation for turning out practical and well rounded graduates thanks to an insistence its students start with a broad base covering the arts, sciences and technical areas, then specialise later.

Financials, inadequate by his standards, but typical of a worker in the town of Sulwith, so unlikely to be bribable. Not after being raised by Catra Beren.

"Her name?"

"Sarwenna Beren," said the com.

"Pretty." Not the kind of name he'd expected from Catra Beren, but he liked the sound of it. It suited that hint of intrigue in her face. In other circumstances, he might have explored it further, but not today. Not when they must be on opposite sides of an unpleasant necessity.

"This is what those solar arrays are killing," his brother had said to him the last time they'd both visited a Solaris solar field, a bitter anger in his eyes as his fingers dug into the dirt and pulled up a slug-like creature. The billyup was unique to the drier parts of the plains. "Change the arrays and find other ways of making money. You can make the Old Man do it, if anyone can, but if Solaris keeps on spreading out over these lands, they will become deadlands in truth."

Caleb and his Survey had won that argument, and now Ethan had to tell a town that their future was about to crash into oblivion.

Below him, a cluster of buildings huddled for shelter in the space between the low range of hills and the single landing pad of the town. He swallowed and set the controls for landing.

A crowd of officials stood waiting as he walked down the ramp from his flyer. He'd been taught well by his father and smacked on the smile that said all was well and he was in charge. It worked, in a fashion, but he suspected it was mostly fear of what he'd come to say keeping them in check.

"Shall we go down to the solar field?" he said to the welcoming officials and headed down the road before any could argue. *Choose your ground, boy, and make sure it's Solaris-owned ground.* The maxim had always worked for him in the past, but as he rounded the bend of the road and saw the beginning of the vast swathes of the solar array, he discovered today might not be so simple. A crowd of people stretched across the road, blocking the entrance, people dressed in all manner of clothes. Some wore the logo of Solaris, identifying them as workers in the plant, but the rest came in all shades and styles: crisp business tunics of the type worn by accountants and administrators, the rough overalls of builders and trades contractors, the open-necked tunics of shopkeepers, and the smart but practical suits of teachers and medical staff. The entire workforce of the solar plant and most of the adults in the town, he'd guess.

Their faces turned toward him as he came into sight. Gruff, wary, and too many with belligerently pinched mouths.

At the front, stepping forward into the clear space between him and the crowd, stood one woman, legs square on the ground, hands on hips and a definite upward tilt to her chin. She swept a glance over the crowd arrayed behind her, as if collecting their attention and channelling it through her. These people are mine, said that glance, and I will stand for them.

The daughter of Catra Beren waited to greet him.

The strength of her hit him square in his gut, the hint of intrigue in the file images nothing to the force of the living woman. He'd been right about her face. Strong bones beneath wispy spikes of hair with sun-touched ends. His feet lost their pattern for an instant, and he had to quickly hide a stumble. This woman mustn't see how she affected him. He thrust up his head and fixed his most beguiling work smile on his face. He'd been defusing worker conflicts since his late teens when he started working in Solaris. He increased his stride to throw off the gaggle of officials squawking at his heels and closed on the woman standing at the head of the crowd. Immediately, all those faces behind her switched focus, staring at her as if waiting. As if demanding a miracle from her, came the incongruous thought in his head.

She was taller than he'd realised, coming near up to his chin, with slim curves skimmed by brightly coloured tunic and trousers. His eyes swept over her: hair lit with a thousand lights, a luscious mouth with a secret hiding in the corners, and a body that belonged in dreams.

The kind that had no place here.

He stopped halfway between them, holding up a hand to the company staff behind in a firm order to stay back, then smoothed out the smile on his face as he looked directly at her, changing it to the smile of a boss prepared to listen but not bend. Her chin lifted and the sparkle in her eyes said she was as familiar with the unspoken language of negotiations as he. He waited. If she wanted to talk, she'd have to move toward him. Move enough that both would have to raise their voices to be heard by others.

For a moment, he didn't think she'd do it. Then she glanced at the crowds behind her and stepped forward, thrusting out a hand, and something jolted inside him. Something new and unexpected.

"Ser Winter? Sar Beren, union delegate for this field."

He lifted his hand to clasp hers, giving her the expected formal bow and releasing her after a too brief touch of the warm softness of her skin, then looked closely into her eyes—dark and light, rich brown and warm gold. He gave in to the grin that had been threatening to well up inside since his first sight of her.

"Sar?"

"Short for Sarwenna."

"A pretty name. Why shorten it? Sounds like Ser or Sir."

A satisfied smirk flitted across those fascinating lips. "Yes, it does," she said, "and that suits me fine."

"Is that so?" He turned to take in the rest of the crowd, giving them a practiced wave and a cheery greeting then turned back to her and let his smile slip. "I don't remember making an appointment with the union."

Her voice lifted. "The folks behind me need to hear what you're planning. You going to close down this field?"

He noted the fists set firmly against the curves of her hips and pitched his voice to reach right to the back of her crowd of supporters. "You have to know what we're facing. Everyone on Arcadia does. We've pushed our world to its limit, and the planet is hitting back. Because of this, the Alliance has given our government no choice. We change how we operate, or we lose everything." She said nothing, those fascinating eyes studying him, challenging him. He lowered his voice, taking a step closer and speaking to her only. Before he arrived, he hadn't intended saying anything to her, but this woman demanded honesty, he discovered. "You want to know about jobs. The simple answer is, I don't know yet. That's why I'm here. The best option: we update the solar arrays. We'll have to cut non-tech staff but may need to increase tech staff. On the plus side, changing the array may free up land for other uses."

What kind, he had no idea. Even without the solar arrays, precious little grew out here, and mineral wealth had long since been discounted. But that wasn't for him to find. The company provided generous redundancy packages to help those who lost jobs. With luck, some of them might use it to make new businesses here. He had enough to do saving Solaris.

A boy strolled along the front of the tense crowd, oblivious to them, his eyes on the constantly changing sheets of the solar field.

"And what about him?" said the woman.

"Him?"

She called the boy over. "Hey, Geordie. How's the sky?"

A smile lit the boy's face, as if true happiness were in his grasp. "Good today, Sar. Patterns is good." A wave, and he strolled off, still staring at the top of the arrays and whistling slightly off tune.

Ethan quirked his head in query at Sarwenna. He refused to use that stupid short version. "Geordie?"

A frown on her face said he should know the name.

"Haven't you read the personnel lists? Geordie MacTavie. He's why this field is so efficient."

Ethan couldn't say he was much clearer.

"Geordie sees the light above the solar sheets. He sees patterns, knows when we need to change the alignments. He's why this field is set so accurately." She scowled. "It's what he's best at. All he's good at."

Aah. So one of the workers who would be lost. Some of the staff here had never done any other kind of work.

"Take away those flat sheet arrays, and you take away his whole world."

"There are other array types. Ones that don't cover all the ground, but still give us good solar conversion rates."

"Yeah, but Geordie doesn't know those arrays."

A scuff of dust. The boy was back, and by the look on his face, he'd heard their words. Next minute, Ethan felt a sudden sharp blow to his leg. One that landed on a place too often hit before, and Ethan was suddenly back in a jail cell with a scowling guard standing in the door and four blank walls locking him in. He lifted a hand in defence, then stopped, just in time. A memory. That's all it was.

"You all right?" said the woman, and he cursed inside. The flashbacks came rarely now, but that blow had done it. He gave his head a slight shake, breathing in the hot dusty air. He was home, in the plains. Safe and free.

"Just a long flight up and an early start," he said and hoped she'd believe the explanation.

Then she shrieked, "Geordie, come back."

The boy had done more than hit Ethan in the shin. He'd taken off, running madly down through the array, flitting under the tilted sheets and heading straight out to the desert land beyond.

"Come back," she called again, with a note of panic in her voice he didn't expect. Then that luscious mouth snapped into a grim line and she swivelled around to the men standing nearby. "Bob, set off the alarm. Theo, call up the rescue service. Set watches on every boundary."

"He's just upset. He'll come back when he calms down," said Ethan.

"Upset? You turn his life upside down, and you think he's merely upset? Go back to your shiny office, Ser Winter. We have a boy to rescue."

She began running, throwing words out to the rest of the crowd. "Get in touch with his mother. Tell her we'll bring him home safe."

Even to him, that last bit sounded more wish than promise. He ran after her and grabbed her by the arm.

"Why the panic? If he grew up here, he knows these lands."

She twisted hard, then gave up trying to escape and glared at him. "Yeah, he does. But when Geordie gets panicked, all that knowledge goes missing and he runs to the one place he belongs. The solar arrays and the desert. Only he forgets how to survive there. Last time, it was three days before we found him and he'd nearly died of dehydration. And that time, he had a water bottle on him."

"And he doesn't now?" It was the one thing any plainsman always carried, even just to walk down the street of a town like this.

"That's what he threw at your leg."

Ethan ignored the angry spark in her eyes and made a sudden decision. "My flyer can scan this area better than anything else you've got here. I'll fly it but I need someone who knows this terrain. You coming, Sera Beren?"

She looked into the arrays where the boy had disappeared. Not even the trace of a dust cloud. A twist of that fascinating mouth then, "Yes, I'm coming."

The grim set of her face remained unchanged as she climbed aboard and settled herself into the co-pilot seat. Her hands on the seat twitched and he discreetly locked down the controls and his files. The way she sat said she'd flown before, though none of those flyers would have been of the standard of his. One of the newest off the assembly line, it had features found on few others, installed here because he'd been at Higher School with a son of the manufacturer. One of those was a high-spec heat scanner that could distinguish a human boy from the sun-baked land and oven-high temperatures of the solar sheets.

"Ready," he said, lifting off.

Her hands gripped the arms of her seat, but she merely nodded. He'd taken off straight up and at speed, and maybe that was questionable, but something in him wanted to unsettle this woman. That stone-cold face of hers was getting to him.

Then he told himself not to be such an oaf. He was too old to be scaring girls for a reaction, and this woman didn't deserve it. Even now, her eyes peered anxiously out the window as they hovered low over the arrays. He recognised that look. She wasn't giving up till she had the boy safe in her care again.

He set his scanner to probe and widened the margin. "Which direction would he take?" She pointed left and he swerved gently. "Don't worry. Most teen boys I know live only to fill their stomachs. He'll get hungry soon enough and come home."

"Geordie's not like most boys," she said, staring fixedly out the window.

"In what way, apart from being a genius when it comes to setting solar arrays."

"He's just … not."

There was something in the tone of her voice, and she refused to look at him, staring fixedly ahead. Whoever this boy was and whatever his makeup, she felt responsible for him. Well, he knew what that was like. His brother and mother had been drumming responsibility into him as long as he could remember. For the Solaris workers, for family, for the business if it should, horror of horrors, one day fail. For his younger brother and for Caleb, though he doubted his older brother would thank him for that. Caleb had been standing up for him and Silas since they were all small children, and Ethan had learned young not to get into the kind of fights that left Caleb bleeding or bruised.

"We'll find him," he heard himself promising now. He brought up the tracking schematics and showed her how it worked as he traced the boy's flight from when he bolted into the solar field.

Her eyes widened. "Why does a wealthy solar power businessman need a high spec tracking program?"

He shrugged. "I felt like it." He wasn't about to admit to this woman that the tracking device was part of a sophisticated defence system built into his flyer. Ethan Winter wasn't going to be taken prisoner again, by anyone.

She answered him with silence and a pointed turn of her head to follow the tracking results. The motion was so obvious he had to smile. He was finding this woman made him do that a lot, and always in ways he doubted she'd appreciate. He glanced at her again and caught a swift turn of her head back to the display. Was that a flush on her cheeks?

This mad search may turn out not too bad after all.

CHAPTER TWO

A few hours later, he wasn't so sure. They lost the boy's tracks not far into the array, the heat pattern disappearing as if the boy had never been.

Sarwenna frowned at the screen. "He must have picked up a box cart. At least it'll have water." She sounded no less worried, and Ethan dutifully kept tracking the boy's course.

Without success. Nothing, not even the box cart Sarwenna said he must've taken. A small vehicle used to scoot under the solar array, its heat signal should have been visible to his scanner.

"He'll be using a cool kit," she said to his frustrated demand. "All the carts carry spares. It stops the heat trace."

"So he has water, a cart and protective clothing. Tell me again why you're worried about him."

She frowned and kept peering intently at the screen. "He's Geordie. Normal rules don't apply."

Which made no sense at all but Ethan didn't push it. Not with that furrow carved into the forehead of her stunning face. When the predicted flight path gave no result, he coded in a systematic search pattern over the whole array. Hours later, they neared the north-eastern corner with still no sign of the boy.

"You sure he's human?" His precious state of the art tracker had found zilch. A few ground-dwelling gracks, hardy remnants of a once healthy population, a scattering of Caleb's beloved billyups, and the odd old man buzzer, swooping down to catch a grack that stuck it's head up between the overlapping sheets of the array. But nothing boy-sized. "How well does the boy know this land?"

"As well as anyone," she admitted with a grudging reluctance in her voice."

"Well enough to hide out for months and no one the wiser?"

"Yes. Doesn't mean he'd survive. When he panics, he forgets the important stuff. And you scared him today," she said, turning to glare at him, looking him straight in the face for the first time in hours. And that made him mad too. His sense of the ridiculous had been stretched long past tolerance level.

Suddenly a spatter from the tracker. "Is that his trace?" She lurched forward to peer at the readout.

Finally. If this trip had been some stupid impulse to play hero to impress the girl, it had long worn thin. He linked into the system. "Looks about right." He zoomed in on the signal, quickly picking up the residual trace of a human's passage. "Just to the north of us, right on the edge of the array. Looks like he never ran under the sheets after all," he said in disgust. "He's been tracking along the field's edges all the time."

Suddenly, a blaze of energy smashed through the flyer, setting every hair on his body on edge. "Full shielding," he shouted to the system, and smashed a hand onto the emergency button, activating the crash harnesses "What in shards was that!"

It came again, and this time he held hard to the controls, fighting to keep his flyer level while his fingers flicked through all the emergency protocols. "It's coming from down there."

"Geordie!" she cried. "We have to save him."

"I have to save us first." A lurch sideways as another bolt shot up and grazed the flyer's defences. "Com, get a fix on that energy bolt."

"Coordinates coming through now, boss," said the cool voice of his system. A red-coloured patch appeared on his ground view screen. "An electro-stasis field generated from the marked solar sheet locus."

"The solar field is firing at us?" His jaw dropped. "A Solaris solar field is trying to kill me?"

"The sheets in that locus have been modified to create a linked hyper-concentrating field with a central funnelled core."

He glared at Sarwenna Beren, white-faced beside him. "You said all that boy could do was sense the sun's rays and align the field's settings."

A buck of the ship and his worst fears were realised. His shielding was good, but the energy from this backcountry boy's cannon had damaged it badly. He'd already lost critical systems. "Look at that readout." He flicked his com screen to public view. "That boy of yours is creating a randomly varying beam that my shields can't predict. If he keeps it up, this flyer is done for. Hold tight, and find a landing place for us."

She frowned, screwing up her eyes as she stared out the viewscreen. No histrionics, for which he was heartily thankful. "There's a flat, sandy valley north of here with a sound base layer. It will give us the best cushioning for an unpowered landing."

"I'm patching you into the system. Emergency protocol X31. Give the com the coordinates."

She did as ordered. He looked at the valley she'd identified. Long and wide, with the substratum confirmed by the geotech analysis. The flyer's system gave it a bare positive rating, but it would be enough. Another beam clipped them, just catching his tail. They were nearly out of range.

"Set in the glide curve to landing point," he ordered the com. The graphics came up. It was possible. Just. His fingers clenched in the directional field then raced across the control panel. "Hold tight," he said to the woman beside him.

Sar gripped the arms of her chair and pulled tighter her safety webbing. If only she had her hands on the controls, not this corporate pretty boy. Despite the deep voice that sent shivers through her and those crisp accents, he was too smooth, too like all the others she'd faced off across company tables.

Too handsome to be real.

She hated not being in control.

A shimmer of energy rocked them again. Another bolt. Not from Geordie. He had some special skills, but that energy cannon wasn't in his grab bag. No, she had a good idea who had made those energy bolts and it set every nerve in her body on edge. When she got back, someone was in for a sharp piece of her mind.

If she got back.

A wild rocking hit the flyer. She glanced at the man beside her. His face hadn't changed from the corporate air of assurance he'd been wearing ever since he'd shown up, but his hands on the controls moved expertly and his orders to his com were that of a man in command. He may be a coddled rich boy, too handsome and with eyes that sent a shock through her body every time he turned them on her, but the man knew how to fly. Maybe, just maybe, he could bring them safely through this. She focussed on the forward viewscreen and her hands clenched tighter on the chair.

"A bit to the left. That valley over the next hump."

The flyer veered left. Then a red band came up. She dragged in a breath. "All engines gone?"

"A couple of auxiliaries are still functional but, yeah, we're in an unpowered glide."

"Have you done this before?" she had to ask.

"A few times, but not in an emergency without backup. You'll need to brace when we come in to land."

He might have been discussing the latest price of Solaris energy units, so cool was his voice. Pride forced her to match him, but she would have loved to break down and scream in terror. For once in her life, couldn't she be helpless and broken?

Don't be an idiot, Sar. This is not the time or place, just like all those other times and places.

"Brace."

She grabbed hold at the brisk order. Through the front canopy, the ground rushed up to meet them. Soft sand, with an underlayer of hard rock. His fingers played across the boards.

Out here, you practiced emergency protocols the same way other folks learnt to prepare dinners, and she automatically assumed the crash position. The shock-proof webbing slapped hard to her head and body, as she thrust her feet flat against the floor and her hands clung to the slots on the arms. In a flyer of this pedigree, the frame of her seat would absorb any backlash and keep her safe. She hoped.

She shut her eyes.

A graunching, smashing boom. Creaking metals and a man swearing.

She opened her eyes cautiously and looked through the viewscreens. Gone the rush of the ground toward them. Gone the sky. All she could see in front of her was sand. Millions and millions of grains of sand swallowing them up.

"We're stuck."

"No, you chose well." The corporate smoothness abandoned, his grin breathed triumph at being alive. "The top hatch is clear. We'll have to wait for the sand to settle from the impact, then we can move out."

"By which time, the rescue party should have arrived." She had to smile back at him.

His grin disappeared.

"What's wrong?"

His fingers played across the com sliver on his wrist in increasingly agitated patterns. "My com's out. No send or receive function."

"I have mine," she said, feverishly signalling hers into life and activating the find sequence.

"Check the range."

She brought up the schematics. Then swore. "Nothing. Transmission signal is zero. That's impossible."

He toggled the flyer control then cursed as a screen came up with an unmistakable error warning. "That beam's warped the core of the flyer's system, and it's sending out a blocking signal."

She couldn't believe this. "You must be able to fix it."

"Maybe, once it's back in a town with proper equipment. For now, we're stuck."

"Don't you have a backup beacon."

He nodded. "But it works best from a high point, not down in this bowl. I'll need to get to the top of those hills. What's the temperature outside?"

"Too high to leave now. Staying with the flyer is our best chance of being found."

Strangely, he didn't scoff like she'd expected. Corporate money wranglers always thought they knew best and that field workers knew nothing of the area they lived and worked in daily. So her mother had taught her, and nothing so far had made her think differently.

Until Ethan Winter said: "Agreed." Then spoiled it by adding, "I'm only going to climb that nearest hill. I'll be in direct view of the flyer at all times. You stay and monitor the controls for any change in the com."

Not an option. He wasn't a local, she told him, and this was his flyer, not hers. If anyone was to do something so stupid and contrary to every rule of survival, it should be her. "People who wander off into the desert end up dead, especially people who don't know it."

"I'm not wandering off into the desert, and I've lived on the plains all my life. It's not as dry near my home, but it's no tropical swamp either."

A scowl split that classic Winter face, a break in his composure at last. She dived headlong into it to press her argument. "You're not a nobody. They'll be panicking from here down to Solaris headquarters. Every rescue team available will be out searching for you."

That made him scowl even more, which only told her how true it was.

"How can you be sure they'll look in this area."

She wasn't but refused to admit it. "They can track our last coordinates and use them to work out the best possible search sites."

"If the boy genius who shot at us isn't blocking their signals too."

"Wasn't Geordie," she insisted.

"Someone did. When I get my hands on him…"

"Leave Geordie alone. He's just a scared boy, and he's made you Winters a pile of credits. You owe him far more than he owes you."

"He—" A snap of that rich-boy mouth and a flare of his nostrils. The man gripped onto his chair arms this time. "I'm going up to the top of that hill, with your help or without it. Nowhere else around here is better to set off a beacon or check our coms."

"Then I'm coming with you," she said, sticking out her chin, "and neither of us is leaving this flyer until the sun goes down."

His eyes flared, darkening to the deep green of a stone she'd found once in an icy stream not far from the capital city in the far off northern lands. Clear and sharp, the colour had enchanted her. That stone still lay in a private drawer in her room. She stared at him, caught by the same wonder for a fatal moment, then dropped her gaze sharply as the corners of his mouth tilted. He put up his hands. "Agreed, Sera Sarwenna."

She mustn't let him see what that tilt of his lips did to her. "You have emergency kits?" she said sharply.

"Of course. In the back locker, labelled with E symbols."

She needed to look for herself, whatever he might think of it. Her fingers tugged at the webbing to extricate herself. He watched silently, then finally leaned over to bang at the central button. "They can stick after a shock landing."

She gave the barest head dip of thanks, refusing to be caught by those eyes again, then clambered out of her chair. Behind them, the cockpit was in better order than she'd feared. A few churned up cushions and fittings, but everything else had been held in place by the evac webbing.

It didn't change the fact that they were stranded in the deadlands, days' walk from Sulwith, and with only evac rations and water. She dove into the locker and hauled out two of the backpacks hanging there, pulling out the contents and checking them over.

He was good. Full emergency rations, desert-grade tents, walking poles and connecting nets to keep them together and anchored in the windstorms that battered parts of the plains. Desert protective gear including a water-conserving coverall and wide-brimmed hat. Best of all, a large container of water in each pack, water treatment tablets and spare pouches to carry back-up from the flyer's reservoirs.

"Satisfied, Sera?"

"The name's Sar," she said, gritting her teeth. "We use first names out here."

And that too real smile was back, the one that had her stomach lurching over. "Satisfied … Sarwenna? And the name's Ethan, not Ser Winter, or head office hotshot, or that rakter jerk."

Her cheeks burned. "Yes … Ethan … the kits appear to be quite adequate. And I prefer Sar to Sarwenna."

"But, Sera, I prefer Sarwenna. Such a pretty name." And his smile this time was pure mischief. For an instant, she glimpsed a small boy playing in a schoolyard, and suddenly the distance between their ranks shrank to nothing. She had to smile back.

"The name's still Sar."

A burst of laughter as he watched her settle back into her seat. "I have to set up the standby system links before closing up the flyer. Why don't you try to get some sleep if we're going to be spending the night scrambling up that hill?"

She looked at the viewscreens showing the barren flats surrounding them, then nodded agreement when she could think of no more arguments against his crazy plan. Going any distance in these latitudes without a com wasn't for the novice. "If no one's come to rescue us by nightfall, they don't know where we are."

"You said your local rescue team would check out this basin."

"Only if they know we had to make a crash landing," she finally admitted to him. "Did you get an emergency signal out before we had to land?"

He shook his head. "All channels were blocked by that beam. Your Geordie is either a genius or the naïve puppet of a genius, one I plan to have a talk with when we get back. Arcadia needs that kind of help.

She looked over sharply. "Arcadia? Not Solaris?"

"Yes, Arcadia," said Ethan Winter grimly. "I had a lot of time to think in prison, and a brother nagging me ever since I got out. Arcadia is in trouble, and I mean to make sure both this world and my business survives it."

"Is that a threat or a challenge, Ser Winter?"

He gave her that cool gaze that smacked far too strongly of a rakter's bite. "That's up to you, Sarwenna." Then cut off her attack by the simple tactic of lying back and closing his eyes.

Sleep. A sensible choice if they planned to march in the night but Sar doubted she would find it. Not after that last crack of his. After one long, infuriated glare at his still body, she lay back as well and shut her eyes. A useless endeavour, she discovered. After a while, she gave up any pretence of trying to sleep and switched on the reports waiting to be read. At least the stored section of her com still worked, though with annoying glitches—sudden screen outages and wavering images—but it worked, and she diligently set herself to catching up. The last thing she remembered was a particularly depressing assessment of alternative options for Sulwith.

A hand traced gently down her face, then moved to shake her shoulder. "Time to move, Sera Sarwenna."

"Wha…" Something dug into her back and her neck felt like it had been bolted into a vice. She opened her eyes.

A face marked by a strong mouth and brilliant green eyes. Ethan Winter, with a soft twist of a smile that was nothing like the corporate face he'd worn for the managers on arrival in Sulwith. A smile that she couldn't help returning until she caught herself.

"I slept."

"Yes, Sera Sarwenna. You indisputably did, and a most charming sleeping beauty you make."

It was an old-fashioned and obvious line, but she couldn't smother the flush touching her cheeks or the automatic tilt of her lips. She would not smile at him. "I take it no one called for us." He shook his head, still wearing that too attractive smile. "Time to get going then," she said gruffly.

He began to clamber out of his chair then pulled on his backpack. "Have you tried your com again?"

She lifted her arm and brought up her com screen, fingers uselessly inputting commands. She shook her head. "Same as yours. No outside connection. Loaded files only, and they are playing up."

A frown. "I hope you know this area."

"Yes. It's basic training for out here. Memorise every map available of the local area."

Never leave your flyer. That was another rule drummed into her as long as she could remember. But when your com's out, some rules have to be broken—and they weren't going out of sight of the flyer.

Standing, she pulled on the other backpack. "You think this interference is only around the flyer?"

"I hope it is."

He didn't sound optimistic. Sar wished she'd taken more interest in the obligatory geoscience and tech classes at school. "It has to be. There's nothing else out here to cause it. Not that I know of."

He frowned. "There's a zone near my home where tracking devices are unreliable, thanks to a natural level of static from the active mineral mix found there, but coms still work there. Interference this strong—this is new to me." He hitched his pack higher on his shoulders and gave hers a once over look. "You up for a hike?"

"There's a choice?"

"Not unless you agree to stay here."

"Not happening," she said and couldn't resist a grin as she followed him up the ladder to the emergency hatch.

Grains of sand spilled into the flyer as he shoved the top hatch open. He hauled out then put down a hand to help her up. She thought about refusing—this was her land, not his—then decided that would be stupid. His hand closed around hers. She was surprised to find there was nothing soft about this man's hand. It had the hard ridges that spoke of tough work.

This corporate rich boy hid too many surprises.

Emerging from the flyer, they were greeted by black skies and a thick scattering of stars. Once out, they stood on top of the flyer and looked around. The moons were out already. Jacopus, large and bright, half full yet and still low in the sky with the rest skittering in his shadow like a flock of chicklets yapping at the heels of the boss moon. She smiled at the chasing dots. Only visible out here under the clear desert sky, the minor moons had always spelled home for Sar. Then she looked down. In the waning light of the evening, the angry furrows gouged out by their flyer showed clearly. Most of the ship was buried under the sand, with only the upper canopy poking out.

They had been so lucky.

Beside her, Ethan Winter pulled something from his pack. Rope, thick and silvery in the half-light. "You reckon that sand will support us?"

"Should do, if you walk correctly." Sar had learnt as a small child the careful sliding pattern for crossing loose dunes. "Follow in my footsteps and copy what I do. It'll be easier going once we get off this churned up section."

"Wait up." He began to play out the rope as she was about to step forward. "Just in case," he said, and looped the end around her waist and tied it firmly, checking the knot with a tight frown on his face, then tied the other to the hatch hinge.

She looked at the rope around her waist, then at the tie on the ship. "I do know this country."

"Humour a city boy," he said, and that was so outrageous that a fitting reply failed her utterly.

She began to walk down the flyer lid. As she'd expected, her feet sank into the sand at first, down to the hard metal surface, but as she moved farther out, she changed the pattern of her footfalls, skittering lightly over the surface and never letting her foot settle too long. Sort of a jog-trot-skip, her tutor had told her once. A tug on her waist nearly had her stumbling, and she turned back and scowled. "You want me to sink, Ser Winter?"

He let the rope go slack, although a black scowl on his face told of his reluctance. Soon, she made it to firmer ground, away from the treacherous stuff ploughed up by the crash site, and breathed a bit easier. Finally a tug at her waist said she was at the end of the rope's length. She turned and looked back at the hatch, stamping down on the sand to show him she was on safe ground.

"Now you," she called. "Keep it light and irregular."

He untied the knot from the ship and looped it around his waist. "You sure you can take my weight. I'm a lot bigger than you."

"And I'm a lot stronger and tougher than I look."

He started out with all the technique of a thundering bull nieten. She'd seen a herd of them the one time she'd visited the western plains. Large grazing animals, the bulls stood above her head at mid-back and tromped over the scrublands with all the grace of a transport truck. When Ethan Winter first walked toward her today, it had been with the controlled power of an athlete—tall, muscular and with the easy grace of a man comfortable in his body. She'd been fighting to ignore that first impression ever since. Now, though, he stumbled and began to sink.

"Light on your toes," she yelled, tugging on the rope to yank him back to the surface. "Hop, skip, slide, with no rhythm to it. Nothing to set off a wave of sand."

He grabbed hold of his end of the rope, jerking her forward. A shocked cry of apology erupted from him, but she held strong.

"Dance on the sand," she called again.

"Dancing usually involves keeping to a rhythm," he said caustically as he set off again, his gait much better this time. Relief still had her grabbing hold of him when he finally made it to firm ground.

"You're safe," she said, and whether she told him or herself, she couldn't say.

When she became aware of her hands clinging to his arms, she snatched them back as if scalded by fire. "We better get going."

She tugged uselessly at the rope around her waist.

"Let me."

She felt strong hands circling her waist to pull at the knot and heard a hint of laughter in his voice. She stared firmly at her feet until he'd finished, then uttered a brisk "Thank you," hitched up her pack and stepped forward. "We're about an hour from the hill. Time to get a move on."

A low chuckle sounded behind her. She refused to look back to see whether he followed. Not that she had to. The motion of his feet upon the shifting sand shivered up through her feet and body all through the long slog up the slope.

The sand cover thinned as they neared the base of the hill, and finally they walked on firm ground. It got easier after that. Sar had grown up hiking this country but still had a feeling her thighs would burn tomorrow. A grumpy part of her hoped her corporate boss man would feel the same burn, but she was beginning to suspect he wouldn't suffer at all.

The heat of the day lingered on the rocks as they began the climb. They paused from time to time to check their coms for a signal. After yet another failed test, she straightened up and scowled angrily.

"We should be out of range of interference from the flyer by now."

"Hopefully it's better on the peak. If whatever that beam did to the flyer is blocking the com feeds, we'll need a direct line of sight to the booster station at Sulwith."

She had to stop more often the higher they climbed. It had been too long since she'd hiked. Ethan stopped with her, waiting without word of complaint until she had caught her breath before lifting his own bottle and taking a mere sip. The man had been trained well, trag him.

One last ridge, hands clinging to the rough-edged rocks blocking their way, and they crested the hilltop. She collapsed onto the narrow ledge and he flopped down beside her, pulling out his drink and taking one long slow draw of water from his flask. Then shoved her flask into her hand.

"Drink. That was a tough haul and we have enough to last till help gets here."

If help got here in three days, but the pulsing in her head warned too clearly she needed water. She took an equally long swallow. Enough and not a drop more.

Only when she had recapped her flask did he try his com. A crease formed on his brows as his eyes stared at the space where his screen should have appeared. Another furious tapping. She watched, beginning to feel nervous. "Nothing coming up?"

"Nothing. No visuals, no audio stream, not even a data stream. Try yours."

She tapped her opening sequence onto the com patch on her wrist. She'd had a data stream just after the crash but now… nothing. She tried sending a thought sequence: first the ordinary alert phrase, then the failsafe emergency code. Her com should pick up the brain wave pattern even if it'd been badly damaged.

Nothing. She clamped a hand hard on the patch and tried again. "A com core is indestructible. It was playing up, but it should have repaired itself by now."

His hand grasped his own patch. "Did you get anything?"

She shook her head. "Not even a squawk. It's fried. Whatever that beam did…"

He scowled, sweat drying on his face and his eyes narrowing. "The one you know nothing about."

"You saying I had something to do with it?"

"You're the one who insisted that boy needed to be rescued. Yet turns out he knows the desert well enough to avoid any kind of search."

"He knows how to hide. Doesn't mean he knows how to survive."

"And you, Sera Beren? What was your backup plan to get yourself back home again after stranding me in the middle of the deadlands?"

She shot up. "You think I would deliberately strand you out here? Strand anyone out here?"

"You made it clear you're against me right from the start, Union Representative Sera Beren. So where have you hidden your backup com?"

He was insane. "I haven't got one. We are both stranded out here, and the only rescue coming is the ordinary, rank-and-file search team from Sulwith. They will find us because that's what they do. It's their job." She shoved up her chin. "It's what we do out here."

"Solaris has the latest tech and will be on their way already. They'll find us."

He deliberately turned away to study the horizon. Why, she had no idea. It hadn't changed from the last time they looked. Flat, dry, and broken only by irregular hummocks. In the far distance lay the line of hills sheltering Sulwith and separating the deadlands from the rest of the plains to the west. Hills that killed off any last whiff of rain that had made its way across the main dividing ranges and to the parched lands of the plains. Out here lay true desert, a land Sar loved even in its vicious starkness, but never discounted. As for being stuck here with someone who thinks you're trying to kill him, that wasn't in any training manual.

"Whoever gets here, it won't be until morning. Safer to wait until daylight to find us."

His head turned, eyes holding hers, and she met their scrutiny with everything she dared to keep open inside her. After too long a time, he nodded agreement. "We'll set up the beacons then get some rest for what's left of the night. There's a tent each in these packs."

She could match that cool workmanlike tone. "Put them up on that rock shelf. It's got the best line of sight and protection from the night winds. The rescuers will be looking for a crashed flyer, not lost passengers."

By the rigid set of his chin, this man wasn't used to being told what to do, but he pulled off his pack and pulled out his emergency beacon. "I've set mine to the standard Solaris signal; set yours to the local one."

She had to bite her lip to stop herself saying she knew what to do as well as he. They had hours yet together and the man had helped her up that hill. "I'll get a meal started," she made herself offer after they secured the beacons with the explosive insert pegs.

"Thanks. I'll set up the tents."

The words may have been bitten off, but she couldn't fault him otherwise. So much for her assumption that a tetchy rich boy would expect her to do everything while he stood around looking too handsome for the rugged setting. Then caught herself. *Of course he's looks good. It comes with being born with a huge credit balance and all the best in schools and care.*

And he didn't ask for any of it, said a niggly voice in her head. One she ruthlessly shut down. Self-preservation said she needed walls against this man. *To protect you from what?*

A question she absolutely refused to answer.

In no time, he had both tents set up where she'd suggested and had placed his pack inside the tent at the outer edge of the small rock shelf, with hers in the one tucked against the rock face at the back—the warmer and safer location.

So he was taught manners. Doesn't mean he was taught to value people.

And you were taught to treat people as you find them.

Her teeth clenched. Her inner voice was becoming more annoying than her teenage sister. She straightened, setting out the food on a large rock as a makeshift table. "Dinner's ready."

He gave the tents a last look over then took a seat on the side of the rock opposite her, offering thanks in a tone that had her grimacing. So polite, so formal. The flat surface of the rock between them may as well have been a wall. A taut silence reigned as they chewed their way through the emergency rations. Dry as cardboard and about as tasty, but at least a full mouth gave her an excuse for not speaking. Until she made the mistake of glancing over at the man from Solaris and caught a wry twitch of his mouth.

"They're nutritious, or so I'm told."

"They'll keep you alive," she said carefully back.

"As long as they don't kill you from boredom first."

Sar couldn't supress a chuckle at the old and very hackneyed wisecrack. "Keep eating," she said using the voice of her old training master and won a grin back from the man from Solaris head office.

An easier silence fell after that. She shuffled around to lean back against the rock face behind them, sitting side by side with Ethan Winter as they both stared out into the blackness of the desert. Above, stars winked in and out as the moons tracked slowly up into the night sky and, beside her, his shoulder leaned to meet hers.

"A beautiful place," he murmured with a touch of wonder in his voice.

"It has its moments."

"And it's your home."

A brief head dip. "I've been away but no other place feels right." She'd never admitted that out loud before, though her father knew how she felt. The peace of the night must be getting to her.

Ethan picked up a rock, studying it, then put it down again, carefully placing it exactly where he found it, his fingers lingering over the rough surface and his eyes studying it. "Why are you so against change, when it could mean the difference between saving the town and losing everything here."

His voice was low, careful, as if fearful of breaking their fragile peace, but what he asked mattered too much.

"It depends on the kind of change. The word is you're the business brains of the Winter family, the one who lives and breathes finance. Yet you're about to let the Feds force you to close down a profitable field."

"There's other ways of making money … and this planet is my home. The place where I want to grow old. If I can do some small thing to keep it safe, I will."

A prickle of unease broke through her peace. "Sulwith field is no small thing."

"No, but there are other ways to harvest solar energy and to make money."

That didn't sound good. "What ways?"

"My brother worked with a small village west of our homestead making newer solar collecting systems. As a result they're self-sufficient in energy."

"You mean the brother who doesn't work for Solaris."

"No longer," he agreed dryly. "The Old Man didn't speak to him for months after seeing the first set of sales figures from that area, but that's where the future lies."

"Helping homes and business set up their own solar systems? Is that what you're talking about?" Did he know what he suggested?

And saw him nod.

"It would be the end of Solaris," she exclaimed, hugging her knees for comfort and jerking away from him, leaving her alone in shock. Her town's future, wiped out by one man's word.

"No, it will be the saving of it." He looked at her, eyes steady, and took a last bite of his energy bar. She nearly choked on hers and had to grab at her water bottle. "Think on it, Sarwenna."

"I am, and of the workers you're about to send down the road." Bile rose in her throat and she couldn't keep sitting here, talking as if nothing had changed. Something inside hurt, something barely formed and very personal. She shot up, clinging to the veneer of courtesy she'd been taught. "I'll say good night, Ser Winter."

He stood too. Rich boy manners, rich boy voice, formal and distant. "Sera."

It was the last insult. She slapped the lid back on her canteen. "What happened to Sarwenna?"

"It no longer seems appropriate … and you tell me you do not like it."

"No, I like being called Sar."

He shook his head. "Can't do it."

Because you don't trust or like me, Ser high and mighty Winter. "Try," She snapped back.

"Goodnight, Sera Beren."

She shoved her canteen back on her belt. "Being stranded out here wasn't on my list of must-do tasks for today, but you know what? If it makes you think twice about those of us who live in the desert, and stops you shutting down the Sulwith array, then I'm downright thrilled you have to put up with a night away from your rich boy luxuries."

His hands clenched and his face darkened, the planes of it all too sharply standing out. "My luxuries? Do you ever follow the vidcasts, Sera Beren?"

Of course she did. The newscasts about his family had plastered the vids for months. "You were in prison during the Survey problems. All Arcadia knows that. But they don't put people like you in ordinary prisons. Five star all the way, I bet."

"Five star? Oh yes, it was that all right. Watch any vid of Aigherach den Coille and ask why a leg break still causes a limp months after being shot when they captured him. An injury that should have been healed within the week by any half-baked medical facility."

He took a step forward and she took one back, putting up her hand in a reflex she couldn't help.

It stopped him immediately, his face a flash of white. "My apologies, Sera Beren. Go to bed. You have my promise you will be safe."

She stared at his hands, clenched tight at his side, then slowly tracked her gaze up that hard body, that grim set of spine and head. She tugged at her neckline.

"And I can trust you?" she whispered.

"Oh, stars." He sat abruptly on their barely cleared table, slumping down as if in shock. "Go, please. Your tent is…"

"The one on the inside, next to the rock face. Yes, I know. The best position. It wasn't necessary. This is my home region and I know it better than you."

"And your hometown only exists because of Solaris, which makes you my responsibility." He looked up then, and suddenly she couldn't attack him any longer.

"Good night, "she said, and slunk into her tent, aware of having failed. Who or what, she couldn't say, and it was a long time before sleep claimed her. A man's face hung in her mind, long after she heard a shuffling, slow step as Ethan Winter made his way to his tent and crawled inside.

A face stripped of pride and rent with pain. She had done that to him. A cold wind shivered up the side of the hill and she prayed, strongly and desperately, that their rescuers arrived before she had to face that look again.

CHAPTER THREE

Ethan crawled out of his tent as the first rays of the sun hit the rock and promised another blistering day. He guessed he'd had some sleep. Not much, but it would have to do. It was all he could manage after last night.

What was it about Sarwenna Beren that she could strip bare what he hid so well from most people? Only the brothers den Coille knew of the snivelling coward hiding under his executive veneer, and he'd learned the hard way to trust the brothers with his life. All of them had scars from their time in prison.

But Sarwenna Beren should never have seen his.

Then he saw she was up already, standing on the rock edge. Her body was outlined by the early light and the impact of it hit him slam in his chest. Last night, he decided he'd imagined her effect on him. So much for false comfort.

She faced out, staring west toward Sulwith town. Toward her home. He made himself turn away and look south instead, to the start of the solar array already shimmering under the sun and reaching greedily up to soak up the first rays. A shining blanket smothering the land below it, said Caleb. Modernise, said his brother, before someone makes you.

Before they destroy Solaris.

Someone had already tried. The corrupt managers in Caleb's beloved Survey had briefly usurped power and seized control of Solaris. Ethan could not forget that the same logo Caleb wore so proudly on his shirt matched the one on the uniforms of the guards who had thrown Ethan into a pitch black cell and kicked him in the ribs as they did it.

The guards and the greedy department heads might have been removed—last Ethan heard, they had all been shipped off to a remote island prison to await trial—but Ethan would never forget what those months had taught him or the damage they had done to his beloved company by their greed and stupidity. These days, the government watched Solaris always. It had to. Deputy Malgrave's warning at The Junction only echoed what her superiors told the Arcadian Council: Restore the environmental balance of your world or the Alliance will take control and forcibly remove all Arcadians. They would lose their home planet forever.

His father didn't believe them. Nor, it seemed, did this woman.

He walked over to stand beside her. "Nothing on your com yet?"

She turned and shook her head then suddenly squinted into the distance. "There's a speck out west. I think rescue is on its way."

He followed her pointing finger, south of Sulwith and near the start of the solar array. So could be either Solaris or a local ship. "Time to pack up."

He went to his beacon first, checking the signal. Still strong, still as he'd left it. So she hadn't done anything to change that. Not that he'd expected her to. Not after her courage and blunt speech yesterday. She was the kind to attack head on, not by stealth, but somebody had made that attacking beam that had nearly killed them and had fried their coms.

He finished his packing, then waited for her to add the last of her kit to its bag. Her deft movements proved yet again her familiarity with this land and its risks. She stretched up, her kit stowed expertly at her feet, and he offered her a ration bar, letting his fingers drift across hers. "Want some breakfast, or what passes for it?"

"Thanks," her voice said, but her face closed tight against him as she snatched her hand back and her eyes watched the approaching dot. She took a mouthful, chewed it slowly as if concentrating on each bite, then swallowed. She lifted her hand, as if to take another bite, but let it drift downward, eyes still fixed on the horizon. "What will you do about the solar array?" she asked in a too careful voice.

He stood beside her, deliberately close enough to disturb that rigid composure. Being shut out by this woman felt all kinds of wrong. "I don't make decisions until I have all the information."

"You have your credit balance. Isn't that all that counts?"

"No, Sera, it is not."

The dot had got bigger. Too big for a local carrier, he reckoned, and let a smile touch his lips. He was going to win one bet at least.

"It's coming from Sulwith," she said, as if reading his thoughts.

He turned with a grin. "Wait."

Suddenly, a whoosh of air above them. Shadow and heat, racing overhead. Another flyer, coming in cloaked and suddenly dropping its shielding.

He shoved at Sarwenna, throwing them both behind the nearest boulder. A flash of scorching fire as the rocky ledge disappeared.

Sarwenna gasped. "We were standing there."

"Yes, and this boulder is next. Move."

He grabbed her hand, and they were running down the slope. Twisting, slithering in behind any kind of cover they could find.

Away from the peak, out of sight. Away from the precious beacons, but the next flash destroyed that hope too. Gone in a cloud of pulverised dust.

A dark hole loomed up in a hillside covered with shattered fill. He pushed her inside, skating in behind her in a clatter of sliding gravel.

"Who was—"

He clamped a hand over her mouth. Then pointed up. Silence, dead silence. That was their best hope of slowing down the search until that other ship arrived. Right now, he badly needed it to be from Solaris. Ever since the Survey takeover, all their flyers were fitted with heavy duty defensive weapons. Winters weren't going to be caught napping twice.

She swept her hand over both their bodies. Their thermal signal? Yes, a problem, but the rocks around here held enough residual heat to confuse the readings and slow the hunt. For a short time.

He strained to hear. Where was the unknown flyer? He'd only caught a glimpse but had recognised the outline and hoped Sarwenna Beren didn't know the various types of military ships as well as he did. Silas had mapped them all while in hiding and downloaded the file to the rest of the family after they were freed. Ethan knew exactly the shape and capacity of any kind of flyer, ground vessel and weapon that could come after him. That black shadow belonged to a Stalker II, the latest stealth, hunter-class flyer. Lethally fast and almost undetectable, it had been developed off world, and imports were restricted to the covert branch of the planet's Federal military.

What were they doing hunting him? And who really sent the bolt that downed his flyer?

Too many questions and no answers. Not unless they survived, and Sarwenna Beren was not going to die because she had the bad luck to be caught out with Ethan Winter.

A whistle of sound from outside. The kind that only came from a low-flying ship on a recon run.

Closer and closer.

He turned his head, trying to see if there was another way out. No such luck. Just a sheer black wall behind them.

Nothing for it. He began to wriggle forward.

Then felt a movement behind him as she began to follow. No. He lifted a hand to Sarwenna. "Stay," he mouthed.

She shook her head.

He had no time to argue. He shoved her back, hard enough to stun her and keep her here. Then sprinted out the hole in the rock, running madly across the open shale field, slithering and falling in a mad slurry of rocks, bruises and slashed cuts, waiting for the burning shots to hit him. Rolling, jumping, zigzagging runs and mad hellion falls. Anything to avoid the tracking blasts.

A sound swooped close above. They followed him. Sarwenna was safe. It was him they hunted. Why, he didn't yet know, but nothing good came to mind.

Caleb and his father had some explaining to do when he got back home.

If he got back home.

Where in tragging hell was their rescue ship?

He swerved again, ignored the flash of pain in his leg as he bashed his knee on a rock, wiped the blood from his already battered face and twisted downhill again.

Close to the bottom now, and ahead lay only flat, sandy plain. Little cover and a knee already swelling up.

"Winters don't surrender." His family's mantra: Winter one, Winters all, chanted in unison before so many playground battles, and Ethan had no intention of surrendering today. Another twist, another slither down the rocky slope sending rocks, sand, shale scattering in all directions. No chance of hiding now. Not with that crashing of debris marking his flight.

"Come on, you tragging flyer." Where was that rescue ship?

Another blast of fire. Too close, the smell of burnt cloth as tracer fire caught him a glancing shot. He twisted again, rolled and fell. Sliding headfirst in a death-defying dive down the last of the long slope. At the bottom, a swivel to the right, away from the blast, eyes searching the rocks and hollows at the base. There, a small gulley running into the desert. A last chance to escape. He threw himself over the edge, crashed down onto the gravel at the bottom, and fell again, skidding downward.

A rock at the bottom met him, another bang on his head and dizziness washed over him.

Get up. Now.

Can't. Nothing left.

Get up, or nothing's what will really be left.

Why must his brother's voice echo in his head when he least wanted it?

Another blast. The next would be his last. He scrambled to his feet, desperately lurching away, waiting for that burn in the back of his neck and the refuge of eternal dark.

Then…

Silence.

No, another whoosh of sound.

A different shadow over head, one with a welcome outline and a crackle of fire power. Solaris had arrived, all weapons blazing. He collapsed onto the ground and waited.

It didn't take them long. The unknown flyer roared off into the distance at the Solaris flyer's approach. He would have loved to have a working com to order the Solaris ship after that unknown flyer, but Sar needed help. He thrust his good leg against a rock and used his hands to lever himself up so he was standing as the hatch lowered and his rescuers ran out. A familiar figure led the charge, ignoring all protocol, as usual, and pulling out a scanner as she reached him. Doc Marsten had been fixing up the mess the brothers made of themselves as long as he remembered.

"Stretcher, now. Sit down, Ser Ethan, before you fall down."

"Good to see you, too, Doc. Thought you would have had enough of patching up Winters by now."

The woman growled at him to stop talking and start doing as he was told. "Good thing for you I was on holiday a bit south of here. The team picked me up on the way through."

He wished he could obey her. "You need to get up that slope. There's a small cavity beneath a boulder near the top of this shale slide and an injured woman inside."

The doctor waved the stretcher forward and pushed him on the chest in that way of hers that had him toppling onto the receiving depths before he could do anything about it. "Lie down like I told you." She turned to the security man coming up behind. "You heard the Ser. Get another stretcher and a flitter up that slope." She looked down at Ethan again. "Her com out too?"

"Yes. You'll need to follow her body heat. She may be unconscious."

"And why would that be?"

Ethan felt a flush rise up in his face. "I gave her a bit of a tap. It was the only way to stop her following me," he added defensively. "That flyer would have killed her if she'd tried to run."

"Like it nearly killed you, Ser Ethan," said the head of security, as he snapped out orders to the second team bringing up another stretcher. "Less heroics by Winter sons would make my job a lot easier."

"Yeah, and we just love being shot at." Ethan gave him his usual hand flip. Joff was another he'd known since boyhood, and he'd heard similar gripes many times before. After this day, the familiarity of it had him grinning madly.

"And Joff, not a word about that flyer to anyone in Sulwith or Dridust. Not yet," he added, suddenly serious. This whole situation had a definite smell to it, and he needed more facts before he let it go public. No point warning his enemies.

The team carrying the second stretcher came down the slope, and he saw Sarwenna Beren struggling to sit up despite the restraining field the medics had thrown over her.

"I'm fine," he heard her claiming, "and a sight better than Ethan Winter will be when I get my hands on him."

She was all right, despite his rough treatment. A weight lifted from his heart as the troopers loaded them in the flyer and secured them in the med bay. She glared at him and struggled even harder to sit up. "You slugged me!"

"I did," he said, unable to resist stirring the wernet's nest, though his eyes guiltily traced the swelling on her forehead. "You're still alive to plague me, at least."

"I'm going to do tragging more than plague you when we get back to town. You and Solaris are going to pay for every single bruise on my body."

"With holographic evidence to support it?"

Her eyes flashed at him, letting him know what she thought of his words or his highly inappropriate chuckle, but she was alive and safe. He'd spent enough time in the med wards after his release from prison to make a fair stab at reading medical data, and hers said she'd suffered bruising and a mild concussion only. If someone could make her take it easy, she'd be fully fit again in a week or so.

If someone could make her take it easy. A good thing he had unfinished business in Sulwith—after he got back home and found out what in the depths was going on here. He quickly ordered his team to report her safe to Sulwith once they were in the air, then demanded a spare com and began to schedule all the other calls waiting for his attention.

Doc Marsten took one look at the com and switched up the strength of the restraining field, sending him flat back into the stretcher. "Ignore him, Sera Beren. His head took too many bangs on his way down that slope." He tried to grab the com she'd twitched out of his hand, only to receive a stern glare. "You, Ser Ethan, need to concentrate on healing your own injuries, not flirting with a woman who had the sense to stay under cover or bothering with calls that can wait till you're safe in Dridust." She frowned and glanced across at Sarwenna. "As for you, Sera Beren, I suspect your debt to Ser Winter outweighs anything he owes you. He did save your life by knocking you out."

Ethan hated the red flush on her face and sudden shock. "It was me they were after," he told the doc. "Of course I left her there."

That had Sarwenna suddenly jerking up again, only to be pushed back by the Doc, but didn't stop her hot words. "You what? Don't you dare put your life at risk to save me ever again!"

Not a promise he was going to make. The thought of that determined jaw and smart mouth silenced horrified him. He shut his eyes and ignored her.

"Ethan Winter!"

He kept his eyes shut and chuckled silently. Suddenly, he felt a whole lot better and gave in to the niggling drowsiness of the stretcher's systems. Next he knew, a warm darkness welcomed him in.

The Doc had tranked him.

Sar looked across and saw that Ethan Winter's eyes were still shut. His face no longer wore that edge of laughter and his lips lifted in a soft tilt as if even in sleep something amused him.

She raised an eyebrow at the doctor.

The woman smiled. "Tranking's the only way to shut up a Winter when they're determined on something."

"Is what he said true? He knew that flyer was trying to kill him when he took off like that?"

"If Ethan said it, then it's true. He's the sensible one of the Winter's, believe it or not, and usually only takes risks when there's no other option."

"He risked his life to save me." She'd accused him of it but it was only now that the reality of it hit her full in the gut. No one had a right to cut him down like that. She would fight Ethan Winter with words and relish every minute of it; she would not side against him with an unknown enemy bent on who knew what.

"The flyer that attacked us…?"

"Got clean away. This is a medic rescue ship, not a hunter class, and that's what you were up against, according to our security scans. How Ethan survived that race down the mountain, only he and the fates know."

Sar shifted uncomfortably. "He was hurt?"

"They got him once. Just a tracer burn, thankfully. He's banged his head, scraped up his body and twisted his knee, but none of it is permanent as long as he rests up. I'll run a full scan while he's out to it." Then a grin on the older woman's face. "At least he can't do anything stupid, like ordering us after that flyer. Give a Winter a chance, and they take over any operation, and we need to get him back to Solaris headquarters."

"We're going where?" A sudden panic and she clenched the sides of the stretcher. "I need to get back to Sulwith."

"And you will … after you are fully fit again."

What about Geordie? "I have responsibilities. People who need me."

The woman's voice was firm. "Plenty of others to handle it. Let me finish checking you over and start treatment of those bumps. Security can link you back through to Sulwith base one we've got Ethan safely at headquarters."

Sar had grown up around enough strong women to recognise when she was beaten. "Solaris flies me straight back here after that. I can recuperate better in my own town than among strangers."

The woman's mouth quirked and her eyes sparkled. "Agreed, Sera Beren." She lifted her com. "Pilot, we're ready to depart."

The doctor kept Ethan Winter unconscious all that long trip west, but she agreed to let Sar off her stretcher as long as she didn't leave the med bay. Sar picked the seat by the window, peering out to where the sun shone down on bare rocks and golden sands. Sulwith sat on the border between the grass and scrublands that covered most of the plains and the deadlands at the dry heart of the continent. There, the grasses had long since been burned off by the sun and searing winds.

Not dead though, despite the name. Not to one born to it. Small creatures skittered over the surface even in the hottest part of the day, and the daily war for survival played out in every nook and crevice of the tough land. Dried up lumps sprang to short and brilliant life on the rare times the precious rain fell, and small, weedy plants poked through cracks in the rocks, soaking up the morning dew then huddling back into the ground as the sun burned across the sky. The blazing sun that powered the richest array in all the Solaris empire, and Sar meant to see Sulwith kept that place. Not one single worker would she lose to this latest government madness.

Now they flew over tough grasses and bumpy hills nearing Dridust, the largest town in the plains. The man who slept beside her lived a few hours southwest of here, but that was Winter heartland, and Winters guarded fiercely who they allowed to visit there. The flyer tracked up an almost dry riverbed and hovered over a large white building, glaring iridescent in the day's heat. A stupid design for this region, she'd always thought, half blinding any who caught it at the wrong angle, but it was unmissable. Solaris Hospital, main medical centre for the region, provided by the munificence of this man's family and directly attached to Solaris headquarters. Whether it was for the convenience of Solaris staff or to drill home the importance of the company to this region, Sar had never been able to decide.

Halfway through the trip, a crewman came back to see her. "We've heard from Sulwith. That boy you were looking for has been found."

"Geordie. Is he all right?"

The crewman glanced at the com message on his wrist. "A few bruises and minor dehydration, the report says, but nothing serious."

A heavy weight left her. "Thank you," she said. The man gave a brisk half-bow before heading back to the front of the cabin. So something good had come out of this disaster. Geordie was safe.

Just as they were about to land, the Doc brought Ethan Winter out of his induced sleep. He struggled up, far too quickly throwing off the effects of the trank. "One day, Doc…" he threatened.

The woman merely laughed. "You've been saying that to me for years."

"And you ignore me every time." Then he saw Sar stand up from her seat by the window. "Doc, what do you mean letting her wander around like that? What if she falls and knocks herself out again?"

Sar froze and the Doc's eyes widened. "The Sera is in no danger and a sight better off than you, young Ethan."

Sar saw the tightness of his jaw as his eyes traced the bruise on her head and the scrape on her hand. "Please, Sera, will you lie back down on the stretcher and buckle in for landing?"

Usually, she would have argued, but something in the hint of vulnerability in those green eyes had her meekly complying. She sat down in the nearest chair. No one was carrying her out of here on a stretcher like some desperately injured victim.

Like Ethan Winter, who had nearly died to save her.

He scowled at the seat, but his hands unclenched once she slotted the strapping closed. A tight pinch of his mouth as he submitted to the Doc securing him for landing, then he suddenly looked across at her, his face deadly serious.

"Whatever you're asked, not a word about that other flyer. We got hurt in an accident. That's the story until I find out what in all sands is going on here."

Then they landed and chaos erupted. A platoon of security troops and medical staff surged into the med bay as soon as the hatch opened, surrounding Ethan Winter's stretcher and bristling with palmed weapons facing outward. The security chief on the flyer joined the new troops amid a jostling of authorities and rigid shoulders until Ethan stopped it all with a short command.

"Stand down. And clear this crowd out of here, Joff. The Doc is mad enough at me already."

Surprisingly, the big man obeyed, with a crunch of eyebrows and a scowl. "You heard the boss," he said to the new platoon. "Line up outside. No one gets near the Ser until he's safely inside the secured wing of that hospital."

"That goes for Sera Beren too."

Ethan Winter's command had her slapping off her strapping and jumping up, her head shaking in denial. A simple check-up then she was out of here, she'd been told.

"That flyer was shooting at both of us, Sera."

Before she could utter a word, the doc pushed her back onto a stretcher and the troops surrounded both of them. The doc put a hand on her chest and activated the restraining field. "If you want to keep Ethan Winter safe, you'll do as they say. You can't keep up with the guards if they need to make a run for it."

Which left her no room for refusal.

The stretchers slid out of the flyer and into the hospital ward at full power, the guards jogging beside them and constantly on the lookout for trouble. Then they were inside, racing down pristine corridors, through a scanner field and into a ward where she was deposited in a room. The troops surrounding Ethan's stretcher kept moving.

"Hey, stop." A string of curses in that high-rank voice of his rocked against the walls.

"Orders from the top," said the security chief and the doctor shoved him back down as he struggled against the restraints.

"If anything happens to her," she heard him growl as his stretcher carried on up the corridor. Her hand reached out impulsively as he disappeared and the doors of her room swung shut, until all she had left was the memory of his voice, lingering in the air. "I'll be back. Don't do anything stupid."

Like get up and walk out of here? That was exactly what she intended until she tried the doors and discovered they were security locked. The room was beautiful, like no hospital room she'd ever seen, with a top of the line cleansing unit, an ever changing display on the walls of the plains, an entertainment and food station that looked to be state of the art, and a bed that was wide and comfortable. But that door locked her in.

By the time someone answered her repeated yells, she was beyond furious. The poor girl in a nurse's uniform looked ready to scurry right out of the room again. Only the burly guard beside her kept both her and Sar exactly where they were.

"I have a few bruises and a bang on my head, that's all. Why is that door locked?"

"Orders, Sera." The big guard gave nothing away, the deep rumble of his voice flat and final. The little nurse refused to meet her eye, fixedly concentrating on checking her readings and testing the healing strips. She could have done that from her workstation.

As for the big guard, his eyes never left her.

They think you tried to kill their boss. The realisation hit in a thud. How did they think she planned to make it home after she'd crashed with Ethan or with a fried com? As for that other flyer, it had definitely been firing at both of them.

Yet these troops didn't know about that, and Sar found herself in uncomfortable agreement with Ethan Winter. The fewer who knew about that unknown flyer, the better. She glared at the nurse working on her injuries. "Just finish and let me out of here."

All that achieved was scaring the nurse. The poor girl acted as nervous as Sar felt, fumbling the scanner and hurrying through dressing the worst of Sar's scrapes with a healing skin set in a seriously skewed pattern. Sar's own medic back at Sulwith would have a very snarky comment about that when—if—she made it back.

Then they left her alone again, with only her fears for company and a locked door to keep out the world. They didn't even leave her a replacement com sliver to track time. She glared at the door and swore, deliberately building up anger. How dare these Dridust big shots think a deadlands woman would give up so easily.

First on her list, get clean again. She turned to the too luxurious cleansing unit. After a few attempts, she managed to figure out the basic controls and let the scouring waves and gentle warm drafts scrub away all the grit and jangled nerves. At the end, she stepped out to discover her battered clothes had been sucked away into the cleaning chute and replaced with a smart set of city wear. Gallingly, they fit beautifully. The nicest clothes she'd ever worn, but she would have preferred her own back.

Anonymous. That's how she felt as the hours dragged on and nothing changed. Her parents would be frantic.

No, they wouldn't. Given the level of efficiency surrounding her, she had no doubt that a reassuring message had been sent back to them as promised. Sera Beren is receiving the best possible care available and will be returning to Sulwith once recovered.

Whenever that was.

Suddenly, a sliding of the door and a flurry of people poured into the room. Ethan Winter marched in their middle looking as if nothing had happened. Hair, clothes, skin, spotless. Only his walk had a slight hitch to it … and his wrist carried a shiny new com patch.

Around him flurried a crowd of medics, security troopers, and fussing administrators.

"Out," he ordered in that I-expect-to-be-obeyed voice of his. The nearest guard hissed furiously back. Ethan flung up his hand.

"Sera Beren is an innocent victim in this, and I owe her a debt of gratitude for helping me in what could have been a difficult situation." He stared down the trooper, waiting with an implacable gaze until the rest of the mob shuffled awkwardly, then slowly walked out. He slammed the door on them and locked it shut.

Against them, or to keep her in? Sar sat on the bed, knees tucked up and watching him as he walked toward her.

A sudden crease on his forehead, no sooner glimpsed than wiped away to be replaced by that too smooth corporate smile. She glared at it, and it vanished abruptly.

"My apologies, Sera. I hadn't realised they'd kept you here. I had thought—"

"What? That they'd given me a quick scan and a ticket home then sent me on my way?"

"No. That you'd been properly treated and sent home by personal flyer with a medic to accompany you." He took a step forward. "Your injuries. How bad are they?"

"You tell me. I'm sure you've seen my readouts."

He saw no point hiding it. "You got hurt because you were with me."

"That's not what your security thinks."

"For which you have my apologies. After the difficulties of the last few months, Solaris security tends to act first, ask questions later."

He lifted his wrist and spoke a few words into his com. "I've sent for your doctors. Once they clear you, tell me what you want to do and I will arrange it. Personally."

Did she believe him? She had no reason to yet she nodded acceptance and saw his face relax. "Thank you," she felt compelled to add. She looked pointedly at the door. "I'm sure you have plenty of others needing you."

He smiled and touched his com, releasing the door lock. "But none as beautiful as you, Sera. Or as intriguing."

Which left her blushing. She did not blush. A sound at the door and the doctor arrived. "Just go," she said to Ethan Winter.

"Timing," he muttered and scowled at the doctor, who stopped suddenly as if waiting for permission from Ethan. He waved her in. "I'll see you before you leave, Sera Beren. And that's a request, not an order."

After seeing the way he ordered everyone here around, and the way they let him? The man spent his life throwing orders around. Stiffly, she thanked him and waited for him to leave. The door snicked shut and she let the doctor take over. At the end of it, the woman told her exactly the same as the doctor in the rescue team, none of which she didn't know already. She had bruises and a head knock. Rest and report in to the Sulwith medics immediately if she became faint, had vision disturbances or any other sign that Ethan Winter's shove had caused more than a minor knock to her head. Why she had to come all the way to Dridust to be told that, she had no idea. Finally the doctor stopped talking.

"So I'm clear to go?"

"Yes, Sera."

"Then I'll be on my way. Who do I talk to about getting home again?"

The doctor touched her com and the door opened.

"That would be me," said Ethan Winter, striding in through the door.

Her mouth dropped open. "Have you been waiting outside this room?"

"I knew you'd need a lift and the team investigating my crashed flyer is leaving soon. I asked them to wait so they could take you with them."

It sounded too plausible. "Thank you," she forced out. "And the solar array, and the other matter?"

"Will have to wait. I don't make decisions without information and, unfortunately, my fact-finding trip was cut short."

"Sorry," she muttered, only to have him step forward and take her hand.

"I didn't mean it like that. Being with me put your life at risk. I don't forget that easily, Sera Sarwenna. About that other matter, not a word to anyone. I don't want you put at risk again."

"You're going to have me watched."

A shrug in half apology. "It's necessary. For your safety and for my peace of mind." A sudden fleeting twist of his mouth and a hint of vulnerability in his eyes. Then the moment passed. Another man came into the room. "Graffin here is my chief assistant. He will see to everything for you. I'll be back in Sulwith soon, and I hope we can get to know each other in better circumstances."

She half-heartedly tugged her hand. He let it drop, and it felt as if she had lost an anchor. "I will still fight you on the solar array. I will protect the jobs of my workers."

The serious face disappeared as his lips tilted up at the corners. "I wouldn't expect any less, Sera.

Then he was out of the room and gone.

CHAPTER FOUR

That startled look on Sarwenna's face had Ethan chuckling as he strode down the corridors of the hospital and stayed with him as he flew west across the plains to the Winter homestead. Then he landed and saw his older brother's flyer sitting on the landing pad and lost all delight. He marched up the front steps of the homestead and slapped a palm on the door control.

The short man who opened the door looked as close to upset as he'd ever seen their butler. "The front door, young Ethan?"

He should have used the family's side entrance but wasn't in the mood to today. "Is the old man in, James?"

"The Ser is in the family sitting room with your mother, Ser Ethan."

"Young Ethan will do fine, James. I haven't cut the family, not yet."

He should have known not to try such tactics on James. The man had known him since he was a squalling baby. Looking as formal as when greeting the seediest lobbyist to the house, James pointed a hand down the hallway. "You know the way still, I assume, Ser."

Ethan was reduced to a shamefaced and muttered "Yes." He thanked James in a suitably penitent voice and added placating him to the long list of tasks waiting till he had the time or energy.

The sound of raised voices greeted him from the sitting room. Caleb's measured tones, louder than usual and with an edge of frustration, countered by his father in full bluster mode. Just what he needed. He slapped a palm on the door and shoved it open.

"Business as usual, I see," he said to the faces swivelling toward him.

"What are you doing out of hospital?" demanded his mother. She patted him down, ordered him to walk as she peered intently at the injured leg, and checked out his face and hands. Faint scars still showed, but not the cuts and bruises. He'd told the Doc to use her fullest regen program. He couldn't hide the limp, but it would mend in a few days.

"That union woman should be locked up," said his father, brushing off Caleb and marching up to him. "She'd better not think she'll get away with luring a Winter into a trap."

"Sera Beren has nothing to do with this."

"You sure?" said Caleb. "The unions are fighting every single change we propose."

Ethan braced against the force of nature that was his brother. Hair the colour of the dried out grasses of the plains and eyes as sharp as the midday sky, Caleb always reminded him of the Jack Robber bird that hunted the plains, the natural lord of the land who missed nothing. He was the most like their father in both looks and presence but totally opposed in views. Ethan snatched a breath and determined to hold on to his temper. Not easy when Caleb stared him down while his father was demanding Sarwenna Beren be arrested and interrogated to find out who'd set her up.

"No one, father. She'd attack us head-on, not this underhand nonsense."

His father opened his mouth to argue and Ethan chopped his hand down to stop him. "Investigate her discreetly, but do not harass her. You'll only set her against us and we don't need that kind of trouble, or do you want to lose more credits on that field than necessary?"

Credits, the magic talisman that ruled his father, or so Ethan had always believed.

"I don't care what you say, son. That woman is a suspect in the attack on you and will be watched. By Solaris as well as those useless Federal police." Then a malicious smile twisted his father's mouth, and Ethan's heart jolted. "We won't be losing credits, as it happens. That field is too important to change. We can fiddle with lesser ones to keep the Feds happy, but no one expects us to go broke simply to make a politician look good."

Ethan suddenly understood the loud voices. "Did you learn nothing in prison, Pa? You read your execution order, the same as the rest of us. This isn't about making politicians look good."

"I've been telling him that for months," growled Caleb. "Maybe you can talk some sense—or credits—into him."

Suddenly the all clear from the hospital felt more like a sentence than a reprieve. "Don't ask me to fight your battles, brother. You've a whole city of politicians and departmental boffins to do that for you." He wasn't about to let Caleb force his hand, not today or any other day. As for his father… "What's this about Sulwith, Pa? I haven't finished my evaluation yet. Who are you telling we're not changing anything there?" He clutched hold of the nearest chair, suddenly in need of support. "We're already offside with the locals. You'll have me walking back into a real cluster mess."

"Sit down, Ethan."

Not even his father disobeyed his mother when she used that tone. Ethan took a seat on the chair, partly because he wasn't sure how much longer he could stand.

"You two as well," he said to his brother and father. "I'm not arguing with you while you stand over me."

Caleb threw himself into a chair opposite, but it took a glare from their mother before the Old Man sat down in his usual chair, an excessively padded and embellished behemoth that always reminded Ethan of a throne of honour, set in the prime position in the room where he could keep his eye fixed on everyone else around him.

"Report, then," said his father.

Ethan had dealt too often with his father's power games to be intimidated by him. "You'll have seen the recordings, including the one of the flyer that attacked us."

A twitch from his father and a grunt from Caleb, from which Ethan guessed that under the bluster they were as worried as he.

"Has security found anything yet?" he asked.

A grim set to his father's mouth. "Not much you didn't know already. Our ship scan identified it as a Stalker II variant. A few differences from the official version, but that's not unusual for a Federal craft. You sure it attacked you?"

"Hard to mistake someone shooting at you. Luckily, they only had pinpoint weapons. Any broad sweep cannons and I wouldn't be here now."

"It's not a Federal flyer," said Caleb. "After the trouble my ex-bosses stirred up, the government ramped up the weaponry on all our vessels. All Fed attack flyers have cannons now."

A sudden sinking in Ethan's stomach. Caleb had a good ear for trouble and access to a level of information Ethan couldn't hope to reach. "How can any non-Federal outfit import a flyer like that without detection. Not the kind of thing you can shove in a trade or diplomatic pouch."

Caleb grimaced. "They'd need good connections and deep pockets."

Stating the obvious wasn't much help to Ethan. "Find out who," he said to his brother. "You're the one on the inside with the powers up in Urbis."

Caleb ignored the jibe. "Anyone involved with this will be well hidden. The Council is still on high alert for any attempt to subvert federal property—things or people."

Ethan turned to his father. "And you, Pa. What about your connections and associates?"

His father's brows shot together. "You accusing me of trying to kill my own son?"

"No, sir, but what about your cronies. The ones who haven't forgiven the Survey or Federals for interfering with their business."

His father's mouth tightened and Caleb's jaw went rigid. Ethan refused to feel guilty. Someone had tried to kill both him and Sarwenna Beren.

"Talk to them," he said. Silence fell, painful and awkward. Too many walls stood between his father and brother, too many differences they avoided discussing. Their opposed loyalties sat top of that list.

"What about the first crash? The one that grounded my flyer? That beam came from our own solar field."

"The initial report is in from the lab. I called in at head office on the way here," said Caleb. "I'm sending you the file now."

Ethan tapped his com patch then glanced at the files loading up. "These are confidential Solaris records. You don't work for the company anymore."

"I called in a few favours and got the lab to keep the details quiet. The summary says they're passing it off as an engine fault."

Ethan gave his brother a pointed look and got a shrug in return. Use it if you want but keep me out of it the shrug said. Hopefully, it also meant Caleb hadn't passed it on to the Survey yet.

He skimmed through the report, past the summary and into the hidden bulk of it. He'd learned long ago that company summaries usually said what would upset the boss the least. There wasn't a lot new, but they had managed to extract footage of the attack beam, though the techs' jargon gave little away. He suspected it was their way of saying they were as much in the dark as he was.

He stopped at a section and sent it across to Caleb's com. "Ever seen anything like this?"

Caleb pulled up his screen and scrolled through it. Suddenly his hands clenched. "You lost power and com transmissions?"

Survivor guilt. That's what the psychologists called it. Neither Caleb nor their younger brother Silas had been captured with the rest of the family, and it had created a barrier Ethan was beyond trying to broach. "A classic glide and dump landing. Luckily Sera Beren knew where to put down. We had sand to cushion us and hard rock below to keep us from being buried."

His brother knew enough about geology to understand the risks they'd faced. Ethan tensed, but a glance at their mother bought Caleb's silence for now. He recognised the jut of her chin though. His mother tolerated no threat to her sons.

"Sera Beren appears to have possessed a deal of convenient local knowledge."

Ethan stiffened. "We owe her a debt, Mother, not further harassment. And don't forget the Feds are watching us."

"Just what I've been telling Pa," growled Caleb.

For a rare moment, it seemed he and his brother were on the same side even if their reasons were as different as ever. He pushed forward.

"I'm going back up tomorrow to finish my evaluation. We can't give the Feds an excuse to claim we ignored facts if we leave it unchanged.'"

"You're not going near that place," his mother snapped.

At the same time, Caleb shot up. "That field has to be changed. Right now, that blanket of solar panels is threatening the survival of three ground dwelling animals and a whole raft of plants. And here's me thinking you'd finally seen sense, brother."

So much for Caleb supporting him. Just once, he wished his brother would try diplomacy instead of jumping head on into a confrontation with the Old Man. "I will finish my site evaluation and talk to the people there. After that, Solaris can make an informed decision on what to do next. If you have any helpful suggestions, brother, put them up then or stay out of it."

His mother glared at both of them. "That's enough. Caleb, I expect your support for Solaris on this. Ethan, you will listen to your father, and you will not be going back to a place where someone has tried to kill you."

"I work for the Survey, mother,'" snapped Caleb, at exactly the same time as Ethan barked an emphatic, "No."

"I am going back to Sulwith, Mother, and I will find out who shot at me and what they used. And Pa, hold off any announcement about the Sulwith field until I get back. I don't need the Feds on my tail while I do my work. That unknown flyer says we've enough trouble with someone high up."

His father had that stubborn look on his face. "Solaris decides what's best for the business, not some opinionated official from Urbis and definitely not some cowardly undercover bunch of agitators. Caleb beat back one lot of jumped-up officials last time, and Solaris will beat them this time."

"Last time, they had us all within a sliver of the executioner's chamber before Caleb and the Feds rescued us."

"Scared, boy? Take a security detail with you."

As if he'd thought to go back without one. "The Feds don't need blunt force to destroy Solaris. They can tangle us up so badly in the courts we won't stand a chance. Or do you think to run this business without a decent line of credit?"

His father leaned forward and planted his hands square on the arms of his chair. "The banks wouldn't dare."

"They would, and will. All that's needed is a hint of Federal controls on their borrowings and they'll roll over quicker than Jack Robber can bring down a gandy."

For a long, long moment, his father held his gaze, mouth straight, and those heavy eyes arrowed onto him. Finally, he agreed. "I'll hold off any announcement for ten days. That's more than enough time to collect some helpful facts. Generations of Winter toil built this company and we are not handing it over to anyone."

Ethan eyed his father, wishing, as so often before, to have avoided this meeting. "Arcadia is my home world, and it's one on which I intend to grow old. We can't fight the Alliance and the planet. I'll check out the Sulwith field and send in my report, based on what I find there."

"That field stays as it is. Put that in your report or don't bother coming back. You want to stay in Solaris; you write what's best for Solaris."

"What, you'll sack me?"

"Don't push me boy."

Just once, couldn't his father listen? On one side, he had Caleb glaring at him; on the other, his father glowering; and all the while, his mother's fingers twitched her gown in the tic that had appeared after her imprisonment.

"I'll leave tomorrow and see what's there," he said, stifling a need to shift in his chair and hoping he was up to it.

"I'm coming with you," said Caleb.

Which sent the room into yet another uproar, only this time his mother led the storm of protests. Caleb ignored it all, and when Ethan strode out the next morning to his flyer, his brother stood waiting beside it, along with his father and mother. Ethan had grown up thinking nothing would ever trouble the air of assurance that was as much a part of his mother as her unique fragrance. Prison had changed that, and today her eyes showed traces of red and she clutched at both their hands as she said her goodbyes.

Ethan gently disengaged her hands. "We're only going to Sulwith. We will be on Winter lands at all times, my flyer is fully tracked and a security detail is following us on backup." Quite a way back, but he didn't tell his mother that. On this mission, Ethan needed space to work.

"That's enough, Helena. The boys have work to do, or Ethan does. Why Caleb thinks he needs to hare off up there is another story. Unless he's finally remembered what name he carries."

"I never forget it, Pa, or what planet I'm born to. Winters don't rule the whole world."

The same jibes, every time his brother came home. Ethan slapped open the hatch. "I'll send through a preliminary report as soon as I can. Not a word about Sulwith until then."

He had little hope of success in that. Sol Winter never backed down. A scowl from the Old Man was all he got today. Ethan lifted a hand in farewell and marched into his flyer, barely waiting until Caleb was seated in the co-pilot's chair and strapped down before lifting off in a whoosh of power.

"Why you're here is beyond me," he said to his brother as they rose high above their home. "What about your wife? Have you told her you've taken a whim to head out into the deadlands?" His brother's quick frown was the first positive of the day, and he couldn't resist a follow up. "You could always ask her to join us. Not a tree in sight, but I'm sure she could endure it for a day or so."

Caleb's wife, Fee den Coille, needed rain and the feel of a living tree underfoot as badly as any of her brothers. Fee managed to survive her new life on the plains only with the promise of the fancy house Caleb was building them on the foothills of the western mountains, right under the last of the tree cover.

"I'm coming, brother," said Caleb, "and that's final. You were shot at. Twice. I intend to find out who did it."

"You what? No, don't tell me. I really don't feel like a lecture today. If you're coming, leave the Survey and politics behind."

He urged the flyer forward and listened with a far too juvenile glee to his brother's grunt as they were both slammed back into their seats.

"Not happening, brother," said Caleb as soon as he could talk. "If the Old Man's playing stupid games, then both he and the locals need a reminder of exactly why Solaris and Sulwith have to change."

Ethan turned and glared at Caleb. "You including me in that, brother?"

Caleb gave him his big brother look. "Not yet. Hopefully not ever, but we'll see."

"What, you think I arranged for that stealth flyer to take pot shots at me as cover for some kind of scheme? Do you trust anybody or is it only your own family you think is plotting against you?"

"Don't be stupid."

Exactly what Ethan didn't need to hear. His brother had said that to him as a boy whenever Ethan got mad at him. "You want me to show you her medical file? Or maybe you think I beat up on women just for the pleasure of it."

"What the trag are you on about now?"

"Sarwenna Beren. I assume you accessed her medical file, including the bruises I gave her to keep her safe in that cave."

"Aaargh." Caleb threw up a hand. "For the record, I'm well aware that was a piece of chivalrous lunacy. I'm not accusing you of staging anything. Nor the Old Man either."

"But you think he's involved in something?" Ethan furiously reviewed that too brief interview with his parents. His Mother? No, she was too distressed, the fear she'd learned in prison still gripping her tight.

The Old Man then? His father was one of the most devious people he knew, with the possible exception of Bram den Coille, head of the Den Coille conglomerate and father to his friends, the den Coille brothers, making him Caleb's father-in-law.

Would the Old Man have let himself become entangled in a plot that put his own sons at risk? Was he that angry at the authorities?

He scowled, unable to answer. "That flyer hunting us. It was no Federal flyer."

Caleb grunted, as if in a kind of agreement. "I've sent a query through to some friends in Urbis. And yes, I did warn them to keep it under wraps for now."

This time, it was Ethan who grunted. "Pa wouldn't do anything like this."

"To you? His ever loyal son? And that wasn't meant as a criticism."

Maybe, but it had Ethan clenching his hands on the controls, wishing they were safely on land where he could show his brother exactly what he thought of that crack.

Caleb's eyes followed Ethan's hands. A long sigh followed. "I know what you've done for this company, and how much it means to you. Whether the Old Man would go so far as to betray it and you…?" His mouth twisted into a grim frown and he leaned back, watching as Ethan set his flyer heading east to the flat sands of the Sulwith field.

Talk after that was intermittent. Not long into the journey, Caleb cut off further protest by the simple expedient of closing his eyes and falling asleep. Or giving a skilled facsimile of it, Ethan cursed silently.

He stayed like that until they began the approach to Sulwith over the blinding sheets of the solar array. One moment, Caleb lay arms crossed and seemingly oblivious. The next, he sat up and peered through the forward canopy, then swore softly.

"The Old Man can't think he'll get away with leaving this field untouched."

"He's got a point. This field makes Solaris as much money as the next ten arrays combined, and it has a uniquely skilled workforce." Like Sarwenna's precious Geordie. He'd checked as soon as he had access to a com in Dridust and been given the message they'd received for Sarwenna during the trip. The boy had been found coming back into town under the cover of the array sheets, despite Sarwenna's claims he would be lost and confused.

And where was Sarwenna Beren now?

Caleb leaned forward, staring at the array "That first shot came from the northern margin, with the second from north of that?" Ethan nodded. "Care to take a look, brother?"

"Fly straight there and let them take another pot-shot at us?" Their mother would have a heart attack.

"Not your style," agreed Caleb, "but I would like a look at those sites without a local escort."

He had a point, but Ethan had no desire to fall prey to that beam again. He sent a coded order to his security details in the following flyer to stay high and hold position, then eased sideways as if trying to avoid the solar array below. The change in thermals over an array was real enough that avoiding direct flights over them wasn't unusual. Soon they were flying low over the eastern rim and tracking up to the northern edge. Caleb stared out the side windows.

"Something down there?"

Caleb didn't break his study of the ground below. "No. That's the problem."

"So? This is the deadlands."

"By name only. Billyups love country like this, as do a whole host of other species, but there should be some ground cover, at least around the margins of the field. There was when man first came to this planet."

Ethan was in no mood for another of his brother's lectures. "Tell Father. Maybe you can get him to change his mind."

"Isn't that your job? You're the one who's made a lifetime study of manipulating him to get what you want. Remember that flyer you wrangled out of him in senior school?"

Ethan's mouth dropped open. "There's a trag of a difference between a flyer and a whole business empire."

Caleb swivelled on him. "You want another crisis like the last one? I can't promise to drag your sorry carcasses out of the executioner's grasp a second time."

Ethan made a show of concentrating on flying but knew his brother wouldn't be fooled. Any Solaris flyer used by the brothers had the latest inflight autopilots fitted. "Of course I don't, but changing Solaris is like changing the path of a big blow. You're the expert on the environmental risks we face, and yet you can't stop the Old Man trying to worm out of making any changes. Didn't you hear him today? He thinks he can leave Sulwith untouched and get away with it. The Council won't tolerate that for long."

"Then make him change, brother."

Ethan refused to answer. Caleb hadn't seen the inside of a prison cell.

Solaris is going to be so strong no two-bit official ever tries something like that again. Their father's first words to Ethan after the Feds had sprung them from captivity. Sol Winter was born a fighter, and all prison had taught him was to fight harder. He'd fallen back on every trick learned in a long history in business to cement Solaris' position as the most powerful energy company on the planet.

Except it wasn't going to work. Not this time. Caleb was right; Solaris must change or be doomed. But how to change? That Ethan was still figuring out.

The northern edge of the array lay below them. A sharp line between bright swathes of solar sheets on one side and the golden dustiness of the deadlands on the other. Ethan flew higher to avoid curious eyes and swung obliquely out from the array and toward the dry valley where Sar had directed him to land. Solaris scanners had this area under surveillance, but his flyer wouldn't trigger an alarm. They should stay undetected. He hoped.

Caleb watched him. "Try tracking across the far wash to make it look like you're hunting for a com-dead flyer."

"It's still com dead?" Ethan hadn't got to that part of the report.

"Yeah, and to do that to that fancy piece of hardware of yours is quite a feat."

"What about the core log? Any signs of being tampered with?"

"Nothing in the report. Not that I've read."

So best to assume it had been. Silently, they looped around the edge of the field below, dipping and slipping around the fingers of hillocks until they lay just out of sight of the array. Ethan settled the flyer into a fold in the hill and under a solid rock bluff.

Caleb peered up, then leaned forward and tabbed into the ship's scanner. Next minute, an image formed of the density of the rock above them.

Ethan waved a hand through the scan field. "Solid as they come. It's not going to come down on us. Sands, you're jumpy these days."

"Just cautious."

This from the man who'd marched his Survey staff into Urbis and defied the whole planetary government. Ethan grunted in disgust. "We're safe. You coming, or staying huddled in hiding here?"

Another of those big brother looks before Caleb stood up and strode out the hatch.

A short walk later, they both crouched by a short dune near the closest of the solar sheets. Attached to silvery poles, each one held a series of thin sheets angling up the pole and catching every ray of sun. Moving gently, they interlocked one on top of another forming a solid catchment shield.

Caleb peered outward, frowning. "This the area the shot came from?"

"Best I can figure." Ethan angled his com screen toward his brother. "The lab team managed to extract a segment of the attack from my old com."

Caleb's frown deepened as he watched the replay. "That was some beam."

"Yeah. Not sure whether I want to lock up the brakka who built it or put him on the payroll."

"Find out who it is first."

Unfortunately, Ethan had only one lead so far to who might help him do that and he wasn't ready to discuss it with Caleb. Not yet. "I'm setting the Winter shield to stop the scanners seeing us."

It did help being a Winter, occasionally. He set the program and waited to confirm that they were both shielded. His father had a pathological distrust of most people, including those who worked for him, and had developed the program years ago to let the family check out operations on the quiet. The com gave the all clear and he lifted a hand to signal Caleb.

Hugging the ground, they stole over the hump of sand and ran swiftly to the array, sliding under the sheltering sheets. Both of them pulled on the cooling coveralls that were standard gear on any flyer heading into the deadlands. The heat under the arrays could be deadly to unprotected visitors. Then Ethan set his com to scan the sheets while Caleb peered closely at each pole. The underside of the sheets showed only a black, non-reflective surface, and too soon they both were forced to activate the light beam in their coms. Caleb had done the same as he had, setting the beam to the minimum necessary and angled downward to stop being seen by an observer.

His brother had got sneaky.

The sheets came so low down the poles that they had to crouch, and only the com and the line of sharp light on the northern edge of the field kept Ethan from complete disorientation. He set his com to scan the poles, peering closely at each sheet and its coupling to the central pole. All smooth, all shiny, all exactly as they should be.

"Send up a bot," said Caleb, sounding as frustrated as Ethan.

"You think I carry surveillance equipment with me all the time?"

"On this trip? Stop quibbling. I don't care how illegal whatever you've got with you is. Just use it."

For an instant, Ethan wondered at the tic on his brother's face. He hadn't wanted to reveal all his tricks, unsure what held Caleb's loyalty, but another glare and he pulled out the micro-bot from his tunic pouch and sent it to worm its way up through the overlapping sheets to scan them from above.

After a while, he linked the results through to his brother's com, receiving a raised eyebrow in reply. "You think I know nothing of what goes on in my own father's company labs?" said Caleb. "Where do you think I spent most school holidays when I wasn't roaming out on the plains."

Ethan gave a half shrug in apology. "Next you'll be telling me you helped develop these bots and never said a word of them to the Survey."

A half smile, dry and tight. "I'm better on ecosystem engineering. Give me plants and animals. These have Silas's touch."

And yes, he was right in that too. Or had been until their youngest brother spent months hiding out on the plains with Caleb's Survey field staff, safe from the claws of the Survey's false bosses. A time Ethan and Caleb usually avoided discussing. "Maybe before," said Ethan, "but now he's as focussed on the madness you're creating on the plains as he was on the technical stuff."

"He feels useful. He'll get back to himself one day. Just needs time. For now, he reckons he owes a duty to the memory of Ben."

Another subject they usually avoided. Maybe the heat was getting to them both, or the frustration. Ben Crane had been a boy a few years behind Ethan at school, bright as blazes and with a cheeky grin Ethan would remember till the day he died. Ben had been killed trying to save the youngest den Coille brother from capture.

Ethan doubted Caleb would ever forgive his youngest brother-in-law for that death. Caleb's guilt at failing to protect Ben had nearly split him from the wife he loved so dearly. Fee den Coille was a force of nature who had somehow tamed his stubborn brother, but Ben had been a child of nature who should never have died so young.

Caleb must have been thinking the same. His mouth suddenly set straight and he concentrated again on the com reports. They worked in silence for a long time after that, moving methodically through the field.

Just when Ethan had nearly given up, his brother touched him on the arm, then pointed up the pole in front of him.

Ethan peered upward.

There, beside the arm joint to the topmost sheet. A tiny scratch, new and black against the shiny surface.

"You said the beam came from a cluster of sheets?"

Ethan was already examining the rest of the pole. "Yes. They rotated to form a cone-like funnel, with the beam coming from the middle.

Another scratch, at the same height as the first.

"It will be a circle," said Caleb.

They each took a pole next to the scratched one, Caleb going one way, Ethan the other, circling until they met back at the first pole. Ethan grinned at his brother, and Caleb grinned back, just like when they were boys.

"In the same place?"

"Yes," said Ethan. "All marked in exactly the same place. Something was attached to those poles."

"So what was it, and who took it away," said Caleb, crouching down to examine the ground.

The beam's creators had tried to hide their passing, but it didn't take the brothers long to find the tell-tale sweepings of dirt showing the passing of a ground cart. The low profile skimmers were the most common way of travelling under the solar sheets and would have been invisible from above. But Ethan and Caleb had spent many teenage years tracking animals and stock over the plains near their home.

"They're not even trying to lay a false trail," said Ethan after a while.

Caleb bent down to check the path. "Right back to town."

Which meant Sarwenna Beren probably had a good idea who would be in it, and it wasn't the boy who'd run off into the solar array. Or maybe the boy was a ruse and she was part of a plot against him. But why would someone brilliant enough to build a beam that baffled the best experts in Solaris leave a trail a first schooler could follow? Sarwenna had been with him, so it wasn't her in the skimmer, but could she be part of it?

No. The denial was instinctive, one he refused to second guess.

Caleb gave a last look at the tracks. "It's clear where they're going. No point following to see if they come out somewhere else, or do you fancy walking all the way back to town, brother."

He grimaced, already feeling a twinge in his bent back. "Not in these fields. They weren't built for Winter-size people."

Together, they headed back to the field's edge, both breathing a sigh of relief when they emerged and could stand upright again. They still had a slog back to where they'd hidden the flyer, and the sun was getting uncomfortably hot. Ethan grinned. They'd better walk quicker then. He pulled out his canteen and took a short swig, just enough to wet his mouth and keep him going. Caleb glanced over.

"Good to see you haven't forgotten everything I drilled into that thick head of yours," he said, pulling out his own canteen and copying Ethan's actions.

"I never forget anything, big brother. Including who always beat you home when old Jim took us out on trekking lessons."

A smile, the nearest to an honest grin he'd seen from Caleb since…

No, don't spoil the moment.

They hugged the edge of the solar arrays until they were opposite the spur hiding their flyer, then both ducked and ran, swerving this way and that, till they gained the cover of the hill and it was safe to disengage the Winter shield. Back in the flyer and buckled down, Ethan turned to Caleb. "We check out the crash site, then onto the hilltop where the Stalker attacked us, before heading into Sulwith. Agree?"

Caleb gave a brief nod, a grim set to his mouth that found an echo in Ethan. Sarwenna Beren had some explaining to do. She and whoever it was she was hiding. The unknown genius had come near to killing both Ethan and Sar, and he planned to make it crystal clear to her quite how close they'd come.

Arriving at the crash site only made him more resolved. The Solaris investigations team had secured the flyer, making sure it wouldn't be lost in the next sandstorm, and inside, everything had been scanned and swiped clean, according to the report on file.

He set his flyer in a hover and they tubed down to the top hatch, switching off the security field and pulling the hatch carefully open. What he thought to find inside, not even he could say. But he prowled over the whole of the interior as zealously as his brother.

"Get this thing to let me in, will you," said Caleb, scowling at the control panel.

"Don't bother. Our investigators will have scoured through everything in the data banks already."

"Not with a Survey scanner they haven't."

"Only if you give me a full download of anything you find."

The words came automatically, and just like that the wall between them was back. Caleb straightened, studying him with all the wisdom of the few years separating them. "Agreed."

That look spoke true, or it used to, and the Survey's research labs had certainly been proven the superior in cunning to any corporate lab. Nor did Ethan want to consider what it meant if he no longer trusted his brother's word. He tapped in the required sequence and linked his com to Caleb's.

"You're in now. No limits," he said and hoped to hell he'd done the right thing. He hoped it even more as he watched the lines on Caleb's face tighten as he studied the scan results.

"Haven't you got enough yet or isn't the Survey's wonder tech so great after all."

"Oh, it's good," said Caleb, still intently focussed on his readouts. He had them in privacy mode, so all Ethan could see was his brother's frowns.

"You promised to share what you found." He reached out the wrist with his com patch to demand access.

Caleb looked up from his data, as if assessing the situation, and for a long moment Ethan held his breath. Suddenly, a whole lot more than a bunch of technical figures was at stake. Caleb's eyes narrowed, and Ethan jerked back as if hit.

The frown on Caleb's face twisted. "Yes, I promised."

Ethan had a sudden feeling Caleb meant a whole lot more. What, he wasn't sure. But Caleb linked through to his com and a screed of charts and schematic diagrams erupted into Ethan's screen space, filling the tense moment. Luckily, he'd been taught enough basic mechanics to pick out the engine diagnostics.

"It's completely fried," he concluded in disgust. "The control module is totally scrambled, and the crash damaged those shafts so badly they'll need complete re-tooling."

"As for the comlink system, that's as bad," agreed Caleb. He flicked through to the coms file and after much muttering and brow creasing, Ethan managed to work out what his brother meant. Nothing mechanical this time. Nothing so simple. This time, the entire program had been altered, creating a new blocking field that should not be there.

"So how do we remove that shield."

Caleb leaned back. "No idea," he said in disgust. "Not unless we find whoever put it there and get them to take it out."

"What about our lab's so-called experts? Don't they have a solution?"

"They didn't get a proper fix on the shield, let alone find a way to remove it. My Survey scanner is better than theirs. It's more sensitive to certain emissions."

"Then use it to work out what kind of field this is. It's a starting point at least."

"Yeah, a starting point. One I can take back to Urbis central labs and hope they can find the answers. That is, after they send down a full review panel and take control of this whole array. Is that what you want?"

No, he did not. "The Old Man would go into overdrive."

That got a dry twitch of Caleb's lips. He supposed there was a funny side to this. Maybe the cursed Survey could fix his flyer, but no way was he letting them take over Solaris property. Not again.

"So we'd better find the tragging genius who caused this."

Before that, they had to check out the hilltop where an unknown, Federal-styled flyer had tried to kill both him and Sarwenna Beren. The one that had let her escape and hunted him.

CHAPTER FIVE

Sar had never been so pleased to see Sulwith coming up on the horizon. The flyer was comfortable, of the kind she'd expect from Solaris head office, the trip smooth, and it took half the time she was used to, but few spoke to her, and she caught too many surreptitious glares from the corner of her eye.

"I did nothing," she wanted to scream, but the hard core of her refused to show it. They could think what they like. She had not tried to hurt their precious Winter heir.

But someone had. Two lots of someones. And the first someone, the one who fired that beam, had to be a local. Not Geordie, but…

She jerked up in her seat and leaned toward the window, thanking the sands for the sight of the landing field coming up under them. A short time later, she unlatched her webbing and jumped up to escape from this Winter craft.

Only they made her wait for the Solaris technical crew to collect their gear and get out of the craft first. She was a mere hitchhiker, even if Ethan Winter's very superior assistant had organised her ride up here. Finally, she was free to march toward the hatch, only to be greeted by a too familiar face.

"Doc Kaybee," she muttered. "Just great."

"Yes, it is," said the grey-haired woman with a cheerful smile and a no-nonsense look in her eyes. "I had a vidcall from a very officious young man telling me a patient would need my urgent attention when this flyer arrived. Imagine my surprise when he told me the patient's name. To think a girl I delivered as a baby hadn't thought to call me herself. What have you been up to, young Sar?"

"Chasing Geordie. He panicked and headed into the field."

If Sar thought to distract the doctor, she failed completely.

"Huh, that boy. They picked him up last evening, thank the sands, frightened out of what wits he has and a sight lucky to be found when he was. Close to exhaustion, but still alive. He'd remembered enough of the desert tricks we'd pummelled into him, unlike some people. Last I saw him, he was tucking into his ma's best pie and none the worse for his adventure bar a bit of sunburn on that too pointy nose of his. As for you, young Sar, you sit right down on this stretcher and we'll get you to my clinic."

"I can walk," protested Sar.

"Yes, and I can still dance a fandarro. Doesn't mean I should do it right now. Sit." Nor did the doctor give her a chance to argue, toppling Sar back down on the stretcher with a well placed shove and ignoring Sar's mutterings.

She was spending far too much time on stretchers. "Just don't bother Da with this."

"He's waiting at the clinic. Seemed better than having him cause a stir here."

That was so unlike her calm and staunch Da that Sar could only stare. The doctor chuckled.

"Would you rather we'd let your mother know?"

"Sands, no," said Sar, suitably horrified. Dragging her mother away from her duties in Urbis was bad enough. Telling her one of children had been injured would bring on the kind of ruckus her family dreaded most.

Geordie was safe. That was something, and she'd find out the rest soon enough.

Thankfully, only her father waited for her on the beaten up benches and rough finished walls of the hospital waiting room. As usual, he said little, simply ran an eye over her, from head to toe, taking in every bump and hitch in her walk.

"She's fine, Rhyn," said Doc Kaybee from behind her. "Could have been much worse, but that Winter boy has a good helping of sense, and she's had some fancy healing work from the meds down in Dridust."

A slight twist of his mouth, then her father pulled her in and gave her one of his brief but thorough hugs. The smell of earth and the sun clung to him as always and, finally, Sar felt safe again, in a way she hadn't felt since that beam shot at Ethan Winter's flyer and his too acute eyes had watched her face for a reaction.

"Let's get you home," he said in his quiet voice.

"The young ones?"

"Waiting at home for you," he said. "Your sister has even cooked your favourite dinner."

"She has?"

He gave a chuckle. "Unfortunately, your brothers mistook it for the scraps for the chappers and threw it out to them."

"Oh, thank the stars." Her sister may be a genius at many things but cooking was not one of them.

They were all home and safe. When she walked in the door, a riot broke out as her two brothers and sister raced to envelope her in the biggest of hugs. Daff and Finn led the charge, with Finn beating his older brother by a hand's breadth. Still only up to her waist, Finn was the darling of the whole family, but the grin on

Daff's face as he nudged her shoulder was as dear, while to one side, her sister Ari's early teen self-importance lasted only a moment before she collapsed on Sar's other shoulder.

"They said…"

Sar had one arm free still. She put it round her sister's shoulders. "I'm fine, Ari. No one was permanently injured. Well, maybe the pride of Ser Winter, but nothing else. He has a bit of a limp and I have some interesting bumps and an exciting adventure to tell tales about. Not so bad a result."

"How could you treat it like nothing?" Ari flung away from her and rushed from the room, sobbing loudly.

Finn peered after her and Daff gave a huff. "She having one of those teenage things," he said to their father.

"Yes, Daff, I suspect she is. Now, let your sister sit down while I find what we have for dinner then I'll go sort her out."

Sar put out a hand. "You get dinner; I'll see to Ari."

Her father shook his head. "She's got it into her head that she somehow caused your crash with all her railing against the changes they want to make here." He gave that slow smile of his. "Ari might be able to do a lot that amazes me but changing a Winter's mind is something not even she can manage."

"She could do it if they were made of nuts and bolts," said Daff loyally, and Finn nodded his head vigorously. It was true. Ari could make any mechanical device dance to her command. It was the human side of her world she currently had trouble with.

Sar gave in. She loved her sister dearly but dealing with teenage histrionics was more than she could cope with after everything else.

"Right," she said, waving her father down the hallway. "Now, have you two left anything edible in the food prepper for the rest of us?"

"Course we did. Da got in some proper food and the food banks are chock full. Well, almost."

"I did nuffing," said Finn, to his brother's elbowing.

Sar didn't feel up to refereeing a squabble between her baby brothers either. "I can see the smudge on your mouth," she told Finn, "and the crumbs on your top," she added to Daff. She opened up the first cooler drawer to find what her father had laid in.

Proper food, as the boys so precisely said. She breathed in, savouring the smells filling the room. Fresh greens, a selection of fruits, with her favourite gaura nestling in the middle, and the special stone-ground flours made by old auntie Baffin down in the town centre. A mix of native and Earth-sourced grains, the flour made a deliciously nutty flapjack that the whole family loved. She checked the boys' choices, flicked her finger through the screen to make a few sensible changes while ignoring their theatrical groans, then set them to organising the table.

By the time her father and Ari came back, with Ari's face looking suspiciously scrubbed, the old slab table set into the family alcove welcomed them with plates, some flowers Finn had insisted on bringing in from their small indoor garden and thrusting haphazardly into a handy jug, and the familiar cutlery that slipped into Sar's hand as if made for it. With the lamp set to a warm glow and the richly coloured rugs and coverings her mother loved bringing life to the cream stone walls and floors, the room shone with cheer and the comfortable glow of a well loved home.

A place where she could finally relax. She needed that so badly, and deliberately chose to ignore Ari's unusual quiet.

She'd worry about it tomorrow.

But Ari stayed quiet all evening, and when she made her excuses early and slipped off to her room, Sar knew she couldn't leave it longer. She waited till Da was busy with the nightly adventure of persuading two energetic boys to calm down and go to bed, then slipped after Ari.

A quiet touch on her sister's door pad. When no welcoming whoosh of the door followed, she tried the usual code. Ari had changed it again, but Da had wised up to that long ago. Sar entered the override code that only she and Da knew.

Her sister sat hunched over her desk, com screen activated, but she blanked it out before Sar had any chance of seeing what was on it.

Sar started with the gentlest and most caring voice she could summon. "Are you all right?"

"Why wouldn't I be?"

"No reason, but it's not like you to disappear so early."

"I have homework to do," was the ungracious reply from the depths of a head of hair that hid any sign of her sister's face.

Sar gave up on being nice. "Where were you yesterday, Ari. When Geordie ran off."

That worked. Her sister rounded on her, chin stuck out and eyes defiant. "Looking for him, like everyone else after that stupid Winter man frightened him with his talk of closing our field."

"Ser Winter spoke only the truth." One that Sar would fight till the end.

"He's going to wreck everything. Those Winters have enough credits all ready. This field's too good to change."

"Not according to the government in Urbis."

"Them too," said her sister with such loathing in her voice that the half-formed misgiving in Sar's head flared into full blown dismay.

"Where exactly were you, Ari? When Ethan Winter's flyer crashed with me inside it, thanks to a strange beam, where were you then?"

Her sister shot out of her chair, arms clamped tight about her body and misery filling her eyes.

"Looking for Geordie," she yelled. "And that's all I'm going to tell you. You're safe, Isn't that enough?"

Sar studied her sister's face, noted the set of her chin and the too rigidly held shoulders. Ari could smile and laugh with all the vibrant joy of her youth but right now, she was blind to joy and something held her tight in the grip of teenage agony. An agony Sar could do nothing about. Not when Ari's chin thrust forward like that.

"Get some sleep and we'll talk again another time," she said in the contained voice that usually deflated a defiant Ari. Not today, though, that stuck-out chin telling Sar more than she wanted to know. More than she dreaded knowing.

"Until tomorrow," she finally said, and quietly let herself out of her sister's room before restoring the lock on the control pad.

Tomorrow, though, turned out to be too busy to have time to talk to anyone.

"The Winters are on their way. Both brothers," was the first Sar heard as she stepped into her office in the town's community centre, little more than an alcove off the main rooms. Marget, the town's information clerk and general gossip monger served as receptionist for the union as well. Which meant any confidential business had to be handled well away from the office, and Sar had taken to staking out a table at the local tavern near the change of shift times, one discreetly off the main room for any workers wanting a quiet chat. This morning, she'd hoped to catch some quiet time at the office to figure out what to do about this latest threat to her town.

Then she'd walked in the door and Marget had made her pronouncement with all the glee of a desert predator cornering its prey.

"Which ones?" said Sar curtly, not caring that her tone would give Marget more fuel for gossip. "There are three of them."

"The two that matter, of course. The deputy head of the whole outfit, Ethan Winter, and Caleb Winter himself. The one who works for the Survey and betrayed his family to the Survey troops."

"No, he didn't." Sar should have known not to expect the woman to understand what had happened up in Urbis. "They're both coming, you said. Is that official?"

Marget madly bobbed her over-curled hair. "It came over the comcast first thing. They'll be here in a couple of hours."

Great. Just what she needed. "I'll get onto the town councillors and find out what's planned," she said, resigning herself to the inevitable.

She strode out into the still cool morning air. A slight dew clung to the hardy bushes edging the small garden in the front of the hall, and a trail of the tiny glitchits tracked from their burrow under the edge of the hall to the precious droplets on the top side of the leaves. In no time, the small bugs could fill a surprisingly large reservoir of water deep in the passages of their home colony, carried microdroplet by microdroplet on the top of the pair of secondary limbs at the front of each body. She carefully stepped over the black line, remembering an old rhyme from childhood.

Step on a glitchit and next you'll get

A twitchit, a twatchit, a two bit cretchit.

Very bad luck, was what her father said the old rhyme meant, and she really didn't need any more of that.

Nor did what met her at the council office help any. The town's mayor had been chosen more for his genial good nature than any knack for organisation. She finally managed to pin down his assistant. "When do they arrive, and who exactly is meeting them?"

Gabrallie looked panic stricken. "Won't someone from the company be doing that? This is a Solaris visit, not a civic one."

"If they shut down that array, they shut down the town."

It got her a promise of some councillors at the landing field but what happened afterward appeared to be a mystery. A Solaris problem, was the general consensus among the council admin staff, busy trying to slip out the door before she could pin them down or discussing what to wear for this latest Winter visitation. Sar had to throttle down her disgust.

"What about food? Or does Sulwith no longer care about hospitality?"

That had Gabrallie blushing in shame. "I'll organise something," she mumbled.

No one else offered to help, and Sar had to be satisfied. At least she could trust Gabrallie to rustle up a welcome spread that wouldn't embarrass the town. Her pride would see to that. Sar gave up on the rest and marched over to the local Solaris office.

"Sar, baby. What brings you here today. You'd better not be stirring up trouble."

Sar grinned at the elderly man behind the counter. Old Rab had been here longer than anyone could remember. At one time, he ran the array repair shop, but these days, he perched himself in the front office as a self-appointed custodian. If you wanted to talk to anyone in the front office, including your own father, you had to go through Old Rab.

"Is Da in?"

"With two Winters on their way? Of course not, young Sar. He's down at the workshop making sure everything's in place and all the workers spruced up and working hard. The whole field is running sweeter than you'd believe today."

Sar snorted. "Or than a Winter would believe."

A deep chuckle that Sar had always loved. "Your father has been around longer than any young Winter sprout. Now the old man, old Sol Winter. Him, you wouldn't fool."

Sar had a feeling that fooling Ethan Winter would be equally difficult. "So what's the plan when they arrive? Is Tom Crabster inside?"

Not today either, she learned. The Sulwith field manager was busy making sure all the array vehicles had been properly spruced up and looking fit to carry the heirs to the Solaris empire. He'd have been better making sure the field's figures and records looked as shiny bright, thought Sar, but said nothing. She followed meekly after Old Rab to her father's office at the rear of the maintenance building. Tom Crabster may be the site manager, but it was her father who kept everything going, regardless of the latest management brainwave. Her father and Geordie were the true secrets behind the profitability of the Sulwith Solar Field.

No, her father, Geordie, and her sister Ari. Her sister who might be… No, don't think it. Not yet.

Her father sat in his usual position at his battered desk, screen open and fingers madly flicking between schematics and figures.

"Hey, Da."

A slow smile lit up his round face. "Hey yourself, little girl."

"Not so little these days," she said wryly.

"You'll always be my little girl," he said in their old familiar banter. "What brings you down here."

She grimaced. "You've heard?"

"That the Winters are coming. Of course," he said in that placid voice of his.

"And the staff? How are they taking it?"

"The staff are all working as they should be." Her father raised an eyebrow. "What else would they be doing."

"Fretting about their jobs."

"When they have concrete reason, they can start worrying. Until then, we have a solar plant to run."

"And Geordie?"

Her father did frown at that with a twist to his mouth. "He was lucky yesterday. But how often can his luck hold? Thankfully, Ari managed to calm him down enough to believe no one is taking his solar field away from him. If Ethan Winter has half the business brain his work suggests, that's a promise we can keep."

Sar wondered if her father was being deliberately obtuse. She took the chair on the other side of his desk. "What about the government up in Urbis? Caleb Winter works for the Survey. He's the brother who rejected all Sol Winter's offers to help run Solaris."

"The brother who designed those roof sheets for the Winter home village that beat any design anyone else has come up with in Arcadia. That village feeds into the Solaris system and hasn't drawn down a smig of power from outside sources since Caleb installed those roofscapes. The boy has as good a brain as any of his brothers; he just uses it a bit differently."

"Yeah," said Sar in her driest voice.

"Yes, young lady. Nor is he coming here to hurt us. He's got enough to do with that new wife of his, building a home and setting up that fancy lake system the Survey is installing out on the Winter grazing plains."

"If he's so busy, why is he taking time he doesn't have to come up here and poke into our business."

Her father cocked his head at her. "Because someone tried to kill his brother. Or that's what he thinks, and when it comes to family, he's as much a Winter as any of them, despite what last year may have looked like."

Everyone on the plains knew that, even if the stupid vidcasters up in Urbis thought Caleb Winter and his wife had betrayed their families last year. Well, they sort of had, but they had also saved them in the end, and that's what counted.

"All right," she conceded, "but what else is he going to do while he's here? The Survey wants to change all the Solaris solar fields, including this one, and he doesn't seem like a man easily distracted."

Her father leaned onto his crossed hands. "Not from all reports. Not that he's wrong." Her gasp of shock had her father looking up sharply. "This field does need to change. You must know that. Given the ultimatum the government says they've had from the Alliance, we have no choice."

Yes, Sar had heard of the ultimatum. Turn around the increasing problems with the environmental balance on their planet, or the Alliance will do it for them, as well as forcibly removing the current population who'd failed to fix their home world. Arcadia couldn't stand against the might of the other Alliance worlds. She scowled back. "How about the Alliance tell us what we're to do about the men and women who lose their jobs. There's no place in Sulwith for the jobless. Where do you go when the type of solar sheet you've worked on your whole life is no longer used?

"You learn how to do a new job, and you learn fast," said her father.

Sar gaped. Her father had spent his entire working life helping any family who came to him in need.

"Yes, I did just say that. You think it's easy for me to look our staff in the face each day and know that change is coming, whether they're ready or not? Some things you can't fight and the truth of what's happening to our world is one of those things. We change, or no one will have a job here, or a home. It'll be too hot, too dry and too tragging uncomfortable."

Sar had never heard such words from her father before and she had no idea what to say.

"Da—"

"Don't fight me on this, please, Wennie-mine."

"The staff. The men and women. They can't—"

"Yes, they can … and must."

She shook her head again and saw pain darken his eyes. The same pain she'd seen as a small child every time he came home after watching her mother leave to fly back to her work in Urbis. Sar still remembered the fierce joy she'd felt when her mother lost her seat on the Federal Assembly and came home to them. She hadn't seen that look in her father's eyes again until the day a few months past when her mother won her seat back and set out on that flyer again.

She had never seen it put there by her. Worse, she could do nothing to banish it. She put up a hand and began to walk out.

"Sar. Wait."

She stopped, shaking her head. "My union members. They trust me to help them."

"You will, but think carefully how you do it. That's all I ask."

Her father so rarely asked outright for her help. Together, they had raised her family, but always he let her do what she could and soldiered on with the rest. She had learned years ago to look for the small signs that said he needed a hand. How could she deny him now? She put out a hand, reached for the chair behind her and eased down into it.

"I will," she said, in a thin voice she barely recognised. "I will think, but…" She took a deep breath. "When do the Winters arrive?"

His hand reached out and his work-scarred palm engulfed hers. She squeezed back and he let her hand drop, easing back in his own chair and answering her spoken question instead of the one in her heart.

"They left the Winter homestead at first light, so will be here for lunch. Marget tells me she has that under control."

"Hopefully. Gabrallie is in charge of it."

"Good. Whatever their faults, she and Marget always put on a fine spread."

A tentative smile from her father, but he still studied her. Not in the least fooled, she'd guess, but willing to give her time to consider.

She doubted any amount of time would change anything. All she could do was forge on. "I take it you have the plant ready for inspection?"

He nodded with that quiet assurance of his. "Everyone knows their job and is doing it. The Winters will have no cause for complaint when it comes to Sulwith staff or equipment."

"They never have," she couldn't help adding.

"No, but before this, all they'd worried about is the profit. Now, the stakes have changed."

Her father's eyes fixed on her face. She forced her face muscles into a calm reassurance and returned his look. "So we make sure those changes aren't more drastic than needed."

"Exactly."

Her father had never been one to waste words. He let his tone speak for him. Today, it held a weight of expectation, one she couldn't promise to deliver on. She mumbled something about checking in with the union subbies and got out of there.

Escaping her father's office. She was on her own in this, and that hurt something deep inside.

The whoosh of a flyer overhead found her standing on the landing pad waiting for the Winter ship to arrive. Marget and Gabrallie hadn't failed the town, and a fine feast waited in the town hall, but there was enough needing to be done to keep Sar occupied till the last moment before the Winters arrived. She hectically chased one chore after another, too busy to brood. Then a sleek shape descended and landed with pinpoint precision on their dusty landing field.

Ethan Winter in the pilot's seat, no doubt. That landing after the attack had been a piece of talented flying.

The hatch opened and the brothers walked down the ramp. She had to blink. She'd seen them together in enough vidcasts but the reality was a different matter. Two renderings of the same prototype, walking side by side. Both tall, but Ethan was leaner, and with browner hair and skin a shade lighter than his brother's. Thanks to working mainly behind a desk, she'd guess, while Caleb Winter scrabbled in that giant puddle of his out on the plains. Only their eyes distinguished them. Caleb's were a bright blue, remarkable in their own way but missing the stunning power of his brother's clear green.

What both shared today was the look in those eyes, assessing and waiting to be convinced they could trust you.

At least it was an honest start ... because they couldn't.

CHAPTER SIX

She stood waiting for him again. Ethan knew a disorienting sense of having been here before, with the desert breeze tugging at those enticing wisps of hair and bringing him the scents of hot sand and warm skin. Except this time those stunning eyes were filled with a wary distrust and her arms hugged her body tight. His gut clenched.

"Is that her?" said Caleb.

"Her?"

"The union foxllar you tangled with last time. The one sitting so conveniently beside you when your flyer failed and who told you where to land."

He scowled at his brother. "She could have been killed too."

"In that plane, and with your training as a pilot?"

"She wasn't to know that." He flashed a glare at the scepticism on Caleb's face. "I'm not that useless at reading people. She was as shocked by that Stalker's attack as I was, and we'd have been in serious trouble if she hadn't guided me down to a safe landing site."

A half shrug from his brother, but at least Caleb said nothing more. Sarwenna stayed back this time as a gaggle of Solaris and town officials bustled forward. Nor dare he single her out, forced instead to waste time with the kind of empty blatherings he'd been trained in since childhood. Only the quality of the feast they'd laid on in welcome held back his temper. Someone in this backwater could cook. By the end of it, he'd rendered the officials twice as polite and sweating hard. Yes, I'm hunting and you better help me if you want to keep your cushy jobs.

Ethan had studied the accounts and reports from this place. The too smooth manager wasn't the man who kept the field going. Somewhere behind the scenes was someone who knew the plant in a way this bootlicker never could. Ethan let the talk continue until they reached what passed for accommodation in the town, then dismissed the manager, telling him they wanted to settle in.

He shook the man's hand, forcing himself to endure the sweaty palm. "We will meet again at the end of the workday," he told him. "You'll be in your office then?"

At the very fulsome assurance that of course he would, Ethan lifted a hand to cut off the flood and turned to follow Caleb inside. No chance yet to talk to Sarwenna, apart from a strangled greeting in the welcoming line up. She'd slipped away as soon as the feast ended, but she wouldn't escape him so easily, and not only because he wanted to see her again. She was hiding something, and he intended to find out what.

"An interesting woman."

He'd barely made it to the shared lounge area of their rooms and Caleb was at him already. "Who?"

"Your union woman."

He really didn't need this. "You can't know what she's like. You never talked to her."

"No, she made sure of it. So why is she working so hard to avoid us?

"I don't know, but I do know she's not the one who made that beam."

"I'll go along with that, but she knows something."

That stopped him. "You didn't talk to her."

"No, but there's nothing in her file to suggest she's capable of it. What's more, the local management treated her like they always do union reps. An irritating necessity they have to put up with. If she'd been responsible for that beam, they'd be scared silly."

Ethan had to take a seat at that, pulling out a drink from the nearby dispenser. He lifted his boot and pushed the other chair across to Caleb to stop him glaring down at him. "You actually notice there are people in your precious ecosystem?"

A cool chuckle as his brother sat down. "I've always noticed the people. They're the ones causing all the problems. And I've been managing a Survey team for years, not to mention having two crazy kid brothers who tried to get into trouble anytime we responsible ones turned our backs."

Ethan's mouth dropped open. He remembered too many tricks Caleb had pulled as a child.

"You trying to manage me, brother?" he said.

"Did it work? You looked about ready to snap the head off that poor manager."

"If that man is running anything around here apart from the welcome party, I'll be very surprised."

"A frontman, agreed, but a smooth one." A fleeting grin from Caleb. The kind Ethan had learned to thoroughly mistrust. "So who is running this field and doing a fine job of it from all accounts. Good enough to make the Old Man go up against the Feds in Urbis and play all sorts of stupid games to keep it just like it is."

It was a question, and one Ethan refused to answer. "He is our father."

"And as stubborn and pig-headed as ever."

"Mother always said you take after him."

Caleb gave that the consideration it deserved. "He must know he can't win this one."

That might be true, but Caleb had never seen the inside of a prison cell or been at the mercy of a bunch of thugs. Not like their father—or Ethan. "It's Solaris business. I'm only here to gather facts," Ethan said.

Caleb stared back at him. Then his face closed over in a way it had never done when they were boys but was becoming all too familiar these days. "I have work to do."

A slam of a hand against a door panel and Caleb stormed from the room. Ethan watched the door close after him and wished stupidly for time to shift backward. A boy's wish.

He also had work to do, but he stayed, slowly sipping his drink and feeling the burn of it going down to lodge in his stomach in an uneasy stew with the questions churning there. He ought to be out there finding out what was going on, like Caleb was.

Like his brother from the Survey was.

"Tragging sands."

Ethan slammed the drink down on the nearest table, grabbed his stuff and slammed out of the room.

"Which way did my brother go?" he demanded of the man idling behind the reception counter.

"Down the street to the main offices, Ser Winter," said the man. He hadn't been on duty when they'd booked in, but Ethan wasn't surprised to be recognised. The whole town knew who they were and why they were here.

So his brother should be easy to find.

Should be. Ethan traipsed over half the town and in and out of Solaris offices and workrooms with no sign of his wily brother. All he got were hints and vague hand wavings.

"Up there."

"Just missed him, Ser."

"He was heading that way, Ser Winter."

Either his brother had marched over the whole town simultaneously or the townsfolk were hiding him from Ethan, and he had a fair idea why. His single-minded brother wasn't above letting them think Ethan was the one behind the threat to shut the place down rather than his precious Survey and all the other officials up in Urbis. Not if it suited his purposes.

Didn't anyone in this benighted town have two brain cells to rub together?

He shoved his toe against a stone and sent it flying off into the nearest wall. That was it. He'd wasted enough time on his devious brother. If he really wanted to help Ethan, he'd be up in Urbis finding out who owned that Stalker flyer instead of interfering here. He whirled around and set off for the main Sulwith workshop. Didn't the townsfolk know that one wrong move by Solaris would bring the Feds down on this place in full regulatory force. Ethan had to find an alternative, and quickly. Had to find out what made Sulwith so successful, what to change and what to keep.

The see-saw of needs that had driven him ever since the Federal marshals had sprung him from prison and he'd discovered that the business he'd loved all his life was on the brink of disaster. His family had to change or lose everything.

Caleb had warned them so many times over the years, but his father refused to listen and prison had only made him more stubborn. To his brother, the demise of Solaris was an unfortunate consequence. He'd never said the words outright, not to Ethan or the family, but all his actions showed his priorities. Planet first. That was Caleb.

As for their younger brother, Silas was too mixed up at the moment to know what he wanted to do.

Only Ethan was left to save Solaris.

"Do you want to be a poor Arcadian or a poorer refugee?" Caleb had said to him once, "because that's the alternative the Alliance of Worlds is offering us."

It had silenced Ethan, as it had been meant to do, but it hadn't taken away the anger simmering inside.

Nothing would. Not with his memories of those months in prison, waiting to die.

No, don't go back there. He thumped down viciously onto his thigh. He would find a way out of this, find a way to save Solaris and stay on this planet. Maybe even find a way to keep his family's respect.

Give up on their love, too, said his head, but his heart hadn't gone there yet. A strong-willed bunch of fiercely independent individuals, they may be, but they were the only family he had.

And you're different.

No, I just hide it better. A sudden grin touched his mouth, swiping away the gloom, and he slapped the control panel of the door giving direct access to the workshop at the back of the main office block, shamelessly using the override Winter function. It was his family's workshop, and he wasn't about to ask anyone's permission to enter it.

He failed to surprise the staff inside. A smiling old man bustled forward as soon as the door slid open, thrusting forward a hand.

"Welcome, welcome, young Ser Winter. Good to see a man who goes straight to the heart of a place without bothering with front office formalities."

Ethan wasn't sure if the man was scolding him for overturning proper procedure or congratulating him. He chose to act as if it was the latter.

"Thank you, ...?"

"Rab Koor, Ser, but everyone calls me Old Rab. You need anything, you just ask me."

And I will make sure you get the official line, suspected Ethan, but he smiled warmly and allowed the old man to lead him on through to the main workshop office.

"You'll be wanting to talk to Rhyn Beren. He knows most of what goes on around here," said the man.

"Beren? Any relation to Sera Beren of the union?"

A chuckle. "Young Sar? Her Da, for his sins," said Rab. "Along with three young 'uns as well. A good Da he be too. He's had to, with a wife like Sera Catra."

Ethan allowed himself a slight quirk of his lips. "The local Councillor for the Federal Assembly? The one who used to be union head for Sulwith but recently won the seat for the Deadlands?"

"Won it back again," the old man said. "A fine woman, but that big chamber in Urbis can barely keep up with her. Rhyn and those childlins may miss her like crazy, but the town is a sight more peaceful these days." The man leaned over, wheezing with laughter at his joke.

"So her daughter took over the union."

"She's been doing all the leg work for years, as well as helping her Da with the young ones, so who better. We're all mighty pleased she agreed to it."

Which sounded as much like a warning as the rest of the man's words. Old Rab he might call himself, but this was no old fool of a man.

"Right, here we are," his guide announced, palming a solid door at the other side of the entry way and pushing it open. On the other side stood a large barn of a room. A solid floor and walls stacked with shelves holding bins of stuff. Some he recognised as the fittings for repairs to the array; others, he had no idea. He knew the basics of the technical side of the field—their father had made all his sons serve holidays working in the various fields—but mechanics was not his passion. He knew what he needed, which was a sight more than his father realised, but not the intricacies the quiet man behind the far bench must know.

Solidly built, brown hair and a round face burnished by years of the harsh desert sun, there was something very sound about the man. Someone you could rely on, said the work-scarred strength in his hand and the squarely placed legs on the floor.

"Rhyn Beren," he said, shaking Ethan's hand with a brief but firm clasp.

"The workshop supervisor," added Rab with a knowing look that set off Ethan's inbuilt alarm. Could Sarwenna Beren's father be the man responsible for making Solaris so many credits? Was that why she was so dead set against him? Everyone put personal ahead of duty. Hadn't his years of tutoring by his father taught him that?

Sarwenna Beren seemed different, though, and if she couldn't be trusted in this…

No, leave it. Time to get a certain union organiser out of his head.

"Good to meet you, Ser," said Ethan, falling back on all the hard lessons of his training to plaster on a congenial smile. "Word is you're the one to talk to about what really happens around here."

A placid lift of the corners of the man's mouth, but not much else. "I run the workshop and keep things going, if that's what you mean, Ser Winter. I understand you're here to find out how this field works."

That, and a bit more, but he wasn't going to tell Rhyn Beren that until he knew him a whole lot better. "Just the things affecting profitability," he said. "I'm a balance sheet man, as you've no doubt heard."

The man looked at him, then gave a small shake of his head, as if amused, but let the fiction pass. "You'll be wanting to see the staff and output files then?"

"I've read them, all the ones on file at least. Are there more?"

Ethan held his breath for a moment. Then a slight creasing about the man's eyes. "If there are, I haven't seen them," said the man. "So you want to know what's behind all those tables and numbers."

"If you have time."

A chuckle. "For a Winter? Of course I have."

Ethan felt his own mouth lift in a grin. He was beginning to like this man.

The man set down the scanner he'd been fixing and gestured toward a flat, box-like vehicle. "This way, Ser."

The box cart skimmer was the same as the ones used on all the Solaris fields to travel under the solar arrays. A skimmer that would match the tracks he and Caleb had seen under the panels earlier.

"The sun's still high enough to make the heat levels under the sheets a risk. Better put this on." He handed Ethan a loose coverall made of a shimmering light cloth.

Ethan used cooling coveralls routinely to regulate body temperature as he'd done on his and Caleb's foray into the solar field on the way here. The fabric of this was different, but he thought nothing of it as he pulled it on, only to be stunned when he sealed shut the seam. A cool breeze whispered over his skin and the air around his body hovered at a pleasantly mild temperature, like enough to an evening stroll around his mother's garden.

"You make these here?"

The man had pulled on his own coverall. "A local came up with the design."

"Give me his name when we get back. I'd like to make him an offer if they work as well as they seem to."

"Doubt he'd be interested," the man mumbled, then strode to the box cart and took the controls. "We'd better get going."

Ethan's inner alarm sounded again. The man had just shut him out as firmly as ever his mother could. This town held too many secrets and Ethan was growing increasingly determined to break them open.

The visit to the field turned out much as any other, complete with the usual spiel trotted out for a head office bigshot with little interest in how the credits were made. Ethan had a game he played, ranking the level of banality and schmooze he must endure. By the end, he was pleasantly surprised to find that Rhyn Beren ranked very low on schmooze. The man knew the field, cared a lot about the technical side of the business and little about the credits, but had a sure grasp of the necessity of making a profit and how to manage it most effectively. Also, he had some interesting ideas about how to change the field. Not something Ethan had expected to find in Sulwith or from a union organiser's family.

"So the workshop could expand to make domestic units?" he asked Ser Beren carefully.

"Slowly. It depends on the field. Cutting maintenance to concentrate on making other things will only cut the field's efficiency for little gain. Need to balance them," said the man.

"You have some ideas for new units?"

The reply this time was more careful. "Maybe. The odd concept plan to pass onto the lab down at Dridust."

Ethan had a feeling those plans were rather more than concept sketches but said nothing. Not yet. He decided on a gamble. He gave the man the coordinates of the section the beam came from. Once there, they both climbed out of the box cart and he pointed out the marks to Rhyn and told him of the accident.

The man went quiet, and Ethan held his breath. "You know what could have made those?"

"No." Short, brief and unequivocal, but Ethan could swear the tech man had some notions in his head. Too quiet, even for this contained man. Ethan watched as the supervisor stroked a finger over each mark, feeling the same slight roughness as he and Caleb had.

"I'll ask around, but I haven't seen anything like this," the man said, looking at the sheet supports rather than Ethan. "Time we got back now."

Evening was coming on so the man was right, but Ethan wondered if that was all that drove their sudden flight back to the workshop. Once inside, the man took back the clever coverall, and Ethan suddenly felt the real heat of this dry region again.

"A very clever device," he said, fingers running over the unique cloth.

"It does the job. Now, if you'll excuse me, my family will be waiting for me."

A brusque handshake, a sign to Ethan to leave the shop ahead of him so he could lock up, then the man said his good nights and strode off.

Ethan watched Rhyn's rapidly disappearing back. Not a run, not even a scurry, but the man's legs covered the ground with definite haste. He soon disappeared around a corner of a building, looking like a man relieved to escape his head office visitor.

"There you are," said a voice behind him.

Ethan turned to find his brother strolling up the opposite alley, a young girl beside him.

"Here I am," agreed Ethan, "but where in all sands have you been?" He bowed slightly to the girl. A stubby, brown-haired urchin, barely in her teens but with that typical curl to her lips at facing a strange adult. Caleb put a hand on her shoulder.

"Meet my guide to this fascinating town. Ari, my brother, Ethan Winter. Ari found me when I was getting hopelessly lost in the streets of this place and has been a big help in showing me around."

Caleb had never been lost anywhere that Ethan could remember. He looked sharply at his brother but gave the girl a polite smile. "Thank you, Sera. That was very kind of you."

The glint in Caleb's eyes said he understood exactly what Ethan was thinking as he turned to the girl with a formal bow. "I've commandeered you quite long enough, Sera. I suspect it's past time you were home again. My warmest thanks for your help, and I bid you good night."

"Yeah," he thought the girl grunted. "You want some help again tomorrow?" she added, looking at his brother with bright eyes. "There's some more places I can show you."

"Thank you, but I will have to forego the honour," said his brother with the smooth diplomacy he possessed but rarely bothered to use.

"Right then. See ya."

Her face had fallen, but Ethan didn't think she'd been defeated, watching the girl as she swirled around and stumped off, shoulders hunched in the usual way of the youthful.

Once she'd gone from sight, he lifted an eye to his brother. "That girl has a crush on you."

Caleb's mouth lifted in that dubious grin. "On the Survey more like. The girl's as smart as they come and is dreaming of bigger and better. She'd make a good recruit. She knows this land and loves mechanics."

"So shouldn't you have seen her safely home and talked to her parents. You do know everyone in town would have noticed you with her."

"And not one looked the least concerned. Unlike you, little brother, these people know I'm a trustworthy married man ... and the girl refused my offer to see her to her door. For some reason, she very badly didn't want me to know who she is."

"Then we better find out." He began to hurry after the girl, but his brother's arm shot out and stopped him.

"Already dealt with," said Caleb, "and you can thank the Survey lab staff when you're next up in Urbis."

Never happening, brother.

"You have a tracker on her?"

A smug grin from Caleb. "Time to repair to our rooms." Very definitely, if Caleb was about to use Survey technology. He sent the plant manager a quick apology and cancelled their meeting.

Ethan slammed shut the control panel on the door of their suite as soon as they got inside and set the controls to the full security lock. Unbreakable except for an emergency. "So where does she live."

His brother had already activated the holo-field from his com and was staring down at the town. Ethan joined him, thrusting back his qualms and concentrating on the layout of the town.

A funny sort of place, one that seemed to have grown like a living organism rather than through any outsiders' plan, stretching up into the gullies cutting into the hills behind and huddling as close as possible to both sides of the sharp-edged spur thrusting out from the main line of the hills. All that could be seen from the top down was a series of flat roofs and tented canopies, most with some kind of furniture and a predator screen showing up as a shimmering of light energy in the holo-field. He gestured to Caleb, and his brother switched off the distracting readings.

"There," said Caleb, his com zeroing down on a street close to the main cliff. The red dot signalling their prey paused at the door of a house looking much like its neighbours. Maybe a bit bigger, but nothing otherwise to differentiate it.

Then she was inside.

"The artisan quarter," said Ethan. "Home to independent contractors. Most of these houses are owner-occupied."

"You think she's not from a Solaris family? Look again, Ethan."

Caleb brought up the details of the occupants of the house. Main householder: Rhyn Beren, workshop supervisor for the Solaris array.

"What is the man who all but runs our solar array doing living here, rather than in the very comfortable homes we provide for our management staff?"

"Your company, little brother. And he doesn't run the array. He's the workshop supervisor, the man in charge of maintenance and day to day problems, but not the manager."

"You met Tom Crabster when we landed. You really think he's the one making the decisions around here?"

"No, but far be it from me to tell you how to run your company."

"Our company. Your shareholding is the same as mine, and the Old Man is still in charge, in case you haven't noticed."

Which nicely twisted that incipient grin on his brother's mouth.

Ethan looked at the readout again. "I'd just met Rhyn Beren when you found me this afternoon. He seemed a straight shooter and a man comfortable in his place."

"Mmm. That's the talk around town too."

"And what else do they say?"

"Rhyn Beren runs the array, runs it clean, and makes sure the workers are well looked after, unlike Tom Crabster. He has to; his wife and daughter would tell him soon enough if he didn't."

"Representative Catra Beren and their daughter, current union organiser Sera Sarwenna Beren."

"Is that her full name? Everyone just talks of young Sar. Won't she let you call her that?"

"Sarwenna suits her better," said Ethan, and cursed the flush crawling up his face and the grin on his brother's face. "So who else lives there," he said with a glare.

A chuckle, then Caleb relented. "Only the younger siblings. The mother is mostly up in Urbis, and Sar and her father seem to be their day-to-day caregivers. Arionna Beren, around thirteen standard years and known as Ari; Daffin Beren, known as Daff, ten standard years; and Finneas Beren, eight standard years, known as Finn or that little devil, depending on what he's been up to. They all appear to be well liked by the townsfolk, as though they have been unofficially adopted by them all.

Ethan watched the red dot. "Bring up the other occupants in the house, with their bio-reading."

The red dot showed up first with a brief image of the urchin he'd met earlier. "The sister, Ari."

Caleb agreed. "And there, in what I assume is a shared bedroom—the two younger boys." An orange light after their images. A third light paced up the street outside. An older man, his pace steady and set. "Your workshop supervisor, Rhyn Beren."

"Sarwenna will be still at the union office and we know their mother is up in Urbis."

What in all the sand bugs was going on here? Too many Berens popping up for Ethan's comfort. "You said young Ari is bright but she's far too young to be our saboteur. That beam was seriously sophisticated."

"Your supervisor? He'd have the technical knowledge."

Ethan shook his head. "He's hiding something, but he'd have known his daughter was on that flyer with me. He's not the kind either."

"Bringing us back to young Ari." Caleb touched his com, bringing up the schematic of the Beren house and following the red dot. "Kitchen first. Definitely a teenager."

"You didn't think to feed her?"

A scowl at that. "Of course I did. Repeatedly. She's only just finished a double nieten sandwich with all the extras. The takeout bar in town is apparently second to none."

"Grease, gossip and a gaggle of young ones?"

"Yeah," agreed his brother.

The red dot moved to the pantry, food slot and chiller cabinet. It took a fair while, but finally Ari must have decided she had enough food to keep her going and the red dot moved.

"Bedroom," said Caleb, "and she's set the door lock."

Ethan thought back to some of his conversations with the den Coille brothers and the trials of looking after teenage sisters— particularly their younger sister, the strong-willed dynamo who had grown up to become his brother's wife. Sometimes, he was very glad his parents had given him only brothers.

Suddenly, the field wavered.

"Sands," muttered Caleb reaching for his com. Another shimmering, a wavering in an out. "Signals breaking up."

Interference? Couldn't be. Caleb's com was Survey issue, even more impenetrable than Ethan's. He yawned. It had been a long day.

His legs began to crumble. He slapped his com.

"Caleb…"

His brother crumpled to the ground and Ethan reached out.

Blackness.

CHAPTER SEVEN

Sar's squad alarm went off. "Code one in the Winter suite." She'd been avoiding the brothers all day, but this had her heart racing and reaching for her rescue pack. She'd been an active member of Sulwith's search and rescue squad since she left college, and her response was automatic.

"Position update," she ordered through her com as soon as she arrived at the hotel.

Gas, sneaking in through the air purifying ducts. By all the sands!

She ran in the doors and banged on the chute to take her up, yelling to her squad boss as she reached the main guest quarters. "Any idea what we're dealing with, Tai?"

"The doc's onto it. She's running an analysis now.

Thank the sands someone was onto it.

She grabbed out her mask and the equipment she'd need for an environmental leak and joined the rest of the squad just as they broke through the room's lock, Tai in charge in front.

"You, you and you." He pointed to three senior members of the squad. "Full haz mode. We don't know what we're dealing with, and some of those knock-down drugs are flammable."

Sar was practically dancing, frustrated at being left out of the entry group. Nor could she argue with Tai, not when it could risk lives, but she very badly needed to see what was happening in that suite.

"Found them, boss," came over the com. "Both alive, but unconscious. Breathing a bit slow, heart rate down, but all other ratings are normal."

Sar felt her legs sag under her. Tai noticed and waved her back. "Take a seat, Sar. We don't need you collapsing as well, not when you're so soon out of hospital."

I'm fine, she signalled with a turned up thumb. She must not be ordered out of here. Tai glared, then gave up. They'd been at school together and he'd learned long ago how stubborn she could be. She stood well off to the side of the doorway to keep him happy.

The doc arrived, with stretchers and a full resuss kit.

"Safe to come in?" the doc sent over the com.

"Yes, scanners are reading the air as safe now," came back from the entry squad.

Doc Kaybee disappeared into the room, and Sar discovered she was holding her breath. Eyes glued to the suite door, she forced each breath in and out, fighting to quell the panic rising inside her.

How many rescues have you been on? This is no different.

Then the stretchers were coming out, and she saw the still bodies of both Winters., and knew it was indeed different.

"They all right?" said Tai.

"Will be, when I get them back to the clinic" said the doc as she marched quickly beside the stretchers, scanner constantly monitoring one brother then the other.

He looked so still.

Brill Devenay of the Solaris engineering group stalked behind the stretchers with an angry scowl on his face. The resident chemical specialist in the town, he was the squad's expert on hazardous chemical leaks.

"Know what we're dealing with?" asked Tai, putting an arm out to stop the furious march of the engineer. The man shook him off.

"Yes, I tragging well do. Some fool thought it'd be funny to slip a vial of akintoside into the air filters."

Brill powered after the stretchers, unmoved by the gasps around him. All the squad had basic medical training. They needed it in a small town this far from outside help and with too many young and fit workers ever ready to pull the stupidest of stunts.

But this one…

Akintoside in small doses was a popular upper, leaving the taker calmer and less stressed. But the effects were highly variable, causing a mild euphoria in one, while the same dose could kill another. A boy in Sar's graduating class had been one. Sar would never forget his laughter, and the awful silence when it stopped that far off night. A bunch of friends goofing off after their last tests. That's all that night was supposed to be.

Who in Sulwith had introduced this dangerous drug into the suite of two men here to decide the whole future of the town? Images of Ethan Winter's smile when he'd been teasing her, keeping her morale up after the crash, jarred with the silence of that mechanical stretcher moving into the ambulance. She badly wanted to be at the hospital, watching over him, but first she must find out what had happened and who had done this.

Within minutes, the town's sole justice officer marched back in the door. Her search and rescue boss, Tai Meynard, protective gear gone and back in uniform, with behind him the chief Solaris safety officer—the one person in town with experience in forensics and who could do the preliminary tests here.

Tai noticed her. "Get home. This is over."

"Sorry, Tai, but I'm staying."

He scowled. "This is a big enough mess as it is. We don't need the union shoving its nose in as well. I've already had to put a call through to Solaris head office. They're on their way and absolutely furious. Get out of here."

She had no choice. Not when Tai put it like that. She stomped out, then did a quick switch of direction and slipped into the small alcove by the main downshaft from the brothers' floor. The one the justice team would have to come back down. She stayed hidden until she saw Tai emerge from the shaft and march off down the hall, the scowl on his face blacker than when he'd entered. Beside him and looking equally black stood Moline Granth, the Solaris safety officer. A middle-aged, short set, woman with an uncanny ability to steer a logical path through any puzzle set her. Sar followed them silently, keeping out of sight. They paused at the main entrance.

"You'll get me the final results tomorrow morning?" Tai said.

"Best I can do, anyway," said Moline. "Head office will have a full panel of their top specialists with them when they arrive, so I've only taken superficial scans. Nothing done to upset their readings."

"No one's getting into that room till they get here, but I need something before Solaris arrives and seals any information down tight. I'd appreciate it if you get those results through to me before you look at any orders from head office."

A dry chuckle from Moline. "Far too late to be checking work coms."

Tai lifted a hand in thanks. "Till tomorrow," and walked back up the hall, heading to the suite. Not surprising, thought Sar. He'd have set up security cams and blocks on that room far more accurate than a pair of human eyes, but Tai liked to have hands on in his work. He'd be running guard on that room for the night.

The shaft door swooshed shut, and Sar hurried out of hiding. She caught up with Moline halfway down the street.

"Hey Moline, bit of excitement there tonight."

The woman barely paused. "A fine evening to you too, young Sar. And no, I am not going to tell you what I found in that room."

"I—"

"Don't even try. I've known you since you were a baby in crawlers."

"I have to know this." She'd crash landed with Ethan Winter and, with his help, survived an attack by a fully armed, fighting flyer. Now, someone had tried to hurt him. Maybe someone she knew. A shard of horror shoved up from the back of her brain, and she shoved it back just as hard.

"No," said Moline in her no-nonsense voice. "Keep the union out of this."

"Please, that man may have saved my life."

Moline stopped, eyeing her closely. "This is personal for you?"

She shook her head, hoping it looked convincing. "Ethan Winter is an arrogant head office honcho, but there's a good man inside him. The union fights clean. This isn't how we operate and you know that."

Moline eyed her closely and Sar tried to look as innocent as possible. All that did was make Moline chuckle. "Don't worry. This is an inside job—I'd bet my life on it—but I doubt it's some misguided idiot from the union. Whoever slipped that vial into this room had a detailed schematic of the entire building system. This had thought, planning, and real money behind it."

Moline's words echoed the thought hiding inside her. A job done by a genius, but with heavy credit backing. She knew two engineering geniuses too well for comfort, but only one of them was crazy enough to think this scheme a good idea.

She thanked Moline, slipping into the automatic manners drilled into her by her mother but, as soon as she'd said goodbye to the older woman and watched her round the next corner, Sar swung sharply around and raced through every back street to get home.

In the side door and up the stairs. It was late, but hopefully Ari wouldn't be asleep yet. Waking a teenager was high on the list of things Sar knew not to attempt unless desperate.

Right now, desperate worked. Scared senseless worked better.

She palmed the door and thrust it back, marched noisily into the room, and grabbed her sister by the shoulder.

"Wha... wha..."

"Where were you this morning, Ari?"

"Wha..."

Sar shook her, waiting impatiently for the shrouds of sleep to vanish from her sister's eyes. "This morning. Where were you?"

Ari shoved her hand off, struggling to sit up. "School of course. Where else would I be?"

"Not experimenting with the hotel's ventilation systems."

"What? Go away, Sar. You've lost the plot." Ari firmly pulled up the cover and shut her eyes. Sar shook her shoulder again and pulled the covers back too quickly for her sister to grab them back.

"That homework project of yours last night. What was it?"

Ari struggled to sit up properly this time and glared back at her. "Have you been working too hard? You're raving."

"Two guests of the hotel were found unconscious tonight. Two very important guests." Was that a flicker of something in Ari's eyes? "Ethan and Caleb Winter have been taken to the main medical clinic. They're going to be furious when they wake up, and Sulwith will pay ... if they wake up."

Her sister's chin shot forward, her teeth clenched and her lower lip pushed forward in a sulky glare. "Who cares? I bet they were drinking."

"No, they were not. They'd been working all day and only just returned to their suite. When they didn't ring for dinner, hotel management became concerned enough to override the door controls."

That lower lip thrust farther forward and her sister looked even less interested in helping. Sar was getting seriously frightened. "Tell me you had nothing to do with it, Ari … and make me believe it. You've the brains, sands know, and you know that building inside out. You're certainly capable of this. Something, thank the stars, those Winters don't know yet. Who would suspect a schoolgirl?"

The mouth might be sulking like a teenager, but Ari couldn't deceive the sister who had helped raise her. Not with that slight tic of her cheek. "You were involved," Sar said heavily, "but not alone. Someone had to provide the materials and the credits. Moline's conclusion, not mine," she added.

The mulish look on her sister's face remained, but her eyes refused to look directly at Sar. Her brilliant young sister was filled with all the passionate and misguided morals of a teenage girl committed to whatever was her latest crusade … and so vulnerable to anyone discovering the genius behind that girlish face. "

She sighed. "The Winter brothers were taken to the medical centre. They were still breathing, last I heard. Doc Kaybee contacted Dridust Hospital and an emergency medical flight is on its way."

The flash of sudden white on her sister's face confirmed everything.

"You were lucky today, Ari. Maybe not tomorrow. I haven't said anything to Da yet, but I can't ignore it."

Ari was nearly in tears, the fright clear in her face, but still she stayed silent. Who in sands had her sister in their coils? Sar had no choice but to accept defeat and leave. The last image of her sister was one tear leaking down an ashen cheek, her funny, smart sister lost inside a terrified body. Someone had done that to her.

Outside, she stood, taking deep breaths as she tried fruitlessly to get her anger under control.

No sound came from her sister's room, and Sar had to leave her, fear shading her steps. She headed for the kitchen. Her father must be home by now. She couldn't solve this one on her own, and while she owed the union a duty, her sister came first. Family. It was the glue that held Sulwith together, and without it, none of the rest mattered.

Da was at the big kitchen table, his workbag beside him and a freshly made cup of dask in front of him, steaming hot and bitter, just the way he liked it at the end of the day. He looked up as she entered, big hands cradling his drink.

"Sar. Take a seat and a deep breath before you bust wide open with whatever's got you in a frizz."

She obeyed the first, grabbing the seat opposite him, but ignored the second. "What do you know about Ari's latest projects?"

Her father lifted his mug, taking a long pull of the hot drink. It should have scalded him but he gave no sign of it, eyes shutting at the end as if seeking a moment's oblivion before opening those warm brown eyes to her. "The ones she's told me about? Working with Geordie on a patch of sheets. She reckons she can get twice the output using the existing sheets so there will be no need to close the field, or to expand it to make it more profitable."

"So she knows we're going to have to change?"

"I thought you didn't agree, that the union was going to fight it."

"If it means job losses, of course we will, but you and those Winters say change is coming, whatever Sulwith wants." A reality she couldn't seem to escape, no matter what her heart wanted, and one she still didn't know what to do about. Right now, though, Ari was her problem.

Her father took another of those long draws of his dask. "Change is coming, and there isn't a blind thing anyone in Sulwith can do to stop it. The planet itself is against you this time, Sar. As for how we change. That's for Sulwith to manage."

"And Ari? Where does she fit? Have you talked about it with her yet?"

"Yes. In broad terms. It's the reason she's looking at those sheets with Geordie."

"Told her what? Enough to frighten her into thinking she may lose her home, her friends, everything she knows and loves?"

A crease of those shaggy brows. "You know better than that, Sar. You've been raising that child with me since she was born."

"She has your brains and Mother's passions. I think she's in trouble, Da."

"Aaah." A long sound filled with comprehension and another line joined the furrows on that tired brow.

Sar swallowed and wished she didn't have to do this. What did she have, except vague feelings and hints of trouble? "She's upstairs, scared witless right now. And got even more scared when I told her about what happened to the Winters. You heard it was akintoside?"

No, he hadn't, said the sudden flare of eyes and the jerk of his mug. "They're in the clinic," he said. "Doc Kaybee is good. They will be safe."

Whether her father was trying to reassure her, or himself, Sar couldn't say. Nor was he stupid, and he knew his younger daughter well. "You tried asking her outright?"

"Not quite. I did try to be subtle," she said to the quirk of her father's eye.

"And you think I can do better?"

"Someone has to. This isn't some kid's stupid crusade. Those are Winters in the clinic, and very smart Winters at that." A slight lift of her father's mouth, but no denial. "I doubt this was her idea. Someone is using her, or the kids around here."

That lift of her father's mouth disappeared. "The question, then, is who. Or more to the point, do they know what she is, or are they merely spreading poison among the teens around here and got lucky when she picked up on it?"

Sar slumped lower in her chair. "If they didn't before, they will now. That beam that brought us down, there was nothing ordinary about that. And Moline is like a desert fratter after prey trying to figure out how that akintoside got into the room."

Her father said nothing for long moments, staring into his mug. What he saw there, she could only guess.

Finally, a deep sigh. "She was full of talk about Caleb this and Caleb that when she came in.

"He wants her for the Survey," she said flatly.

"At a guess, yes."

"You'd let them take her?"

"When she's old enough … and it depends on which Survey comes asking."

Sar had to agree. Few on Arcadia yet trusted Survey Head Office, even though all the past leaders responsible for the criminal abuse of the Survey's powers were firmly locked up in remote prisons. "If she was so impressed, why the attack on the Winters? Yes, whoever is using her is trying to scare the sons from changing Sulwith—"

"That's what they'll have told her anyway."

"—but why carry on with the gas attack if she's changing her mind about the Winters?"

A grim attempt at a smile on her father's face. "About Caleb Winter and the Survey. Not about Solaris' plans to change Sulwith." Her father lifted his mug, considered a mouthful, then put it down. "Too late to stop the attack, is my guess. Moline sent through the rough details before you got home, asking what I thought." He shifted in his seat. "Best bet would be an automatic set-up. A self-enclosed unit spliced into the control unit, set to go off when the sensor showed both Winters were alone in the suite. No connection back to the operator that way."

"And Ari's capable of setting that up?"

A dry look from her father in answer. Of course she was. "Accessing a controlled drug like akintoside, that's another matter."

"Someone gave it to her and suggested what to do with it, but she knows the risks of taking it."

"At her age? Risks are just an invitation to try something. Consequences happen only to others."

Sar gave a chuckle, despite herself. "What do we do about it, then?" Then had a thought. "Her friends won't talk, but her brothers?"

"Would sing like a mountain warbler if they thought it would get their annoying big sister in trouble with me."

It was too late tonight to tackle her brothers. Sar wasn't about to go waking them and raising the problem to something really big in their eyes. Better to tackle it tomorrow morning over breakfast and let them think it was just a stupid prank gone wrong. Any hint that Ari was in real trouble and they'd clam up quick.

She left her father soon after, telling him she was off to bed after all the excitement. She did go to her room, but after restlessly pacing up and down and unable to settle, she pulled on her warm overcloak and slipped out of the house. The house sensors would tell her father she'd left, but hopefully he trusted her to know what she was doing.

She needed to find out if Ethan Winter and his brother were all right.

The streets of the town were quiet. It was that hour between the end of the workday and the start of the night's revels. Most were home eating with family, catching up on the day or getting ready to go out. A half-time hour not quite day or night, perfectly suited to Sar's mood, and her need for discretion.

This was personal, and no one but herself had a right to know about it.

The clinic was as busy as ever. Sar avoided the main clinic entrance and slipped in the side door, shamelessly employing her search and rescue badge to pass the security check. Once inside, though, any hope of staying unnoticed vanished.

"Sar, baby. What are you doing here so late?"

"Hi, Min. I was part of the squad who rescued the Winters and thought I'd call in to see how they are before I headed home."

Min Walters, chief nurse in the emergency triage clinic, was another who'd known Sar since she was a baby. "Just calling in?"

Sar raised her hands in defeat. "I feel responsible for Ethan Winter after crashing in the desert with him. He's not from the deadlands."

Min didn't look convinced, but not from round here was too common a cause of visitors landing in her care for her to bother arguing. "What's a stupid kids' prank got to do with Sulwith being in the deadlands?" she asked.

"Not enough danger for our kids. They have to make it up," said Sar with what she hoped was a believable chuckle. The deadlands could and did kill naïve visitors in too many ways. Danger wasn't something in short supply in Sulwith.

Min raised an eyebrow but waved her in anyway. "Keep it short. Their head of security is due to arrive any time, so don't be here when he comes in. He's bound to be the kind to judge first and ask questions later."

Sar promised Min to remember that, then hurried on before the woman changed her mind.

Then she was outside the door leading to the main treatment rooms holding the Winters. The ones filled with the latest in medical equipment to cover all kinds of near-death incidents on the field. Sun and dehydration weren't the only killers out here. The margin of the deadlands was home to a host of dangerous wildlife unique to the area.

"What's the most precious commodity out here," her father had asked her on her first trek out to the dry and barren lands east of Sulwith.

"Water."

"And what's your body mostly made up of?"

"Water," she'd repeated back in the rote lesson she'd learnt every day of her life since starting school.

"So what does every animal or plant out here see when they see you."

"Water," she'd said, but in a voice barely over a whisper, the truth suddenly coming home to her. From the soaring salk, ruler of the skies, to the scavenging fratter and down to the swarms of tiny bitters and the blood hungry dry litten plants, hiding just below the grains of sand, so many plants and animals waited to pounce on intruding humans. One instant of carelessness could mean the end for any too naïve visitor.

But akintoside was a drug from the big cities, made in underground labs in Urbis. It had no place in the deadlands.

There was a window into the brothers' room and two occupied beds. In one sat Caleb Winter, grim-faced and apparently arguing with his nurses while gesturing with short finger jabs at the other bed.

In that one, a body lay still, and it was only the display panel above it that told her Ethan Winter still lived. She had enough basic training to understand the panel readings: heart rate, breathing—all below normal. As if in stasis, said her suddenly chilled mind.

She shook her head. He would wake up.

Too intent on Ethan, she failed to notice she'd moved to stand in full view through the window. A door opened, a sudden shout, and she turned to run but a large man suddenly appeared behind her.

Solaris security, just as Min had warned. She recognised the man's face from her trip back but didn't know his name.

He knew hers, of course. "Sera Sar Beren, boss. Union organiser and daughter of our workshop supervisor," he said to Caleb Winter, glowering from the doorway of the treatment room.

"The one in the flyer with Ethan when it crashed. Bring her in," said Caleb curtly.

She momentarily thought of protesting, but the hard grip on her arm and the anger flooding Caleb Winter's face kept her mouth firmly shut. No point trying anything. It would only make worse whatever this man was thinking.

Once she was in, Caleb pointed firmly to a spot well away from his brother. Sar couldn't stop herself glancing at Ethan and heard the softest of sounds. His breath, whispering in and out of his lungs. He really did live. The sound made the fact real, and the knot tightly coiled inside her unwound a turn.

Caleb Winter towered over her, an angry finger thrust in front of her face. "What are you doing here?"

Sar thrust back her shoulders. "I wanted to see if Ser Ethan was all right. I was part of the rescue squad."

That had Caleb's eyes narrowing further in suspicion. "Come to finish off the job?"

"No. I had nothing to with this."

"You telling me the union doesn't care what Ethan decides."

"Of course we do, but once Solaris announces any changes, then we'll tell you to your face what we think of it. Not this cowardly attack. That's not how we do things around here."

"No?"

"Cal…"

The softest of mutterings from the bed across the room. Both of them swung around. Caleb Winter strode across the room and Sar followed.

Fingers lifted off the still covering, and she automatically grasped them. They clenched tight on hers and Ethan Winter's eyes opened.

"Not Sarwenna…" Then they closed again, and the quiet breathing of oblivion resumed, but still his fingers clenched hers tightly, clamping down like a vice when she tried to move away.

A man rushed into the room, dressed in a doctor's coat.

"What just happened?"

"This woman—" started Caleb.

"Whatever it was, keep doing it."

The man went to the panel as Sar tried again to tug away from the grip of those fingers.

"Stay right where you are," said the doctor. "Ser Winter, sit down again. Whatever she's doing, it's helping. Ser Ethan's consciousness came up a full level, then plummeted again when she tried to move." He gestured to a nurse. "A chair for the Sera. She's staying."

Caleb Winter glared at her then studied the readout panel. A highly qualified eco-engineer, he appeared able to interpret the display. She wasn't surprised. And yes, the signs were improving.

"Bring me a chair too," said Caleb, "and no, I do not need to go back to bed. Take your tragging readings if you must, then look to my brother."

The doctor's lips twitched but he did as ordered, running his scanner unit over the elder Winter brother but looking ready to take a step back. He checked the readout, then gave a nod.

"Well on the way to recovery. You may want a mild pain killer for the headache but it looks like a normal akintoside recovery. No signs of traumatic susceptibility."

"Unlike my brother."

"He got a much higher dose," said the doctor grimly. "He was standing closest to the prepper. Right next to the delivery point. If you'd ordered something up, both of you would be comatose now."

Sar collapsed back into her chair in shock. She gripped the side of it, keeping her head down to stop the elder Winter brother seeing the effect of the doctor's words. What was Ari thinking? But no, she wasn't thinking, not as an adult.

The fingers of her free hand clenched tighter, hard enough to cause pain. "Will he recover?" she had to ask the doctor.

The man took more readings. "Hopefully. He's gone deeper than I'd like. He needs a reason to come back."

That brought a scowl from Caleb as Sar tried to tug her hand out of Ethan's grasp again; but those fingers held on tight, defying the blank stillness of the rest of Ethan's body.

"Sit still," snapped the doctor, glaring at his readings. "If you're what's needed to make Ser Ethan fight back, then you will stay right where you are."

Caleb yanked his chair to the other side of the bed and sat, his scowl blacker than ever. "Both of us are staying."

The doctor looked like he was going to say something, then thought better of it, shrugging and getting on with his work. Not surprising, given the look on Caleb Winter's face and the size of the security man standing guard at the door. A few more checks, some words with the guardian nurse, then he left with a promise to be back soon.

Sar tried to ignore Caleb, and he did an excellent job of doing the same back. Silence fell on the room but for the soft breathing from the bed and the murmuring hum of the equipment constantly monitoring Ethan.

After a long while, Sar had to move. Her arm had begun to feel like a lead weight, Ethan's fingers spasming over hers every time she tried to change position.

Caleb handed her a pillow. "To support that arm," he said gruffly.

"Thank you."

Then more silence. At one point, a nurse brought them something to eat. Sar tried chewing it but gave up. Everything tasted like sand on her tongue.

Caleb watched her shoving the fork around the plate. "You should eat."

"I will … later."

A sigh, as if to say he'd tried.

More time passed. A sudden sound at the door and a whirlwind erupted into the room. No, another visitor. Small, dark-haired and rushing at Caleb Winter. The woman launched herself at the dour older Winter brother.

"I'm fine, sweetheart," he said to the small dynamo landing on top of him.

Sar could only stare, unsure if she'd heard correctly. That voice wasn't the Caleb Winter of the last few hours. Soft, gentle and suffused with love, he smiled at the small woman currently checking him all over, patting frantically at arms and legs. Then she realised who the newcomer must be: Fee den Coille, wife of Caleb Winter and the other hero of the fight against the rotten Survey heads.

"You promise?" the small woman demanded.

"Would I fail to tell you if I weren't?"

"Like a shot, if you thought it would worry me." she said back. "Your mother commed me as soon as she heard. Why didn't you tell me directly?"

"Because I've only just woken up," said her husband, "and the doctor told me you were on your way."

"Of course I was." The small woman flung her arms around Caleb. "You're really fine?"

"Yes, sweetheart. I'm really fine. You know it takes more than some school kids' prank to down me."

"Prank, huh. Why's Ethan still asleep then?"

The scowl came back. "He got a full dose of the filthy stuff."

Then the woman noticed Sar. She stood up again, one hand still holding on to her husband, but with a sudden look on her face that made Sar believe all the stories told of Fee den Coille Winter.

"Sar Beren," she said, extending her free hand to introduce herself. The small woman looked at it, then at her husband.

"The local union organiser. Ethan won't let her go. It's the only sign he's shown."

The woman's face became as unreadable as her husband's but she extended a hand. The merest of touches, fingertip to fingertip. "Sera."

Silence fell on the room again.

CHAPTER EIGHT

Ethan fought the darkness. One link, one solid point pierced the haze. He reached out, grabbed hold of that one point, and knew that if he let go, he would be lost forever.

Then blackness fell again, but his hand clung to that point.

Later, sound intruded. Breathing. Not his own. A scent he knew but couldn't remember.

Then another sound, a soft voice coming from the solid point keeping him safe.

Slowly, slowly, he made sense of what he heard, what he felt.

He opened his eyes.

Sarwenna sat on the chair beside him, head slumped onto her shoulder, a crease marring those strongly shaped brows. Her arm sat awkwardly, her hand caught in his. He tried to lift his head to see why that was. Then groaned.

Her eyes shot open, and another face looked at him.

"Ethan."

"You're awake."

The first voice was the soft song of his dreams; the second came from his brother's face, filled with relief.

Another sound, footsteps thudding into the room, and a stranger's face thrust the two familiar faces back.

He reared up.

Then the hand in his twisted free and came to rest on his shoulder. "It's the doctor. Please, let him examine you," said Sarwenna, and he subsided.

A scanner wave passed over him, a familiar ripple tracing along his body as the waves soaked through and checked his internals. "Well?" he demanded at the end.

"You were lucky, Ser." The man wore the stern look of all doctors giving unpalatable advice. "A few days rest and you should be back to normal."

Rest? "I've got work waiting for me."

A growl. That was Caleb. "You heard the man, Ethan. You're staying right where you are. Let me take care of this for now."

"You want nothing to do with Solaris."

"As you pointed out, I still own as many shares as you do. I can find out what you need as well as you can."

True, to a degree—some things, maybe even better—but the memories of running stupidly down a shifting slope of rock and gravel as a flyer took pot shots cut at him. His brother must not become a target too. "Just get facts; make no promises." He tried to lift his head. All he managed was a few fingerbreadths off the sleeper pillow, only to see a familiar grin on his brother's face … and another familiar face.

"You're here too," he said in disgust to his sister-in-law. He liked Fee and thought she was the best thing that had ever happened to his brother, but she had a bad habit of seeing far too much sometimes.

Then he felt Sar move away from him. "Time to leave you with your family, Ser Ethan."

"No…" Don't leave me, not yet, he wanted to say.

Across the bed, his brother watched him. "Stay a little longer, Sera," Caleb said softly. "Wait till my brother settles properly. Then I'll walk you out."

"I shouldn't…"

A nurse bustled in and settled it, much to Ethan's dismay. "Ser Winter needs sleep. He still has a long recovery in front of him. A few minutes more, then you must all say goodnight."

Sarwenna had no choice but to wait for his brother, much to Ethan's satisfaction. Anything else would have looked too ungracious. She sat and Ethan drank in the sight of her. From her blunt-cut nails to her firm curves, those warm eyes and the wispy spikes of hair. A style she probably thought of as a no-nonsense cut, but which instead enhanced the strong bones and unique beauty of her face. The woman intrigued him. More, with her he felt free of fear in a way he hadn't known since the soldiers had barged into the Winter homestead on that long-ago night. Sarwenna Beren would fight for her own, and if he was one…

A buzz sounded. He automatically glanced at his com, then saw Caleb and Fee both pulling up their screens. "What is it?"

Caleb scowled. "Nothing. Just a glitch at the lake." Which meant the Survey's precious lake project near Caleb's home in the foothills of the western ranges. The mountains dividing Winter lands from den Coille.

Fee was scowling as well. "I can go; you stay here."

"No need for that," said Ethan hastily at the thought of his elder brother babysitting him.

"Try again, Ethan. You've been nearly killed twice in this place."

"And Solaris security must now be here in full strength."

A grim tilt of his brother's lips. "Joff arrived earlier," he confirmed, "and his people are swarming all over the place."

"Then go save the world and leave me to save Solaris."

"I don't give a nanoglit for Solaris, as you well know, but I've been dragging your hide out of trouble since you were a kid. Not about to stop now."

"Then it's long past time you did."

Fee touched Caleb's arm, and his brother's lips snapped shut. Interesting. A year ago, this argument would have descended into a shouting match if not an actual brawl. For a long moment, he and his brother locked eyes, each refusing to back down. But finally, unbelievably, Caleb took a step back.

"I'll have a word with Joff before I leave," he said.

"You'll only be repeating what Mother's already told him."

Which brought a slight lift to the grim set of Caleb's mouth. "No stupid poking into anything beyond Sulwith. Survey Central can do any snooping far better than you can. I'll get onto them as soon as I lift off."

"Any help appreciated," acknowledged Ethan. Caleb had a point. He might mistrust them but Survey Central was about as slippery as they came. "I'll send the schematics from the report through to Silas too, once the Solaris team has finished examining the wreck."

Caleb nodded agreement. Their baby brother could make any com program sit up and sing to him. He took a reluctant step back then grasped Ethan's arm in a firm clasp. One solid grip before dropping it gently back on the sleeper.

"Be careful." A grimace, a lift of his hand in farewell, and strangely, a nod to Sarwenna still standing on the far side of the bed, and he left, holding tightly to Fee's hand.

"I better go too. You need to sleep," said Sarwenna.

I need you. The thought was instinctive. She tugged to free her hand, and he had to force his fingers to open when all he wanted to do was slam shut the door and lock the control panel to keep her here.

"Will you come back again?" he said awkwardly.

She'd stepped away from him, half turning to leave. "If you like," she said softly. "If your security let me."

"Of course they will."

She opened her mouth, then seemed to think better of it and moved toward the door. He pulled himself up. The silence, her reticence was wrong. Not in this woman who had stood in the middle of the road at the head of her union and faced up to the man from Solaris.

Her hand touched the open door.

"Caleb will make sure you get home safely," he said and received a grim nod from his brother behind her.

A wry lift of her eyebrows and a slight quirk of her lips. Yes, that was the real Sarwenna Beren. Then she stopped in the doorway, head high. "I'll be back tomorrow."

She stepped back and the door closed on her.

He was alone except for the myriad of sensors watching every move of his body.

He opened his com. "Graffin, in here now. And bring Joff from Security with you."

Ethan Winter may not consider her a security risk, but the man waiting with Caleb Winter when Sar walked out of the room clearly thought otherwise. Big and hulky, he blocked her way out.

"A word, Sera, if you please."

Sar knew an order when she heard one. "Your boss is safe from me," she protested.

"That's for us to decide. Please step this way." He pointed down a side corridor to a woman waiting outside a room at the end. Sar balked.

"You're not serious?"

The man's arm thrust out toward the room while his big body blocked any attempt to escape down the corridor.

"You can't just kidnap me. This is my town. A nurse or doctor will be along any moment and make you leave."

"Please, Sera. It's necessary," said Caleb. "Our security will see you safely home afterwards."

The big man kept his arm out and his face motionless.

It had been a bluff anyway. In Sulwith, Solaris ruled. No one was coming to her aid. They probably wouldn't even tell her father. She shoved her head high and marched down to the equally silent woman, brushing past her into the room.

The examination was quick, clinical and thorough. The woman said little apart from the odd request to move a limb or remove a garment, but it still left Sar feeling soiled and guilty.

No, more guilty. If what she suspected was true, her own passionate words railing against changes to the solar array had led directly to this latest attack on Ethan Winter. The one that could have killed him.

That thought kept her silent while she submitted to the humiliating procedure.

At the end, the woman handed back her com and her shoes. "All clear, Sera. You have been granted as necessary access to Ser Winter. Solaris trusts you will not abuse it. You may go."

No point arguing. Not against the stone wall of the woman's face. Sar shoved her feet into her shoes and walked out of the room, head forced high and heart pounding. The big security guard still stood outside Ethan Winter's door and his hand lifted to stop her approach then pointed her down the corridor to the clinic's back entrance.

She was dismissed.

Outside the clinic, the first sunlight of the day touched the walls of the town, but the chill of a desert night still clung to the streets. A woman stepped into view and flashed a Solaris logo. The promised security, clearly. Sar hugged her arms around her body as the woman silently followed her home. Sar did her best to ignore her, too shocked to do anything else, and if she hurried, she could slip into the house in time to catch her brothers at breakfast. When she eased open the back door, only her father sat at the table, an untouched bowl in front of him.

The touch of cold air must have alerted him. He looked up, eyes dark and face drawn. "Sar. You're home."

"Of course I'm home," she said brightly. "Don't tell me you sat up all night waiting for me."

"I heard… The Solaris security chief and his team arrived in town last night. The night staff called me. They're everywhere, asking questions, and—"

"I was at the clinic with Ethan Winter. He's awake and will make a full recovery."

Her father dropped his face in his hands. "Thank the sands for that."

His voice was muffled, but she caught the desperation in it. It wasn't for Ethan Winter her father gave thanks. No, it was for his town, his people, most of all his family.

"Ari?" she asked, her voice pitching too high.

Her father lifted his head, his face taking on its usual calm demeanour, but the memory of fear clung to the drawn lines. "In bed. I checked her only an hour ago."

"We're safe, Da. We're all safe, and you and I are going to make sure we stay that way."

A nod. "Whatever your sister may have done."

She reached across and closed her hand over his. "Together."

He looked down at the bowl in front of him.

"Eat up, Da," she said softly. "I'll get the boys' breakfast."

"As long as you get to bed after. You look like you've been up all night."

She nodded with a weak chuckle. "Let's hope it was worth it."

A night spent keeping Ethan Winter on the living side of the final divide? Nothing in her regretted that.

A shriek of laughter from down the hall stopped her thoughts from straying farther down a path she wasn't yet sure she wanted to follow, or if she even had a choice of refusing.

"I'm starving," announced Finn, as he did every morning after far too many hours without sustenance. Daff didn't bother with words. He plunked himself at the table and pulled the control pad over. Sar had to whip in quickly before he plugged in to something sweet, gooey and lacking any nutritional value.

"Aww, Sar."

"Breakfast is the most…"

"…important meal of the day," the two intoned together, looking about as innocent as skulking fratters. Two bowls filled with cereal, fruit and frachen in front of them, they stopped the chorus and set to.

No point talking to them yet, Sar knew, and smiled. Her father pulled up his com and browsed through the day's news and work schedule, as was his normal habit. Everything normal, routine, relaxing for her brothers.

"Any sign of Ari getting up?" said Sar after a while.

The boys looked at her in disgust.

"Still asleep, or not ready to come down yet."

"Nah, she'll be piling that smelly sludge all over her face," said Daff. "She'll be hours yet."

"And then she'll grab all the best things from the prepper and take them back to her room. How come she's allowed to eat that stuff for breakfast and we're not," said Finn.

"Because she's already done more of her growing than you have. Do you want to end up a scratchit of a nib kid?"

Daff shook his head, but Finn didn't look convinced. "Just a small dollop of—"

"No. And not for Ari either if she ever decides to show her face. What does she do up there?"

"Talking with her friends on that new comcast room," said Daff. "The one all the town girls are nutty about."

"Oh," said Sar, working hard to keep her voice as flat and unconcerned as possible. "A new comcast room is it? Talking about makeup and the latest clothes and stuff, I suppose."

"Yeah, mostly," said Daff, with a hint of guardedness in his voice. "Silly stuff."

"What silly stuff," said their father, breaking into the conversation for the first time. "Anything for your poor old Da to worry about, young Daff? Maybe I better have a nosy at it."

"Nah," said Daff too hastily. "It's just girls' stuff, says Ari, and they don't let in old people like you or Sar anyway."

Da raised his eyes at that. "Sounds like I definitely need to have a look at it. Any idea how to get in unnoticed?"

He looked at Finn. Her baby brother's eyes sparkled at the question. Nothing he liked more than a puzzle, and especially one shared with his father. "We can start straight after breakfast," he said, jiggling with excitement and shovelling spoonfuls into his mouth. Sar put a hand on his spoon.

"Slow down. You'll choke if you keep eating like that. That com room won't disappear before you finish."

Finn's bottom jiggled harder, but he did make a show of chewing his current mouthful before shovelling another one in. In no time, his plate was empty and he rushed to bang his dishes into the cleaning unit. "Ready, Da?"

His father chuckled, slowly rising. "Guess I am, son. Dig out one of the throwaway coms. No point taking chances on an unknown comsite." Finn's jiggling went into overdrive at the chance to poke into a risky site, and their father grinned at him, then at her. "You want to have a nosy too, Sar. We might need an expert to translate this room."

Finn's mouth dropped open. "Why her?"

"Cause she's female, numblewits," said Daff between mouthfuls.

"Yeah, but she's not a girl. She's too old."

"I was once," she said, and gave her brother a poke. "I bet you can't hack this com room. Not if it's for girls."

For once she turned out to be right. Finn's devious tricks could outwit most com sites, but this one had obstacles he couldn't fathom. Fortunately, Sar wasn't too long removed from her own teenage years, as she grandly told him when she finally figured out how to get through the most devious trap. "It's obviously that second door. Set the planter by the left side of it."

Finn scowled up at her. "Nothing special 'bout that one. It'll be the third on the left."

Sar shook her head. "Wrong shade."

Finn and her father both turned to stare.

"No self-respecting girl would have a door that colour. But that second door? That is stunning and the shape of it is crying out for that planter box."

They both shook their heads, but Finn had been stuck here far longer than he could tolerate. He linked to the second door and moved the planter as she'd suggested. Then grunted in disgust when the door opened.

"Welcome, guests. Come in, please and take a seat."

The voice of the com room set Sar's hair on edge. Too smooth and unctuous, too seductive to be allowed anywhere near her baby sister. She glanced at her father and saw the same set jaw as hers.

When she'd been a young girl, though, she would have been enthralled by it. Someone had some explaining to do.

"Now we're in, can you find out what happens here," she said to Finn. Her young brother wasn't as cocky as at the start, but his instincts were as good as ever. As was her father's for making them use a throwaway com, unlinked to anything in the house. She wouldn't want this site to infect anything she valued.

The feeling only increased as they wandered through the room's phases. The early ones were much like those in any teen girls' room. Fashions, celebrities, glitz and sparkle. Harmless candy fluff, a fun diversion populated by the usual collection of teenage avatars: overly made-up young women with exaggerated curves and dressed in the kind of outfits their families would have banned on sight.

They then went deeper and into rooms skating closer and closer to the censor ratings with their dark hints of domination. A clever young man with a sneer on his face ordered the avatars into a grove hung with silky drapes and soft ropes, complete with a slinky, overstuffed couch on which he reclined as he gave his orders.

A fantasy unicorn, straight from the files of ancient mythology, complete with steel brackets hanging from its mane.

A queen sitting in splendour on a throne of blackest stone, with a cruel smile on her face and surrounded by a glittering court of avatars, each eager to be the one at the front she deigned to notice.

Finn had kept their presence hidden till now, but suddenly a wall blocked their way. Sar saw a door. "Open it," she said to Finn.

"Open what?"

"The door—the one surrounded by flowers."

"Can't see it," he said.

Her father shook his head too. "Looks like you're on your own from here on. This is for girls only."

A gender-locked site? She'd heard of them but hadn't expected one to intrude into her family home. "Can you ghost me, Da. This is no place for Finn. And keep the link open for a quick exit."

"We'll try," was all her father could promise with little hope in his voice. She was on her own. She took a breath and put out a hand to the simulation. The door opened, and she entered another phase of rooms.

This one was starker. Images of Sulwith wove past her in a maze of ominously shaded simulations. Flashes of the Solaris solar arrays cut into harshly lit extracts from vidcasts of the march on the capital by the Survey field staff. The march that had ended their senior managers' grasp for power and saved Ethan Winter's life. He had been imprisoned and scheduled for execution on trumped-up charges that were thrown out by the Federal Assembly thanks to his brother Caleb's evidence.

What were these doing in a teen com room?

At the end of the maze, a group of avatars crowded around a tall post, among them one dressed in stark black with a mask of glittering ambrosite streaked with lines of ochre. A mask exactly like the Dryden festival mask taking pride of place on Ari's bedroom wall. Sar stepped back into the shadows of the phase. With luck, Finn and Da could keep her invisible, but she wasn't about to bet everything on it. Not in a program that broke too many conventions and dripped of wrongness.

Unlike the early phases, no sound came to her from this inner com room. No whisper of voice or music, no rustle of leaves or pace of feet. But the mouths of the girls opened and closed as their bodies jerked in a parody of a dance. Their heads all twisted up to the top of the pole where a series of holo-images flashed by in a hypnotic kaleidoscope of scenes: beautiful women and handsome men, smiling with their mouths but empty of eyes, draped across stunning flyers and relaxing in gorgeous rooms; the brittle laughter of workers, coms activated in a babble of voices as they worked in an office the mirror of any of the corporate ones she'd visited on union business, fighting for the rights of workers too often left behind in the struggle for corporate profits. Offices like those of Solaris, glimpsed once on a trip to Dridust, sleek and shiny, removed from the outside world with pampered air and smooth surfaces untouched by the dust of the real world of the plains.

A nirvana of wealth and success.

Other images came in glimpses through windows, sparkling clean at first then abruptly changed. Windows filled with snarling faces, with hands clawing for entry, mouths open and shouting, with shrieks demanding ... what?

Faces shockingly familiar. Faces from the newscasts. Two she'd seen only a short while ago. Caleb Winter and Fee den Coille, almost unrecognisable in their rage.

Propaganda. A simple word, but it didn't cover this outrage. She wished she could see her sister's face, see whether she believed this foul twisting of truth.

Then the avatars turned and began to move forward, to move toward her. Time to leave. She slapped at the door. Nothing happened. A thump, a closed fist hammering on that virtual doorway keeping her from safety.

Nothing.

There were stories of what happened to gamers locked in a program that turned against them.

She kicked at the door, slapped and punched it again. Come on, Finn. Don't fail me now.

She stepped back then rushed forward and rammed her shoulder against it. Finally, the door slid open a fraction. She grabbed at the gap, shoved hard against it, and pushed her way back to the outer room.

Her father rushed forward.

"Get us out of here. Now."

Moments later, virtual reality vanished and the welcome lines of the breakfast room solidified around them. Sar heaved in a deep breath of relief.

"Someone's playing them, and it's not good," she said before collapsing into a chair.

"Ari?"

"She's there, in that last room. We have to get her out, now. Whoever created this site cares nothing for the girls following them."

Her father turned to Finn and Daff. "Boys, cut the com access to Ari's room, then get ready for school."

Daff looked up from a bowl of mush, one that looked suspiciously like a sweet cream that definitely wasn't on the breakfast menu.

"Now, Daff," said their father in a voice he rarely used but which all of his children knew to instantly obey. The one that called them to stand together as a family. He'd last used that voice when their mother won back her seat in the Assembly. The exuberant blast of the desert that was their mother, as much the heart of their home as their father was the rock on which it stood, was about to leave them for months at a time. Lost again to the lure of the halls of power in Urbis.

Daff and Finn scurried off to the study and in no time Sar and her father were alone in the kitchen. "Tell me," said Da.

At the end of her recitation, her father leaned back in his chair, lines scouring his forehead. "There's a reason our laws control underage com room content. At her age, she's ripe for something like this."

"But who's behind it and what are they after? If only I could hear what's going on in that inner room."

"You're not going back in, and that's final," added her father as she opened her mouth to argue. "I'll not risk losing two daughters to this. Ari's com access is now officially restricted."

Sar nodded. Her father had done the same to her once during those vulnerable teen years, but nothing she had slipped into had been like this room with its dangerous, callous abuse of a young girl's passion for a cause and for excitement.

Her father reached out and patted her hand. "We'll get her out, and keep her out," he promised. "And then, we will find out who's behind it."

A sound from the hallway, a snarl eerily like a foxllar frustrated of its prey. Then a tousled head and a mass of hormones erupted into the room.

"Morning, Ari," said their father dryly.

"Those brats. Where are they? They cut me off."

"Cut who off what, and which brats. There are only brothers and sisters in this house."

"Finn and Daff. They pulled the plug on me, yanked me away from my friends. What will I tell them?"

Sar sometimes wondered if Ari's phenomenal mental abilities were focussed too much on technical gadgetry. She seemed remarkably slow when it came to handling other people.

Their father merely pulled his cup closer and picked up his spoon. "I think you better leave this room and re-enter it when you can speak normal, polite Standard rather than the language of the gutter." His voice was even and firm, with no sign of upset. Sar could only wonder at his patience.

Ari stopped in the doorway, hair flying askew and the favourite jumper she always slept in drooping off one shoulder. She looked a mess. "You're going to let them get away with it?"

Da lifted an eye to her. "When I hear they have broken any house rules, I will take the appropriate action. If you are referring to them cutting your com access, that was on my orders…"

Ari's mouth dropped open. "Da!"

"…as it appears you are accessing a com room that is not within the agreed bounds of what you know is suitable for your age."

"Not— They've been spying on me!"

"No, they have been helping me check on the com room that has been holding your attention to an unhealthy degree. And what we found was a site that causes me serious concern. Your com access is blocked until I am satisfied you will restrict your adventures to suitable sites and levels of interaction."

Ari glared, setting her mouth in mulish defiance. "I'll just use a friend's com."

Her father remained as calm and stoic as ever. Sar knew too well how infuriating—and how impossible to counter—that was. "You won't, you know. I am setting a universal alert to your com entry, one which will immediately block you if you use it for other than accepted educational or communication purposes."

"Educational, communication…" Ari's raised her hands in the air and cut down in a slash. "You can't mean it. No fun at all?"

Sar would have felt sorry for her if she didn't have the foul touch of that inner room in her mind still. "There are all kinds of fun," she said, "and most don't include causing harm to yourself or others."

Ari turned her head in shock. "You—"

"Yes, I went into that room. I am female and not much past being young," she said to the dark eyes and clenched hands of her sister. "That is no place where I want to hang out, nor is it one for my sister."

"It's just fun. And talking about stuff. Things that matter."

"That's not what it looked like to me."

A sulky pout warped her sister's face. "What would you know anyway. You're supposed to be fighting for your union members, but all you can do is moon round after Ethan Winter. Just 'cause he's rich—"

Shock held Sar speechless. Mooning round? Could Ari really think that? Or, worse, had she heard talk like that around town?

Her father rose. "That's quite enough, Ari. When you have learned to see past simplistic slogans to the complexities of reality, you may pass comment on how your sister manages a testing work situation. Until then, you can help by telling me how you came to log into this particular com room and who told you about it."

The pout worsened, Ari setting her mouth in a stubbornly mulish line as she slung herself into a chair and grabbed at the prepper control pad.

Da sat himself down opposite, hands crossed on the table. "Ari?"

Ari reached over and grabbed at the bowl sitting in the prepper slot. She pulled it over toward her, then jumped up and slammed open the pantry shelf, pulling out her favourite syrup. She poured a lethal dose of carbohydrate filler all over the once healthy bowl contents.

"Ari?" Da sat with arms folded, waiting.

Ari munched on a spoonful, staring fixedly at the table. Then shoved her chair back. "It was a bunch of girls at school. They'd heard about it and said it was totally reb."

"Which girls," said Da.

"You don't know them."

The first true words Ari had said. Sar watched her face, waiting for change.

Then another pout. "Fine," she said. "It was Jarek, Phinnea and Marshea. Their dad transferred here when we were little kids, and now he's telling them they'll have to transfer out again. Back to where their folks live, up north in Urbis."

Sar vaguely remembered a girl in Ari's class with clumpy blond hair that was permanently draped over her face as if to hide the person behind it. She hung around a group Ari had always wanted to belong to but could never get accepted by. Not when she routinely topped her class in any science or mathematics exam.

The other two names she hadn't heard.

"Their father's name?" said Da.

"Drocash. Ser Drocash."

"Aah. Maxell Drocash. The second-shift metallurgy technician."

Sar vaguely remembered the name from her union lists. Mostly because the man had recently and very publicly pulled out of the union, claiming it was no more than a front for the bosses and worked for their good rather than that of the workers. In the process, he'd taken a few others with him and caused more strife than Sar needed when she was new to her position. She discreetly pulled up his profile notes on a private com link.

There were the girls from school and their ages. She sent the link through to her father's com. He was busy with Ari still. Her sister had filled another bowl with foods she knew unsuitable, then defiantly said she was off to her room.

"When you have finished breakfast."

"I have. This is a snack. I need to get ready."

Da fortunately had the sense not to go down dead ends. "Make sure you put the bowl in the washer before you leave." He activated the news feed of his scroll and picked up his mug as if nothing had happened. He held it in both hands, staring into the depths of its contents for long after Ari had left the room. Finally, Sar tapped the table and pointed at his com feed, pinging him to pick up her message.

"Sorry." He blinked and put down his mug before bringing up the Drocash files and reading them through.

"Jarek and Marshea Drocash would be Phinnea's older sisters," Sar said. "More than old enough to access the com rooms for those wanting to manipulate the tensions on Arcadia for their own gain."

"And their father is no fan of the Winters."

"Nor of me," she said, grimacing. "He told me clearly enough he won't be waiting around for me and the union to save his job."

"As if you could," said her father.

Maybe not, but she'd go down trying. Saving her members' jobs was what she did. "We'll see what happens once Ethan Winter is up and about again."

A sigh from the depths of her father's heart. "You can't stop time, Wennie. Sulwith must change to survive. Fighting that will hurt you and do nothing for your union members."

"Let's concentrate on saving Ari."

Another sigh, deeper than before, and his hand reached out for hers. "I'm not your enemy, Wennie mine."

"No, of course not."

But he was no longer the father to whom she could tell everything.

CHAPTER NINE

Ethan glared angrily at the doctor. "I'm fully recovered and have work to do. Give me the all clear to get out of here."

"Your mother ordered a full check-over before you take one step from this room, and your security head backed her up."

"Mother's not here and security take their orders from me."

Doc Marsten lifted an unimpressed eyebrow and carried on poking at him with her scanner.

She finally put it down. "You've still got a way to go before you're back to full strength, but I guess you're better out there than fretting into stupidity in here. You're free to go."

"Yes!" He activated his com. "Graffin, what's taking so long. Get in here now with proper clothes. And send the latest reports through to my com." Paranoid about any threat to her sons since her time in prison, his mother had put a temporary block on his links to Solaris but Graffin had his own com pathways.

His assistant strolled into the room, looking far too innocent, as if he hadn't deliberately delayed obeying Ethan's earlier calls until the doctors could come in and plague him with their scanners.

"About time," he growled.

Doc Marsten ignored him and began issuing instructions to Graffin.

"You do know that man works for me?"

"He works for Solaris and the Winters," she said serenely. "I'll return to check on your progress in a few days' time. I trust you will be sensible meanwhile."

Ethan flipped his hand at her. As soon as the door shut, he grabbed for his clothes. Graffin looked horrified at his haste, but Ethan had too many unfinished questions waiting for answers.

Starting with finding out the truth behind one too-beautiful-by-half union representative.

By day's end, all he'd collected was a pile of dead ends and a galling dose of frustration. The people of Sulwith were polite enough. Of course they were when their future depended on keeping the Winters happy, but what they felt or intended hid behind too many smiling masks. All he had to go on was his gut and a painfully developed ability to read faces as well as words. A skill he'd been learning from his father since he could barely talk.

Caleb and Fee had left in the night, after one more visit to give him so many warnings about keeping safe that Ethan finally snapped at his brother to get going before he personally shoved him on to the flyer. Unfortunately, that left him with no one to talk to about his findings. Particularly why one woman in particular had spent the entire day avoiding him.

"Graffin, find Sera Beren."

"The Sera is finished for the day and has left no record of her evening's schedule."

"So find her. That's your job, and one you're usually tragging good at."

Normally, Ethan would have enjoyed the slight twitch of his too proper assistant's lips, but tonight he was fed up and tired. He'd known as soon as he saw that blanket of silvery sheets covering the ground that the field had to be changed drastically, and sooner rather than later. It hadn't needed Caleb's self-righteous observations to tell Ethan the land below was dying. Sometimes, he wished his brother would remember this planet was Ethan's home too. He'd spent as much time as Caleb exploring the wild parts of the plains as a child.

But Solaris was Ethan's heart as it would never be for Caleb. His brother had told him many times of the patterns in the land and its living things that fascinated him, yet he failed to see the same patterns in the living entity that was Solaris. The constant interplay between the figures and the reality behind those figures, the dynamic tension between what made credits today and what would make them tomorrow.

Right now, Solaris was in the same danger as the planet. The old man claimed they would have to choose between saving the planet or saving Solaris. He was wrong. Solaris had to change. That he accepted, but it could survive.

And would. About that, Ethan was determined.

Not that he'd let any of his thoughts seep out in his talks with the folk of Sulwith. "Nothing's been decided yet," he said, again and again. Sarwenna Beren would have seen through the ploy within minutes, and maybe some of the townsfolk did too but, for now, they were prepared to bide their time and wait for his announcement. Not that he was welcome here, and he mustn't fool himself into believing otherwise.

Sarwenna Beren's place wasn't as set in stone as he'd first supposed either. She was too new and too untried, despite her years working as her mother's offsider. The polite distancing of some when her name came up suggested that they wondered whether she was as committed to the town's future as she claimed. It didn't help that the story of her night in the clinic bringing him back from oblivion had done the rounds already.

No wonder she'd been avoiding him. Then a thought. Her father worked for Solaris. He couldn't refuse to see a Winter son, and what could be more reasonable than that Ethan should sound out the head of the techs here, outside the office.

"Graffin, we're going visiting. Find me something to take along as a gift and try to find some flowers that won't wilt in this heat."

A twitch marred his assistant's perfect face. "Yes, Ser," he said in his most precise voice. Graffin had many praiseworthy attributes—an ability to find whatever Ethan needed in the most unlikely of places being one of them—but his assistant was not a fan of roughing it, and staying in a small, dead end town like Sulwith definitely came within that definition.

His otherwise excellent assistant was true to expectations and soon had him walking through the town with a bottle of best Sylerian and an artlessly wrapped bouquet of flowers in his arms. Not too expensive, tasteful but not over the top, and wrapped in a plain white sheath with only one soft lavender cord as decoration.

"Any more risks warning the Sera of an underlying intent, Ser." Graffin had said with a poker face. Ethan chose not to comment, merely thanking his assistant and confirming he was now off duty. For once, a hint of a smile had cracked Graffin's face as he hastily bowed himself out of the room before Ethan could make any more requests.

Ethan soon came to the unprepossessing frontage of the Beren home. He placed his hand on the door panel.

"Ser Ethan Winter, to see Ser Beren regarding the Sulwith plant. I have a couple of questions for him."

Unsurprisingly, his name had been coded into the house system and after a brief pause, the door opened and a voice welcomed him inside, followed moments later by the appearance of Rhyn Beren.

"Ser Winter. Please, come in."

He suspected affability was built into the workroom supervisor's psyche but was still surprised at the man's welcome. He'd expected at least a hint of his daughter's withdrawal. "I know it's late, Ser Beren, but I would appreciate a few moments of your time. To review the plant schedules."

A slight smile touched Ser Beren's face. Ethan brought out the flowers. "For your daughter," he said noncommittally. Her father gave a short smile, one Ethan couldn't interpret, then passed the flowers over to the household drone to put in a vase. "My daughter will enjoy these when she returns home. It's rare enough to see such flowers out here and she will cherish them."

Ethan looked at him suspiciously. Amusement or a subtle warning? Either was awkward, and he said nothing, following Rhyn Beren into the main sitting area and taking the seat the man waved him toward.

Once they were seated, Rhyn pulled up his com spreadsheets readily enough and laid them out in a field overlying the low table set there. Ethan made a show of studying the figures and graphs, but he'd seen all these reports before. Tonight, he was more interested in Sarwenna Beren. Unfortunately, there was still no sign of her.

He made a show of looking down at the data fields, one finger tracing a table of figures and filtering out the pertinent details.

"Biodiversity under the fields has fallen incrementally in recent years? It matches with my brother's views on the field."

"That it must be closed immediately, I suppose. It's the usual Survey line."

"That it must change, and soon," corrected Ethan, "if these figures are accurate. Are they from our own people or from Federal sources in Urbis?"

"Our own. They're real. Rock solid," said the Sulwith man. Ethan looked up sharply. Dead pan flat, but a tired endurance underlay the voice, as if the man had lived with these truths for too long and fought them all the way.

"Anyone else in town seen these?"

"Ser Crabster and the local head of the research unit that produced them. She was sent them by the team from Dridust under strict confidentiality." Ethan raised an eyebrow. "Her staff had supplied the raw data and the chief analyst needed her corroboration before finalising the report. She hasn't told anyone else."

"You're sure of that?"

The man gave a tight smile and nodded his head. "If she had, the union would have been banging on Tom Crabster's door within minutes. And my daughter would have marched straight into my office."

"Aah." Ethan understood that complex smile. He studied the man before him, reviewed all he'd read of him and what he had seen today of the local operations, and suddenly made a decision. He set his elbows on his knees, clasping his hands, and leaned forward. Before he'd come here, all he'd thought of was the solar field and the business changes needed, but now he'd met the people working it.

"The field must change, yes. I agree with my brother on that one, although our father hasn't accepted it. Which means the town needs an alternative, another way of making a profit from Sulwith that the Old Man will accept before the Feds come here and shut us down regardless. Everyone loses then. Solaris, all the Sulwith workers, and the rest of the townsfolk who rely on their credits for income. Do you have any ideas?"

The man said nothing, but Ethan could swear he saw a glimpse of something in those eyes. Hope, wariness and maybe, just maybe a spark of excitement. But the wariness held sway.

"What's your father's opinion on this, young Ser?"

Ethan grimaced. "As you'd guess. The Old Man was born a fighter and dreams in balance sheets. The ones from yesterday and today."

"And thinks they'll follow the same patterns tomorrow?"

Ethan looked the workshop supervisor square in the eye. "Yes."

He kept holding the man's eye, watched as the stoical face creased into a grim hint of a smile. Then a deep breath, as if the man was shoring up his courage. Ethan held his breath.

"But they won't," said Rhyn Beren of the Sulwith field. "Not if the news from Urbis is true."

Ethan drew in a breath, deep and hard. "True, and probably worse than you've heard."

Rhyn stared at the data sheets. "I came here first as a young man, before our children were born. My wife … you've probably seen her on the vidcasts?"

Ethan allowed himself a quick lift of lips, a slight hint of amusement. Word was no one could say who most dreaded the return of Sera Beren to the Federal Assembly: the opposition parties or her own. Catra Beren tolerated no impediments to what she termed ensuring her constituents received the rights they were due. Everyone else called it plain bullheadedness.

How much of that had her daughter inherited?

"Your wife is a very effective representative for her constituents," he said in a bland voice.

"A thorn stuck in the backside of every bigwig in Urbis, you mean."

Ethan had to laugh at that. "She and my father have clashed more than a time or two."

"And on this?"

Ethan's laugh cut off. "On this, they're probably on the same side for the first time ever. My father wants to keep the field as it is. The largest asset in the Solaris balance sheet, a shining jewel and a monument to the glory of the company."

"And you?"

The man looked as wary as Ethan felt. "My father and your wife are wrong. The Survey and the Alliance are only stating fact. Arcadia can't take anymore. We change, or we lose our home. My brother Caleb is right in this. I didn't use to believe him but prison gives you time to think. I did a lot of report reading when I came out. Now, it's up to those of us in the business community who recognise that truth to find a way through it. Unless we do, everyone depending on Solaris for their livelihood might as well leave Arcadia in an Alliance evac ship. There'll be nothing for them here."

He'd said it. Announced out loud to a Solaris employee the truth of Solaris future paths.

Rhyn Beren would have made a good strategos player. He nodded slowly, no surprise on his face. "How can I help you?"

Not the answer he'd been expecting. "And if it means the death of Sulwith?"

A grim twist of the man's mouth. "That's my daughter's view, but Sulwith is only a place. It's the people of Sulwith who count, and change is not an end, only a new kind of beginning."

A faint spark of hope lit inside Ethan. For so long he'd had to hide his innermost thoughts, and now the supervisor echoed ideas that had churned inside him for so many years.

He would have liked to tell Rhyn's daughter of his dreams too, but she had made her position clear. Yet the memory of her hand binding him to life was imprinted in his bones.

"Thank you," he said to Sarwenna's father. "It means a lot. We do have a small unit in the research lab that's been doing some work with the Survey." Not something he or Caleb had let their father know about. "Can I tell them to contact you?"

The man gave a slow yes of agreement.

"And your daughter?"

Another of those wry twists. "Works for the union, not Solaris."

"Aah. Not a word then."

A faint trace of a frown touched the man's face and Ethan knew a pang of guilt. Ethan suspected the man wasn't in the habit of keeping secrets from his eldest daughter. "Not yet," he said.

"What will you do next?" Rhyn asked now, switching topics from one Ethan guessed struck too close to home. "These attacks against you can't continue. One day, they'll succeed in killing you."

A good question, and not one Ethan had an answer to. Too many unsolved mysteries. The strange flyer that targeted them, the gas attack, the unknown beam. He might find the locals responsible, but the ones behind them… The attacks were too sophisticated and too costly. They spoke of serious brain power and a pile of credits, the kind unlikely to be found in a town this small.

Ethan grimaced. "I'm going to need help on this one." There was only one person he could think of with the technical craftiness. If he'd agree to come.

Silas arrived the next morning, much to Ethan's shock. "Right, brother, what's so important that has Caleb practically ordering me out here," said his baby brother with a curl of lip and a wariness that had never been there before.

"You hear about my accident?"

"The one that happened when you pulled one of your flash flying tricks to scare the union girl? Yeah, I heard about it."

"That's a story, not fact."

"Says who?"

Ethan sighed. "Let me show you. Or are you scared to fly with me now?"

A scowling, "Don't be a total moron," was his answer. After that, his little brother climbed into the flyer and stared straight ahead. He said nothing until they cleared the solar field and began to head north. "There's life down there, you know," said Silas.

"So Caleb tells me."

"And the Old Man?"

"Is digging his heels in."

"You and the Old Man can't win this one."

"I already said the field needs to change," said Ethan, stung by Silas' ready assumptions about Ethan's loyalty.

"You'll go with the Old Man and Solaris. You always do."

"I go with Solaris," said Ethan.

Silas humphed loudly and slouched back in his seat. Ethan was relieved to spot the crash site. Anything to break the silence.

The Solaris recovery unit had set a support field around the flyer, but Silas still eyed the encroaching sands dubiously.

"You set down there?"

"It seemed the best option at the time."

"Said who?"

He didn't bother telling Si it was Sarwenna Beren. Not when his dead flat voice said he'd already guessed. "There's a hard pan underneath, but enough liquidity in the sand on top to cushion the impact." Si looked no more convinced. "I'm alive and so is she, thanks to her advice. Our tech department confirms it too."

Silas didn't look convinced and Ethan gave up trying. Yet his brother blaming Sarwenna rankled. Why, he refused to think, concentrating on the tricky descent instead. He put his flyer into hover mode, set the jets to diffuse output to stop damage to the craft below and held it at a point as far as possible above the crashed flyer. Soon they both glided down the airshafts to gently slide into the open hatch of the crashed vessel.

At first, Silas moved gingerly through the cabin but soon the lack of movement must have reassured him, and he set to testing the controls. Luckily, the repair crew hadn't touched anything yet, held off by Ethan's orders and the investigating team. The flyer was as dead as ever.

Silas started with a routine check, attempting to fire up the control panel. After a time, an unusual crease appeared across the bridge of his nose and he punched harder at his scanner and the controls.

The flyer stayed stubbornly silent.

"It's been like this since that beam hit you?"

Ethan nodded. "All flight and external coms gone, but basic life support, internal coms and the mechanical steering mechanisms still working."

The crease deepened but a familiar light lit up his brother's eyes. A tech wizard, Silas couldn't resist a new challenge. He punched a few more commands into the control panel, swore loudly, sat back and stared at it with a faraway look in his eyes, then leaned forward and played an arpeggio of orders into the main control screen.

"Got ya!"

Suddenly, a shimmer of light and Ethan recognised the image forming. Somehow his little brother had got the flyer to spew up the incident records, something that had frustrated the Solaris' investigator team, despite all their expertise.

"How'd you do that?"

Silas flexed his fingers, wiggling them with unholy glee. "Professional secret, big brother. Just call me a genius."

Ethan groaned. His little brother was back in all his cocky smugness.

A series of schematics appeared in a holoview. Most meant little to Ethan, but Si marched around the display, muttering and periodically dipping low to peer at the images of the flyer from below. His fingers wriggled again and the view changed to the solar field.

A flash, and the beam that had nearly killed Ethan and Sarwenna shot up through the image, straight to the back of his flyer.

Right toward the central core, missing the main propulsion unit by a mere sliver of space.

"That beam could have blown this whole craft to eternity."

"It could," agreed Silas, "but it didn't."

"Sheer luck," said Ethan, a cold feeling settling in his stomach.

His brother shook his head. "Not luck. Not with that degree of precision. Whoever designed and sent that beam knew exactly what they were doing."

"Can you pinpoint the origin?"

Silas nodded, pulling up a locus on the solar field image and setting the coordinates into the data bank.

Ethan recognised those figures. He lifted his hand over his com patch and sent a file through to Si's com. "This is where we found the markings on the solar support struts."

Si's fingers wriggled again, feeding Ethan's figures into the existing data bank. Then he sat back, looking at the new result with a grim set to his mouth. "They match."

Ethan wasn't surprised. "So what was attached to those struts and who put it there? Ever seen anything like this before?"

Silas slowly shook his head, but that look on his face said a memory stirred somewhere in his brain. He chewed at his lip, staring into nothingness, but then shook his head with a disgusted grunt. "Not like this, but... Get me back to base. I need to check something in the lab database and I need a more secure link than one remoting from here."

"We can use the link in the local manager's office, but I don't want to tell him why."

"No reason you should be telling a mere plant manager what you're about. Not when you're the anointed wonder heir to the whole company."

"Not me, as you well know. The Old Man hasn't given up on Caleb taking over after him."

"Last I heard Caleb was too busy sorting out the Survey to want any role in the company. Everyone else know it's you."

"Tell the Old Man," scowled Ethan again.

Silas gave a flippant wave of his hand. "Life's too short."

Ethan had to give way, with a grunt of laughter. "You win. Finish up here, and we're off into town where you can scour through confidential Solaris records to your heart's content. Only don't, by all the shifting sands, let the Old Man know what you're up to."

"Done, and on the way you can take me to meet this woman Caleb talked about. The one you insisted stay beside you when that gas had you knocked out and spilling all your deepest secrets."

Ethan groaned.

CHAPTER TEN

Sar's day started no better than the day before ended. A pack of angry workers parked in her office demanding she tell them their jobs were safe.

"You'll know what's happening here as soon as I do, once Ethan Winter recovers and finishes his assessment."

"We're not the ones spending nights holding hands with him," snapped a woman at the rear, backed up by a chorus of muttered Yeahs.

"I know who pays my salary, and it isn't Solaris," she said sharply. "You think I'm about to let this town disappear off the map? I was born here, and that's not something you can say, Martia Frappen, or many of the rest of you." She glared around the room. "If I had any idea what that man intends for this place, I'd tell you, and that's a promise. Or is the word of a Beren not good enough now?"

"Your father; your mother: sure as the hottest sands. They earned it."

"And you've watched me grow up, Jack Mattheson," she said to the gruff-faced man in the front. One of her father's most trusted technicians, she'd played with his tools as a young girl and for years now had made sure his wife got the medicine keeping her alive. "Don't you stand there and tell me you don't know what my word's worth."

After too long a rumpus of back and forth, a headache beat a tattoo behind her eyes and the heat in the room finally wore itself out. She slumped down in her seat as the workers stomped out of the room.

"You promise you'll let us know as soon as you find out anything," said Jack, the last in the room.

"I promise, and what's more, I'll be doing everything I can to make sure you and every other member has a job after it."

"Here in Sulwith?"

She forced herself to meet his eyes. "If I can," she said softly. "If I can."

The brief nod and the droop of his mouth said he understood. Jack and the rest of the other workers needed truth, and that's what she'd given him. All she could give him.

He left and the room echoed with the silence of retreat. For the rest of the day, she kept to her office and concentrated on the pile of work waiting for her. Finally, Marget poked her nose around the corner. "Time to go home, Sar. Mooching in here won't help anyone. Go and get some food in your stomach, a good blast of air in your lungs, and a decent night's sleep."

Sar wished she had enough energy to argue. Not that her self-appointed nanny would listen anyway and the woman was right, blast the sands. She flipped shut the file she'd been staring at and hauled herself out of the chair.

"I'm on my com if anyone needs me.'"

"You'd turn that off too if you had the sense your father gave you. Too much of your mother in you, that's your problem."

She was too tired to bite back. "Just tell them," she said and escaped out the door.

"We've got visitors."

The jubilant shriek greeted Sar as she arrived home, and her heart plummeted.

"What visitors?"

Her brothers grabbed hold of her bag and tugged her into the family room. Rising from the best seat in the room stood Ethan Winter, a cautious smile on his face and a glint of something in his eyes. Another man rose from the chair beside him; a leaner, younger version, tanned and with the crinkled sun lines on his face of a man who spends his time outdoors. In his face was assessment and a sparkle of laughter.

"Sarwenna," said Ethan. His voice was soft and his eyes fixed on hers with a warm glow that brought an answering warmth in her. His hand gestured to the younger man. "My brother, Silas. I thought he might be of some use in solving the mystery of the beam that shot us down."

Sar's guts clenched tight, all warmth banished, and she had to force a smile on her face. "That's kind of you, Ser Winter. Are you an engineer?"

The younger man grinned. "Nah, just a student of com systems."

"Si's been tinkering around the Solaris internal systems since he was a kid," said Ethan. "He apparently does have a string of qualifications but the general belief in the family is he charmed his way into them."

Finn was near to hopping where he stood. "You like com stuff?"

Sar groaned inwardly. Her youngest brother loved nothing better than messing around in com systems and talking to anyone he could find about it. In a town like Sulwith, he'd long ago worked through the few who could match him. Right now, he was looking at Silas Winter as if he were the biggest, brightest feast day present ever.

Worse still, the youngest Winter brother was grinning back. "You got something to show me?"

"Don't bother Ser Winter, Finn."

Too late. Her brother had already grabbed hold of the young man's sleeve and was literally dragging him from the room.

"If you'll excuse us," said Silas, near to laughter.

"My apologies for my son," said her father, belatedly stepping into the breach. "Finn, I'm sure our visitor has better things to do than tinker around in our house system."

"No he doesn't," pronounced Finn.

"It's all right, Ser Beren," said Silas, letting himself be pulled out of the room and down the hallway to Finn's bedroom, a place decked out with the kind of com links that not even their father could decipher. Sar saw disaster looming.

The sounds of giggles and the sight of Daff sidling out of the room soon after did nothing to help. She tried to make the kind of polite conversation her mother had drummed into her, but her mind was only half on what Ethan and her father said. A chuckle of laughter interrupted their murmurings and she looked up sharply.

"Did I miss something?"

"Only the entire question and answer," said Ethan. "I asked if you've recovered from your ordeal with me. Then decided you must have since it bothered you so little you completely ignored any mention of it. Your father agreed."

She had to blush. "It's just … the boys can be very insistent. Your brother must need rescuing by now."

Another chuckle. "Probably, but they will do him good. Shall we go and watch his struggles?"

She stood before thinking better of it and caught a quick frown from her father. The only saving grace of the whole evening was Ari's staying out of the way as she continued sulking in her room. Just then her darling sister chose to come and investigate the strange noises in the house.

"Finn appears to have found someone to inveigle into joining him in his com explorations," said her father to Ari's grumpy question. Then he indicated Ethan. "Make your bows to our visitor. Ser Ethan Winter of Solaris head office. Ser Winter, my younger daughter Arionna."

"We've met," said Ethan, to Sar's surprise, standing and giving her sister the full bow to a grown woman of worth. "Your sister was kind enough to act as guide to my brother Caleb on his first day here. He spoke highly of her service to him. Greetings, Sera Arionna."

Ari blushed. A genuine, honest to sands blush, and even smiled at Ethan. Sar's racing heart slowed a fraction. Maybe they'd get through this visit without mishap.

"He also spoke highly of her understanding of engineering and mechanical matters. I think he wanted to recruit you for the Survey, Sera. It's lucky you're too young for them to snatch you up yet," added Ethan, and Sar's heart began to race again.

"Ari is young, as you say," said her father in his most placid voice, the one he used to soothe frayed tempers and fraught work rushes. "Time enough to think about what she wants to do with her life when she finishes school and has done all the other things a growing girl needs to enjoy."

Ethan nodded to her father with a smile and sat down again. "As you say, time enough. If she's interested in the Survey, though, I'm sure my brother will put in a word for her."

He glanced at Sar and she forced a smile onto her face. Not that she could fool herself into thinking he was lulled by it. Not when his eyes stopped on her mouth and a slight frown momentarily traced his lips. She had to fight to keep the smile on her face, which only brought a twitch to those lips and a suspicious glint in his eyes. Fortunately, he chose to turn back to Ari and her father, asking about the town and how long they'd lived there. Innocent enough, but the tension tying her gut in knots wound tighter.

Silas and her brothers erupted back into the room. Daff was near frothing and Finn kept hopping up and down.

"He's Crakato. He's Crakato!"

What could have set them off now? "That's nice."

"No, Sar, he's The Crakato." Daff was almost as dizzy as Finn.

"Yes, Crakato, you said that already." She glared at her father and Ethan as they doubled over with laughter, then at their visitor. "And who might Crakato be?" she said to Silas Winter.

He shrugged, with the merest of pained glances at his brother. "I occasionally dabble in Deadgulch Alley."

That name she did recognise. The latest craze in com games and one to which her brothers were both addicted for some unknown reason. She'd checked it out with her father and he'd said it was harmless, despite the bloodcurdling fights.

"Dabble," gasped Ethan. "Plays every instant possible and pours his heart into it, more like."

Finn was nodding madly. "Yeah, he's the Crakato. Only the best of the best in the whole Deadgulch Alley 'verse."

Silas grinned and lifted his hands up in surrender while Ethan fell to laughing like a maniac. Fine for him. He didn't have a sister playing around in questionable com rooms or who might be involved in nasty plots against him. Plots about which Sar must make sure he stayed ignorant.

She hadn't taken into account her brothers, though. Finn was still jumping up and down. "Sar, he can help us with Ari's room. If anyone can find out the mods behind it, Crakato can," he said, looking ridiculously pleased with himself considering he'd just thrown Ari into the heart of the dead sands.

"Finn, Ser Winter isn't interested in a teen girls' com room," said her father.

"A com room? What's the story, young Finn," said Ethan, and Silas' grin disappeared as his eyes narrowed in interest.

"Nothing, Sar said quickly. "Merely a room she's been hanging out in."

"Till you and Dad blocked me," said Ari, reverting to type as a sulky teenage brat. What had happened to the sweet little girl who'd been her baby sister. "It's just a room for me and my friends, nothing special. I'll be the only one in my class who's blocked."

Ethan Winter's face wore the expression Sar was learning to dread; the do tell me more look he used when wheedling information from a target. He'd tried it on her, briefly, in the Dridust hospital and, more successfully, on the townsfolk at his welcome gathering. Now it was fixed on her sister. So bland, so nice, so amiable. Nothing in his voice or face to warn Ari to stay silent. All Sar could hope was a guilty conscience set her on guard.

"Your father sounds like our mother," said Silas.

Ethan chuckled. "Since you were hacking into adult-rated com rooms when still in first school, she had good reason."

Silas's grin widened. "They had the best outer shields. Much more fun to break than the ones mother let me at."

"That's it, that's it," yelled Finn, fists clenching tight in excitement. "You should see the shields on Ari's one. It's got double blinds and triple catch traps, and there's a real gender switch at the last barrier. I couldn't crack it. We had to send Sar in." Ari's mouth dropped open then she hastily shut it. As for their darling baby brother, he was looking at the youngest Winter like someone about to make all his dreams come true. "I bet you could break it," he said.

Silas' eyes lit up.

"No, Silas. We have work to do," said Ethan hastily. "We only came to ask Sera Sarwenna if she remembered any details of that beam."

Sar glanced sharply at him. His voice sounded honest enough, but she was beginning to distrust Ethan Winter when he had a goal in mind.

"A gender barrier," said Silas. "Haven't tried to break one of those in—"

Ethan groaned but Silas ignored him.

"Come on, young Finn. Let's have a nosy." With which, their visitor disappeared with her brothers into the den.

Ethan raised a hand. "My apologies. Silas has a one-track mind when it comes to com systems. I can try physically dragging him out of there, but I doubt I'd have much luck. Not till he breaks into that site. I do hope there's nothing in it too embarrassing, Sera Ari?"

Sar couldn't miss the quick flick of fear in Ari's eyes as she ducked her head and shook it in denial. "No. Just stuff."

Her father frowned "Stuff you shouldn't be accessing for years yet. Now, don't you have homework to finish young lady?"

Ari looked rebellious but then, to Sar's utter relief, mumbled a gruff "Guess so." She hunched her shoulders, gave a quick sideways glance toward the den then slouched out of the room. Sar's hand clutched the side of her chair as she watched her go, feeling as if she'd run from one corner of the solar array to the other.

Her father and Ethan stood as Ari left. With the slam of her door upstairs, Da collapsed back into his chair and waved at Ethan to sit down again. "My apologies. I'm afraid Finn can be very one-eyed when he's set on something. Few others in Sulwith share his passion for solving com riddles, and he's still very young.

Ethan had on that company smile again. "No problem, Ser Beren. Your Finn reminds me of Silas at the same age."

"Maybe, but he tends to lose sight of time. Can I offer you something to drink while we wait?"

Ethan shook his head. "If your Finn's anything like Silas, they'll be some time. Would you mind if I took a walk around the town while we wait? What with everything that's happened, I haven't had a chance yet to get a feel for anything beyond the solar field." Then he looked in her direction with a definite challenge in his eye. "Maybe Sera Sarwenna would like to come along and show me what's at risk for the people here."

Walk through the town, in full gaze of anyone in the streets, and with no one else to deflect his questions while his brother investigated her sister's com room?

She went to shake her head, but no brilliant excuse came to mind. Nothing that wouldn't look even more suspicious. Her father opened his mouth, but Ethan spoke first.

"It's all right, Sera Sarwenna. It's no doubt the end of a long day for you. I shouldn't have asked." He stood. "I'll be back a bit later to collect Silas before he upsets your brothers' bedtime schedule too badly."

Before she knew what she was doing, Sar leapt up. "No, I'll come."

Her father's mouth dropped open, but she ignored him. Not when she had no idea why she'd done it.

"Take a wrap," he said. "The night air can creep up on you this time of year."

"I'll be careful," she said to her father's silent warning.

Ethan held out his arm for her, that tragging company face masking any thoughts as he made polite noises of farewell. But she'd seen the quick smile, swiftly erased. The same smile she'd seen that night in the desert. The one that felt real and that spoke to something inside her.

"I'll look after her," he promised her father.

If only she could trust that promise.

She tried to steer him away from busy thoroughfares, filled with townsfolk enjoying the cool of the evening after the day's heat. Strolling through town or meeting up with friends was a favourite pastime, but so was gossip and, in a small town like this, talk multiplied like a breeding glitchit's nest. Ethan wore a twisted smile as he blocked every one of her moves.

"That street looks interesting." He wandered past a bar filled with a crowd of gawking workers newly off shift, despite her obvious attempt to steer them into the empty street that detoured around the back of it. He simply laid a hand over hers where it rested on his arm and shifted direction, asking far too solicitously whether she was warm enough.

"Quite, thank you." She couldn't pull her hand away. An open struggle with the man would only add to the gossip. Or that's what she told herself. "Are you deliberately trying to get me offside with my members."

He suddenly ground to a halt and lifted his hands away from her. "I wasn't thinking. How bad is it?"

"Nothing I can't handle," she muttered back.

"Please, forgive my selfishness." He started walking again, veering away from the busy street and into the nearest back lane. Few windows faced onto it. She was safe from scrutiny. So why did she feel so guilty?

They continued walking but he made no attempt to take her hand and their talk was only of the town. Questions from him and comments on points of interest from her. Nothing personal, nothing threatening. Nothing real.

A small park met them around a corner, one holding little more than a stunted shrub and a bed of the local flowers drooping in the heat. Another few months and a rare burst of colour would welcome the onset of the long awaited cooler season. A time when, hopefully, a burst of rain would shatter the silence of the desert. It didn't happen every cool season, but maybe this year?

Not if Caleb Winter's predictions were right.

Suddenly she wished her hand still lay on Ethan's arm.

He stopped to stare at the bed of straggly plants. Then straightened, a grimace twisting his mouth. "This isn't working. I need to see the whole town, not these little pieces that don't make sense. Is there somewhere with a view over it all?"

The sun had begun to set and his face lay in shadow, yet she felt him watching her. She nodded slowly as if caught.

"There's a bluff above the town. The steps up to it start a short way from here." The fingertip of the hills reached right into the middle of the town, overlooking the whole place. No one else was likely to be up there at this hour. Later, when the moons were higher, but not yet.

He smiled, the movement of his lips breaking the webs around his face. "Lead on, Sera."

"I have a name."

"Yes, you do. Lead on, Sarwenna."

Something about the way he said her name stroked down her body and set her nerves on fire. He took her hand, his strong fingers linking with hers and she was too happy to feel their firm grasp again to protest. She led him across the small park and down the track to the start of the bluff climb.

Halfway up the rocky steps, he paused and looked back at the town.

Was he pausing for breath? It had only been a day since he'd been in a hospital bed recovering from the gas attack. She tried to pull her hand from his but his fingers clamped down and he turned to look at her.

She blushed red, feeling like the worst kind of selfish idiot. "I'm sorry. I didn't think."

That real smile lit his face. "Presumably, you know what you're talking about."

"You. This climb. It's too much to expect."

"Too much for the recovering invalid, you mean. I assure you, my dear Sarwenna, I'm not that fragile."

"Yes, but…"

His other arm lifted and pulled her closer. "Whatever you're thinking, forget it. This is the best time I've had since arriving here."

He touched a hand to her cheek and his head bent. Then his lips gently touched her cheek. A peck only, but the warm smell of him wrapped around her and she leaned in closer. A short gasp of surprised laughter came from him.

She stepped back as if burnt and heard the trace of a sigh. He pulled away his arm, tugging at her hand again. "Come along, my dear Sarwenna. Let's see what lies at the top of this hill."

They were off again, climbing up before she could protest, her hand firmly clasped in his as he pulled her up the rocky steps.

It had been a peck only. It meant nothing.

At the top, she walked toward the tip of the hill, to the point where you could see the whole town laid out all around the base of the rocky protrusion.

He came up beside her and let his gaze take in the full circle of the town. His eyes settled on the company headquarters, then traced over the streets and alleyways.

"It's compact, I know, but there's water in an aquifer coming out of the hillside and we prefer to stay close to it. The streets go where they need to."

His hand still held hers, and neither made any move to change that. Now, she felt the smallest pressure of fingers.

"The town grew to suit peoples' needs?"

"Yes, I guess. It works for us."

"Mmm."

What that meant, she didn't know. It didn't sound like the slighting she'd half expected from a man who'd grown up at the renowned Winter homestead and regularly visited Urbis.

She offered him a swig of her water, and watched as he took the requisite sips, the muscles in his neck working as he swallowed each mouthful.

"Thanks," he said, passing the canteen back and waited while she took a drink, feeling suddenly as if her mouth was coated in sand. "Want to sit?"

"Oh. Thank you."

There was a lip of rock at the top of the bluff forming a hollow that made a natural seat. They settled into it, legs dangling over the still warm face of the rock, and looked down on the town lights beckoning below. It was a place she often came when she needed to think or to gather her strength after yet another tussle with her members. Tonight, the hollow felt as if made for the both of them, and it seemed only natural to settle into the curve of his shoulder. He lifted his arm, pulling her in closer, and something about the peace of the evening and the isolation had her accepting it. She turned to look at him, the strong lines of his face brought to stark relief by the evening shadows, and met his eyes studying her. Pools of dark velvet, they met her own and she was caught.

"Sarwenna." A soft murmur, barely above a whisper, but the sound of it arched through her.

She leaned closer, lifting up her face and her hand lifted to his neck, playing in the strands of hair touching his tunic collar. A deep groan, as she pulled his head down.

What she intended, she couldn't say. What she got was far more. A kiss of mouth and tongue, heart and spirit, as his warm lips met hers and set fire to all her carefully built defences. His hands held her head as his mouth angled to deepen the kiss and she drowned in the feel of his body, her hands lifting to cling to the hard muscles of his arms.

It was much later before she surfaced and leaned back into the rock, needing the solid touch of the warm stone as an anchor. He let her go slowly and those darkened eyes still watched her.

"I won't apologise," he said. "I've wanted to kiss you since that first day on the landing strip."

She shook her head. "It was mutual but not very wise."

How it made her feel, she wasn't ready to discuss. Not yet. Maybe not ever. He watched her in silence, then leaned in and caught her lips again, the magic as strong as ever.

Afterward, he took her hand, fingers playing a gentle seduction in her palm, and his other arm pulled her into his shoulder. "This isn't over," he said, then turned back to the town and waited till she recovered enough to relax against him. Ethan and Sarwenna, not

Ser Winter and union rep Sar Beren. But they were those people too.

It wasn't over, not yet, but it should never have started. She eased back from his hold, desperate to regain herself and unsure at first whether it was possible. He went still, his eyes studying her as his mouth twitched. Then a sigh and he eased back too, leaning into the rock behind as if needing an anchor. He lifted his arm from her shoulder, but his hand kept hold of hers.

"When you're ready," he murmured, then leaned forward.

His head turned slowly, taking in the whole town. His other hand lifted to point downward, and his voice when he spoke was soft with the touch of the evening's quiet. As if the kiss had never happened. She wasn't fooled but was relieved. She found herself leaning closer into his body, unable to let him go despite what her head told her was sensible.

"So that's the company office," he said, pointing, and the rumble of his voice resonated through her. "There's the hall where you have your offices and next to it, the town's main shopping centre. All in a tidy package. That was planned at least, but the rest of it…" His foot tapped on the rock as he gazed down. "Who lives there, in that row of smaller houses below the company office block."

She didn't need to look to know where he pointed. A utilitarian block of single bedroom units someone had once tried to titivate with a mix of colours that had fortunately now faded into the streetscape of the buildings around it. "Those are for the in-and-outers. Single staff who come in for their workdays then fly out again on their off days. They're not really homes, more a bunk house. It's the reason we offer a six day on, four off work cycle option."

"And those who live here permanently?"

"Can work that too, but most prefer a split cycle. Four on, one off then either repeat, if they're single, or three on and two off if they have families, to match the school cycle." He'd known that but guessed he needed to hear her say it. To speak for the town.

"The Solaris workers' families live near your house mostly?"

She nodded. "Da prefers to live where he can get a feel for what's happening rather than up with the managers and business owners."

His eyes went to the wide streets in the area close to the fold of the hills where they met this bluff. The Fold, they called it in Sulwith. Sheltered from the worst of the scouring winds that swept through the area and with longer hours of shade thanks to the hills behind, the area was considered a premium residential district. Her father and mother had flatly refused to live there.

"It's home. We like it," was all she said.

"More convenient too?"

She nodded. She'd grown up running in these streets and playing all kinds of games with children from every part of Sulwith, including The Fold. The rambunctious glee of the outer streets was far more fun than their so-proper streets. With only one first school and every child in higher school having to share tutors and com channels, any adult attempt to maintain a social divide soon failed.

To Sár and her family, such a divide had no place in a town like Sulwith. Too small, too far from any other settlement; when trouble came, it must be fixed by the town. Even those who lived in the Fold recognised that. The houses may be bigger, with yards and the occasional garden, but her mother had solved that problem too, creating a small inner courtyard at their home that mimicked the gardens up in Urbis that she had grown to love while serving there.

Or that her mother claimed they mimicked. Sar had discovered the heart-breaking difference on her first trip to the northern metropolis as Mama's assistant. She still remembered her shock at seeing a giant baullnia tree and the beauty of the delicate beith tree in the main Urbis park. Trees that came from the mountain homeland of this man's sister-in-law, Fee den Coille Winter.

Ethan shot her a swift glance but thankfully said nothing, keeping up his study of the town below. Could she risk letting him into her life? Risk her family and all those depending on her? Yet it was so easy to keep talking, to tell him too much, and she could still feel the touch of those firm lips against hers.

No, keep to business. She was the union representative; he was the man from Solaris come to shut down her members' work and her town.

"It's a simple enough layout really," she said in a neutral voice; "town centre and public buildings on the solar field side of town, family and permanent housing behind, leading back into the hillside, and the schools are just below us, about halfway to the Fold."

He gave no sign of noticing her withdrawal, but that meant nothing, she was learning. "The Fold is on both sides of this outcrop?" he asked instead.

She shook her head. "The Fold proper is on the north side. It gets more shade there. The south side gets some from the bluff farther south but it's not as high as this outcrop so at the hottest time of year it tends to bake down there."

He tilted his head round to look back. Few plants grew there and the buildings all carried the silver coating of the heaviest duty heat repellent finish. Her own home had it on the south side only; the north was painted in a warm ochre that set off the desert bushes her mother had planted there to soften the lines of it. "Every house is connected by a series of underground tunnels and has an underground suite to retreat to in the worst of the sandstorms, but those in the South Fold tend to have bigger ones and they're used more often. Folks who live there like their privacy better than their comforts, and if you like tramping in the evenings, there's a good track up to the hills just behind it. The South Fold is a good part of town for temp families too—cheaper rents. That street a block back from the hillside is all Solaris owned."

He gave a brisk nod, as if settling her words into some map of his own building inside his head. The lights below had brightened, necklets of gemstones shining among the houses and tracing the curving patterns of the streets. For a stranger, Sulwith was an easy town to get lost in despite its size, or so the transients claimed.

"The in-and-outers," said Ethan Winter, eerily echoing her thoughts. "Do they mix in with the town much."

"Some," she said warily. "Most are interested only in making their stash and moving back west to a more settled town."

His gaze suddenly sharpened. "They cause trouble?"

"Nothing the town can't handle. You met our Justice Officer yesterday. Tai Meynard, head of search and rescue, and the law around here. He's expert at stopping anything before it gets too out of hand."

"All work, no play? I'd be surprised if that succeeds."

She had to smile. "We'd never get anyone to come out here if we did that." Her chin lifted. "See that patch of very bright lights, just beyond the singles row and off the main road down to the solar field?"

His eyes followed down to a jangling patchwork of multicoloured bar lights and shop signs.

"The strip. It's not big, but it's enough. Tai has an office right in the middle, as well as his main desk in a room in the town hall. They keep it down there, don't hurt anyone, locals or in-and-outer, and he's happy. All the strip businesses have a link to him and know he'll be there when they call, with backup if needed—and the workers know that if he's called in, Tom Crabster is the next person on Tai's com list. The money here is too good for them to risk that."

"So you think Solaris pays well. Nice to hear you approve of something we do."

The words shattered the fragile link forming between them. He spoke lightly enough but she couldn't ignore his meaning. She jerked free of him, suddenly cold.

Hand open and mouth grim, he sat up. "I meant nothing, Sarwenna."

"But you are Solaris, first and last. Thank you for reminding me."

"I am of Solaris. My father is Solaris; he's the one who makes the big decisions."

"That's not what we hear. They say you dream business plans and spreadsheets. Or are you saying Solaris doesn't matter to you?"

A shake of his head. He pulled up the knee opposite her, hands gripping tight as his dark eyes focussed on her. "Solaris matters. I will do everything I can to make sure Solaris survives what is happening on Arcadia. I also know, though, that Solaris has to change to survive and that a company is made of more than business plans and spreadsheets. It's my own family for a start. Winters are Solaris, the reason my parents and I nearly died at the hands of the rogue Survey head office staff."

"The Survey your brother works for."

"Yes, but their head office forgot the Survey isn't only its top tier. It's the frontline staff and their unbroken history of commitment to this planet and its people. We can't make a similar mistake for Solaris."

"And your father?"

A dry gust of brittle laughter. "Is going to make tragging sure no one ever gets to threaten him, his family, or his company ever again."

Sar's face flushed. That last bit had been truth, a truth this man hadn't meant to share. Not by the way his hand suddenly clenched shut. "I … I had no right to ask that."

His head twisted away from her. "Prison … it changed us."

"You," she whispered.

"Yes." Short, brief and sounding like it had been torn from deep inside him. Something lodged in her gut, something too scary to be examined, and she suddenly lost her courage.

He eased down his leg and pulled back to sit against the lip of rock behind them. A harsh breath and he turned slowly back to face her. She could have cried at the change in his face. At the loss of the man who had come so close to baring his soul. The heir to Solaris faced her now.

"What is it about change that scares you so much?" he said. "Why won't you even look at other options for this field and how your people can adapt to them?"

He started to smile, but she recognised it and put up a hand. Not his business mask. His face stilled, any trace of a smile wiped clear.

"What kind of options," she finally dredged up the courage to say. "What are your plans for this field and Solaris?"

"You want the management line?"

She reached deep to find more steel. "No," she said. "What does Ethan Winter plan for this field. You've been here long enough and talked to plenty of people."

"When someone wasn't trying to kill or incapacitate me. That tends to distract the mind."

She dropped her head, but his hand reached out, then paused. As if fearful to touch, and that hurt. She had learned too much tonight. Most importantly, that, yes, he was both Solaris and Ethan. Both the boss she must face across a table and the man who had risked his life for her on that mountain top. That was the man she wanted and set both her hands around his. With a shuddering sigh, he lifted his other arm and pulled her closer, head buried in her shoulder.

"I'm sorry," she said, as his arms tightened and he clung tight to her.

Then he suddenly twisted away and sneezed—a paroxysm of sneezing that wouldn't stop no matter how hard he tried. She had to giggle, the kind of manic giggling that came from nerves stretched too tight.

"I am truly sorry," she said when his sneezing died down. "It's Ari's latest must-have teen accessory, a scent bulb in a brooch. It got caught between us and broke. Daff insisted on me trying it out to see if it's the reason she's turned so silly. I told him it's just her age, but he didn't believe me."

He pulled out a mesh from his pocket and wiped his eyes and nose, leaning back as if gasping for air, then chuckled. "For your father's sake, tell her to keep using it. No one's going to come too close to her while she's wearing that."

She grinned back and pulled out a mesh to capture the fragments of bulb and wipe away the worst of it. "I'll get rid of it in the cleaner as soon as I get home." That brought a full and truly gorgeous smile to his face. "Not for that reason, idiot." She tried to pull back, still feeling laughter bubbling inside her, but his arms were stronger than she'd guessed. He leaned closer, giving her a short but devastating kiss, then his arms relaxed and he released her.

"Of your own free will, Sarwenna. Always," he said, so softly she wondered if she'd heard him.

The laughter had shattered the distance between them, and now she could ask her question. "So what does Ethan Winter dream of for Sulwith and Solaris."

She held her breath, wondering if he would answer. At first, no. His arm still enclosed her shoulders but his gaze locked on the town below, to the ribbons of light and the increasing number of homes with shining doorways of welcome as the shops and offices darkened for the night. Then he leaned forward.

"Up here, it all looks so simple. A doll's house town with stick figure inhabitants. But that's not the reality."

She held her breath, waiting for what came next.

"One day in prison, a guard came and told us we were scheduled to be executed. He had this stupid grin on his face, as if the news had made his day. None of us had ever done anything to him. It didn't matter. To him, we were the big ones of the world who had always treated him as a nobody; now it was his turn to be the big one. We were just faceless stick figures."

"Like the ones down below?"

"Exactly like. It's something I can never forget or I let that guard win. Business isn't only profit and loss cycles, watching trends and trying to keep one step ahead. It's also that man down there heading off for a night on the town and dreaming of a win in cards or love. It's that same fool stumbling home late tonight and dragging himself out of bed tomorrow, only to repeat his day all over again. It's that mother down there calling for her child to come inside now or they'll be sorry. It's Tom Crabster walking home to his big house in The Fold and your father being welcomed home after spending a day making sure the Sulwith solar plant keeps making money for me and my family—and for all the other families depending on it for their livelihood, for the very basics of life: food, clothes, a roof over their heads and secure credits in the bank for a stormy day."

He turned then and caught her suddenly dropped jaw. His lips tilted in a wry twist. "Tom Crabster is a good front man. He looks the part and gives a fine speech, but he couldn't keep one of our smallest plants in credit. Your father keeps Sulwith going. He's the one with the technical expertise and the people skills to make sure that the right equipment and the right people are matched and ready to produce. It's a common enough situation, and one no company boss is going to interfere with. There's only one true rule in business: if it works, don't muck it up."

She squirmed at the cynicism in his voice so soon after giving her words she'd never expected to hear from a rich businessman. Ethan Winter represented a class of men and women she and her mother had spent their working lives fighting against. Now he asked her to see his side of the divide. To see the man, not the class, and she didn't know if she could do that. What did that make her? But if she let the Winter heir become a real man with his own drives, passions, and dreams, how could she keep fighting him for the passions and dreams of her members?

"You say don't muck it up, but that's exactly what my gut tells me you're planning for Sulwith. This is a huge plant, the biggest in Solaris, and from what the union can work out, it's your most profitable thanks to the expertise and hard work of my members."

He let his arm slip from her shoulders and turned his body to face hers. But he hadn't withdrawn. Not fully. He caught her hands and lifted them, studying the palm of first one then the other. Soft hands. That's what he'd see. Not the hands of a woman who spent any time in real physical work. Not like her members.

Not like his, as the surprisingly rough ridges of his hands held hers, one thumb stroking the soft hollow of her palm over and over.

"The Sulwith solar plant is all of those things, but it's also a solid mass of sheeting covering an area near as big as Urbis itself and everything under those sheets is dead. My brother Caleb has been shoving the cost of that down my throat for years." His fingers paused and his gaze lifted a moment. Then a swallow. "I thought I'd have to wait. Work away in the background, keeping Solaris going until my father cedes control."

A dry gust of laughter. No, she couldn't see Sol Winter doing that either.

He set down her hands, placing them carefully back in her lap. "Prison and Caleb changed that when he exposed the truth behind all those hidden Survey workers. Yes, I will protect Solaris, will make it the best, most viable company I can, but our planet needs help, and if we Arcadians don't change, we won't have a world to call home. If our stupidity makes this planet uninhabitable for people, Solaris is dead as surely as the land beneath those sheets."

"And your father agrees with you?"

That twisted quirk of his mouth again, only this time there was little amusement in it. "No. He's dead set on ensuring nothing changes. That Solaris makes as much money as possible so we are strong enough that no one ever threatens us again."

She leaned forward and her hands slipped back into his. "Yet isn't he right? Solaris is the single largest supplier of energy on this whole continent. We'd go dark without the power cells from all those sheets covering land you call dead."

"It is dead. I've seen the lab analyses, the ones from our own labs as well as my brother's Survey labs. Not only that, but Caleb shoved the timeline eco-patterns of the surrounding lands under my nose last time I ventured out to see what he's up to with those lakes of his. Sulwith is right on the edge of the deadlands. A hundred years ago, the deadlands started a full day's drive from here, and in another fifty years without any change, the deadlands will stretch tragging near to Dridust itself."

"So your brother says."

"No, not just him and the Survey. After I came back, I asked Solaris' best ecologists to run the historic survey images for me. They matched Caleb's. I can only assume his projections were as accurate."

"It changes nothing, not here, not today." She pulled back and hugged herself tight. "We need energy. Solaris needs to make money and my people need work. Today, not in some mythical fifty years. Sulwith's children will go hungry today without work for their parents, regardless of what might happen when those same children are grown and grey-haired."

"And that's the quandary." His hand lifted toward her, as if seeking to reclaim the vanishing trace of that faint bond, but then dropped. A sigh rose from deep inside him. "How do we live through the changes that have to be made?"

She wished she had the courage to take up his hand again ... but how could she when they stood on opposite sides of the words falling between them. "You must have some answers or why would you be here? Why not simply follow your father's orders and leave us in peace to keep making money for Solaris?"

"Because he's wrong."

So simple, so real. The grim twist of his mouth echoed the dread in her heart.

"Energy creation doesn't have to be done by one big company. Each one of those houses, the streets, the water pipes and the public buildings. All of them can be collectors of energy. Some for their own use; some to feed into a bigger collective."

"You'll really take Solaris out of solar fields!" She stared at him in shock. "If your bankers find out, they'll force you out quicker than a Jack Robber's dive."

"Maybe, maybe not.'"

She bobbed her head vigorously. "Yes, they will. You're talking about dismantling an empire."

"Not … quite. The bankers trust my father, and they are starting to trust me … hopefully enough to get them to hold off till the new business lines come onstream."

"So what exactly are you talking about? Sulwith field gone. And the other fields, all gone too?"

He shook his head. "Not if we can find ways to mitigate their effects."

"Oh, and how are you going to do that. Break them up into pieces so small they might as well be closed down." She had to gasp for a breath. What he proposed…

He broke in before she could say it, leaning forward urgently. "We change how we collect the sun. Sulwith field is huge, but that's not the reason it's so profitable. It's how it's run. So far, all I've figured out is that your father is one hell of a supervisor, but that can't be all there is to it. You said your Geordie can read the sun like no one else, and maybe that's the difference."

Sar's breath stopped in her throat. Don't ask, please don't ask.

He studied her face and she eased back into the shadows. Thank the sands the sun had finally set. He turned to gaze out from the ledge and she could breathe again. She turned to see what he was looking at and caught the glimmer of light as the last rays of the sun lit up the solar field. A shimmering carpet of colour stretching in glowing wonder to the horizon and beyond.

"A pretty sight, but not a scientifically effective sight," said his voice beside her. "The design of the sheets in use here was surpassed years ago. The newer sheets are smaller and with wider spaces between to allow the local ecosystems to recover."

"Expensive too," she said.

"My father's reply, every time I suggest changes," said Ethan Winter, "but the newer sheets create more energy and need less maintenance."

"And fewer workers."

"Yes, fewer workers. Which is where point-of-use systems come into play. People need energy; they just don't need it to come from a single, corporate source. It can come from their own homes, and we can sell them the equipment to make it. From what I've seen, there's a workforce here no company in its right mind would want to lose, so how do we use them?"

"You can't build a factory out here. Too far from your markets and too expensive to supply," she said flatly.

"Maybe not. You already have regular transports taking out the energy packs. We can modify the schedules and flyer types to cope with equipment."

She shot up, suddenly sickened. "Don't give me that. Shipping home appliances from way out here is never going to be a viable proposition. Not like the energy packs. Their value far outweighs anything you're talking about." She thrust her hands on her hips. "What is this? False hope to lull the union rep and keep her onside. Is that what this whole evening's been about?"

He stood slowly, his eyes never leaving her face. "No. It was me talking to a beautiful woman who I hoped—just hoped, mind you—might look past my family name."

She'd begun to think the same, until he tried to get her to believe in his new future for her home. A future based on a mirage. She didn't know which was worse. The anger boiling up in her or the sick grief churning her gut.

"Thank you for your company, Ser Winter, but my brothers are due to go to bed soon and my father will be needing my help. I trust you can find your own way back to your quarters." She gave him a curt bow, then fled. He had a light system and a map on his com. He could find his own way back.

.And all the way down the steps, hurrying so fast she nearly tripped, she heard that deep, resonant voice of his voice calling her back.

CHAPTER ELEVEN

Ethan cursed soundly as she fled. He'd driven her to a mad flight down rough and rocky steps. She'd break her neck if she wasn't careful.

"Sarwenna! Stop, please. Wait."

By a sliver of moonlight he caught sight of her, hurtling at the stairs. He began to run, moving silently, using every bit of tracking stealth drummed into him by old Jim on those long ago days out on the plains, hunting game on the hard ground.

What if she fell? He hurried down the stairs, listening always for the beat of her feet on the uneven stone. Then the sound of her feet changed as she reached the dust-coated, plascrete path at the base of the hill and his heartbeat eased. Another glimpse, silhouetted in a streetlight and a quick turn of her head. Did she guess he followed her?

Around the streets they raced, down a twist and back again. Always staying close enough to keep her safe but far enough back not to spook her. Let her think she could lose him in the sprawling maze of streets. Then he reached the end of an alley and discovered she'd done just that. Disappeared right from in the middle of a deserted backstreet with all doorways closed. Back down the street he charged, into the next alley then up another, listening always for familiar steps, a huff of strained breathing, anything to show where she'd gone.

Nothing. He finally came to a stop at the end of a small laneway between two major streets filling up with night traffic. After dark was the time for outdoor eating and for partying. She could easily slip into a crowd and be lost to him.

She had to be safe; this was her hometown. If he said it often enough, it might come true. He ranged through the streets, hoping for a glimpse of her and trying to come up with a credible excuse to bail her up in her home. Knock on her door and confess to Rhyn Beren he'd driven his daughter to flee into the night to escape him, and was she safe home? Yes, that would go down well.

She must be home. Defeated, he turned and headed back to his rooms, slamming open the door to his quarters. The sight of his brother sprawled in the best chair in the room only made it worse.

"Comfortable?" he snarled at Silas.

"Yeah, I wanted nothing more than to wait all night for you to get your executive self back here. And don't bother going to the Beren household again. Not after the state Sera Beren was in when she returned home."

His gut clenched. "She was fine when I left her." Angry, upset, but physically all right.

"White as a shellbar and refusing to talk. What in all the sands did you do to her?"

"We had a misunderstanding," said Ethan, guilt churning him.

"Yeah, looked like it, and now you stroll in here after leaving me to take the brunt of your mess back there."

The curt tone finally got through to Ethan. "There's something else? Trouble?"

"Could be."

Two short words. Precise and taut, like a bucket of ice dumping over Ethan when he was already drowning. Hate it or not, Sarwenna Beren would have to wait. "You broke the code on that com room of Ari's?"

"Yes, I broke the code, and if I had a sister, she wouldn't be allowed within a sector's width of a site like that. Good thing her father shut down her access."

Ethan threw himself into the other chair and dredged up all the patience he could muster. "It's a cover for something?"

"Something very nasty," confirmed Silas. "Those girls are being brainwashed into thinking they're part of a secret resistance against the Alliance's lies. The program's words, not mine," he added.

"Can we talk them out of it?"

"Reason with a teenage girl convinced she's a heroine in a twisted horror tale? Yeah, love to see that."

Ethan shifted in his chair then stood and headed to the prepper bar, needing something to get him through this. "You want something to eat?"

"After spending hours in com geek heaven with a genius brat of a kid?" His mouth twisted grimly. "Point me at it."

Ethan punched his order into the control panel then switched it to Silas' com signal. "Genius? How high?"

"Near to off the scale in the stuff he likes. But definitely still a kid. He thinks com systems are toys designed solely for him to play with.

"Like you, you mean."

Silas had the grace to laugh. His meal appeared. A huge helping of proteins and stodge, with a side dish of his favourite spicy sweet sauce. "What?" said Silas between mouthfuls. "I've been working."

Ethan grabbed his own plate and slumped into his chair. "Turned out so was I," he said, as disgusted with himself as he was Silas' piled up plate of junk food.

"The elder sister? She's your suspect?"

He shook his head, reluctant to discuss Sarwenna Beren with Silas. "She's not capable of creating that beam. But her father might be, and now you tell me the brother is a genius in coms."

"Yes, but not mechanics. And her father…" Silas shovelled down another mouthful and Ethan had to wait for him to finish it. "He's straight. I'd swear it," he said finally.

Ethan thought the same but wasn't prepared yet to dismiss anyone. "Someone made that beam and Rhyn Beren is the brains behind this field. He's the one running it, and that means he's no engineering sluggard."

Silas nodded slowly. "I looked at the readouts of that beam. It's not my field—Caleb would confirm it better—but that flash of power was aimed without thought of the consequences. That's not Rhyn's way. My guess on that beam; it was meant to scare you off, not kill you."

"Speaking as the one who got shot down, that's not what it felt like. Without Sarwenna's local knowledge, who knows what would have happened when I tried to land us."

"Exactly. He would have known you had Sera Beren on board, and I'll tell you now that man lives for his family. You can't fake that kind of thing."

"Our father lives for his family, he tells us."

"So that we can take over his precious Solaris after him and make sure his name isn't forgotten. Not the same thing."

His father was more complicated than that, but it had taken him prison to realise it. And prison wasn't something he could discuss with Silas.

"All right. Not Rhyn Beren. My gut says you're right, but my head says don't rule out anyone."

"There's another genius in that family, according to Finn. Their sister Ari."

Ethan lifted his eyebrows. "The sulky teen?"

"The one who's currently com-grounded, yes, that one. Remember what I was like when Mother did the same to me."

Ethan gave a snort, a vivid memory coming back of his usually laughing kid brother flying into a full-scale rage and kicking everything in his room into oblivion. Their mother had shut the door on the ruckus, then calmly told Silas he would be allowed to come out again once his room had been restored to exactly what it had looked like before he threw a childish tantrum. He'd half expected Silas to choke, he was so furious.

"Caleb did say he'd like to recruit her for the Survey," Ethan said.

"Daff elbowed his brother hard in the side as soon as Finn said it, and the kid clammed up quick. He looked to be near to tears, so I had to pretend not to be interested. Both boys believe she's a genius, and they definitely didn't want a Winter to know about it."

"A genius who's been hanging out in a com room aiming to subvert the teen girls here into some kind of rebellion." Ethan's first reaction was to dismiss the idea as too outlandish, but remembering the smiling kid he'd first met with Caleb before going to her home and finding a sulky teen, he chewed it over again. "That beam is beyond anything our labs have come up with. She's incredibly young to have done that."

"And you've always told me this field's tuning could be magic it's so precise. That means there's some serious brain power working here. Her father runs the field but he's out as a suspect and

Finn's too young and not mechanically minded. It's the systems he's passionate about, not the physical equipment."

"That beam had to have been made somewhere, and by a person with access to some seriously advanced tech. We're talking more than a passionate girl with a knack for mechanics."

"A girl caught up in a com room that's more like a scary cult indoctrination site when you get past the outer barriers," said Silas.

"Am I supposed to congratulate you on your expertise now?"

Silas waved a hand angrily. "Those inner rooms are protected by the kind of locks no teen girl's site should need. The kind that would keep out most parents. Sar made it in because she had Finn's help, and she's not far enough removed in age to be blocked."

"Her name's Sarwenna," said Ethan automatically, and then cursed silently at the twitch of his brother's mouth. They needed to concentrate on the business at hand "You recognise anything about the programming?"

"Noooo. Not exactly."

A first kick of hope. "You've seen something like it before."

Si leaned back in his chair, eyes distant. Then gave a frustrated grunt. "Not like this, but the patterning of it, the layering. I've seen that before."

"Where?"

"It was before the Survey problems. When the Old Man had me checking out the other local corporates."

Spying on competing corporates wasn't unusual for their father, but a sudden foreboding lodged in Ethan's gut. "Which one?"

"Our friends across the mountains. The Den Coille company."

"Cut it," said Ethan sharply. "I spent months in custody with the den Coille brothers. Not one of them is into the exploitation of vulnerable young women."

Silas shook his head. "Calm down. I'm not accusing your buddies of anything. What I'm talking about is the type of coding used in the system blocks." He screwed up his face, thinking, and Ethan had to clamp down on his frustration. His brother would answer when he was ready, not before.

Silas' hand tapped on the chair, rhythmic and irritating. Ethan stood, needing to move. He ordered more food from the prepper. Rubbish food, filled with unhealthy fats and too much of everything bad for a body. Just what they needed tonight.

Silas reached out a hand and opened his mouth to eat. Ethan copied him, even as Si paused with a plate in mid-air. "Got it," he announced. "It was in a report I was looking over a while back. We'd intercepted a system upgrade from den Coille for their latest expansion drive."

"Written by whom," said Ethan, waiting tensely.

"Seolta den Coille," said Silas.

Seolta mar Bram an Scathach den Coille. The one den Coille brother he'd never quite trusted. "You're telling me the den Coille brothers are sabotaging any changes to Sulwith, and are prepared to kill me to achieve it?"

"Woah!" Silas dropped his plate with a clatter. "That's one hell of a leap. All I'm saying is this program has a pattern like one Seolta den Coille wrote. He's the only den Coille brother capable of anything close to it."

"Yeah, and the one most loyal to their company. He's also the one most like his father, as wily in business as he is gifted in com programs."

Their own father was an unscrupulous son of the sands but Bram den Coille had a cool-headed streak of cunning that not even Sol Winter could match.

"If Seolta's involved in something this big, his father will be too," said Ethan. Something was beginning to smell rotten and Ethan had a bad feeling it had a multi-corporate stench to it. "Not a word of this to Father," he said. "Not yet … and wipe that frown off your face. I'm trying to protect him and Solaris, believe it or not."

"He's not involved. Not if it would hurt one of us," said Silas stubbornly.

"Do I think he planned the attacks? No, not even the Old Man would do that. Would he agree to some unspecified warning that will bully me out of changing anything here? Maybe, maybe not."

Si grunted and shoved his plate away. Ethan didn't blame him. He no longer felt hungry either.

"That beam that hit your flyer? We can't just ignore it."

"We won't," said Ethan grimly.

Silas suddenly looked worried. "You have a plan."

"Yes, brother, I do."

"Well?" Silas shifted, eyes narrowed and his mouth set dead straight "Out with it. Don't you dare try to protect me. I had enough of that from Caleb when he sent me into hiding."

Ethan gave a sudden whoosh of breath. "You wanted to be caught and thrown into prison with the rest of us?"

"Don't be stupid," said his baby brother.

"Good, because knowing you and Caleb were free was the only thing that got Mother through the whole disaster. Which you'd know if you spent more time at the homestead."

Silas shook his head angrily. "Not now."

Ethan studied him, seeing, as so many times before, the guilt in his brother's eyes. "You helped me get through it too, you know. Every time I saw the pain etched into Aigherach den Coille's face, I thanked the stars it wasn't you."

"My point exactly. All the den Coille's were taken. They came close to being wiped out. So maybe they're more set on making someone pay for it. This could be a den Coille plot only. No one else has anything to do with it, including the Old Man."

Ethan couldn't take away the sudden hope in his brother's voice. "Maybe," he said non-committally. Not that he believed it, not about the rest of the den Coille brothers. Seolta, though… "I'll talk to Cumchdach and see what he says."

"By com link, I hope. No going into their territory. Not till we know more."

"I've no choice. You can hack any link, and I suspect young Finn is well on the way to doing the same. Whoever made that site is just as good. Or do you want me to rely on you being better than them?"

"Only the best on this continent," said Silas with a sudden grin, as quickly lost. "You will be careful?"

That Ethan could promise and saw the relief on Si's face. "And while I'm away, you can have some more fun with Finn and Daff. See if you can't lure Sera Ari into joining you."

Another quick grin. "Who knows what we'll find."

The next morning, Ethan left Sulwith early, before there was any chance of Sarwenna Beren being up and about. He did not want to lie to her. Not yet. Not ever. Silas had agreed to stay on for a few days on the pretext of exploring the area, to play games with two boys who were fast succumbing to an unhealthy fit of hero worship.

"Have another check on the readings from that beam that shot at us too, will you? See whether anything else looks familiar."

"Will do," said Silas, looking more like the young brother Ethan remembered before the Survey troops has crashed their way into the Winter home. He'd told Silas to run that night, and Silas had obeyed, but sometimes Ethan thought his brother would never forgive him for it.

He clapped a hand on Si's shoulder. "It's good to have you back onside, little bro."

Si went bright scarlet, but his hand lifted briefly to grasp Ethan's and he gave a single nod of his head.

Then he stepped back. "Go find out what those tragging mountain climbers have been up to."

A wave of his hand and Ethan stepped into his flyer. In no time, he'd left behind the deadland margins and was over the scrub and straw-coloured grasses of the plains. Ahead lay the towering mountains that split the continent in two. On this side, the dry, rain-starved plains and desert spread in a huge sweep toward the far coast. On the other side, wet forestlands sprawled down the mountainside and across the narrow margin to the grey, swirling seas of the Western Ocean. Only the bravest fishermen dared take on the fast-moving currents that hugged the treacherous coastline here. Away up north, those same currents deposited a rich load of nutrients into the northern seas, and fishing settlements sprang up wherever a bay offered shelter to the fishing fleets.

Ethan had once suggested Solaris expand its interests there. From his father's reaction, you'd have thought he'd suggested disbanding the company completely, but Ethan had quietly invested some of his own funds into the fleets. One of the many outside interests he'd picked up over the years.

Financially, he didn't need Solaris. Something he'd never told his father, although he suspected Caleb had an idea of it. Thanks to those widespread investments, Ethan had access to a stream of financial news lost to his father.

All called for change. All said the planet had no other option.

He'd thought the den Coille brothers understood that as well as he did.

The mountain ridges rose up in a ragged battlement ahead, clouds swirling around the razorback peaks and sleety rain starting to bucket down on his craft. Not for the first time this trip, he wished he had his own flyer under him. He'd flown that enough that it felt like a second skin. He had no idea what this flyer would do when challenged.

You read the schematics when the Old Man bought it.

Maybe, but it was a long time since he'd taken the route over the mountains, and the last time was on what the den Coille brothers termed a fine, sunny day. By which they meant the winds were down to a brisk howl and the occasional patch of clear sky broke through the grey cover. Today, the winds roared down the slopes at gale strength and the storm clouds hurled themselves at his flyer in a battery of icy fury that had him calling on every gram of pilot training he possessed.

Up and over the top, then down the tree-cloaked slopes on the far side.

Suddenly a screeching siren exploded into his audiofeed.

"This is protected air space. Identify and hold position."

Ethan slapped open his public link. "You read my ID the second I breached den Coille airspace. Cut that racket and get Cumchdach online to clear me through."

That brought a very formal voice back online. Ethan could almost see the curl of the man's lip. "Hold your position, Ser den Winter. Any unauthorised approach to the city limits will result in retaliation."

An alarm rang from his ship security system. "What the—" A red warning screech and his shields suddenly came on at full strength just as a blast of a plasma cannon shot past his bow. "Watch where you're firing that thing," he yelled into the com, even as his fingers raced to tap out Cumchdach's personal code and he pulled the flyer up to a high hover.

"You were warned, Ethan mar Sol an Helena den Winter. Cumchdach mar Bram an Scathach den Coille has been advised of your request."

Trag it. Mountain folk addressing plainsmen by their full honorific never ended well. Didn't that fool at the other end of the com know he'd been imprisoned with the den Coille brothers? Their people knew he could be trusted.

A signal through his com, and Ethan accepted with a sigh of relief. "Cumchdach, what kind of a welcome do you call this?"

"The kind you give an uninvited visitor after a strange flyer attacks our new plantings."

Ethan didn't need to ask which plantings. Cumchdach wasn't talking about new festia saplings, the swamp-loving producer of the nutritious pollen that was the basis of the den Coille wealth. Plantings of festia already coated too much of the western slopes, increasing the moisture levels in the local atmosphere and worsening the rain disparity on both sides of the ranges. The Federal government, through the cursed Survey, had forced the den Coilles to start changing to less damaging plantings under the control of the local Survey field staff. The ones headed by Fee den Coille Winter, his eldest brother's new wife.

Cumchdach had shown Ethan the Survey's economic spreadsheets and their data on projected damage if no change was made. There had already been a disastrous mudslide recently that took out a big lump of Manascraoch but that made little difference. Just as in Sulwith, too many feared the new plantings, worried for their jobs and their families, and armed guards had to patrol each new plantation.

Unlike the Solaris and Sulwith situation though, the head of Den Coille had accepted the warnings of the Federal government. Bram den Coille had no reason to love the Survey or be thankful to his Survey daughter, but he was also a pragmatist. Fee had been co-opted into helping his people find a new economic direction.

Bram den Coille was also supposed to have taught his people to work with plainsmen.

"None of our people have fired on you," he said to Cumchdach.

"You sure of that? What about the Old Man."

"He has no reason to attack den Coille country." A statement he hoped was true, even if it avoided the point.

"Maybe. You know him better than we do. But this is no time for a social visit."

Ethan switched his com to a tightly secured private band. "It's no social call. I need to talk to you and your father—alone."

Cumchdach's mouth tightened. "Not now, Ethan."

"Your attacker; was it a Stealth II?"

"A Stealth— Yes. Why?"

"Because one came tragging near to killing me out at the Sulwith solar field."

The crease deepened on Cumchdach's mouth and he studied Ethan's face closely. Then let out a long, slow hoo. "I'm sending you the coordinates for the family's secure docking platform. Father, Seolta and I will meet you there."

"No, just you and Bram. No Seolta."

"No." Flat and final.

"It's important, Cumber. You, your father, and that's all. I'm unarmed and I'll drop my security shields if you promise not to fire on me again."

A slight twist of Cumchdach's mouth at the pet name Ethan had taken to calling him in prison. At first it had been solely to annoy the mountain man, then later as their friendship grew against their enemies, it became a part of the front both adopted to keep the other brothers' spirits up.

Ethan hadn't called him that since the day the Federal troops had freed them all from the Survey prison. The day Ethan's brother Caleb had roused the frontline Survey staff to rise up against their managers and wrench back control of the Survey from their crooked top brass.

Cumchdach gave a brusque wave of his hand and Ethan nodded back. Moments later, he was hovering above a tight cluster of treetops as a platform rose into view. A green light came through his com and Ethan set his craft down on the private landing pad of the den Coille's house. He still remembered his awe when he'd first seen the famed house. A wonder of architecture that wound its way through a huge baullnia tree in an astounding piece of engineering. All the buildings in the treetop city that was Manascraoch were similar. Mountain folk were happiest with a flexible tree branch under their feet and hated the feel of solid ground. Not surprising when the ground below their trees was a spongy and cold bogland. Give him the sand and stone of the plains any day. Right now, he eyed the flimsy-looking platform with the trepidation he could never banish when landing here. It didn't look big or strong enough to hold a land skimmer let alone a full-sized flyer.

They land here all the time. Stop procrastinating.

He snapped off his harness and set his com to run a tight security lock on his flyer. He was beginning to have a bad feeling about this trip.

When he stepped out of the hatch, he came face to face with a full squad of den Coille guards, standing in a circle around him and blocking him from Cumchdach and Bram den Coille. Not one of the squad, or either of the den Coilles, gave a smile in welcome and, suddenly, it felt like he'd been caught in the boggy mountain ground. He slowly lifted his arms, hand facing out.

"There's no need for this," he said.

Cumchdach went to step forward but the guards blocked him, and his father put a hand on his sleeve.

"How did you know that was a Stealth II attacking us," said the dark-eyed man who ran the Den Coille business empire.

"Because one attacked me when I was inspecting a solar field we're told needs to change."

"And will you?"

Ethan shook his head. "That's confidential business information. My report is finished, but the local workers deserve to know the outcome first."

Bram den Coille studied him with those too acute eyes of his. Ethan didn't trust the man but did respect him. He stared back, hoping he looked as staunch and resolute as the Den Coille head.

Finally Bram gave a short nod. "As is proper. Guards, stand down. Ser Winter will be accompanying us to the operations room. Ser Ethan, you will submit to a body scan and unlock your flyer to our security scans."

Cumchdach turned abruptly to his father, speaking urgently. Unfortunately, Ethan couldn't hear a thing, and his gut twisted harder. If Bram had ordered a sensory shield around him and his people, they really were spooked. Or had chosen a side and it wasn't with the Federal government or the planet.

He'd expected a body scan as soon as he saw the guards, but his flyer too? Not one of the guards had lowered their weapon, and too many fingers hovered above firing buttons. Bram clamped his hand down tighter on Cumchdach's arm, despite his son's continued protests.

"A scan of your flyer, Ser Winter. Unlock it to us, or this ends now."

Ethan had no choice. He held out his wrist and very, very slowly brought the other hand across to hover over his com patch. Then set in the code to unlock his flyer. A nod to the troops. "It's open to you. Don't break anything. I've already lost one flyer to this business."

The weapons still held, still faced him, but the two troopers on the outside edge broke off and came around behind him. At a cold nudge of metal in his back, he stepped away from the flyer, away from any kind of escape route. A lighter sound of footsteps marched up his flyer's ramp. The woman of the pair he guessed, which meant the man stood right behind him. Ethan was bigger than most mountain folk—Winters were built tall and lean—but this man was a trained Den Coille trooper and could probably beat him cold. Ethan stood very still, eyes fixed on Cumchdach as he tried to shame him into apologising for this.

But Cumchdach was his father's son as much as Ethan belonged to the Winter clan. He might give his father a look of disgust as they all waited for the scan results, but he met Ethan's stare with no trace of apology.

Finally a step behind him again. "The flyer is clean."

That cold nudge of metal again, and the rest of the troop pointed their weapons at Ethan.

"The operations room, Ser Ethan," said the senior trooper.

The man behind pushed as Ethan began to follow the circling squad of troopers. They led him across the platform and down the nearest corridor, walking after the two den Coilles.

Down a flight of steps, along more corridors and up and down more steps, around the trunk of the baullnia and under branches and walkways. Caleb had told him once of his own march under guard through the den Coille stronghold. "There is a logic to the place, but it's also an easy building for a man to get lost in if that's what they want." After so many ups and downs, Ethan barely knew whether he was still high in the canopy or close to ground level.

Finally they stopped at a door. The guards shoved him through the entrance, pushing him against the far wall and running a scanner far too closely over him. Nothing friendly about the hands that patted and prodded him either. Did they think he came in armed with a full offensive screen? He'd come to talk to a friend.

A yank at his hands, a last shove in his guts, then they shocked him by walking out.

He leaned against the wall to catch his breath and sourly watched as the sparking of lights across the doorway told of a confinement force field. One touch of those sparkly lights and Ethan would suffer a very nasty burn. At least the room had windows, though all he could see through them were leaves and grey sky.

He watched in disgust as the two den Coille's walked through the field unharmed. "It's DNA coded?"

Cumchdach nodded but said nothing as he propped himself against the flanking wall, leaving his father to walk closer to Ethan. A brave move, given the anger stirring in Ethan.

He lunged forward, ready to give the man a taste of the humiliation he'd dumped on Ethan.

Nothing. He was stuck, adhered to that far wall as if by a high capacity magnet. He struggled to get free. Nothing again. He stopped, fighting hard to keep his temper.

"You will explain yourself, young den Winter," said Bram den Coille. "Are you a threat to den Coille's?"

"Not me," said Ethan.

"But my son is?"

"Seolta? I hope not, but I don't know for sure. That's why I came here. I needed to talk to Cumchdach about a com program Silas is looking at for me."

"To do with the attack by a Stealth II you claim you came under."

"That I did come under." The thick mugginess of the room's climate setting left a slick of sweat on his neck, and he longed for a breath of hot desert air and wide open sky.

"Where, exactly," said Bram den Coille, as Cumchdach left off holding up his wall and came to stand beside his father.

"Just off the far northeast corner of our Sulwith field. It's full desert country and empty of anything but wind and sand. No reason for a Federal Stealth to be patrolling there."

"You're sure it was a Stealth?" said Cumchdach, breaking his silence at last.

"After what happened to us last cycle? We've talked about this plenty of times. I know the outline of every Federal ship, land vessel, weapon type and uniform. No one takes us by surprise again." Cumchdach looked nothing like the man he'd learned to trust in prison. A man from whom he'd come to expect logical thought and plain common sense. "We're supposed to be on the same side."

"Yet you come in here immediately after an attack and accuse Seolta of attacking you."

Ethan strove hard for patience. "I did not." He looked at the door. "I only asked that he not be part of this discussion, not yet."

Cumchdach frowned. "Sounds like an accusation to me. Seolta is my brother—"

"And my son, and an integral part of Den Coille. Any slur on his name is a slur on all of us." Bram looked angrier than ever.

"Just listen," said Ethan.

Bram's fists closed, but Cumchdach said nothing. Both men glared at him and he waited tensely.

"All right," said Cumchdach at long last. "If you're not accusing Seolta of anything, what are you telling us?

Ethan sighed in relief. "Not only did I come under attack from a Stealth II; just before that, my flyer got shot down by a beam of a kind I've never seen before."

Cumchdach's mouth dropped open and Bram waited.

"I called Silas up to Sulwith to look into it. As part of it, we had to check out a suspect com room, one of the nastier ones. One that may be involved with agitating opposition to any changes at that field."

"And the Stealth attack…"

"May or may not be linked."

"So you're not accusing Seolta of being a party to an attack on your business, or on us," said Bram.

"Not directly. But Silas said that room's com program had similarities to one he remembered in the past, when Solaris and Den Coille were in opposition.

"Were enemies. Yeah," said Cumchdach, "but that doesn't mean you go accusing a den Coille of trying to kill you."

"Would you just listen?"

"If there's a reason to."

Ethan gritted his teeth. "Both of you know how angry Seolta was by the time we were released. He still is, from what I've seen."

"Angry enough to attack his own kind. Is that what you're saying?" said Bram.

"I don't know," said Ethan, "but what if I'm right. What if he is involved in some way? Or is working with some group without knowing their real end game?"

For the first time, there was an easing on Cumchdach's face. "He is angry. We've both tried to get him to talk about what happened and haven't got anywhere."

Bram looked unconvinced. "Doesn't mean I'm going to stop trusting my own son. As for suggesting Seolta doesn't have a tragging good grasp on what he's doing… Not Seolta."

Ethan had to concede that one. Shrewd and cunning, Seolta den Coille was the most politically astute of all the brothers. Ethan had never quite trusted him, but he did respect his abilities. Seolta would know everything possible about any group he went into business with.

"When it comes to com systems, Silas is about as good as they get. He's been playing in our systems since before he could talk properly," he said.

"Seolta grew up writing com programmes," said Bram. "He doesn't leave a trace if he doesn't want to."

"Maybe he wasn't directly involved in this. Maybe someone has conned him," Ethan said.

Cumchdach shook his head. "Not Seolta."

Ethan thought it unlikely too, but now wasn't the time to say that. "I'm not saying he is doing anything. Just that a com program has structural similarities to one he designed." He was saying a great deal more than that, but right now he was calling on every trace of diplomatic double-talk he could come up with.

Unfortunately, Cumchdach knew him too well. His face closed up and he stepped back, with a nod to his father. Bram looked at Ethan then at his son and followed. Again that annoying sensory shield as the two men talked, then argued.

At the end, Bram den Coille stayed back and Cumchdach approached. "Transmit everything you have. Let us have a look at it, then we'll talk again."

Ethan looked past him to Bram den Coille. The man nodded and activated his com. The door opened and the guards returned. They surrounded Ethan and the force sticking him to that tragging wall suddenly vanished, leaving him to stumble awkwardly onto one knee.

One guard grabbed one arm, the second his other arm. "We will talk soon," said Bram den Coille, dark eyes narrow.

Ethan nodded and turned to Cumchdach. "The usual place?"

"Yes," said Cumchdach.

"No," said Bram as the guards began marching Ethan out the door.

Cumchdach grabbed for his father's arm. "No?"

Ethan couldn't see what came next as the guards hauled him out the door and turned to the right, marching him rapidly down the hallway.

"What in…" he heard from Cumchdach. Followed by running steps. "Guards, turn him around."

"Your father's orders," said the trooper in the lead.

"You can't do this. Not to—"

The guards kept dragging him on, Cumchdach arguing with them every step of the way, and Ethan began to get a bad feeling. Along another corridor and a sudden switch to a hallway he'd never been down before. Gone were the friendly mountain walls of living wood and soft colours. This was harsh grey plascrete. Clinical and ominous.

Around another corner, and they shoved him to a single room at the end—a room with no window, the only exit the one they tried to force him through and a tell-tale too white light shining from the roof panel.

"That's a cell." A cold wave of horror swept through him. Too many memories invaded his head, a wash of panic threatening to overwhelm him. Not again. Not ever again.

"You can't do this," said Cumchdach.

Ethan grabbed for the door frame. "Not in there. Not going. No," he shouted.

Another shove, a punch in his side that left him stumbling forward and out of breath for one vital moment.

"You have a single com band. Transmit your message," said the lead guard. "When we get the records, the Ser will see about releasing you."

The door slammed behind him, the lights dimmed, and he heard the unmistakable sound of a security screen slamming over it. They had locked him in.

He shut his eyes. Only that made it possible for him to get up again, but then he made the mistake of opening them, of seeing the four walls surrounding him, knowing that behind him the door was locked and could not be opened by him.

He was in a cell.

Nothing in this room was under his control. Including his body. The world stopped and so did he.

He froze, feet square on the floor and head turned to the one small sliver of light coming under the door, the one crack leading to the outside world and freedom.

Outside, he vaguely heard a sound, heard someone shouting. He heard words and understood they must make sense, but they couldn't get past the walls surrounding him. The walls coming closer and closer, ready to smother him.

"Open this door, now. Get him out of there."

A mumbled No. The one word he understood. Guards loved that word.

"Don't do this, Da."

Then a scrabbling behind him. A whoosh of sound.

The walls moved in, hovering closer, crushingly close.

A hand on his shoulder. "Eshta, it's me. Cumber. The door is open. Hold on, you're getting out."

Someone pushed him closer to the walls. "Don't. Close, too close."

Hands caught at him, turned him around with a violent shove. "Eshta, the door. It's open. You're free to walk through."

The words began to make a kind of sense. The walls still moved in, but there was a patch of white light. A break in those moving walls. He stumbled forward, reaching for it. Putting one foot in front of the other.

Then he was out, but more walls waited, pushing him back.

"Open that far door. Now."

His feet followed the voice's commands, but the walls still surrounded him, still moved closer and closer.

Then he was running, stumbling, falling toward the smell of living greenery and pungent dirt.

"Nearly there, Eshta."

Another footfall. One step after another, through a tunnel. Soft rain falling on his face. Something above him, a brush of green, and a squelching beneath his feet. Trees. Leaves. Mud. Sky.

Outside.

No walls here.

He breathed in—once, twice—deep and desperate.

"That's it. Like that, Eshta."

"Cumber, is that you."

"Of course it is, you stupid big lummock. Who else would pull you out of trouble?"

The words might sound harsh, but Ethan heard the touch of tears in them. He breathed in again, breathed out, fixed his eyes on the soaring trees around him and the glimpse of sky above.

More people came in behind him. What must they think? These people were not friends, and they had seen his hidden weakness. Had seen him fail.

Then a deeper voice. Bram den Coille, said the robotic memory centre in his brain.

"What happened back there?"

"I tried to tell you. He can't take a cell. Not after… In prison, the guards used it to control us. Ethan had no brother there."

"Cumchdach. Tell me."

Bram den Coille had been imprisoned too. Like Ethan, like his sons, he'd been sentenced to execution thanks to the false testimony of the one-time Survey bosses. But only the den Coille brothers and Ethan had been held in the Survey prison in Urbis central. Both sets of parents and Cumchdach's eldest sister had been held in a routine Federal prison, far from the city. Not pleasant, but with normal prison jailers.

Not so the new troops employed by the disgraced Survey managers.

"Whenever we looked like causing trouble, they would pull out Aigherach and force him to try to walk on that leg of his. It's why the fractures never healed."

"And they didn't think that would work for Ethan?"

"It did, but they wouldn't believe it," Ethan said. His voice sounded husky, strained as if from long disuse. A mere whisper.

"What did they do?" said Bram.

Thankfully, Cumchdach took back the telling of it. "Ethan stepped in front of a guard trying to bully Aigherach. They shut him in a sensory deprivation room and kept him there for three weeks. When he came out…"

"…I was barely sane," said Ethan, pulling on every speck of courage he possessed. "It's why … I can't take closed rooms. Not small ones without windows I can see out of."

"But in prison. There's no windows facing outward in that block." A touch of horror in the senior den Coille's voice. "I know. I made sure our people were in the team that scoured that place and seized any kind of evidence against the vermin who dared to threaten my family."

"Luckily the Federal troops broke us out soon after that. Mostly … I can operate normally, but sometimes…"

Bram cleared his throat. "It seems apologies are in order, Ethan mar Sol an Helena den Winter."

Ethan lifted a hand. "No need." He risked a glance at Cumchdach's father. The man looked as serious as he'd seen him, but whether that meant he now trusted Ethan…

"My sons are still watched. Our whole family is."

"The same goes for Winters and Solaris, but I came to Cumchdach with this first. It hasn't gone beyond me and Silas."

"Not even your other brother?"

Caleb, this man's son-in-law and apparently no more trusted than before he'd worked to free them all. Bram den Coille no doubt blamed Caleb for getting them thrown in prison in the first place, and there was too much of an element of truth in that for Ethan to dispute it. "He's checking out the Urbis end, but no, he doesn't know about this yet."

"Will you tell him?"

Ethan had to think about that one. Not tell the big brother who had looked out for Ethan and Silas since the day they were born.

"Winters are tight," he said. "We don't keep secrets from each other. This … yes, I will be telling him."

He took a breath, holding onto the freedom of air and sky as long as he could.

Bram and Cumchdach murmured together.

"He is family, both to me and now to the den Coilles," Ethan reminded them.

"True," said Cumchdach, but he's also Survey."

"As is your sister."

Cumchdach's eyes darkened and Bram jerked back as if slapped. So maybe reminding them Fee had chosen the Survey and Arcadia over family wasn't the brightest thing to have said now, but he couldn't claim to be thinking rationally. Another deep breath. How long before they threw him back in that hell hole of a cell?

"My daughter's loyalties are not under discussion," said Bram stiffly. "Only Seolta's, I understand."

Ethan interjected. "May be under discussion."

"You came here to ask me to spy on my brother?" said Cumchdach.

"No." It wasn't like that. Yes it was. "All right, yes. Before he gets deeper into something that's a whole lot bigger than he realises."

"Seolta is neither naïve nor easily duped," said Bram.

"But he is angry," said Cumchdach slowly. "Enough to grab at anything to get back at the people who near killed him and all of us?"

Bram clamped his lips together, eyeing Ethan, who began to sweat again. Don't show fear in front of them, not again. You can survive that cell.

"Father?"

Ethan felt like begging too, but the last time he'd opened his mouth he'd only made things worse.

Finally, Bram drew in a breath. "We will discuss this. Cumchdach and I."

"And Seolta?"

"That is for us to decide, not for a Winter. Transmit to Cumchdach all the information you have. Then it is time for you to leave, Ser Winter. A skimmer will take you back to your flyer."

Ethan let out a whoosh of breath. No corridors, no closed rooms. "Thank you."

Bram gave a brisk nod and swung around to leave, then stopped. "And, Ser Winter, it would not be wise to return to Manascraoch. Not until this matter is resolved."

CHAPTER TWELVE

That brother was in her home again. Just what she needed. Sar slammed her bag down on the entrance bench, shoved off her boots and marched down the hallway, following the sound of a small boy's laughter and the deeper chuckle of a near grown man. Then she found them.

"You're here again, Ser Winter."

Silas Winter dropped his feet down from the table, hastily shoved a plate of crumbled biscuits under a nearby cushion, and plastered on a smile, the kind that no doubt worked with his mother when caught out. Except she wasn't his mother; she was Finn and Daff's big sister. The sight of Daff curled up on the seat beside the tall plainsman and Finn lost inside his latest com puzzle was the final straw.

"Have you two finished your homework?"

Daff peered around the far side of Silas Winter. "Aww, Sar. Not yet. It's dumb stuff anyway. Si says we can learn far more by just doing."

Si had the good sense to look guilty. "That's not quite what I said."

"Yes, it is," said Daff staunchly, and Silas had to raise his hands in defeat.

"I may have said something like that," he admitted, and straightened up as she glared at him. "Come on, boys. Your sister's right. Homework's important. I can come back tomorrow."

At that, Finn jerked up from his com field. "You can't go yet. We haven't finished working out this shield pattern."

"And what pattern would that be?" She stuck her hands on her hips, the only way to keep them from flapping uselessly at the intruder, then realised her mistake as the light in Finn's eyes warned he was about to launch into a long and complicated explanation of the glories of his latest target. She was too aware of just which shield pattern currently enthralled him. Ari's decidedly suspect com room.

"It's late, dinner will be on the table soon, and I'm sure Ser Winter has other places to be."

"Not tonight, Sera," said the annoying young man. "If that was an invitation to dinner, it's gratefully accepted. Hotel food is fine enough for the odd night, but there's nothing like a good honest home meal."

Sar's mouth dropped open, totally outflanked. Finn grinned in delight, and Daff did a big fist bump. "Yes, and after dinner we can beat you at Deadgulch Alley."

"As if," said Silas, sounding no older than her brothers. "You're on."

Her brothers shrieked in excitement and it seemed she had no choice. "We would be pleased to have your company," she said stiffly.

A sound at the door and her father bustled in.

"Da, Si's staying for dinner and we're gonna play Deadgulch Alley."

"That's nice."

Sar looked sharply at her father. He'd barely heard Daff.

"Not if you keep bothering the Ser," she threatened the boys.

Her father heard her this time. "'Ser Winter can stay or go as he pleases, and you boys can mind your manners.

Just then, Geordie erupted into the room. Sar paid him no attention. The boy practically lived at their house when Ari was home. Then she took in the look on his face.

"Geordie, what is it?"

He jabbed a finger toward the desert. "Big storm. Lock down. Big one coming. Find Ari."

"She's upstairs. Go and tell her what's happening. Does your mother know you're here?"

He shook his head and she signed in resignation to Daff. "Send his mother a com message, then start preparations."

"For what?" said their unwanted visitor.

"A storm's coming, a big one. You'll have to stay here."

"Just because a boy comes in frightened by a few dust whirlies?"

"Geordie knows the sky," pronounced Finn, already packing up.

Silas rose as if to leave. She put out an arm but her father beat her. "No one's going anywhere, Ser Winter. You're stuck here for the duration. The only safe way back is through the tunnels, and they are restricted to use by the emergency services in a storm."

He stared. Didn't he know of the underground network of tunnels connecting everyone in the town, used when it was too hot to walk in the streets? In a big storm, they mustn't get clogged by pedestrians. Everyone in town knew the rules on that.

"There's been no alarm—"

Suddenly, an eerie wail echoed through the house and ricocheted through the town, setting every hair on edge.

"What in the darks." Silas shot toward the door.

Her father blocked him. "Too late. You're staying, son." He pulled up the emergency channel on his com.

Sar was already shutting down the outer window covers while the boys had rushed to their rooms to grab what they needed. "How bad?" she asked her father.

"Building still. Could go to category ten, say the reports."

Silas stopped trying to shove past him. "Category ten? That's a tragging big blow. We get some of those back home."

She shook her head as her fingers played their tune on the prepper controls, updating the basement food supplies.

"Not just wind. A sandstorm."

"It will flay the skin from your bones," shrieked Daff, grinning madly.

"Which is why I want you boys down in that basement, quick and sharp," said their father, fingers flicking through the main house controls to lock everything down into storm mode. "Where's Ari?"

"Here," said a voice from the stairs, and Sar breathed a sigh of relief. She'd been worried whether she'd have to ask Finn to eject her from the banned com room. Finn could bypass a parental block, and she hadn't been sure Ari couldn't do the same.

Then she looked at her sister's face and gave another sigh of relief. The sulky teen was banished, the emergency siren overriding teen hormones for a girl raised on the deadlands border.

"The stairs to the basement are through that door, Ser Winter. We don't use the shafts in emergencies," Sar said, turning to her other headache.

"What can I do to help," he said, sounding as briskly efficient as his brother.

She had no choice but to accept the offer. Not in a sandstorm like this one. All she could do was hope nothing else happened in the coming hours of close contact. "Bring that box and set the coms to closed cycle. Outside communications will be down until this is over and the atmospheric electrical activity can interfere with our com systems if we don't isolate them."

"On it, as soon as I send through a message to Ethan."

The first claws of the storm had begun to batter at the window shields as they hurried down to the basement. Last preparations done, her father slammed closed the basement shields and the underground lights flickered into life at the bottom of the stairs.

Sar had been through more sandstorms than she could remember, but this one was as bad as any she'd known. Even in the closed underground rooms, she could feel the bone-deep vibration of the winds hurling the desert sands against their sanctuary. A hum that set the hairs on her body on end.

"She's a bad one," said Silas Winter beside her, idly playing a com game. She could feel him watching her and the rest of the family but also noted the abrupt tapping of his fingers in the control field. The man wasn't as calm as he made out. Not surprising in someone barely out of boyhood. Or in a man who'd spent months hiding from his enemies, and she suddenly wondered how often he'd had to wait in a hideout like this for danger to pass.

No, don't go there. She couldn't afford sympathy, not for a man who threatened her family. Tonight was hard enough. The two boys hadn't seen enough storms to understand how bad this one was, but Ari flinched with each battering shudder, eyes constantly flitting to the overhead lights despite knowing they were safe down here. The basement rooms ran on a backup auxiliary cycle, powered by a storage cell in the back room and isolated from the main house feed. Losing power was the one thing Sar wasn't worried about.

Not until the lights gave an uncertain flicker.

Sar jumped straight to her feet without thinking. "What in the sands was that?"

Silas was staring at the ceiling panels. "A power surge from atmospheric static?"

"This system is double-isolated and self-governing. It's insulated from power surges," said Ari, staring at the ceiling panels, nerves vanished, and the business-like look on her face had Sar's stomach churning. You know nothing of power systems. Don't do it.

A stupid wish when her family's life depended on those systems. Her father had more sense. "Ari, switch to the auxiliary back up," he threw over his shoulder as he marched out of the room, just as the lights gave another shimmer then blacked out completely. Sar only took a breath again when the panels stuttered back to life.

Finn made a bolt for Sar's side, followed a shade slower by Daff. She put an arm around each of them. "Your coms can give you a backup beam," she reminded them. It made little difference.

"The lights have never gone out before," said Daff. Finn clung on tighter. "What else will stop."

"Nothing," said a cool voice across the room. "Not when we have the workshop supervisor here to keep everything going," said Silas Winter.

Finn's face brightened. "And Ari."

Sar could have groaned.

A puff of dust from the main vents and another flickering of lights. No time to try distracting the outsider. "Ari, onto it," she ordered.

"You do the vents; I'll check the lights," said her father to a brisk nod from her sister as she slapped her com into life and began a scan.

Silas Winter's head jerked up at that. He said nothing, just watched closely and Sar had the nasty feeling he'd seen the final piece of a puzzle lock into place.

She could do nothing about it, nothing to stop Ari exposing herself. Lose the air supply and none of them would be getting out of here. But why today, why now in a system that had been built by her father and Ari and had never failed before?

She needed to move. "Finn, Daff. You hungry?" A silly question—they were always hungry—but the boys' vigorous head nodding gave her an excuse to start pulling out items from the prepper's store. "Time for some first-principle cooking lessons," she announced to a cheer from both of them, as they forgot their fear. Mostly because of their trust in Da and Ari, she had to admit.

The basement had a built-in hot pad with its own power supply. No point stressing the energy system further by using the prepper when the systems were playing up.

"Pancakes," voted Daff.

"With draspa berries and mushies," put in Finn.

She could only nod, too conscious of Silas Winter watching her sister and father work on the ventilation system. The food had almost no nutritional value except providing energy, but making it would keep the two boys occupied for a considerable time.

After a while, Silas wandered over. "Anything I can do to help? Your father and sister seem to have the power supply problem under control, and I'm a systems expert, not an engineer."

If that was a question, she chose to ignore it, passing him a large spoon and a bowl of rehydrated draspa berries. "Two scoops into each bowl. Then turn the mixture over slowly."

She demonstrated what she meant on the third bowl in front of her as the two boys measured out the rest of the ingredients, Finn with his tongue caught between his teeth and looking far too young to be the systems genius who had broken into Ari's com room. Silas gave her a grin as he turned the mixture like an old hand. "I used to help our cook. The kitchen was the most fun place in the whole house."

She forced herself to smile back. "Then you can help Daff with pouring the pancakes while Finn and I make the mushies."

Silas had made pancakes before, she discovered, and Daff enjoyed showing a fellow male how their hot pad worked. Soon, the two were deep in discussion over the merits of their pad versus the portable stove Silas had used on camping expeditions out on the plains, followed by increasingly taller stories of making a primitive campfire in ever worsening conditions without burning down the dry grasslands or the desert scrub.

All through the boys' laughter, though, she couldn't miss the Winter son's glances at the control board where her father and Ari worked, wielding com scans and laser drive units like others worked an artist's stylus.

Finally, Ari leaned back and her father gave a pleased grunt.

"That should hold it," he said.

Silas Winter looked up from the hot pad where he and Daff carefully monitored the latest pancake. "All fixed?"

"Appears to be," said her father, eying the now steady stream of light from the ceiling and the clear ventilation currents.

"What was the problem," said the man from the core of Solaris.

Her father shrugged, but Ari wasn't as savvy. "The alternating coupling unit had got stuck. We had to route around it."

Sar jumped in before her sister could launch into a more damning explanation. "That's good. Now wash up and we'll have these pancakes ready in no time. Ser Winter, how are you and Daff going over there?"

An amused smile accompanied his reply. "Take a seat. One more flip and they're done."

Sar gritted her teeth and wished she could turf him out, but the storm still roared outside. They'd be all together for hours yet. More than long enough for the man to interrogate her sister under the guise of charming her. He was so tragging helpful. Once they all finished devouring the pancakes, he offered to help her father and Ari as they ran a full check on the basement power set up. The man was even better than Finn with com systems, and her youngest brother hung on his every word as the Winter man took him through the steps of each program. It gave Sar nightmare visions of having their house systems modified by a first schooler. But Silas did make Ari and her father's work easier, and that was a good thing if it gave him less time to discover what her sister was capable of. He talked to her, too, as they worked. Ari soaked it up, and not even her father's judicious interruptions could stop her artlessly explaining to Silas what she was doing.

"Ari can make any machine do what she wants," said Finn proudly. "Her and Geordie tuned up the solar field so it's the best performing field in all of the plains. Isn't that right, Da."

"They had some good ideas and Geordie has a special gift for sensing the sun," said her father in his light and even voice. It had no effect on Finn.

"Yeah, they make that field hum. That's what everyone in town says. Bet that's why you're here, isn't it, Silas." Finn always got on first name terms with anyone he liked.

"I only came along for the ride with Ethan."

"He knows nothing of fields," pronounced Finn, "not like you."

"Not true," said Silas loyally. "Just not as interested in the technical stuff." Sar wasn't so sure of the truth of that, but part of her liked Silas springing to Ethan's defence, even against a small child. A part of her that said Ethan Winter needed defending, which made no sense. What she should do is get Silas to admit why he was really in town, but she couldn't do that to Finn. Her baby brother didn't need to be worried about losing his home. Not yet.

By the time morning came and the sandstorm had finally worn out its fury, Sar had been forced to watch her family parade themselves in all their cursed abilities. Finn was a coms system addict and Ari could fix anything. Daff would one day be a talented administrator, his skills honed by a childhood spent diverting Finn from some of his more radical ideas and bridging the divide between Ari and the world. If she let him, and that wasn't often these days. Only their father could move between all of them, thanks to the absolute trust all his children had in his love and approval.

She'd packed the boys off to their beds at the first yawn, but it didn't help. All she could hope was that Silas wouldn't tell his brother everything he'd learned, but that was wishful thinking. Ethan Winter would pick up on all the nuances and come to the kind of conclusions that Sar most feared.

He was going to close them down. Everything her father had told her, and what Ethan had let slip, convinced her of that. All the worst fears of her members come true, their homes and the lives they knew lost, despite the promises she'd made them. And afterward? How could she protect her family and the workers who looked to her?

Especially when she wasn't sure she could protect her own heart. Not after that evening on the bluff.

No, too much thinking. The storm had passed and she had things to do.

"Finn, Daff, Ari; you know the drill. Get to it."

It didn't stop the wrangling after being locked up together far too long, but they'd been brought up in the deadlands and set to packing up the basement even as they kept arguing.

"Is too the longest blow we've had," said Finn.

"What would you know, sprat."

"Don't be childish, you two," said Ari with a slop of big sister condescension. "It was a big blow, but not the biggest ever. Check your com records."

"Was it worse than usual?" said a voice from behind her. "We have big blows at home," said Silas Winter, "and they can kill if you're caught out in them."

"Big enough, I guess. Da would know more than me. If you'll excuse me, I have to recheck the stores down here. We always restock straight after a storm."

Her father put a hand on the young man's shoulder. "Never know when the next one will come, and they're getting stronger and more frequent. Don't worry, though. This field can stand up to them. The Winters aren't going broke soon."

A red flush washed over Silas' face. "My family is aware that there are worse things than losing your wealth, Ser Beren."

"I guess you are, after last cycle's events," said her father. "For now, we can leave Sar and the others to finish up here. You're welcome to come with me to check on the field and make sure our people are safe."

Silas Winter may be young, but Sar didn't make the mistake of thinking him naïve. He'd had to grow up quickly in the recent troubles, hiding out with Caleb Winter's field staff for months while the renegade officials in head office hunted him. She guessed that's where the deep tan on his face came from, as well as the old eyes taking in the rooms and her family before giving a slow nod. "Thank you. Ethan will be grateful for the report."

"And when is he coming back?" Sar couldn't stop herself asking.

The very faintest of tilts of his mouth. "Shortly. The storm forced him to stay overnight at Tollic but he left there first thing."

She'd had to ask. "That's nice," she mumbled, or something like it, and hastily waved them off as she hurried toward the storage cupboards. As far as she was concerned, Ethan Winter could stay away. The longer he did; the longer the field was safe.

And the longer the weight of family secrets hung over her.

It was a considerable time later before she was free to leave the shelter, emerging into the murky half-light that always followed a sandstorm. She looked skyward, breathing in short shallow bursts to avoid coating her throat and nose with the lingering dust, but revelling in the orange glow in the sky. A sign of promise, a sign that said you have survived.

A loud bellow from the end of the street shattered her peace.

"Sar Beren. Whose side are you on?" Maxell Drocash, in all his spiteful fury.

"Are your family all safe, Maxell?"

A scowl from the man. "We know what to do in a sandstorm. But what you did before the storm. That's not right. Not to me, and not to the other workers on this site."

"Oh?" she said in the most reasonable voice she could muster. "You're now the union delegate, are you? Has there been a vote no one told me about? Because it was my name on the winning ballot at the last election."

"That voting stuff means nothing with the talk going 'round town. They're saying you're Ethan Winter's latest clutch buddy. You planning on winning him around with pillow talk, or looking to land yourself a good bed when the Winters close down this town?"

"What's that crud-infested brain of yours on about, Drocash?"

"You were seen up on Bluff peak with him, and it wasn't to talk union stuff neither. Not by all accounts."

The man stuck his face right into hers, and she had to bring every part of her body under rigid control to stop the reflex step backward. "You spied on us? Or are you just repeating scum talk making the rounds. Look at who's doing the talking Ser Drocash, before you start accusing me of selling out the union."

She would love to accuse him of being involved with his daughters' luring Ari into that sleazy com room, but the risk was too great. They had to find out what linked the girls with the low-life wernets manipulating Ari and the other teens in the town. Stopping those brakka blood suckers was more important than fending off the despicable Drocash.

"Go home, make sure your family and street are safe. You can stick your nose into other business once this town and its people are all provided for. That's what real Sulwith people do."

Suddenly, the man crumpled to the ground in front of her. Then he was hauled up again by a furious Ethan Winter. "And what Solaris employees do, instead of harassing a woman in front of her own home."

Another shake, and Ethan dropped the man to the ground. "Collect your pay and get out of Sulwith before I set the town's law on you."

Drocash proved to have a smidgeon of bluster left. "Winters don't own everything around here. This is a public street."

"Don't push me, brakka. Public enough that enough others saw you verbally abusing this woman and can swear to it."

"Stop it, the pair of you." She had to shout to be heard. "Ser Drocash, we're finished here. I'll answer to the union when and if I'm called to do so." The man glared at her as he struggled up. One foul word she refused to listen to and he slouched off, promising all kinds of retribution in a garbled mumble. She swung on Ethan Winter, torn between wanting to fling her arms around him in thanks or rage at his high-handed intervention. Drocash really had something to talk about now.

"I was handling it, Ser Winter. It's my job to handle it. He wasn't hurting me, only yelling. It's what members do sometimes. A union is a democracy. They are allowed to disagree with me."

Ethan's green eyes shone so dark they looked black and his hands grasped her shoulders as if to ward off any more attackers. "Disagree, yes. Abuse, no."

"It was only words."

"No one talks to you like that. No one."

"Including you. As Ser Drocash's representative, I will be filing an official complaint of unjustified dismissal."

"You'll defend him after what he said?"

"Yes. I will. It's my job and he's my responsibility. He's also a particularly good metallurgy technician, and he doesn't need to be a pleasant team member to do that. You have no grounds to dismiss him."

"I sure as tragging sands do. The man threatened you."

"Not physically. Not yet. You dismiss him and my credibility is destroyed. How can I get the workers to trust me if they think I'll run off to Solaris' bosses every time it gets tough? I'm a grown woman, not an Urbis patsy doll, and you have no right to treat me otherwise."

He drew back as if stung and his hands dropped from her. "My apologies, Sera Beren." He dipped his head in stiff salute. "I won't bother you further. If you'll excuse me, I have to check the solar field for damage."

He swung around to walk away.

"No, wait," she called.

He ignored her and kept walking.

She had work to do. All the usual post-storm tasks in a town where everyone, right down to the smallest child, had an assigned role whenever nature did its worst. Hers was to check on the homes in this block for damage, follow up on the other union families, and assign work crews to make any emergency repairs. The rest would be prioritised over the coming months, but right now, families must be made safe.

No time to stare regretfully after the Solaris boss.

With each bang on a door, each query to a household that had survived this time, she saw the face of the man she'd sent packing. The man who had come to her aid when she needed him, at the cost to his company of a worker they could ill afford to lose. Drocash might be a nasty piece of work and his daughters a quicksand trap waiting for a victim, but he was also a skilled technician. Sulwith had never figured as most workers' preferred location, and the current uncertainty surrounding the field only exacerbated that.

Ethan Winter needed the man. Yet he'd put her first, and that had all kinds of alarms going off in her head. Not least because of that jolt of relief at hearing his voice.

She'd been so glad to see him.

CHAPTER THIRTEEN

Ethan bent to check the next solar supporting pole. Plenty of others could have done the job but right now he needed the mindless task.

Run your hand over the shaft, feel the tiny abrasions no scan could pick up, then scan the rest for internal damage. Log the result and move on to the next one.

So far, two-thirds of the field had been damaged by the sandstorm. He and the other workers moved methodically through the worst hit sections.

"You don't need to be doing that, Ser Winter." The section maintenance tech working with him looked as put out as he'd been when Ethan first attached himself to the man's team. Ethan wasn't sure whether the tech was more worried about working with a boss or Ethan's lack of competence.

"I've done it plenty of times before," he assured the man. "The Old Man believes in his sons knowing all parts of the business."

The man shrugged, as if making a jibe on the stupidity of the rich. "We've another day of this to go."

"I'll do one more block, then get out of your way."

The man tried to hide his relief but he was about as successful as Ethan had been with Sarwenna Beren.

He'd let her down, had diminished her by his words, and knew it as soon as he'd said them. A union rep hears hard talk like that man's all the time.

Not as slanderous, though; not as personal. A blazing pyre of anger at the man's slurs still raged in Ethan's belly.

No one talked to her like that.

She'd looked so shocked at the man's abuse … and so hurt by Ethan's intrusion, as if he'd shown her as little respect as that brakka workman.

The man was finished with Solaris, and Ethan didn't care how critical he might be to the Sulwith field. He was gone for his own protection. Ethan didn't trust himself if the man spread any more of his filthy slander against Sarwenna, his beautiful, strong, upright woman, debased by the words of a no-account gutter-dweller.

Was he any better? She'd been handling it, and he had failed to respect it. That's what kept him out here, powering from one pole to the next, one more damaged sheet to add to the growing multitude.

Another change needed for all the Solaris fields. Sheets that stood up to the more violent storms Caleb warned him were coming.

Finally, sanity hit, along with a wrenching headache and a sick feeling in his gut as the first waves of fury wore themselves out. With sanity came the realisation he couldn't just sack the brakka technician. Treat the man as he deserved and Sarwenna paid the price. Her name would be on everyone's tongue as causing it. The sick feeling in his gut trebled.

"I'm going back to the main office to write up the initial report," he said to the supervisor.

"Thank you for your help here, Ser."

The man looked so relieved Ethan decided to add a bonus to his next pay for handling the boss well when the boss had been acting like an idiot. He grabbed the nearest sled and hurtled back at full power to the office. The rush of speed made no difference, though, and he slammed into the office feeling as surly as when he'd started, thumping down into the manager's chair without care whether or not it put out the man. Tough, Ethan needed the space.

Silas arrived soon after, curt-faced and looking as sour as Ethan felt. "A bad storm, for certain. You going to do something about it, or just let those sheets rot while you grouse about the place?"

"I've just come in from checking the outer field."

Ethan thrust out a foot to shove the second chair toward his brother. Silas flung himself into the proffered seat. "I heard all about it. The big man from Dridust playing local repair boy."

Ethan stiffened. "More help than you standing around playing with your com."

"You think? My com has been working on a certain file while you play at workman and avoid answering the question everyone in Sulwith is waiting on. You've no right to keep hard-working Solaris staff dangling while you figure out whether you want to do your job or keep union Rep Sera Beren sweet."

Ethan had been itching for a fight since that wernet slug bait had mouthed off at Sarwenna. He flung himself out of the chair and right at his brother. "Take that back."

Silas had learned more in the desert with Caleb's Survey troop than how to appreciate the plains' unique plants and herbs, and for the first time in many years, Ethan found himself on the back foot with his baby brother. With muscles honed to a hard edge by days slogging over the plains and working on the lake site, Silas was no pushover. It didn't stop Ethan. Only made him more eager.

The Winter boys had been wrestling since they were first schoolers, to the despair of their so proper mother and their father's delight; but Silas was the baby, and they'd always pulled their moves against him. Not today. A long, brangling brawl didn't finish until a lamp came to a crashing end when they rolled against a cabinet. The noise echoed through the office. A loud crack sent an explosion of small particles rocketing across the room to cover both of them in grit. Ethan released his hold, pulling himself up and grabbing his knees as his head dropped and he gasped for breath. Beside him, Silas did the same, then looked up with a face scattered with tiny cuts. Ethan burst into a great rollicking laugh.

Silas grinned back. "You're not too pretty yourself."

"And you've sprouted some muscles, baby brother."

"Necessity, in Caleb's crew. You've been stuck inside too long." A sudden gasp and Silas' laughter froze in mid breath. "Oh, sands, I didn't think."

Ethan glared. "You mean, too many months stuck in a prison cell while you and Caleb stayed free under the light of the sun. Tragging hell, Silas, I've been out of that cell for months and it wasn't you who put me there."

"I ran away when you were taken."

"Yes, because I told you to. So stop feeling guilty, because, brother, I've had more than enough of it. You ran to warn Caleb, just as I told you."

"I was still safe while you—"

"Came tragging near to being killed. Yes. But that's history. Now to make sure it wasn't all for nothing…" He threw a large, battered cushion, at his brother. It caught Silas square on the jaw just as he leaned sideways, sending him toppling over in a heap on the floor and scowling up at Ethan.

"Hey, no fair."

"It worked, little brother. Wily old men's tricks always beat young muscles, and don't you forget it."

"Watch out. You'll soon be using a cane and bleating about grey hairs."

Silas wasn't that much younger than Ethan, but Ethan had a small measure of height over him and Silas still hadn't grown into his full breadth. A shove from Silas, answered by a push from Ethan, and then they threw their arms over each other's shoulder, both grinning madly.

"We'll call it a draw," said Ethan. "Now, come and help me finish sorting out the storm damage, then we're going to figure out what the tragging hell is going on. Someone isn't too happy about the direction I'm taking Solaris is my guess, and I intend to find out who."

"What about the Sulwith field? You made your decision days ago, so when are you going to let the locals know the outcome?"

"When it suits me. There's a few bad wernets need shaking loose first."

Silas groaned and gave him another shove. "One day, you'll give me a straight answer."

Ethan grinned back. Maybe, but not today.

"One thing you ought to know, big brother. The other genius in this town."

Cold reality swamped Ethan. "Yes?"

"Ari Beren is better than her father. Finn Beren is one out of the file for com systems, but Ari can fix anything, he tells me, and she and her father stopped a major air supply failure during the storm."

Ethan's heart just about stopped. "In the Beren's house? What kind of failure?"

"The worst kind." Silas's face had gone deadly serious. "Any other house, and we'd be talking funerals. But Rhyn and Ari fixed it. I watched them working. Her father talks to her like an equal and the girl stops scowling as soon as she gets a tool kit in her hand."

Ethan was still getting over that word funeral. "Doesn't mean she's a genius, just that she likes mechanics," he said curtly.

"Her father has run this field better than any other field in Solaris. You said it yourself."

"So he's the one who's the genius."

Silas shook his head. "Rhyn asked Ari too many times what to do next. She was the one who worked out how to make the repairs, not him."

Ethan felt like swearing. He didn't want to believe his brother, but Ari Beren had been targeted by that com room, and someone very clever had designed the beam that brought down his flyer. "I'll have her watched." He'd do more than that, but Silas didn't need to know details of that. No one was getting a chance to hurt anyone in the Beren household. Especially not Sarwenna Beren. "Tell me exactly what happened. Then this town needs our help."

The town and solar field had been badly hit. Ethan set Silas to coordinating the restoration of the external com links while he made his way through the damage reports and did a reconnoitre of the town.

Sulwith had been hit by storms plenty of times before, and the townsfolk were well versed in what to do. As he walked the streets, there was no sign of panic or despair. The odd person doffed a finger at him, but mostly they ignored him, too intent on their work. The place was like a nest of critchits, each person busy with their assigned job to restore the whole. They didn't need him or Silas, but this was a Solaris town, and that made him responsible for its recovery. He knew exactly the income of most people in the town, and Solaris provided their disaster insurance, mostly because few other companies would touch it. By the looks of the broken walls and gouged out streets, insurance wouldn't be enough this time. They were going to need help from the Solaris coffers. Silas had said Daff told him the storm was strong enough to flay a man to the bone, and the boy was right.

Ethan made at last for the town council offices. The same one that harboured the union office. The woman at the front counter looked him up and down while her hands kept tapping on her com.

"Who you want to see? Sar or the mayor."

He could feel his back stiffening. "The mayor," he said. "I'd be surprised if Sera Beren was here."

The woman cackled. "You're right there, Ser Winter. She's up the back of the Southside, checking on a worker's widow who lives up there."

Ethan stopped mid-stride. "Checking on… Hasn't there been a com muster?"

"Too early yet. Com musters only work if you've got a proper intercom system working, and that's waiting on young Finn and Ari."

"I'll talk to the mayor later. This needs fixing now. Tell my brother Silas what you need. He's back at our hotel. He can help."

The woman looked unimpressed.

"Finn Beren idolises him," he added, "and dragged him into helping out with a com puzzle he couldn't solve."

The woman's face cleared. "In that case, thank you, Ser Winter. I'll give Sam at the hotel a comcall right away."

Ethan's sense of importance had taken a lot of knocks since he'd come to this outland settlement, but he had to laugh at this latest. Needing the backing of a school-age child took some beating. His word was generally good anywhere on the plains.

He set out for the Southside area of town, hunting Sarwenna. It wasn't a big town so it shouldn't take long.

He hadn't counted on finding so many damaged homes on his way. Most had repairs under way, but when he came upon an older woman breathlessly dragging away the mess of her front facia and huffing under the weight of each load, he had to stop and help.

"It's all right, Ser. My sons will be here, soon as they fix up their own homes."

"I know they will," he soothed her, "but how about I make their work a bit easier?"

From the looks of the rough colouring on the battered front wall, he doubted any sons were coming any time soon, but he wasn't about to take away the woman's pride. She'd lost too much to the storm already.

It cost him time he didn't have, but he refused to worry about it, and the smile on the woman's face when he cleared the worst of the mess made it worthwhile. "I'll make sure a crew comes by to finish it off and secure your building till it's fixed properly. Make sure you remember to input your insurance claim."

The smile disappeared from her face, but she nodded and politely thanked him. Too politely.

"You do have insurance cover, Sera?"

"Of course, of course," she said, but something about the flatness of her voice sent a warning prickle up Ethan's back.

"I'll make sure it's processed among the first batches."

Again, that too polite thank you, and he added checking on her file to his growing list of jobs when he made it back to the office. Why would anyone in a deadlands border town skimp on their insurance cover? Especially when Solaris offered a generously discounted cover to anyone who lived in a Solaris field town?

He left her, too many unanswered questions jostling for space in his head, and he needed to find Sarwenna Beren to have some of them answered.

Or so he told himself.

A block up, he came to a young boy and a teenage girl patching up a shattered and scoured-out roof edge, balancing on the shakiest of makeshift ladders—an old chair set on a battered table with one leg rocking against the uneven paving of the broken street edging.

"Get down from there, you two, before you fall down and break your parents' hearts."

The boy looked down at him as if he'd lost his mind. "Floods can come after sandstorms. That's what Da says."

"Then your Da can get up there and fix the roof."

This time it was the girl who looked down at him with a too old look in her eyes. "He's inside. Can't come out."

"Can't see. Not since the last storm. Everyone in town knows that." The boy scowled at him.

"Why not?" said Ethan.

"Got caught out in the field when the storm hit," said the girl in a flat voice.

"Yeah. Geordie had disappeared and no one else can warn us in time."

More questions. Ethan groped for what he could manage for now. "Your Da's sand blind? If that's the case, you should have help here. Solaris covers injuries like that."

The boy peered down at him, mouth agape. "Don't you know nothing? Da's a contractor, not an em-ploy-ee. Solaris don't care nothing for us kind."

It had the tone of words heard and too often repeated. Too much of truth sat in the glare of the boy and the tired defeat in the girl's shoulders as she turned back to mending the broken roof.

Ethan drew in a breath and set his hands on his hips. "You two are getting down from there, right now."

He'd been ordering people about since his early teens thanks to the Old Man's training methods. Throw you into a management post and watch you sink in quicksand summed up his father's method. After the first humiliating post, Ethan learned to walk tall and miss the traps, and now had the stance and voice to make these children obey him. Slowly, they climbed down. Ethan set them as far away from their crazy stack of makeshift supports as he could, then cleared away the rubble and set the table safely in the streets with no wobbles. Thanks to his height, he wouldn't need the even more shaky chair on top, and scrambled up to check out the roof edge.

He could see why they'd risked injury to fix it. The sand had piled up in the grooves of the edging, blocking any hope of drainage and scouring cracks into the underwall space. The next good blow would have left the house filled with sand.

"Get me some filler and a patching tool."

The boy scurried off while the girl stayed to watch, eyes scrunched down in wary scrutiny. "You know what you're doing, Ser?"

"Yes, I do. I've helped out in plenty of maintenance crews." Another part of the Old Man's training he'd never thought to feel grateful for.

The boy arrived back with the oldest and least reliable patcher he'd ever seen. The power pack sputtered into shaky life and he set it dubiously against the edging hollow. At the end, he looked back down the roof line and had to admit the patcher had done its work. The line might be skewed, the finish spattered with droplets of filler, but the edging looked leak-free and strong enough to keep out the elements. The girl still watched with arms crossed and suspicion in her eyes, but the boy grinned beside her. Ethan handed back the patcher.

"Mind if I come in and have a word with your father. Let him know the house is secure again."

"Yeah, we mind," said the girl, but her brother had already whirled around and started running inside, yelling at the top of his voice.

"Da, Da, we fixed it. The man fixed it."

Ethan didn't share his confidence but he followed them both into the house, unwilling to say anything to dampen the boy's enthusiasm. From the looks of the inside of the house, enough had already been dished out to this pair. Everything was tidy, the signs of storm damage hastily cleared from the front rooms where the roof edging must have failed, yet nothing looked loved. Dull walls, unpolished tables, chipped edgings on the walls. A house with an active young boy in it never looked pristine, but they did usually look cheerful.

The children led him into the family kitchen. Someone had tried to paint a brave flower on the far wall and a child's artwork graced the screen above the family table, but defeat hung heavy over the room.

Then Ethan saw the man slumped in a large chair by the cooler. His head lifted to the boy's calls and a smile woke in his face, but it did little to soften the mass of scarring that ran across his eyes and down a cheek. Sand burn. Ethan had seen it once before. The tiny grains burrowed deep into the skin, impossible to remove without a top-notch healing unit, and even then the scarring could not be completely eliminated.

This man had been in a unit, by the looks of the pink puckering of new skin over part of the burn, but not a top notch one. Angry whorls of raised skin marred his chin, and where his eyes should be stood only a patchwork of scarred knobs.

Ethan scuffed his feet deliberately loudly. "Good evening, Ser. A fine pair of children you have here."

The man turned unerringly to where Ethan stood. So the blindness had been long enough for him to start adapting to it. Not that he should have to. Urbis had facilities in plenty to restore sight and this town wasn't that remote from help.

"Thank you, Ser. Your name, if you please."

"It's the Winter man," piped in his son. "The one who's going to shut us down."

Ethan sputtered. "Nothing's decided yet."

The girl grunted. "You are, though, and everyone will leave town so even Ma's work won't save us."

The man said nothing to his children's words, but the grooves on his face deepened. "Leave the man alone, Mairi. What Ser Winter decides is none of our business."

It was, but these people deserved better than false promises. "The town will hear the final decision in a few days," was all he dared and saw immediately how well they understood. "Can I do anything more for you to repair the storm damage?" he said anyway.

"Thank you, Ser, but we will manage fine," said the girl.

"No, thank you," said the man.

Not even the boy spoke up, the light in his young eyes dimmed as he clung to his father. "We'll manage," he muttered.

Even if the boy had been a better liar, Ethan had only to look at the roughened door margins, the potential leaks in the walls and ceilings, the haphazard piles in the front room where precious possessions had been shoved away from fragile walls to know this family needed help. But their closed faces gave him no way in.

"Your mother. Will she be home soon?"

The girl shrugged. "Depends."

The man put a hand on his daughter's arm. "My wife is a nurse at the hospital. She'll be busy there a few hours yet."

"Please give her my regards and if there is anything Solaris can do, let me know. Or, better, see Rhyn Beren and ask him to send me word."

The girl's brows rose and for the first time a light flickered in her eyes. "Not old Crabster?"

Ethan shook his head. "Rhyn's more practical, from what I've seen."

The slightest of smiles lifted the man's face. "That he be," he agreed. "Thank you, Ser."

Ethan had no choice but to doff his hand and leave them, effectively dismissed.

Turmoil stewed in his chest. He'd gone hunting for Sarwenna to make sure she was safe. That hadn't changed—worry for her a constant niggle at the base of his brain—but right now he also had some very pointed questions for the union rep.

The first woman had said she was up in the Southside. So probably doing the same as he was: helping those hit by the storm. He'd never doubted she meant well by her people.

There was an old saying about good intentions, and Ethan had faced too many years of frustrated attempts to change Solaris to tolerate woolly do-gooding here.

That's not Sarwenna.

Tell that to the old woman and to those children.

He finally tracked her down in a narrow alleyway between two faceless block buildings. The few windows that opened to the streets hid behind closed shutters and the outer walls gave no clue whether they were homes or workplaces.

A small child skipped through the far doorway. So, homes. She stopped when she saw him, stuck her thumb in her mouth and stared. He crouched down so as not to scare her.

"Have you seen Sera Sarwenna Beren?" he said in his softest, least boss-man voice. The girl looked blankly back.

"Is Sar here?"

The thumb came out and small ringlets bobbed vigorously.

"Inside your house?"

A sideways shake of the ringlets this time, and the thumb slid back to its comforting home.

"Where is Sar then? Can you show me?"

The child stared round-eyed, as if deciding whether to trust him. Then a slow nod. She lifted one grubby hand and swivelled around, pointing back through the doorway she'd just come out of.

Not her house then, but Sarwenna was inside. Ethan nearly chuckled out loud but restrained himself and thanked the small girl very solemnly. "Is your Ma inside with her."

A shake of her head.

"You're on your way home?"

A nod.

"Can you show me where your home is? If I give you my hand, can you take me there?"

A smile at last. He appeared to have passed some kind of test. Her hand reached for his and he took the small fingers. She led him out the alley and across the next street to a small doorway on the far side. He had to duck to get under the lintel, but once inside a blessed coolness struck him.

It was hot, this part of town, as Sarwenna had said. Hence the scarcity of windows and the solid walls, he guessed. He followed his small guide to a walled courtyard in the rear of the building. A woman bent over a tub in the corner, coaxing a small plant back to life with trickles of water and sweet words.

He cleared his throat. "Excuse me, Sera. Does this young lady belong here?"

Of course she did, running up to hug the woman's leg and turn that solemn look back on him again.

The woman stood, startled, then blushed scarlet. "Oh. Thank you. Dressa, you know you're not supposed to run off without telling me."

The girl showed no sign of guilt, giving her mother's legs a warm hug. "Sar, Sar."

"Sar had you. Well, that's all right then, but you still have to tell me." She straightened up. "My apologies if she's been bothering you, Ser."

He lifted a hand, palm out. "On the contrary, she's been a big help to me. Is there anything you need before I'm on my way?"

She gave a distracted smile and a slight head bob. "Thank you, but no. We were lucky compared to some, and my husband is in the town centre now fixing up things. Ser…"

"Ethan. Ethan Winter." Then could have cursed at the tide of white chasing away all light from her face.

"Ma?" said a small voice from her knees.

"I'll take my leave, and please let the main office know if you need anything," said Ethan, retreating to polite inanities and making his hasty way out of the house.

Was everyone in this town scared of him?

He marched down the street and back through the alleyway to the plain building, looking for Sarwenna. When he'd started this mad mission, it was to make sure she was safe, to reassure that coiled up part of him that she had survived the hellish clouds of windblown sand he'd seen coming in on his flyer's rangeviewer.

Now, he had questions, and she'd better have answers. A spike of hair and a familiar voice giving orders gave him his target.

He had a few orders for her, and it was long past time she stopped talking and started looking and listening.

Cared about these people, did she?

Then he saw her, and his first thought had nothing to do with orders or telling her where she'd gone wrong.

"You're safe."

Her head swivelled and her eyes went wide with shock. "You're back." A hand brushed ineffectively at the dust coating her cheek and the other pulled at her overalls.

Then he took in where she stood. "What do you think you're doing?"

Though why he asked, he had no idea. Tool in hand, knee deep in a tottering wall threatening to fall at any moment as she scoured away the damaged plascrete, it was plain as sands and no different from what he'd been doing on his trek here. His hand still itched to grab the heavy tool from her hand.

A head appeared beside her, scowling. "Trouble, Sar?" said the man.

"No, no. Nate, meet Ethan Winter. Ser Winter's brother was caught and stayed with us during the storm."

The scowl deepened but the man twitched a respectful hand to his head. "Ser Winter."

Ethan gave the man the briefest of nods. Right now, he was interested only in Sar. She'd stepped away from the wall, thank the sands. "Silas made it through safely, thanks to your family's swift thinking."

"Swi— Oh." Her lips shut tight.

The man looked from Sarwenna to Ethan. "Something happened?"

"A minor malfunction during the storm. Nothing serious. Da fixed it."

"A major stoppage in your ventilation system is what Silas said. And your sister Ari was the main repairer."

"Ari was there? That's all right then," said the man Nate. Did everyone in the town know about the girl?

"It wasn't that serious," Sarwenna tried, glaring at both him and the man Nate. "If that was all you came about, Ser Winter?"

"Not all. I need a word with you."

Nate crossed his arms and stood like a block.

"Just a short discussion, that's all," said Ethan. "About union and Solaris business. In private."

The man looked set to object, but Sarwenna studied Ethan and finally gave him the other man a short nod. Nate had no choice but to walk away.

"I'll be just on the other side of the wall. A shout away." Then he disappeared from sight.

Sar straightened, tool held protectively in front of her. "You wanted a word, Ser Winter?"

"The name's Ethan, and that ventilation malfunction? You could have died in that storm."

Shock bleached her face. "A bit of a glitch, that's all."

"Silas called it sabotage … and said your sister is an engineering genius."

She gasped. "She's talented, yes, but she's only a schoolgirl. It was a routine malfunction. Da fixed it and Ari helped."

"And this field runs like a precision timepiece by sheer good luck? Drop it, Sarwenna. I'm not in the mood."

All the colour came flooding back to her face. "Not in the mood? You think Sulwith should bow down and quake because a Winter is not in the mood? You forget, I don't work for Solaris. I have more than enough of your people needing my help right now, though, including the workers who live in this building."

His fingers tapped furiously in his com search. An in-and-outer hostel, said his com of the building. That's who she was helping? The fit, the strong singletons without any bond to the town. Not the families he'd seen on his trek to find her.

"The workers can fix this place themselves. There are plenty of others in town who can't and need your help more. Or don't they vote in the next election?"

"Not these workers. Tom Crabster has ordered them all to report to the solar field. Only once that's operable can they get back here, and meanwhile all their personal belongings, all their gear, is exposed to the elements and any who like to help themselves to it. Let alone checking that no one is buried under this tragging mess."

"I should have known he was involved, but don't take me for a fool. A full muster of all Solaris employees was the first job of the field manager, and I've already checked that it's in progress. That's what being a Winter means. I'll get the list as soon as it's done, and not even Tom Crabster is stupid enough to send me a made up list. These workers will be looked after, unlike the woman I saw a few blocks back or the small child wandering the streets because her mother has no one else to look out for her."

"Wander… You mean wee Dressa. Let me tell you, Ser mighty Winter…" Sarwenna drew herself up, looking as if about to explode. "Everyone knows exactly who she is and keeps an eye on her. As for the other families you saw…"

"The ones I stopped to help, since no one else seemed interested. Which is why it's taken me so long to find you."

A fisted hand flung into the air. "You say you stopped to help. This town's not perfect, but we do look after our own—union and non-union—including after a storm bigger than anyone remembers.

We have a mayor, a law office, council representatives. I can't look after everyone."

He would have folded right then, the heartfelt grief she couldn't keep out of her voice too real. But Sarwenna Beren wasn't the kind to give up, and she clutched that tragging tool tighter and lifted her chin. "Since you know so much more about it than I do, why don't you go show this town how to look after its own. I have work to do."

She turned her back on him. Lifted up that too heavy tool and started to work again, setting the vibrations to maximum and flinging stones and blocks aside to get to the broken wall below.

He stared at that rigid back and cursed as a wayward rock nearly caught him. She heard him, by the sudden twitch of her head, but didn't stop, thrusting that too heavy rammer dangerously at the wall in a way that had his heart clenching.

If she kept that up, she'd hurt herself. Maybe he should leave her to it.

And she's given you a choice, fool?

She's safe.

CHAPTER FOURTEEN

Sar heard the footsteps as Ethan Winter left. She refused to turn around to watch him, but each step echoed right inside her. She dashed up a hand and brushed away the stupid tears smudging her view of the wall.

What did he expect? Marching in here and claiming she didn't care about her town. After spending all morning doing the best she could for all those clamouring for her to fix things, she'd welcomed the call to help out at the in-and-outers hostel. No fraught dramas, no families wanting her to make it all right again, no one demanding she save the solar field and all its jobs by stopping the tidal wave of change thundering down on Sulwith whether they liked it or not.

You sound like you've given up.

Had she? How could she do that to her members, all those still looking to her to protect the lives they had built in defiance of the deadlands? Generations had lived out their lives here, had developed and built the best and largest solar field in all the Solaris empire. Workers who knew no other way to put food on their tables and a roof over their families' heads. Learn a new way, her father said. Not so easy for too many of those looking to her for protection.

Few made a fortune here, but they worked hard and had a good life, mostly, including the ones she helped to escape Tom Crabster's manipulations and constant attempts to shift work from union staff to vulnerable contractors. The union workers did what they could for those on the outside. Earning enough to live on left little time or credits to pay for retraining or thinking of different ways to earn a living. The night of the storm, she'd tossed in her shelter bed, counting options, turning over ideas and discarding one after another, realising in the lonely stretches that she would have to find alternatives for her people.

What had done that? When her father said change had to come? When she learned that Ethan Winter's helter-skelter run down that slope being chased by an unknown flyer was to protect her? When Finn and Ari seized on Silas Winter as some kind of heroic saviour?

Slam, bash, scrape out the rubble from the wreckage.

A stone ricocheted off a wall and smashed onto her foot. "Aaah." Her years in Urbis acting as her mother's second had taught her more than politics. Curse words from every filthy backstreet erupted from her mouth, and it wasn't till she heard a gasped "Sar Beren" from behind her that she remembered she wasn't alone.

She'd felt alone and abandoned ever since Ethan's footsteps left her.

These footsteps were lighter in tread. "Sorry," she muttered to Emilia, the house matron of the hostel coming down from the top floors with another load of broken fittings. She picked up the crusher again and aimed it at the pile of stones blocking the doorway to the outer courtyard, biting on her lip and refusing to give in to the ache in her foot.

Then she made the mistake of trying to step closer and the foot crumbled under her.

"Sar, put that tool down now. I'm calling the medics."

Sar sat heavily on the nearest block. She had no choice. It was sit down or fall down, but she shook her head at letting Emilia call the medics. "They're busy enough already. That storm blew up too quickly for everyone to make it to the proper shelters in time."

Emilia had never been a good listener. "Sit still. Wait there and I'll get help."

The woman bustled out of the room intent on her mission. Fat chance she had of finding anyone to help today. Not for a stupid injury caused by her own idiocy. If Ethan Winter hadn't made her so tragging angry, it would never have happened.

She swiped at the dust coating her cheeks, hating the dampness smearing them, and leaned back against the pile of rocks with eyes shut. Just a few moments. What harm could it do? It had been so long since she'd stood still.

The footsteps came back. The light ones of the matron, with another heavy tread beside her. She'd found someone.

Then the pattern of those footsteps intruded, the familiar sound of them, and she opened her eyes just as Ethan Winter scooped her up in his arms and lifted her away from the dust and mess.

"I said you shouldn't be working here, but you didn't have to get yourself hurt to prove me right."

An edge coated his words yet his arms cradled her gently, and he held her legs close to him, supporting her foot without pressuring it.

"It's just a bruise. I dropped a rock on it."

"Yes, and I just happened to be in the neighbourhood. Your face is white as plas sheet."

He refused to listen to any of her protests, marching with her through the streets like a rescued prize. At the hospital doors, she struggled so much he had to let her down, gently, keeping an arm around her shoulders to take her weight.

"I can't go in there. There are real people needing help."

"Like you. Or can you suddenly walk?"

She scowled at him but had no answer. He swung her up again, making her feel both ridiculously small and cherished and very embarrassed. Doc Kaybee, straightening from a cot holding a small child, was the first to catch sight of her.

"Sar, what have you done to yourself."

"Nothing much, just a bruised foot. Please, don't stop."

"Doctor, Sera Beren dropped a sizable piece of rubble on her foot. It needs to be checked for fractures and placed in a healing unit."

Doc Kaybee gave her foot one quick glance. "Not life threatening. Take her out to the waiting room. The nurses will deal with her in due course."

The arms holding her tensed. "You will deal with her now. Winter money paid for this hospital and keeps it going. Do I make myself clear?"

Doc Kaybee stood up again, one hand protectively on the child. "Look around, Ser Winter. This town just endured a category ten storm, and every single person in this room is in urgent need of my skills. Sar can manage with an assist unit for now and knows better than to demand priority care when so many others are more in need."

"She may; I don't. I've already had an earful from the hostel matron about what Sarwenna's been doing since the storm. Helping everyone in town. Now it can help her."

"Ethan. Stop this right now. The Doc is right." What had got into him? Ethan Winter was a power in the plains, his father even more so, but never before had she seen him wield that power so bluntly.

"You're hurt, and for once you're going to let someone else look after you," he said stubbornly.

"It's my job to look after these people. You saw the state of the town."

He ignored her, carrying her over to a momentarily clear bed and placing her on it. "The scan and healing unit, doctor. Treat her, and then you can get on with your other patients."

Doc Kaybee stood slowly, watching Ethan and finally waving a hand at Sar. She bent down to her patient, made a notation on her scanner and checked the child's readings. "You're going to be fine sweetheart. A few days with us and you'll be back playing skipjump with all your friends." A smile and a pat for the tot, then she straightened up, all trace of pleasantry banished from her face. "All right, young man. I'll treat your emergency, then I expect your full cooperation with ensuring the wellbeing of the rest of the patients."

The arms holding her relaxed. "Done."

One more glare, and Doc Kaybee returned to her usual business-like manner. She ran her hands over Sar's foot, firmly enough that Sar couldn't hide the wince, bringing a scowl to Ethan's face, and swept the med scanner over it.

At the end, she turned to Ethan as if Sar existed only as an accessory to their power struggle. "She's fine," said the Doc. "Badly bruised and the tendons have taken a punishing, but nothing broken. All our med units are taken up at present with patients whose lives are at risk. Go through to the nurses and they will put a support field on it. That's the best we can offer. Take it or leave it."

Ethan Winter had money and the weight of Solaris, but Doc Kaybee had been facing down overwhelming odds for years. Sar wasn't surprised when he finally gave way. "There's a field unit in my ship. Will that do?"

"For something like this? Yes, it will do fine, and you might like to make it available for others. We've got a whole wing of minor injuries needing attention so that people can get back to setting this town to rights again."

Sar wondered for an instant if the red flush on Ethan's face heralded an explosion of rage. Then saw his hand tug at his collar.

"Of course," he said stiffly. "Send them down to the landing field … but Sarwenna goes first."

He made sure of it, too, picked her up again and marched her to the head of the line that had formed as soon as word went around of the field unit, pushing ahead of all the more deserving cases behind her and right into the interior of his flyer. It was as well appointed as the first one, the one that had crashed into the desert thanks to that unknown beam, but she should have known a Winter could pull another out of their fleet at will.

"The field unit's back here," he said gruffly.

The waves of the healing scanner enveloped her foot and nothing could stop her melting into the bliss of feeling no pain. Then she turned and looked at the queue of people waiting outside. So many of them.

"How many killed," said Ethan to Doc Kaybee on his open com line as he stared at the queue.

The Doc looked shocked as well she might. "None. What do you take us for, young man?"

"Injured then?"

"Too many," the Doc admitted. "Not what we like around here, but all will mend with time. That's going to be the real cost for my patients. How long out of work for those needing full rehab? That field unit of yours will help with the lesser cases at least. I'll send a nurse to take over. I assume your ship has good security cover for anything of concern in there. You're probably needed elsewhere."

Ethan coloured, but refused to be needled by the doc's dry tone. "Someone has to run things, and Winters have done that for the plains region for a long time."

The Doc's eyebrows soared. Self-appointed she might have said, but the doc was too much of a pragmatist to let personal matters get in the way of her patients' wellbeing.

It was true though. The town would be expecting him to take charge of things.

"They'll be waiting for you up at the Solaris office. I'm fine now," Sar said. "Thank you for your help."

He glared back, mouth tightening. "Don't use that puckered-up tone on me. Not when you're hurt."

She shifted under his frowning eyes. "I've told you. It's nothing. Go look after Solaris affairs. Better yet, go tell the town what you plan for them."

She shouldn't snap at him. The man was being seriously considerate in his own way, but being coddled by him made her too comfortable, and that was all kinds of wrong. She was the one who looked out for others, not the other way around.

That frown twisted. "When I've seen you out of that field unit and able to walk again."

His final word apparently. No matter what Sar said, the man stayed stubbornly by her side. She ordered him to dial the unit to maximum to hurry the healing.

"No."

"That queue out there needs this unit as much as I do. Turn it up, or I'll take over myself."

"You know how to use a unit like this one?"

"Sort of." Then reached for the control panel.

His hand reached for them too.

"Leave it," she said, grabbing his hand away and quickly switching to maximum. Teeth gritted, she held hard to the sidebar as a jolt of energy seared her nerve endings. She couldn't hide a sigh of relief as Ethan grabbed hold of the unit and switched it off.

"Are you trying to fry your foot. You're lucky not to have major burns after using a setting that high."

"You were here to take over if something went wrong, and I trust you not to deliberately hurt me."

A red flush on his face. "Don't tempt me," he muttered, but his voice had softened.

Luckily, the nurse sent by the Doc arrived just then, took one look at both their faces, and grabbed the com. "I'll take care of this now," she said with force. "Ser Winter, they are asking for you down at the main office."

For a moment, Sar thought he might tell the woman to go to the darks out of sheer anger. Then his fingers tapped on his com. "The scanner's yours. The rest of the ship is under lockdown and secured to my com only. I'll leave you to your work."

He straightened, slammed back into the pilot's area and activated a shimmer of lights to mark off the security shield blocking access to the flyer apart from the small passenger area holding the field unit. Then he bowed stiffly to Sar. "You need to go easy on that foot for the next few days. No more working on demolition sites. Get some of your union members to do that for you."

She nodded back as formally. "Thank you for your assistance."

He looked as if she'd shot him in the chest. "Don't."

"I won't hold you up further," she added, refusing to acknowledge the flash in those bright eyes.

"No, mustn't do that. I have such important duties."

He didn't have to sound so hurt. She was trying to be polite.

"Yes, you do," she said deliberately, "like writing up your report and telling this town once and for all what you've decided for them. They deserve the truth. Do they have a future here or not?"

"After that storm? You think they're interested in the future plans for the solar field today?"

"Of course. Do they rebuild or pack up to leave? No one here can afford to waste energy on pointless efforts."

"Pointless… Like mine, you mean, saving you from yourself."

She gaped. "This isn't about me."

"Isn't it?" His eyes bore into her. "You hide behind the union, but what are you doing for these people?"

"Plenty."

A jerk of his head and a huff of disbelief. "Keeping them stuck in the past is what you're doing. Change is coming, and you refuse to see it. You're no different from my father and the other corporate heads."

"Don't you compare me to them!" She'd spent her life fighting the company big heads, from the likes of Tom Crabster up. How dare he.

He thrust his face forward. "Just like."

Everyone stared at them. Sar was beyond caring. Her fists clenched and she opened her mouth to tell this sprig of privilege exactly where he could stick his unwanted opinions.

He put up a hand. "Don't bother. As you so forcefully point out, I have work to do and a town waiting for me to tell them the facts. Which is more than anyone else here has done so far." A curt goodbye and he swung away from her, back rigid and head up.

She watched as he stomped down the ramp, past the silent, waiting queue, all listening intently, then back up the road to the centre of town.

So much of her wanted to chase after him, to apologise and make it right; but too many depended on her, starting with her little sister. Drocash might have put a nasty take on it, but he did have reason to question her loyalty to the town, trag him. She forced herself to turn back to the nurse and ask whether she needed help to organise the patients. A suspiciously careful smile on her face, the nurse agreed that yes, another pair of hands would be a big help.

Sar was safe for a few more hours.

Ethan fumed. That woman could turn him inside out quicker than his father. He stalked up the track, past the first buildings on the outskirts of town and along the road to the council offices. He could have ordered up a skimmer to take him to the offices, but not even in this mood did he consider taking a vehicle away from carrying the injured to help.

Besides, he very desperately needed to walk. To pace off the hot fury boiling in him before he ruined his image with the whole of the town. All thanks to one beautiful, brave and butt-headed woman intent on fighting him at every step. Worst of it all, she was right this time. The town deserved to know what the future held, and Ethan had known what he must decide since he first arrived here. Rhyn Beren may have put it plainer and Caleb set it out more brutally, but change here was inevitable, and Ethan owed the townsfolk the truth.

The whole truth, including what other plans he had for their future. Except that he didn't have any, not yet. Only half-formed ideas and a barely glimpsed vision. A big-picture strategy, that's what he needed as his old business theory teacher would have said with a frown. What are your specifics, boy?

For this town, these people? He wished he knew.

He marched up through the town, anger draining away and reality intruding all too harshly in its wake.

He slowed, one step following another, up the main street of town, past newly broken buildings and sand-scoured pathways. His end point had changed but he didn't realise that until he reached the base of the steps. The ones leading up to the bluff he'd gone to that night with Sarwenna, looking for a place to see the town's layout from above, and where he'd found something unexpected and precious instead.

The railing had disappeared in the storm's fury but he'd grown up clambering around rocky outcroppings and caves near his home. Balancing on these rough but serviceable steps posed little problem, and he welcomed the concentration needed to make the climb. Then he was at the top, looking down at the town.

It had changed under the storm's onslaught, but not as much as he'd expected from his meetings with rubble and disrupted homes. Most houses still held their basic shape and the streets were busy with townsfolk repairing and clearing away debris.

No deaths, but too many injuries thanks to a lack of adequate warning, the town doctor had said.

No deaths, with all this destruction?

He looked at the town again, concentrating on the smaller details. Solaris built and repaired all the service towns on the dry lands of the plains, but Sulwith was at the extreme margin of habitable country according to the company architects and engineers. Caleb had said the same, but now that he thought about it, not as dismissively. What had his brother seen here that he hadn't?

Silas had told Ethan he'd sheltered from the storm in the basement of the Beren house. Not a dank, small room but a full apartment, one with emergency tunnels connecting it to all the other houses.

He sat down on the same ledge where he'd sat with Sarwenna and stared out at the town. Rounded edges, thick walls, and an absence of tall buildings to create wind tunnelling. The rooflines were familiar. They were Caleb's designs from the houses near his home region, the ones that gave passive solar energy and modified the interior more effectively than the conventional Solaris roofing panels provided with the standard Solaris kitsets.

The streets were made of a roughened plascrete coloured a warm sand colour, neither heat absorbers nor reflectors. They would keep a temperature similar to that of the house walls and the flat desert in front of the town. The only area of potential temperature differentials was the flat landing field and the vast spread of the solar panels.

Listen to you. Next you'll be claiming to be an ecoengineer like Caleb. He'd obviously spent too much time hanging around his brother on his trips home from university.

His mouth twisted grimly at the old memory. The loss of his big brother to far-off Urbis had hit him hard. No more did he have Caleb to stand between him and the Old Man.

For most of his early life, Ethan had been the useful second brother, the one on hand to answer his father's bidding, the one who cleaned up the mess after one of the Old Man's blunt reckonings with any employee who failed to deliver perfection.

Frustrating and too often galling, it had taught him what he most wanted to learn. One day, he would run Solaris and make it into a company fit for the future. Caleb's defection to the Ecological Engineering Survey department only kept it at bay, not made it impossible, despite the Old Man clinging to a vain hope his eldest son would come to his senses one day and step back into the company. In the meantime, he allowed Ethan to take over the work that should have come to his brother.

Ethan hadn't minded one bit. He loved Solaris in all its multistranded and living complexity. Solaris was his. His to save, his to make better.

His to make bigger and more complicated than his father ever dreamed. His to negotiate a way through the disaster facing Arcadia and bring it out the other side entire and improved. The Old Man may threaten reprisal if he didn't follow his directions, but he had to trust it was bluster only. He had a report to write and a decision to make. Solaris, or Arcadia. Family profit or the planet?

He leaned an elbow on his knee and propped his head on his fist. The locals had changed this town from the bare bones of the settlement built by Solaris. He could see where the familiar styling had been subtly altered. Buildings and streets warped, shapes changed, the layout bent and twisted.

And the result: a town able to survive a category ten sandstorm with no deaths, even without adequate warning.

If they could do that, what else could they do?

He rose and dusted down his clothes.

Next day, the entire town waited for him in the main plaza before the town hall and Solaris company offices—the only two important buildings in the town. He emerged from the Solaris office onto the wide portico at the front of the building. A heavy silence blanketed the square, ominous in the morning heat as they waited to hear what he had to say.

"Thank you for coming," he started, and felt the tension rocket up. Too conventional, too much the opening of every politician and big wig when coating bad news as good. He took a breath.

"I'll get right to it. The Sulwith field is the biggest in Solaris and the most efficient in output for the type of array used … but it's too big. Federal records show the effect on the regional environment is beyond acceptable levels. Aridity levels have increased and flora and fauna counts have decreased to a point where regional survival of many species is at risk, including those most critical in moderating climate and biodiversity extremes." A breath and a quick scan of the faces. No change, stony and reserved. He battled on. "I'm no scientist, nor are many of you, but we've all seen the vidcasts. Our world is in trouble. Arcadia has to change, and so does business." Now for the tricky bit. "Because of it, the Sulwith arrays must be updated to more modern, higher productivity sheets and the size of the field cut back."

The silence stretched taut, faint mutterings and cries percolating up to him. The crowd held still … for now.

Then it came.

"Will there be job cuts? How many, and who?" A shout from the middle of the crowd, in a voice he knew too well. Sarwenna and the union were here.

He put up a hand. "I am posting the full details of the changes on the Solaris company website as soon as I finish talking. Yes, there will be cuts. Job numbers will be cut by forty percent and the array sheets will be changed to the latest types for this area over a period of two years. The increase in output for each sheet will be used to reduce the land directly covered to no more than thirty percent of the total."

Gasps filled the air.

"As I said, the full details will be available on the Solaris site, along with the support arrangements for those affected. Solaris values the work done by so many for so long and thanks you for your ongoing contributions to the company. The main office will be open for personal queries, or you can contact my office directly. Management have been instructed on what the company expects of them during this transition period, and there is a help kiosk on the Solaris website. You will also find a section for suggestions. This is a town of innovators. The people of Sulwith can put their hands to many things, and Solaris is interested in supporting any job opportunities you come up with." His hands played in his com field. "The site is now live. I will leave you to read the details. Thank you for your time."

Heads bent and Ethan was free to withdraw; but the masochist in him had to stay a few moments, had to watch the changes on their faces. Relief where they still held a job, grief and dawning anger where their future had just vanished. That anger grew and the mutterings and murmurings became shouts and raised fists.

Get out of there now, Ser Winter, said his head of security through his com link and his guards stepped forward to stand in front of him. They were right. This crowd was about to erupt. He stepped back as if in a planned withdrawal, then hurried into the Solaris offices, through the back and into the skimmer waiting there for him.

"Keep a watch for Sarwenna Beren," he ordered his security. "Get her out of there if that crowd turns bad … and no, I don't care what she thinks. Keep her safe."

A short race through the streets and he was in his flyer, lifting above the town with Silas sitting beside him. His security's flyer lifted off straight after. He hoped like all sands the rest of the squad made it safely away. They were the best in Solaris and only the Federal marshals could beat them.

"Time to go home, brother?" said Silas.

Ethan nodded, though he hated looking like he was running away. "And long past time to figure out what's going on here."

As soon as they made transit height, Ethan put a com call through to his assistant, Graffin. "I'm calling a meeting at the company's office in Tollic. Ask Rhyn Beren to get there now, along with anyone he thinks can help. I want the ideas people in Sulwith, the ones with untapped skills and abilities. Ask him to bring Ari Beren and Geordie MacTavie with him—and I mean ask. It's up to Ser Beren whether his daughter and her friend are involved in this."

Tollic was the closest town to Sulwith, an hour's flight west into the plains country. Marginally wetter than Sulwith and with double the population, it was far enough from Sulwith to make a safe meeting place. He would have liked to include Sarwenna Beren, but the risk of her being seen as part of Solaris was too great. He linked through to his head of security. "Joff, status report for Sera Sarwenna."

"In her union office, facing down a crowd of scared and angry workers."

Ethan let loose a string of curses that had even Silas staring open mouthed. "I told you to keep her safe."

"We have one of our people in the crowd. Sera Beren's refused a security squad."

"I didn't tell you to ask her permission," Ethan snapped.

"Didn't. She recognised the squad and told them in no uncertain terms to get out. Reminds me of your mother, sir."

Joff had been with Ethan since second school. "Drop the sir, Joff. You're fooling no one," was the only come back Ethan had. "Do what you can and insert a microdrone to monitor her. And no, I don't give a trag how illegal that is. One person so much as tries to hurt her and you get her out of there."

He heard the laughter in Joff's voice. "Understood, Ser Winter."

It wasn't enough but it was all he could do. Stubborn woman. Always looking out for others and forgetting herself. Which meant, he'd have to look out for her himself.

"Keep her safe or don't bother coming back to Dridust. Ethan Winter out."

One priority, his first priority, met. Now for the meeting. The trip to Tollic didn't take long but was enough time for Ethan to assemble his thoughts: the questions he must ask and the arguments to make. He sent Silas back to Dridust with a Tollic security squad, despite his protests, then marched into the Solaris office to prepare for the meeting.

A few more hours of research left him armed with enough data to shove the iron rod of authority up his back and hopefully keep him in the driving seat of the meeting. The report he'd released to the Sulwith workers had been based on too many facts to deny its truth. The Sulwith solar array had to change, but what came next? Time to face that.

Everyone he'd asked here so arbitrarily waited in the main boardroom for him, even Ari Beren wearing a face filled with trepidation. He squared his shoulders, shoving all other thoughts to the back of his brain. All but one: Sarwenna Beren, a tight, ever present coil in his gut.

"You've heard the broadcast. I'm here to tell you, I meant the last part. Sulwith is a town capable of much more than blindly following Solaris' orders and, from what I'm told, you here are the ones with the ideas and connections to come up with other options for your town.

"And Solaris is going to help us out of pure goodness?" interjected the mayor, bitter and angry as a man whose town had just lost half its income had a right to be.

"Yeah, Solaris is already losing money over this. Why would they throw away more?" came another jibe.

"We won't throw money away, but new investments that promise to survive the coming challenges are a different matter," said Ethan. "That's why you're here. The Sulwith array is the most efficient supplier of bulk solar power. How about shifting that efficiency to local power sources? Create power right where it's used?"

"You're talking solar-plant-in-place. That's been tried before," said a man down the back.

"Yes, and never worked," butted in the woman beside him.

"No, and you want to tell them why, Ser Beren?"

Rhyn Beren looked none too happy at Ethan's singling him out. "Yes, it's been tried, repeatedly. There are many designs out there."

"And why did they fail?" prodded Ethan.

Rhyn gave him a dark look under those strong eyebrows of his. "Because the big companies bought the designs and shut them down. Or the designer couldn't get capital for development."

"Because there is no money in it," pronounced the mayor triumphantly.

"No," said Ethan. "Because there was no money in it for the bulk solar suppliers. It undercuts us and takes away future markets. But what if Solaris moved into making domestic and commercial in-built solar units as well as our involvement in large-scale solar supply. In a region like ours, personal energy production should be part and parcel of every house or office or manufacturing site. The Sulwith power plant workers have a proven record as efficient and capable. You have the energy sources and the work force. You can make solar production units as easily as you make bulk power."

"What about distribution?" said the woman at the back sourly. "It all sounds mighty fine, Ser Winter, but Sulwith is too far off the main cargo routes to be a manufacturing town. The flyer port is big enough for the routine power cell transporters, but you're talking big, multiple-grade carriers. Commercial ones, and Solaris don't own them."

She had a point, a good one. And one he hadn't yet figured out. So admit it.

"You're right, Sera. How to keep the costs of production down to outweigh the increased cost of transport? It's a problem to be solved, one of many. No one is promising easy here."

A choked-off laugh. Then another, and suddenly the room filled with manic chuckles. He'd said the right thing apparently and heaved a sigh of relief.

Suddenly, a commotion at the door and next minute, a woman burst through the troopers guarding the entrance.

"Sarwenna."

"Don't Sarwenna me, Ser Winter. Not after what you just did to the union. Or did you merely forget to tell us about it before you sacked near to half the work force of Sulwith?"

Ethan shoved on his corporate face. "The union received a comfile, the same as everyone else, supporting the workers."

"The same—" She just about spluttered and his heart dropped. So much for vain hopes.

"I can make time for a formal session with the union immediately after this meeting."

"After…" Sparks of fire shot from those gorgeous eyes. "Right now, you and me. Clear everyone else out."

Did that include her father and sister? Not a question he was going to ask. "After this meeting, Sera Beren. Troopers." A lift of his hand and both troopers advanced on her, holding her firmly, no more than that though, after his pointed look to his troopers, and they escorted her from the room, still sputtering and more livid than ever.

The door closed behind her. He chose to ignore the silence in the room, the stunned shock of people whose world had crashed from under them, then been exposed to a spectacle that shook the accepted order. The Winters ran the plains and no one challenged that, not if they wanted the plains and Solaris to survive.

Sarwenna just did.

He shook off the thought. "Ideas, Ser and Sera. How to make Sulwith thrive on more than one industry. Rhyn, can you bring up those plans of yours for a modified solar field?"

The man lifted his head. "You do know that was my daughter, Ser Winter. Where have they taken her?"

"To a side room. She is safe, Ser."

"And locked in there until you decide she can leave?"

He nodded, refusing to feel guilty.

"And that's how you intend to deal with anyone in Sulwith who refuses to go along with you?"

"What? No, of course not."

Rhyn stood up. "Ari, we're leaving." And all around him, the rest stood up to go too.

"No, stop. I asked you here to help your town."

The mayor puffed out his chest. "Yes, we've seen that, Ser Winter. When Solaris is ready to talk redundancy and compensation payments, you can reach me in my town office."

Disaster stared him in the face, and it was all his own fault. Of course he should have talked this over with the union and invited them in, but Sarwenna Beren scrambled every brain cell he possessed.

Don't blame her.

"Please, sit down, all of you. Let me talk to Sera Beren … apologise to her. You're right, I should have brought the union in. But Sera Beren and I—"

He would have put on that smooth smile he'd learned, but the glint in her father's eyes warned him in time. He thrust his fists behind his back, clenching them tight. "The Sera and I have had some … misunderstandings lately."

Rhyn Beren stopped short and Sarwenna's sister suddenly grinned. "They've had a fight."

You're the one who wanted to bring a teenage girl into this.

Yes, because the tragging girl had some serious mechanical talents. He'd just forgotten she also had that highly misplaced sense of humour that infected teenage girls. Rhyn Beren, on the other hand, was old enough to have a much more acute understanding of the situation. Ethan felt the red flush of colour in his cheeks as Sarwenna's father scrutinised him.

"That was personal?" He tilted his head to the door out which Ethan's guards had taken Sarwenna.

"No, no," tried Ethan. Then had to concede. "Maybe, a bit, but I've already discussed some of this with Sarwenna—Sera Beren— and she ignored it."

"Maybe you should explain it better," said her father in a dry voice. "We can wait."

The rest of the room had stopped their exodus to listen and watch, too many smiles tracing undecided faces. Ethan drew in a breath. He had one chance, one small chance. Which meant a very big apology and a pile of grovelling. He lifted a hand toward the chairs in the room. "Please, sit down. I'll have food and drinks sent in."

"And you, Ser Winter?" Rhyn hadn't moved.

"Will be talking to your daughter, Ser Beren."

"Can I watch?" piped up Ari, and a wave of laugher swept the room.

"No, young lady, you cannot," said her father with that quiet smile of his. "Ser Winter does not need an audience. He's going to have a hard enough time of it as is."

More chuckles, and Ethan forced himself to join in. Except that Rhyn Beren hadn't been joking. He left them to the spread Graffin was hastily arranging, and marched out the door, down the hall, down to the next level and around another corner.

He could hear Sarwenna yelling from the start of the hallway.

Sar had never been so furious. Locked in a bare room until this sprig of the bosses decided she could go free. What did he mean treating her like some lost accessory stuck to one side while he did his manly tasks? Did he think he could leave her here to potter around doing something inconsequential as he rearranged the lives of all she held dear?

At last the door opened, and the man himself had the gall to stand there looking at her as if she were the one behaving like a spoilt brat.

"Finished deciding on the fate of my town and my people?"

He wore the look on his face she hated most: the superior smile and carefully blank eyes. The corporate rich-kid look. "The others insist on your joining us. I take it you're willing to listen as well as talk."

That should appease her? "Listen to what? You telling us what's going to happen next. What the mighty Solaris has planned for all of us? Or no, I forgot. This isn't about Sulwith. Solaris and Winters have only one loyalty. Making credits for Solaris. So how are we all going to serve you now, Ser Winter?"

He took one breath, then another. "Are you finished? Because I have a bunch of people out there waiting for you to show some adult leadership."

Had he no idea what she'd been doing today, what she did every day?

"I came in here intending to apologise, Sera Beren, but that was based on an assumption that you might possess a speck of reason."

"You're the one who cut the union out of this. Who failed your employees. My job is to make sure my members are treated fairly by their employer. Solaris signed up for that in every contract made with its staff. So you tell me where I'm lacking in reason. Is it when I expect to be consulted before you sack the majority of my members? No, you'd rather they waited till well down the track so you can play at being the big boy charity and rearrange their whole lives for them."

He caught his hands, clenching them tight in front of him. "I've tried to talk to you about this. Many times."

That night at the bluff. Was he kidding? "No you haven't. Not properly. Not how it's usually done in business. In an office, in the plant, with facts and figure and proper plans." Not dreams or hopes, she might have said. Not tantalising glimpses into the heart of you. "Or were you just playing your big boss games with me too? Manipulating me to make me roll over with whatever Solaris decides for this town."

"No!" It exploded out of him.

She forced herself to carry on. "Because that's what it feels like. Solaris needs the union's help and Ser Ethan Winter knows he has to grovel to get it."

Right now, though, there was precious little sign of grovelling coming her way. Not from the man standing legs akimbo and facing her down, one hand pulling through his hair and the other shoved into his back pocket.

"Yes, I need your help. Your precious townsfolk refuse to discuss anything unless you're fully briefed and join in the meeting. But…" Another vicious tug of his hair. One that had to hurt. He shoved the hand into his other pocket and took a breath. "Whatever is between us … that was real. Is real. And don't tell me you didn't feel it too."

He'd called her bluff and she couldn't deny it. Something about this man… That night on top of the town had been real, she'd swear, and he'd betrayed every moment they'd ever had with his actions today.

"You want my help—me, Sarwenna—or you want the help of union representative, Sar Beren?"

"Both. Yes, right now, I need the union rep." A long drawn out moment. Then a sigh and eyes dark and wide. "When you were hurt… Don't do that to me again. I've been too close before to losing those who matter to me."

A gasp. She suddenly realised: prison. That's what he meant. The stark colour of his face said he hadn't expected those words to come out. Now his eyes clung to hers, waiting for her reply and both his hands were shoved deeper into his pockets. Hiding from her.

"And I'm one of those people now? Someone who matters to you?"

"Yes. Maybe. I don't know. Yes," he said as if torn from deep inside him.

It echoed the churning inside her. A turmoil she couldn't deny, no more than she could deny her attraction for this man. An attraction she had no time or space for. Not when her town teetered on the edge of extinction and too many of those people watched her. His actions said any bond between them was a lie, even as his body told her of its truth. Tense, rigid, face wiped clear of all emotion but for the tight muscles around his mouth and jaw, and those wide, darkened eyes.

She threw up a hand. "You say one thing and do another, hint that I matter to you then treat me as nothing, acting as if I have no part in the future of my town, my home."

"That's work. That's boss and union."

How could he understand so little? "Yes, company man and union woman. That's who I am, who you are, and you can't pick and choose the parts of me you're prepared to like. Just as I can't you."

"You can't? You do feel this thing?"

"Is that all you heard?"

He shook his head. "It was the most important. The one that mattered most to me, and that I can least afford to consider."

"With a roomful of Solaris and Sulwith folk waiting for us to fix our 'little problem' and come back to fix their problems," she said bitterly.

"It is not little, Sarwenna. Not to me," he said quietly, "but I have no answer for us and don't know if we ever will. I wish very much it were otherwise."

"And your actions. Are they unanswerable too, fixed and unchanged?"

He swallowed, tugged at his neckline. "I was wrong. I admit it. The union should have been fully informed of the scale and nature of the changes." He tugged again at his neck, messing up the beautiful line of plackets clasping the outer tunic closed.

"That's not what hurts, not me personally. It's that you didn't tell the union because you didn't trust me to deal with it properly. Isn't that true, Ser Ethan?" He swallowed again, and she could have cried. She put out a hand to the wall, needing the solid feel of it. "I'd known, but hoped—"

"You wouldn't listen to me. Every time I tried to talk about the future, it got turned around to something dark and hard. And you are still hiding things from me. I didn't know what your response would be. What you would land on this town."

"You thought…?" She would never hurt her hometown. Would she? His words had opened a chasm of doubt inside her. Jobs or town? Family or town?

Had she been too set on saving her members' current jobs to look at other options? Her father had hinted at the same. "I would never hurt my town. Not deliberately," the honesty at her core forced her to add. "My members need jobs today, need food on their tables today and tomorrow, not in some nebulous future time."

The lines of his jaw eased a bit. "I do understand that. Better now than when I arrived," he had to admit, "but that storm has wiped out a sizeable chunk of the solar arrays. It forces our hand."

"Whether to rebuild or replace with modified sheets at lower density?"

"Exactly. No sense throwing good credits after outdated systems."

"And your father agrees?"

A deep breath. Those eyes still meeting hers but no longer so dark, no longer so intense. "He has to. The Feds and the Alliance will step in if he refuses. They'll destroy Solaris."

"Oh." He'd said something of it before but never like this. Never so stark, so believable.

"Without Solaris, no one will have a job here." He stepped forward and she felt his presence as if he'd touched her. She stepped back and he lifted his hand in apology. "Will you return with me, Sera Sarwenna? For Sulwith, not for me."

What could she say?

"One more thing, Sera…"

What now? Hadn't he said enough?

"Your sister…" he started and her heart plummeted. "Silas tells me she is a mechanical genius. He also said that incident at your house during the storm was no accident. Sabotage is a harsh word, but in that basement were three people most responsible for the smooth running of the Sulwith solar field."

Sar gasped, then smacked her hand over her mouth.

His hand shot out, touched her then retreated. "I mean her no harm. She's a young girl living out a fantasy someone's fed her, but it looks like someone else might. That beam that brought us down. Is she capable of building it?"

Panic rocketed through her. "She's only a child."

"A child someone tried to kill."

No, not possible, but his implacable voice continued, giving it the lie.

"I thought they were after Silas, or you, or even Finn, but none of you know the secrets of that beam. Ari now… This com room she's been playing in. Is it possible…?"

Sar hugged herself tight. They'd never had a hiccup in the power system before, but sabotage… "It was a big storm, far bigger than we've had before."

"Silas took a look at the com system records for that room. At my request," he added at her gasp of outrage.

"That's…"

"…illegal. I know but so is what he found in that com room. This isn't some ruse to get you onside."

She didn't need his weary denial to accept his words. Too much of it echoed her own worries and suspicions. "Where is Ari now?"

"Back in the meeting room waiting for you, along with your father."

"And the boys?"

"At school, under full Solaris security cover."

"Security. You've had us watched?"

He nodded slowly. "I prefer to call it protection."

She shook her head, unable to take it all in. "I'll come to your meeting as the union rep only. As I should have done from the start. We will have a proper meeting about those notices you sent out. Solaris will negotiate redundancies and re-training offers with the union and you will set up a liaison to advise the independent contractors. Agreed?"

He had no choice and they both knew it. "Agreed."

"As for the … incident. The house systems…"

"It's still under investigation. I have to ask you to say nothing of it yet."

"Of course." She shook her head again, trying to clear away the mists of unreality. No change. "I can't— We will talk about this later. I need…"

His hand came out again and this time it caught hold of hers and stayed there.

CHAPTER FIFTEEN

Dead quiet reigned when they walked back into the meeting room. Ethan drew in a breath and took his seat again. Sarwenna kept walking and took the seat farthest away, on the other side of the room.

He would have liked her beside him.

"Thank you for waiting for us," he said, watching the faces in the room. Seeing who made a point of avoiding looking at Sar and who sent her a discreet glance … which faces sharpened as they did it, which softened with mouths creased in concern.

Her father was one of the ones soft with concern. Then he turned to Ethan and gave him a short nod. A commendation or a warning? Rhyn Beren, he was learning, was a master of the calmly composed front. No doubt living with a family including Ari and two lively boys did that, let alone his famously driven wife, but Ethan would have liked to be able to read the man.

To know what he saw today in Sar's closed face.

Enough. He took a deep breath and stood to face the waiting townsfolk. "Sera Sarwenna and I have agreed to hold a meeting in a few days, once the union members have had time to review their notice packages. Solaris is not about to throw out anyone without support."

"Your father on board with that?" said the mayor dryly.

"It's consistent with Solaris policy, and he put me in charge of this project."

From the looks on their faces, those watching believed that as much as he did. He ploughed on regardless. "Sulwith needs to diversify. To create a sound economic base not reliant only on Solaris. That's the reason I asked you to come here. I'm told you're the ones in Sulwith with ideas. If anyone can come up with ways to help your town survive, it's the people in this room."

Still the carefully masked faces.

"Let me start," Ethan said in an attempt to break through their walls. "I walked through Sulwith after the storm. It was a bad one with little warning, but you got by with relatively minimal damage and no deaths. I've seen the standard plans for Solaris-built towns and Sulwith still shows elements of it, but someone has seriously modified the original designs of the buildings to better fit your location. Who, and how, is what we need to know. Skills like that are highly sought after, and will be more so when the warnings about what faces Arcadia come true."

Nothing. Stubborn, blank faces refusing to answer. Did they think he'd steal their designer from them? Maybe he could try with dollops of credit, but he seriously doubted it would work. Not if they were like the rest who chose this tough place to live. He looked around the room, hiding his desperation and shoving on the smile that had lured business partners to his side before. It only hardened the stiff-mouthed barrier. Finally he looked at Sarwenna, losing the false smile. She met his gaze and gave it back with one equally shielded. No help there, and he was stupid to hope for it.

Then she opened her mouth and his heart thudded. Her voice was cool and distant, a professional, but the words she spoke… She was backing him.

"Myli Oraka. She makes the plans and her team builds the houses. The roof lines and corners come from Darbu Ceiltnek. He's an old man now but he knows this town inside out. He's the best one to talk to about building design. Myli doesn't like talking. Reckons she's too busy to bother."

A chuckle, prosaic and blissfully normal, shattered the tension for good. "Last one who tried got a right piece of her mind," said Rhyn.

Ethan breathed a silent sigh of relief and thought it best not to risk asking where she was. Not yet. He shoved on the nearest he could come to his real smile and leaned back as if enjoying the story.

Seated near to him, the mayor looked thoughtful. "Wonder if she'd look at outside designs. Myli is a right grumblebut when she's bored. Starts looking around the place and thinking up complaints. You reckon you could get some other towns to use her?" He sounded like he was near begging for someone to take her. Ethan decided he definitely had to meet this woman.

"Myli don't travel. Likes her own place too much," said a woman wearing a multi-coloured tunic and hair that had a life of its own.

"She could do it by com," he said, keeping his voice easy and relaxed. "Plenty of Dridust designers refuse to leave town and they still draw up plans for far flung townships."

"That explains a lot," muttered the mayor, and a general chuckle rippled around the room.

Rhyn leaned forward. "Myli's not like them. Likes the deadlands and walks it regularly. She knows this land and the weather patterns. Maybe Ser Winter's brother could spare time to help her with reading the patterns of a new town. He's an ecological engineer, isn't he?"

Ethan nodded. "One of the best. I'm sure he'll be only too happy to help," he promised, ruthlessly ignoring his brother's already hellish workload. Caleb's actions had started this trouble; only fair he helped Ethan sort it out.

"Talking of designers…" The mayor eyed the woman in the multi-coloured tunic.

"Stop right now, Gered Burgaldor." The woman crossed her arms and outright glared at the mayor. "I'm happy enough doing what needs done around here."

"But Maddie, your clothes are smak," piped up Ari.

All the women in the room nodded, even Sarwenna. Ethan studied the woman again. That tunic was like nothing he'd seen before, a mish-mash of colours, but it worked, he suddenly realised. Did something to the woman. His mother would know. He grinned at the thought of strong-arming his very proper mother into working with this backlands town.

First off, she'd have to get the woman to relax enough to show her what she could do. Maddie, as Ari called her, had gone bright scarlet, and the older man beside her chuckled in delight. "Can't hide any more, Maddie darling. Looks like Sulwith has come calling."

After a few hours, Ethan's head rang with ideas. How could a town written off as no more than a base for labourers, be so stuffed full of creativity? Maybe, just maybe, there was a chance to make this work. "Thank you all," he said winding up the day, still in shock that they had trusted him enough to open up. To hope that he understood the reality facing them all, top-house privileged and working prole alike.

Their trust didn't extend to giving him a chance to talk to Sarwenna. A group of townsfolk surrounded her as soon as they left the building and smuggled her out of the offices. To where, he couldn't say. Not yet.

Somewhere safe. He trusted his own security staff and had to believe in their capability. They could do their job better without him. That's what he told himself anyway, but it didn't help. Not this time. At least she'd agreed to meet with him, even if she had insisted on using the union's office. Not a place neutral to both, and definitely not Solaris' office, but it was a meeting.

First though, he had to go back to Dridust and start putting all these ideas into action.

He activated his com. "Graffin, I'm leaving for Dridust on the hour. Wind up everything here, make sure our guests all have transport back to Sulwith, then you head back too."

"I will be at the flyer when you are ready, sir."

"No, it's all right. More important that you sort everything out here with a maximum of courtesy and a minimum of fuss. Cutting your time short will stop that. I'll see you in Dridust."

The too polite reply told Ethan exactly what Graffin thought of being stranded in the back-of-beyond lands, but Ethan also knew there were flyers standing idle in the local hangers his assistant could commandeer and had little sympathy for him. Besides, Ethan needed to fly alone. Security had cleared his flyer, and his craft had a state-of-the-art route scramble installed making it near impossible to track. He met the panicked demands of security to take a guard with a promise to call in immediately if anything looked suspicious and a simple com off linkage cut. They'd send a backup flyer after him as soon as he lost sight of base, but as long as they kept their distance, he could live with that.

He badly needed some alone time, and no amount of miserable looks from his assistant or overly cautious security were going to take it from him. He waved a cheery hand at Graffin as he surreptitiously blocked his com link, then strode out of the building and to the flyer landing pad. In minutes, he'd swept through the pre-flight checks and lifted high above the baking lands below. He lifted to a hover point where he could see the speckled dots of Tollic, Sulwith, with their fields of shimmering light from Solaris solar fields, and out to the ultra-dry deadlands lying beyond the border town.

Desert lands coming closer and closer with each passing day and threatening to engulf it.

His fingers stabbed the controls and, with a surge, he lifted the rest of the way to the upper transit level then headed west, headed home. Yet surprisingly, a part of him regretted leaving the emptiness of the dry lands and sighed at the sight of the first waves of golden grasses and scrubby hollows as he returned to the plains proper. The margins of the deadlands might offer little comfort to humans but the vast emptiness did offer a freedom not found in the commercial coils of Dridust.

You love the business.

The business, yes; the constant jostling and fight to get his ideas listened to in a company tightly controlled by his father, no. As he neared the sprawling complex in Dridust that was the Solaris head office, he felt for the first time a tightening of dread in his spine instead of his usual anticipation.

Why did this battle matter so much more than all the other ones with his father?

The ones you lost, you mean?

Enough. He had a company and a planet to save, and childish wailings wouldn't win him either. He signalled his arrival and set down in his usual slot in the section reserved for family. The Old Man's was in place but no other family flyers. Silas must have gone back to Caleb and the Survey lake site.

A pity. Right now he could do with a brother's presence.

Before he exited, he spent extra time securing his flyer. After the incidents in Sulwith, even Solaris offices no longer felt safe. He locked the hatch, setting it to his retina and DNA print only. Over the top maybe, but he could almost hear his security chief's approval from here.

Stop procrastinating.

No, merely mindful of recent events. Yeah, and the grass had suddenly turned green over all the plains.

He shoved his shoulders back and strode into the building, heading for his father's offices.

A blocked doorway stopped him. He slammed a palm on the control. Nothing. He called up the main admin portal. "Ethan here. We've got a door problem on level three, hall five. Can you activate it from there?"

"Good afternoon, Ser Winter. There is no problem with that door."

"Yes there is. It won't open for me."

"I am sorry, Ser Winter. That corridor is open to Solaris staff only. Family members may use hall two. Shall I send someone to accompany you?"

"Accompany? It's Ethan. Open this door immediately."

"My apologies, Ser Winter, that is not possible. A staff member will be with you shortly."

What in tragging hell? He slammed his hand against the control panel again. All it did was bring one of the heftier members of security hurrying down the hall. The man skidded to a halt, face too carefully blank and a tell-tale bead of sweat on his forehead.

"What's going on here, trooper?" he snapped, and hated the quick blinks and too rigid posture of the man.

"If you will come with me, Ser Winter. Your father has asked that you join him in his office as soon as you arrive."

Sanity at last. "That's where I'm headed as soon as someone lets me through this tragging doorway."

"If you will follow me, please, Ser. This way."

Ethan was getting a nasty feeling. With no other option, he followed the trooper. Down to hall two, pacing through corridors he'd last used when he was no more than a mid-schooler coming with his mother to see his father at work. The family passages. The non-staff family passages. The ones not even Caleb used any more.

By the time they reached his father's offices, Ethan had built up a serious case of thwarted fury. He didn't wait for the formality of linking in and asking permission to enter. Whatever was wrong here, he was still family and the Winter codes opened this door to family. He thrust his fingers against the pad and entered the code, then put a hand in to throw back the too slowly opening door.

"What in tragging sands is going on here, Father?"

"Ah, Ethan. Take a seat, won't you."

He'd heard his father use that condescending tone too often against underlings and business rivals to tolerate it now. "When you've told me what game you're playing."

His father lifted an eyebrow but Ethan ignored it. He stopped right in front of his father's desk, legs apart and looking down on the man he'd worked so hard to impress for so many years. "Enough. Explanations. Now."

His father sat forward, as in control as ever except for the small tic in the side of his face. "What about you explaining the meaning of that extraordinary report from Sulwith. That field is the most profitable in all of Solaris."

"And the most environmentally destructive."

"Says your brother. But not even his precious Survey can expect us to destroy the businesses that keep this world running. Without Solaris energy, the whole plains region will grind to a halt."

Had the Old Man understood nothing of these past months? "Do you want to get us thrown into prison again, this time for good?"

That got the Old Man. He thrust out of his chair and stood glaring back, looking as angry as Ethan. Whether he was, Ethan doubted. No one could be as angry as he felt right now.

"Yes, prison," he growled at his father. "Remember it? Because I certainly do."

"No one is going to throw Winters anywhere."

"And you're going to make sure of it?"

"Yes, boy, I am. Solaris is going to be too big, too rich, and too powerful for anyone to touch us again."

"Not even the Feds? Or are you claiming to be bigger than the Alliance now."

A glower back in answer. Of course he wasn't. Not the Alliance of Settled Worlds, the interplanetary grouping of all the human-colonised worlds. All powerful and fully capable of carrying out its threat to forcibly remove all the human settlers from Arcadia if they did not reverse the growing environmental imbalances threatening the ecological survival of the planet.

An Alliance too powerful for one man or one company to overthrow, no matter how rich or weighty Solaris might become.

"The Alliance can be made to listen to reason," said his father. "The Survey exaggerates."

"No, they don't, and you know it. Sulwith is not sustainable in its present form. Which is why my report included alternatives. Solaris can be so much more than just an energy-making company."

"Hah, that old nonsense again."

"It's not—"

"How about you prove it then, son. Go out into the world and show Solaris how it's done. You're such an expert. You don't need Solaris. Go build your own business."

"And Solaris?"

"I thought I'd made that plain, son. As of now, your position in this company is finished. I warned you about the Sulwith field."

He was bluffing of course. Ethan checked his com links, and his heart stopped a beat. Nothing, no response to any Solaris code except the basic family codes.

"You're out, son. You have no role in Solaris. Go join your brothers, or better still, go play in the city. Solaris doesn't need the kind of trouble you're foisting on us, nor do you. When you've calmed down enough to be safe to have in the company, come back and talk to me."

"And funds. Are you going to cut me off from Solaris credits as well?"

"Of course not," said his father. "Your shares in Solaris are intact and your basic allowance will be forwarded to your account as usual."

Allowance! After all his years of work, all the long hard hours of grind he'd put into keeping Solaris alive and growing.

"Stick your allowance." The thought of touching it, of being diminished to being his father's pensioner, made him sick with disgust. He threw his hands in the air and marched out of the room. "And keep your tragging company," he said with one final slam of the door.

At least his flyer still answered his code. He set it in flight with a whoosh and a swirl of dust, lifting off and setting a course for … where?

He let his hands make the decision and wasn't surprised when they steered him east. His security screamed into action behind him, but he ordered them to stay back, to give him space. If only he could order them to let him go alone.

He lifted higher and drifted across the plains, deeper and deeper into the deadlands border country. He neared Sulwith, coming in south of the town to set a heading east and farther south. His flyer had been fully fuelled up before he left Tollic. In regen mode, he could travel halfway around the planet before it would need a boost.

South and east. Deeper and deeper into the baked, harsh country of the deadlands proper. To the north, the desert gave way to broken scrublands then the towering blocks of the eastern ranges dividing the dry centre of the continent from the northern coastal lands. Set between the western end of these ranges and the towering ones running down the continent and dividing the plains from the west coast forests lay a wide valley leading to the fertile temperate regions of the northern coasts. Prime lands that were home to Urbis, the planet's capital, and the main agricultural regions of this continent. On this side of the continent, the barren spikes of the eastern ranges slashed toward the sky keeping the fertile lands safe from the frontier lands of the central region below.

And us safe from them. Safe from the grasping, grubby games politicians and corporate heads played up there. He'd always thought those ranges a hindrance but now he felt enormously grateful for their sheltering bulwark. Down here, he could breathe. Down here, ideas could grow.

More procrastinating?

He grinned to himself. Then it twisted sideways. His own father had kicked him out of the company he loved. The company he'd been ready to sacrifice anything to save. That had stood between him and Sarwenna. His hand itched for hers and he longed to hear her sharp, pitiless challenges that gave him a reason to fight.

What did he do now?

He slowed his flyer, came in lower and looked for a landing pad. There, a large slab of rock overlooking a barren basin. He put down, barely waiting for the dust to settle before releasing his harness and opening the hatch. Then he walked out.

The heat of the desert hit in a wall of scorching fire. Hotter than Sulwith, hotter than his home on the dry plains, the air pricked at nerves and baked his head. The kind of heat that wasn't safe for man or unshielded machine.

He welcomed it, closing his eyes and lifting his face to the burning sun, feeling the slap of it already biting into his skin …for a moment only before sanity returned and he switched on a personal shade field. He could do with that coverall of Rhyn's. Restless, he walked to the edge of the rock, feeling a swirling of hot air from the bowl below adding to the incineration from the sun. He dialled up the protection of his field and stood, staring out into the nothingness beyond.

No, not nothingness. Caleb had taught him that. He stood silent and still, waiting, as Caleb had taught him. Slowly, slowly, the slight traces of movement returned to the gravels below. A faint shimmer where a small animal ran between rocks. The erratic waving lines covering a patch of orange dirt where the aerial feeding web of a plant rooted far below the surface absorbed the sun's energy then sent it down deep to the rest of the plant. Brittle, short-lived, shrivelling to nothing within a day, the lines of the web were stuffed full of photosynthetic cells to milk the solar energy in their short life, to be replaced overnight by new suckers. A delicate balance between the energy needed to grow new suckers and the gain to the plant from the thin web above ground. A constant battle for life, repeated over and over out here.

And you, will you keep fighting?

The question hung like a dagger in the air. Ethan felt like one of those brittle webs at the end of the day, burnt out and ready to be replaced by someone newer, stronger, more able to keep up the struggle. So many waited for him to return to Sulwith and make good all those promises he'd so rashly made.

They would be all right, for now. Thanks to his father, the jobs from the solar field were safe for tomorrow.

But for how long after that? The Feds couldn't allow the field to stay unchanged, not with the Alliance breathing down their necks. It was a fool's dream to think otherwise, and the Old Man was wrong to peddle it.

He should leave them all to it. Let them live in their false hope of a world where Sulwith stayed untouched. Let Sarwenna's union win.

Sarwenna. A vision shimmered to life of the woman he'd first seen, standing tall and defiant against him. A woman ready to fight for her members and their future.

Can you do less?

Fight his own father? He stared out at the basin, seeing an endless horizon, endless struggle. There is life here. So his brother Caleb kept reminding him, but Caleb was bent on saving the planet, not Solaris. And Silas had thrown his hand in with his oldest brother while he figured out what the turmoil of the Survey battle had made of him. The den Coille brothers were closed to him as well, since he'd accused Seolta of working against the Federation. As for his mother…

He sank to a crouch, thinking of his mother's face as he'd last seen her. So proud, and so tragging scared for her family. All his mother wanted was the survival of all she cared for. What had happened to the strong woman who'd raised him? Had prison permanently damaged something in her, broken the courage and pride that had carried her through life? His mother would sacrifice anything now if only it meant her sons would live.

It was love, but not of a kind Ethan could live with. He'd wondered so often as he grew up whether his mother genuinely loved her children or saw them more as an extension of her own self-worth. Now he wished by all the sands to have her back again. That mother had pushed and prodded, had expected her sons to stand on their own two feet and succeed.

Suddenly the horizon felt impossible to reach. Too far, too hard. Too much of everything, leaving him trapped here in this bleak and empty land. He shoved up from the edge, swung around abruptly and strode back to his flyer.

This time there was no slow dawdling over the lands of his birth. He pushed the flyer up to the swiftest atmospheric zone with the best air currents, set it to maximum speed and logged in a course for the far west. His flyer swept past the longitude of Sulwith and he refused to look down. He'd left a message on file for the town, full of bland platitudes, knowing whatever he said was irrelevant. His father would make all the explanations and nothing Ethan could do would change it.

Coward.

He refused to listen. Not to the niggling words of his conscience, not to all his mother had taught him of manners. Not to any thought of Solaris, the business, and its future.

West, to Caleb. To family who still accepted him, faults and all.

He hoped.

It didn't stop the moment of panic when he landed in the main field behind Caleb's field station. He'd planned to slip quietly into the station and see Caleb in his office without onlookers. No such luck, not in a place stuffed full of people he'd grown up with.

"Ethan. Had enough of screwing over lawyers and banks? Come to do some proper work?"

"Hey, it's the hot shot businessman."

Even from old Bob, the man who'd taught him to ride a horse when he was barely old enough to walk. "You want Caleb or Silas? Hope you remember how to ride."

Ethan groaned. Of course his brothers would be out working, and of course Bob would be the one to meet him. The old stockman had a theory that a hard day's work made a man and used every chance he could to reinforce it. One look at the grin on his face told Ethan there was no point in asking for a skimmer or truck, and he wasn't about to try landing his flyer in the deceptive ground around his brother's lake without permission. As for the jibes from the others, he'd worked stock and trekked side by side with the name callers enough times. He was long past having to prove anything to them.

"You going to saddle up for me?"

Bob just grinned and jerked a thumb at the stable. No, he hadn't thought so. Not the old stockman's style. Ethan grimaced, wishing he felt more up to this. He trudged over to the stable and took comfort in the horses tucked into their stalls. He moved among them, trying their walk, then picked the one that looked the most reliable with an easy gait. Bad enough he had to ride for the first time in too many years; he didn't feel like coping with a temperamental mount of top of everything else. He gave the saddle's girth a last tug and mounted up, heading his horse over to the hut railing. "Which direction?"

Bob sent his gaze over the horse, no doubt checking that Ethan had put everything on properly. A brief nod, then he touched a finger to his com link. "Sent the coordinates to you now," he said. A touch of a hand to his hat, then he turned and slouched back inside the hut.

"Nice to see you too, old man," muttered Ethan. It was so typical of old Bob, Ethan had to smile. He set out across the dry plains to the setting shown on his com.

He'd visited Caleb's lake site before, but this time his com pointed away from that and toward a bank of hills he knew to be riddled with caves and tunnels. Was Caleb still that cautious? The trek out took him through broken country where his com failed more than it worked. Something to do with the local minerals. He wasn't worried. He'd spent his upper school years racing skimmers through the twisting turns of the underground hollows and hidden passageways, so getting lost wasn't a problem. He had to stop to rest his horse in the rough ground, but eventually he emerged and caught the track again, not far from where he'd guessed it would be.

It was late in the day when he caught sight of the field camp. Right on the edge of a small dam that he was sure wasn't there when he was a boy.

His horse caught the scent of fodder and other horses, quickening its tired pace and whinnying as people emerged from the low building on the edge of the dam. A shout and his brother appeared in their midst, unmissable by his height and distinctive Winter colouring. Part of the land, people always said of Caleb, his sandy hair and tanned face merging with the grasses and rocky soils. Next moment, he caught sight of Ethan and strode forward, waiting in front of the crowd for Ethan to bring up his horse.

The whole scene was too eerily similar to how he'd first met Sarwenna Beren.

"Ethan," said Caleb. A wealth of questions lay under that steady voice, but none of it showed. "You're a long way from home. Taking a sabbatical?"

"Something like that," said Ethan, matching his brother's tone. "Need an extra hand?"

"Always." He tilted a head at the woman standing nearby. "Take Ethan's horse, will you? I doubt he's up to bedding it down if he rode here. Long time since my brother last sat on a horse."

Wasn't that the truth? Ethan gratefully slithered off the horse and back onto solid ground and let the woman lead his horse away.

"She'll put your bag into the spare bunk next to mine. Come on in out of the sun. You'll be wanting a drink."

His brother slung an arm around his shoulder, his hand digging in for a moment as if in support, then eased off again, walking Ethan into the welcome shade of the hut and through to his quarters. Fortunately, he kept his pace slow. Ethan wasn't sure if he'd have made it inside otherwise after the hours on horseback.

"Thanks. I'm more out of practice than I realised."

An amused grunt from his brother, but no more was said until the welcoming shade held him safe inside the field hut with its cool refuge and proper climate control. Caleb dialled up the food prepper and shoved him into a seat. Nor would he allow any talk until Ethan had filled his stomach and quenched his thirst, sitting opposite and watching every mouthful his brother took. Ethan felt about ten standards old again.

He finally shoved the plate away and leaned back in his chair.

"So what really brings you here?" asked Caleb.

Ethan stared at the floor, unable to meet his big brother's gaze, but Caleb never let him get away with anything. His foot kicked at Ethan's chair under the table, sending it tumbling backward. Ethan shoved his feet hard against the floor just in time to stop it falling right over. His brother had last used that trick on him at a family dinner more years ago than he cared to remember. His hands clamped down on the table and he glared across at Caleb.

"Thought that would get your attention."

"Yeah," he said, trying to sound like the adult in the room, to no effect.

"What's wrong? Father riding you too hard on that Sulwith deal? Thought you would have finished your report and sewn that one up by now."

Ethan swallowed. "I have. Released the results a couple of days ago."

"And the Old Man wasn't happy?"

Ethan dropped his head again and leaned back in the chair. Caleb's foot shot out and Ethan had to look up. "Not as you'd notice," he said.

"And…"

A deep breath. "He sacked me. I'm out of Solaris."

CHAPTER SIXTEEN

Caleb's chair crashed to the ground as he shot up. "Say again."

"You heard. I'm out."

Caleb grabbed up his chair, swung it over to the table, back to front, and slung a leg over it. He leaned forward over the chair back and fixed his eyes on Ethan with the same intent scrutiny he'd used when they were both in the playground and Ethan had fallen foul of a teacher. "Tell me what he said. Exactly what he said."

"I'm out. Go build my own company, he said."

Caleb's face didn't change.

"You expected this," said Ethan in shock. "Maybe it was even your idea."

"Don't be stupid."

"So why aren't you surprised?"

"It was inevitable. Point is, what are you going to do about it?"

Do? Ethan could barely string together a sentence.

Caleb sighed. "What else did Father say?"

Ethan considered refusing to answer; but what had he come for if it wasn't to talk? He coiled his hands into fists and forced the words out. "Told me I could come back when I'd calmed down enough to be safe. Solaris didn't need the kind of trouble I'm creating nor did I." He took a breath, readying himself to get it all out while he could, but Caleb suddenly straightened.

"Safe? You, or Solaris?"

"Solaris of course. He's wiped me. Told me to go play elsewhere, hasn't he?"

Caleb wasn't listening.

Ethan grabbed another plate and piled it up in the prepper then slumped back at the table, as his brother sat silently opposite, lost in thought. He always did that when problem-solving. Ethan guessed he should be relieved his brother was taking him seriously, but right now he would have preferred words to fill the space. Black depression settled on him.

It was true. His father had kicked him out of Solaris. Had taken away the only life Ethan had ever wanted.

He ploughed through the new pile on his plate, taking no notice of what he ate. Then thrust it into the cleaning chute. Caleb sat silent still with the zoned out gaze that spoke of using his com's personal mode and his fingers playing periodically on the screen zone. Ethan cast him a disgusted look and clomped out of the room, heading for the bedroom set aside for him. Sleep. That's what he needed. Maybe something about this whole crazy thing would make sense in the morning.

No use. Sleep had also deserted him tonight. After a long while, he gave up on pacing his room and went out to the kitchen to make a hot drink. The square at the centre of the compound lay dark under the sky and the stars shone through, tiny pin pricks of light belying the massive distances and huge energy balls behind their sparkles. A bit like the torrent of hurt lying under the words that kept echoing in his head. You're out … out … out…

Stop it. You lost your job, not your life, nor your head, your brain … not even your wealth.

Not that he'd touch his father's pitiful allowance, and the Old Man should have known it. Ethan had amassed enough outside investments over the years to have no need of charity from the family firm.

But Solaris had been his life.

His footsteps echoed in the packed dirt of the square. He stepped softer. He had no desire for company in his misery. Not in the dark wallow of this too long night. He entered the combined kitchen, dining and leisure building, closing the door and checking that the windows were shuttered before bringing up a single beam of light over the food prepper area. He dialled up a hot and bitter cup of dask and lifted it to his mouth, taking one, foolish, burning swill of near-to-boiling liquid.

"Trag it."

A soft click of the door behind him, and he turned, still nursing a burnt lip, and watched his brother walk in, lifting an amused eyebrow at Ethan's curse.

"Couldn't sleep, or trying to figure out how to turn the Old Man's latest quirk into a credit flood for us all?"

Ethan threw him a hand gesture from their boyhood. "Not much chance of that, not anymore."

Caleb lifted an eyebrow in that annoying way of his.

Ethan set down the too hot mug. "He's wrong this time. He can't win, not against the Federal government and the Alliance."

Caleb was dialling himself a mug of dask. "We've both been telling him that for years. Me straight to his face; you in more subtle ways. He's never listened before. At least now, it's no longer your problem."

"Not my problem…"

Caleb shook his head. "Not anymore. Not when you don't have to keep trying to save Solaris. It'll survive for a while longer, of course, but not much. Why don't you set up in opposition? The sands know you've enough ideas to start your own business."

"Start my own…" Ethan gulped another mouthful, this time ignoring the burn and grateful for the bitter lift of the drink. "You want me to finish off Solaris even quicker that it's going down now."

"It's going to happen anyway. Why not take advantage of it?"

"This is Solaris we're talking about. It's our family, our name. Generations of Winters have built that company and made it what it is."

"Only takes one generation to send even the best company to oblivion. Arcadia is changing, and companies that refuse to recognise that are on a one way track to nowhere."

Ethan could barely believe his ears. "You really don't want to take over the company after Father."

"Never did. Tried to tell you both."

"But … you're the eldest."

"The heir, the appointed one?"

"Yes," said Ethan bitterly. It was a fact of life he'd learned to live with. A fact he thought he'd come to terms with, until Caleb saved them all and his father discovered the born leader inside his bleeding-heart son.

"I have no interest in running Solaris," said Caleb flatly. "Never have, never will. Making a business is your thing. I have a planet to save. Which I'd begun to hope you would help with."

"You've accessed my Sulwith report," Ethan suddenly realised.

Caleb nodded. "A good job and a fair reading. I liked the ideas of the townsfolk."

"Much good it did them." Ethan felt empty. A golden husk without substance, one who promised much and delivered absolutely nothing. "He's going to destroy them all. Sulwith, Solaris.

The workers and the scientists, the future of us all." His father had been through prison like him, knew the threat of inaction to their home world, yet had chosen his stubborn, tired old path rather than make the changes Solaris, Sulwith and all the other work sites and small towns needed. "Why?"

"To protect you, is my guess."

Ethan stared. "From what? Success?"

Caleb took a sip of his drink then moved over to one of the puffed up chairs and settled back into it. His chin tilt suggested Ethan take the other. Why not? No reason he couldn't brood in comfort. "I already have a security squad shadowing my every move," he reminded Caleb.

That annoying eyebrow quirk again. "Not that I'd noticed."

"I ordered them home."

"And they left you, just like that?"

Ethan shook his head. "Last I checked, they're in permanent hover above us."

"And you didn't think to warn me we're under Solaris surveillance."

"Figured you'd know anyway and would block them if you objected."

Caleb lifted his mug. "Didn't bother, not this time. There's little to see here, and you need their protection."

Ethan scowled. "No, I don't."

Caleb lurched forward. "So no one's after you? You haven't been attacked by an unknown flyer, near killed by a dose of akintoside and downed by an unknown beam that stranded your flyer? Let alone riling up too many elements in Sulwith and the corporate world with your plans for Solaris's field?"

Ethan couldn't argue. All true, and all still unsolved. He had some ideas, but… "You were supposed to be tracking down leads on the Stealth fighter."

"The Feds are looking into it. Marshal an Fallon owes me."

"No, he doesn't." The senior Federal policeman had led the squad that freed Ethan and the den Coille brothers from prison. It was Ethan who owed Marco an Fallon and his troops a debt he could never repay.

"The Feds need to find out what's happening here," said Caleb uncompromisingly.

Ethan couldn't disagree, but right now he'd had enough of waiting for others to find an answer to his questions. "You seriously think the Old Man sacked me to save my sorry hide?"

"It's a possibility. Maybe more than a possibility."

"From whom?" Ethan lifted his mug, took another long draw of dask. "He came near to dying in prison, same as me. He wouldn't risk going there again. Not even for Solaris." If he said it enough, he might start to believe it. Fact was, his father would do just about anything for Solaris.

But risking its long-term survival to save Ethan's hide? "What in all sands is going on here," he muttered.

His turn to brood. He turned over the disastrous line of events since the first day he landed in Sulwith. "That beam from the solar field. Silas tells me Sarwenna Beren's younger sister is a mechanical genius, and she's also recently been lured into a decidedly suspect com room."

Caleb smacked his mug down on the side table. "Ari? That girl in Sulwith I said would make a good recruit for the Survey?"

Ethan nodded. "Yes, Ari Beren. It's a bright family. The youngest brother, Finn, thinks Silas walks on water, and Silas thinks the kid could grow up to be near as good as Silas at manhandling com systems."

"He the one who cracked the code of that com room?"

Ethan nodded again.

"What's so dangerous about it?"

"Dark hints of eroticism and cult figure worship, all packaged to appeal directly to young women of Ari's age, according to Silas. The ones on the cusp between childhood and full blown teen girl."

"When they live in a fantasy world and latch onto any chance to save the world or be adored?" There may be no sisters in the Winter family but they had girl cousins aplenty. "Which means the ones behind it not only know what makes people tick but are as unscrupulous as all sands."

Ethan agreed. Abusing children to win a corporate battle was about as low as you could get. "They're from the business world," he said flatly. "Have to be to pull this off. And infected with the same greed as those Survey bosses you were up against."

Caleb grimaced in agreement. "The private corporate world doing the dirty. That's your territory."

"The goal's the same."

Caleb nodded. "Power and credits today and blow the generations of tomorrow. Worse, it looks like the Old Man's been suckered into working with them."

Ethan wasn't so sure. The Old Man was near as wily as they came. A bit hot-headed, admittedly. "It's wider," he said slowly, thinking it out as he spoke. "Seolta den Coille may have a finger in it. Silas recognised his touch in the programming of that com room."

Caleb's eyes widened but gave no other sign of what being told about his brother-in-law meant to him or his wife. "We need Silas here," he said grimly. "Seems he knows too much to be able to keep him out of this. Unfortunately."

"He's been through what we have. He deserves a part in it," said Ethan, to a scowl from Caleb.

"He's barely grown."

"Only a year younger than Ben when he put his life on the line. I reckon Silas has earned that right too."

Caleb's scowl deepened, harsh lines bracketing his face. Ethan doubted he'd ever throw off the guilt of young Ben Crane's death. It changed nothing. "He's at the new plantings in the wetlands we're building between here and Lake Ben. I'll call him in."

Some time later, a scruffy and barely awake Silas strolled in, took one look at Ethan, and stopped dead. "What's happened?"

Ethan waved at Caleb to explain, unable to face telling the whole sorry story again.

"The Old Man's lost it," said Silas at the end.

"Caleb thinks he's doing it to save my sorry hide."

Silas thought a moment. "Could be. Sands know you've stirred up enough trouble lately. What about Sar Beren? What does she think of this?"

"Why should she think anything of it?" said Ethan defensively.

Silas ticked points off on his fingers. "She's union, her family is probably up to their necks in whatever is going on, and you're halfway to being nutty on her."

Ethan opened his mouth to deny it. It wasn't true anyway. He was way past halfway.

"Don't bother," said Silas, and "Shut it," said Caleb. "We haven't time to waste on side issues."

But it wasn't, not this time. Ethan had stabbed Sar Beren in the heart with his report. No, not the report. In the way he'd made it public without talking to her first because he was too much of a coward to tell her to her face and watch as she rejected him. "She knows Sulwith and has weight with the town. They listen to her."

"Because of her parents," said Caleb flatly. "Rhyn Beren's senior Solaris staff and anyone who's ever paid any attention to the Federal Assembly knows Catra Beren."

"That battle-axe?!" Silas sat down suddenly and stared. "She's the Beren's mother?"

"Arianna takes after her," said Ethan thinking of the surly teenager clumping down the stairs.

"No she doesn't," said Caleb. "A delightful child."

"She thought you could give her something."

Silas butted in. "You're both right, but Ari hasn't the drive of Sar, or Finn for that matter. Those two run the family, with their father and Daff running protection behind them."

Silas was wrong. Sarwenna was nothing like the fiery Catra; neither as bull-headed nor as hell-driven. More her father's daughter in the way she did things. And yes, her mother's daughter in her commitment and passions.

But the whole of her was unique. Sarwenna Beren, daughter of the deadlands with a pride he never wanted trampled. "They listen to Sarwenna because they trust her. They know she works for them, first, last and always."

"Maybe. Whatever the reason, you should talk to her."

"She's in Sulwith," said Ethan. "Not a place to welcome me at the moment."

"Make them," said Caleb bluntly. "After you get yourself up to Urbis. That's where the secret to this whole carbuncle lies."

Ethan shoved his fists against the arms of his chair. "Central government is your world, not mine."

"Not the wernet bloodsuckers running this operation. They're pure corporate. Your world, your ballpark."

"They're not likely to open up to me now the Old Man's given me the boot."

"Leaving you without a credit to spend…"

"Not quite," admitted Ethan, then felt like throwing something at that slight lift of Caleb's lips. "You knew credits weren't a problem. That's what you were figuring out earlier."

Caleb shrugged with no hint of apology. "I've watched you studying the financial 'casts since you were barely able to tot up the data. You hid them well, but I know you and always assumed you'd have some backup investments out there."

Silas dropped down into the remaining chair. "You mean…"

"Our Solaris reject here is rich enough to keep you and me both."

"Not with the way you spend Survey credits," protested Ethan. "I've seen the scale of your lake developments."

"Does the Old Man know?" Silas demanded.

"Of course he does," said Caleb.

Ethan didn't argue. "He offered me my Solaris allowance."

"Which you immediately refused," said Caleb.

Ethan flipped a hand in a banned playground gesture. "He can pay it into my accounts but I won't be touching it."

"Can I have it?" said Silas.

"When you decide what you're going to do with your life. Your share of Solaris pays you quite enough at the moment, especially if you plan to spend your days mucking around in Caleb's mud holes."

"Regardless," interrupted Caleb, killing the budding wrangle between his younger brothers, "Ethan will be welcomed into Urbis with open arms. With your brain, your experience and those credits to burn, the corporate wernets will be lining up to embrace you."

That wasn't all Caleb meant, he realised with a rush. Let the corporate leeches sucker you into their world and find out who's behind the attacks. That's what Caleb meant, and Ethan grinned.

"Go join them and get them to start flapping their greedy mouths."

"After which, you take it straight to the Feds," warned Caleb. "No more heroics than that. You're trained in business, not subterfuge."

"Unlike you," said Ethan, and chuckled at the flush reddening his brother's cheeks. He'd long known Caleb's Survey training covered a great deal more than planning and nature. The skirmish with the Survey head office had proved it, sending his brother undercover for months as he plotted against the usurpers.

Caleb leaned forward, hands tightly gripped. "I mean it. The people you're up against have already shown they're willing to kill."

"Yes. Specifically, to kill me. So what makes you think they'll suddenly decide I'm harmless and tell me all their secrets."

"Because, little brother, I've watched you managing the Old Man for years, seeming to go along with his plans while you worked to change Solaris piece by piece. You play a long game. This is no different."

Except Sulwith and Arcadia didn't have time for a long game. Not with the damage humans had already done here and with the Alliance breathing down their necks. Caleb knew that as well as anyone, which meant his big brother was still protecting him, trag him.

"And what happens to Solaris while I play games up in Urbis?"

"That's the Old Man's problem."

"Let it fail. Let it rot. Stop all those credits you both use so freely?" Ethan countered. The company he'd spent his life on. All the men and women working so hard to make it succeed, all the families dependent on it for food in their bellies and a roof over their heads? He stood, fists clenched. "Not going to happen, not on my watch."

Caleb waved him to sit down again. "You've no choice."

Ethan stared at him suspiciously. "You playing mind games with me, brother? Conning me into saving the company."

Caleb let out a word from the lowest streets of Urbis. "I don't give a grain of sand whether Solaris survives or falls. I do care about catching whoever is using it to stop us saving our world."

The big divide that would always separate them. Caleb had grown up resenting Solaris, thanks to their father's pressure. Unlike Ethan. A society was made up of big cogs and small, each dependent on people who cared about them to turn those cogs. Solaris was a big cog but not too big to be irreplaceable. Others would line up to take its place but not with the same people or resources. His father refused to recognise that, refused to understand that Solaris couldn't fight a whole world plus an interplanetary agency.

"That's it?"

Caleb made no attempt to apologise. "I can't put Solaris ahead of Arcadia. Nor can you."

"Don't need to." Ethan wondered why he bothered trying to explain. "Solaris can survive, as long as it changes."

"Not going to happen," said Silas, coming down on the side of Caleb as too often these days. "Not with the Old Man in charge. Not now he's kicked you out."

"In order to protect me, according to our big brother here."

Caleb made as if to stand, fists clenching by his sides, then slowly sat down again. "I'm right. You know I am, you're just too thick-headed to agree. How was the Old Man after they released him from prison?"

"Angry as a riled up Jack Robber bird cheated of its prey." Determined that no one could ever catch a Winter out again.

"Angry enough to put Solaris before his family."

"They're the same to him," said Silas, scowling.

"No, not fair," said Ethan, working to put into words the feeling growing in him. "To him, Solaris is what gives Winters power, what makes us who we are. Solaris makes us, and we made it."

"He doesn't purely love the wheeling and dealing?" Caleb lifted that eyebrow again, and Ethan bridled.

"What's wrong if he does?"

"Nothing, if he remembers there's also a world outside Solaris."

"Like you remember there's a world outside your precious Survey?"

Caleb threw a hand in the air. "Gah, it's like talking to a rockface. One minute you're condemning the Old Man, next you're defending him. Just once, can't you try listening to reason?"

"Same to you, brother."

Caleb claimed Ethan could rile him up quicker than anyone else, and the reverse was true for Ethan. They both shot up, glaring at each other.

Silas tried shoving between them and was shoved back down for his efforts. He thrust a hand through his hair and glared up at the both of them. "Just once, could you two try working together instead of bellowing at each other like a pair of juvenile nieten bulls?"

Tell him that, Ethan nearly said, stopping himself just in time. Silas was right. "Sorry," he mumbled. Caleb looked like he'd been knocked on his backside by the apology, giving Ethan a second-hand snib of satisfaction. "You heard me."

"Accepted, and same to you," Caleb muttered back after one awfully long moment.

Silas thrust up again and this time pushed between them to shove first one then the other back into their chairs. "You're both idiots."

Ethan for once had no answer to that and decided not to try. "So what next?"

"You came here for help, didn't you? What do you want?" said Silas, far too reasonably.

"Not money, nothing physical," he growled back.

"To get the Survey to find out what's going on." Caleb had slouched back into the chair, but the scowl on his face hadn't lessened. Silas huffed out a sigh.

"And I'm supposed to be the juvenile around here. Is that what you wanted, Ethan? To have someone else take over and make everything right again."

No." The response was automatic. This mess was his to sort out, his to fix. Then he remembered who he was talking to. "Not really, not at first." A haven, that's all he'd consciously wanted. A place where he still belonged. But subconsciously? He dragged in a breath. "Yes, I came in here ready to chuck over Solaris as easily as the Old Man chucked me over... but Solaris is important to too many people for that. With logic and good will, Solaris can be a leader in making the changes Arcadia needs. Instead, the Old Man is turning it into a fortress where nothing changes."

He breathed in hard, remembering that rigid office and his father's last words, his father's face—and his hands hidden under the desk. "He's afraid of what's to come," he said slowly. "Afraid of being thrown back into that prison cell."

"Like you," said Caleb and all Ethan's carefully constructed defences crumbled. His hands grabbed for the chair arm.

"I've seen you in close spaces," said Caleb gently.

"I can control it," he said, crossing his arms.

Silas opened his mouth, then clamped it shut, sitting down and staring into space. Anywhere but at his pathetic brother.

"All right, yes, I hate closed rooms. I never go into a place without checking where the exit is and being stuck in a room without a window or door is my biggest fear. But I'm handling it, and it's my problem not yours. That's not why I'm here."

"Does whoever is out to get you know about it too," said Caleb, carefully avoiding the fear word.

Ethan shook his head. "The only ones who know are the den Coille brothers, and now you two." That was the wrong thing to say as well. Both his brothers stiffened. "They were in prison with me," he said, trying uselessly to explain. "We shared stuff you can never understand. I can't change that, and you need to deal with it."

Silas hunched down into his chair and Caleb flushed red.

Ethan sighed, feeling suddenly old. "Neither of you put me in that cell. You weren't my jailers, and I've about had enough of you two buttoning up every time it's mentioned." Always this stupid wall between him and his brothers. "I can't change it," he said again, knowing it for the truth and hating it. Because he realised why he'd come here. The den Coilles were barred to him now he'd accused Seolta, and he badly needed his brothers.

Prison had dealt a blow to that. He stood up slowly. "I'm for bed. I'll see you in the morning to say goodbye."

"Sit down, brother." Caleb's voice slashed like a knife through the tension-filled space. "You're going nowhere. Not till we figure out who's after you and what to do about it."

"No point," he shot back, but Caleb had never been one to give up.

"We nearly lost you once. Not going to risk it happening again," he said simply, in the voice that said nothing would stop him. "Sit down."

Ethan didn't know whether he could do this tonight. He was so tragging tired of it all. Too tired to fight. He slumped back down, sitting rigidly and staring at his hands.

"Get him a drink, Silas. Not dask. The strong stuff in the top cupboard."

Ethan took the cup Silas passed to him. He swallowed a mouthful to placate the angry glare from Caleb, then bent forward coughing and spluttering. "What in all sands?" he said once he recovered.

"Old Jim's own mixture. For special occasions only."

"Thank the sands for that. It's lethal."

Caleb gave his slow smile, taking the bottle Silas passed him and sloshing an unhealthy amount into his own mug. "Yeah, it is." He lifted his mug, took a deep draft, and put it down with a loud sigh and a gasp. "Pure poison."

Silas went to grab the bottle. Caleb snatched it back and added a splash of water to Silas's mug before adding the spirit. "Not straight, young man, not yet. You're barely legal."

Silas looked about to argue, but a glance at Ethan's flushed face had him backing down. He took the mug with the diluted spirit, took a cautious sip, then a slow and long one. "That's good stuff," he decided with a smile.

"It is," agreed Caleb. "Now to your problems, Ethan."

Suddenly Ethan knew a strong need to down the whole mug of potent brew. His problems…

"Where to start…"

CHAPTER SEVENTEEN

A day later, Sar still couldn't believe it. All Ethan Winter's fine words and he walks out on them with no word of explanation. When her friends hustled her out of that meeting room, he made not one attempt to stop them.

She'd served her purpose, clearly. All usefulness gone, his pompous aide had organised their trip home and close-mouthed security from Solaris surrounded her, right up to her doorway. Every moment of it she waited, for a word, a signal, the slightest of com touches. Nothing. Ethan Winter stayed silent, leaving her feeling like no more than a forgotten tool in his business negotiations.

She should forget too but couldn't stop brooding. All night, all through a barely touched breakfast, and with every footfall as she stomped through the streets and through the door of her office.

Alternatives. That's what he'd demanded she consider. A tight band of pain circled her head as she marched into her office. The glowing smile on Marget's face was the final insult.

"Have you heard?"

"Heard what?" she snapped.

"The solar field. It's staying as it is. Nothing will change."

Sar stopped short. "Ethan Winter said that?"

Marget waved a hand. "He's yesterday's news. Old Man Winter got so mad when he saw the plans for here, he sacked him. Threw the whole plan out, just like that." The smile dialled up to unbearably smug. "Everything's to stay just as it's always been. Isn't that wonderful?"

Sar muttered something, too stunned to think straight. Wonderful? After yesterday's meeting? After him making her reconsider everything she thought she knew about Sulwith?

Marget just grinned. "We've won, Sar."

Sar forced a smile and pushed past her into the office. She slumped in her chair and activated her com, to be assaulted by a deluge of incoming messages. She ignored all except the important one. The statement from Solaris Central to the union, confirming what Marget had said.

Sulwith Solaris was to continue unchanged. Sol Winter had taken personal control of the Sulwith field and Ethan Winter had chosen to exit Solaris for now while he explored other options. She believed that no more than anyone else. His father had sacked him because he dared to take a different route.

She should be relieved. The union had won. Only … she was no longer so sure about that.

No time to think. A crowd of workers surged into the room, all gleefully repeating the news. Not one asked whether it was sustainable. En route back here, Sar had taken the time to read the latest Alliance reports and Survey briefings.

The Alliance was coming. It was there in every line, every environmental report, in the anger of the front-line Survey staff that day in Urbis when Caleb Winter had exposed the double dealings of the Survey heads, and in the westward march of the greedy deadlands sands. She stared out her office window. Once, it had rained here every cycle. Now, the supply of water was a central plank in any town councillor's election campaign.

In those reports last night, the Alliance was right to give Arcadia an ultimatum. An unadmitted part of her had seen what was happening to her home, but she'd told herself she welcomed the increasing grasp of the desert. She loved those dry, empty places.

To live in them full time was another matter altogether and unless something changed, that was the future Sulwith faced.

"Hey, Sar. Not so glum." A young clerk slapped a hand on her table. "We've won. You beat them. Word is the Old Man proper gave it to that snotty Winter boy. Told him just what he thought of his precious report."

A crowing of laughter on the other side. "Yeah, a kid trying to do a man's job, but his old man set him straight."

That kid had survived months of harsh imprisonment, was a man full grown who had stood up to his captors and faced death at the hands of his enemies. "They disagree, that's all," she said.

The boy looked shocked. "You're not defending him? He tried to take our jobs, but we showed him."

"We?" This boy had stood in the back of the crowd that first day and had done precious little since.

"Yeah. Sulwith workers won't be pushed around." A man in a stained jerkin, swaggering to the front then leaning right over her. Another who had stood in the back on that first day. She had to dig her nails into her palms to keep her temper.

"Solaris has put a stop to the changes for today. Doesn't mean the Feds or Alliance will let things stay as they are," she said.

"Solaris is too big, and our politicians know what's good for them. Back Solaris solar fields or get kicked out of office."

"Yeah, they can go drown their sorrows with Ethan Winter up in Urbis."

Sar glared at the loud-voiced woman and got a dead straight stare back. "Not as if he knows how to do anything else," said the woman. "That boy's been coddled all his life."

Sar remembered a moment when Ethan Winter gave the lie to that. Fear had flashed across his face, to be hastily banished. "The Alliance is real; so is the threat," she said.

A snort of disgust met this. "Come on, folks. Time for a drink. Who'll join me?"

The room echoed with cries of "Me", "I'm with you", a bellicose battery of high spirits and brave claims, and in no time at all, her office was deserted again. Marget stuck her head in the door.

"I'm off to join the rest. Too gloom and doom in here."

"Somebody has to be the grown-up."

"Hah!" A toss of her head, a snatch at her bag and Marget whisked out of the room. A whoosh of the outer door and she was gone.

Sar refused to give in to the impulse to race after her with a biting rejoinder. Mostly because she couldn't think of one. Was she the fool here? She straightened her back, sat more firmly in her office chair and turned to her official com link channel. Work might help.

She'd turned off her union links overnight and sighed at the size of the queue waiting for her. Then saw a newly arrived message planted right at the top.

Old Man Winter in all his glory, lording it in a full size holo image. She switched it quickly to desk display size. It made little difference to the power of the man but at least he wasn't staring down that long Winter nose at her.

"My son has chosen to step down from Solaris management in order to pursue his own business interests."

I bet he did.

"Accordingly, I will be taking personal control of those projects under his watch, including the review of the Sulwith Solar Field."

Sar let the rest of the blitherings wash over her. She'd heard this kind of talk too often before. The only thing unclear from the stock phrases was whether Old Man Winter had done the sacking or they'd had a fight over the direction of Solaris and Ethan had chucked his job and the company in his father's face.

Ethan Winter in a rage and doing something unplanned? No, his father had sacked him.

At the end of the speech, her com blinked red in warning of an appended notification and she started listening again.

"All union representatives are invited to a meeting at the Dridust office in three days to hear further details of the plans for the Sulwith field."

"Hah. There's only one union rep in Sulwith, you old brakka. Me. This is a consolidated field."

She clicked on the invitation link and accepted. Better find out what Solaris had to say. It should be an interesting meeting. Sol Winter was about to learn she couldn't be as easily dismissed as his son.

That night on her walk home, calls and celebrations met her on every street. Cheeky young boys who should have been in bed careered around corners. "Did you hear, Sar? Did you hear?"

Men rolling through the streets, lurching from doorway to doorway. "We're safe, Sar. S'all right now."

Women lifting a glass from the sidewalk tables. "You hear the news, Sar? We're staying, we're all staying."

She lifted a hand to each one, plastered a smile on her face, and avoided each and every invitation to join in the fun. "Work," she told them all. "Details to sort out."

Luckily, no one asked her what details. She opened her own door in relief. Finn and Ari whooped when they saw her. Ari had something white dusting her cheeks and Finn wore a suspiciously clean tunic. Then Daff stuck his head around the corner.

"Sar, you're home. Good." He glared at his brother and sister. "You two finished in here yet?"

"Finished?" Sar looked around the room, taking in the remarkable assortment of decorations plastered on walls, ceiling and any flat surface available, and her heart sank. Every colour of the rainbow covered the once restful walls, highlighted with strange shapes she could only guess were meant to be flowers, intricate creations of multi-faceted shapes that had to have been done by Ari, and a garish and extraordinary conglomeration of objects from all parts of the town that she guessed were Finn's contribution.

And Daff's?

"This way," her second brother said impatiently from the doorway. She followed him with increasing dread, through another door, and into the formal dining room. A room they hadn't used since their mother went back to Urbis. When she was young, this room had bulged with dinner guests, talk echoing off the ceiling, with her mother in the centre of the chaos at one end of the table and her father quietly smiling at the other. She gasped when she walked in. The spirit of those nights was back. A lively dance song started up as she stepped through the doorway; overhead, the brightly sparkling crystals in the light setting shone as they hadn't in years, and that special blend of desert and garden scents beloved of her mother wafted through the vents.

She couldn't help it. Her eyes welled up and tear drops touched her cheeks.

Finn stared in horror. "Don't you like it?"

She reached down and hugged him. "Of course I do. It's perfect. But why?"

"To celebrate, of course," said Ari in the voice of a teen girl faced with adult stupidity. "You beat off Solaris and saved the town. This is us saying congratulations."

Sar wanted to shrivel up inside. "Oh. Thank you. That's lovely of you all. And Da. Where is he?"

"Right behind you, Wennie. Sit down, eat up, then this lot can clean up while you tell me all about it."

He knew. She saw it in that slight pinch at the corner of his mouth. Her father had been the first to ask her to look at the future with new eyes before Ethan Winter forced her to confront it head on. She nodded her thanks, unable to say more, then switched on her big sister smile. It seemed to fool the two boys and Ari at least.

Finally the too bright meal was over and she could retreat to the study with Da. A familiar squabbling echoed from the kitchen as the younger ones tidied up, laughter bubbling up through the shrieks and name calling. That smile. She'd pulled it off.

Then she saw her father's face, saw the crease on his forehead and the frown on his mouth, and she crumpled like a small child. "What's going to happen now?"

The lines on her father's face echoed the ones on her heart as he tilted his head toward the giggling play from the kitchen. "They think we're all saved. And you?"

She shook her head. "That meeting with Ethan Winter… It got me thinking."

Her father nodded slowly. "I took a trip out past the lion rocks the other day. You remember the spot?"

"We used to picnic there. When I was little and Mama was first up in Urbis. You and me."

"I missed her so badly then," a sad smile flitted across her Da's face, "almost as much as I do now."

She took his hand in hers and gave it a squeeze. She'd never understood what lay between her volatile mother and her placid father, but that it was a true love she'd never doubted. A peaceful one, now... "We used to pick jujube berries."

"I looked for them, but they need water and the spring has long since dried up."

She gasped. "It's hidden, safe from the sun." The spring had been little more than a dampness in the sand, buried far under a rocky outcrop and needing hard digging to gain a precious cupful of water., but that water source had been enough. In that small hollow had grown jujube bushes, a few rank grasses, the web-like farantee plant, and a wealth of animal species called it home, from the tiniest of flitting snitchits to wandering natheens, cousin to the grazing nietens of the Winter plains.

"All gone," said her father. "Nothing but dry sand and scouring winds. The emptiness is spreading."

"The field's too big, too complete, too much the wrong kind of solar sheets?"

"All of those," agreed her father.

"You were right, Da, and I was wrong. I did some research. Something I should have done long ago. If we don't change now, in ways we control, the Feds and the Alliance—the planet itself— will make us."

"Yes, Wennie, I'm afraid they will."

Both of them fell silent, until her father dragged himself up from his chair and made for his special locker hidden under the vid-painting on the far wall. He pulled out the bottle he kept there, one he'd had as long as Sar could remember. She'd seem him drink from it only twice: once in celebration on the day her mother said she was coming home, when Sar was but a first-schooler, and again on the day her mother announced she was contesting the regional seat on the Federal Council. The day her Da knew she would be leaving him again.

He poured them both a small glass and she lifted it to her mouth, savouring the familiar smell, even though she hated the taste of it. It made no difference. She swallowed it straight down, same as her Da, and banged her glass down on the table.

"Still as good as ever," wheezed Da.

Sar just gasped, tears starting in her eyes. "As strong as..." she managed to croak. Then had to clutch her head as the full force of the spirits hit. "Ooh. That's it. I'm for bed before I drop right here.

Her father snorted. "I wish..."

"All right, after I read the rest of the comms in my queue."

"From Solaris?"

She nodded solemnly, lifting her glass. "That was first in the queue. Inviting the union up to a meeting in Dridust. Well, ordering more like."

Her father's hand suddenly stopped dead. "You're going, of course?"

"Mmm. No choice. It's the only way to find out what's behind this latest news. What it means for the future of the workers here. At least you'll be there to tell them the real facts."

This time the silence crashed into the space between them in a clatter of desert crystals.

"You will be there?"

A shake of her father's head. "No one's invited me. Not yet."

"They will. It can't have come through yet. Bet it's caught up in a jammed link somewhere."

"Yes, you're probably right."

She knew that carefully bland voice. "I'm not a child, Da."

A sad smile. "No, you're not. You haven't been for a long time."

That fraught silence again, as they both took a sip of the potent liquor.

Her father set his glass carefully on the side of his chair. "If anything changes, anything happens…"

"Nothing will," she said desperately.

"No, but if it does, the boys and Ari come first. Promise me you'll look after them. You'll keep them safe."

"Of course I will. As will you and Mama. Nothing's going to happen."

That night in bed, Sar tossed fitfully, unable to forget her father's words.

If anything happens…

She set out for the Solaris meeting early on a desert morning with the sun still hiding its warming glow and her father's words echoing in her head. No invitation had arrived for him. Tom Crabster, the field manager, had left for Dridust the previous evening. He'd offered Sar a lift in his company flyer, but the thought of being stuck in Dridust and dependent on Solaris for transport home stuck in her throat. She declined, using as few words as possible.

Wait to hear what they propose. Her father's last words of advice. Why had he been left out? Everyone in Sulwith knew her father made the field work, not that credit-pinching windbag, Tom Crabster.

The trip west didn't usually seem so long. Once out of Sulwith's local perimeter, she set the flyer to auto and opened the records she'd uploaded to review before the meeting. Outside her window, the sun sparkled on early morning dew and stained the desert below a stunning rose pink. Each detail, every twig and hollow, stood out as if carved into a stone plaque set under the slanting morning sun, like an old-fashioned etching she'd once seen stored in an ancient archive in Urbis. She drank it all in, committing the shape of her home country to memory. Slowly, the land below changed. She resorted to peering backward out the window, suddenly feeling an urgent need to capture that last sight of desert sand, that last splash of colour on rock walls. Then no more, all lost from sight and replaced with long golden grasses and shrubby pockets of stone and grit between the ever present solar fields. Still dry, but water lived here.

Sulwith country had looked like this once. Holo images preserved in the town archives could be mirror images of the country below. Sulwith should still look like this, but the settlers had changed all that.

Now they must change it back, said the Survey, and said the erratic thump of her heart. Sulwith wasn't the only place on the planet where settlers had altered the climate and ecosystems so dramatically. Among the research reports she'd read after that last meeting with Ethan was one written by his brother Caleb, one that challenged all she'd clung to. So many changes had been made, all over the planet. Small changes, big changes, changes that merged and accumulated, one upon the other, tumbling their home world right to the edge until Arcadia could no longer withstand the onslaught of all those changes.

It had the ring of truth. She'd tried to ignore the drumbeats, to believe that jobs, credits, the economy came first; but credits did not stop the scouring storms or bring back the rains.

Yet credits did put a roof over her workers' heads and pay for the food Sulwith could no longer grow.

She landed at Dridust and still had no idea what to say to Solaris management. She walked across the landing pad and up to the building entrance, furiously discarding one brilliant argument after another. Then she saw the man waiting for her at the entrance and discarded every one of them.

"Good morning, Sera. Welcome to Dridust. They are waiting for you in the meeting room on level five."

"Ser Graffin. I thought…" She'd last seen this man back in Sulwith, making arrangements for the delegates after Ethan Winter's momentous meeting. He'd been Ethan Winter's right hand man.

The man had the cheek to give her the perfunctory bow of management to a supplicant and look down his nose at her. "I've been transferred to Dridust central protocol section. A promotion."

"Congratulations," she choked out.

"Thank you, Sera. If you will follow Wilmena here, she will escort you to the meeting room."

At the meeting room door, her escort stood back and let Sar enter first. She walked in, head held high. The room held the usual suspects. Sol Winter at the head of the table, directly facing the door so every person entering had to bear his immediate scrutiny. Beside him, his accountant and the rest of his cadre of financiers.

She'd expected them: a cluster of moneymen interested in only two things. How much will this cost? What's the profit for Solaris?

Then she saw the others seated at the table. Some were familiar, some not, but near the head, two down from Sol Winter himself, sat a man who shouldn't be here: Maxell Drocash.

"Take a seat, take a seat," boomed out from the head of the table.

She inclined her head. "Greetings, Ser Winter. I trust you and your family are well."

A grunt, an abrupt frown, and he waved her brusquely to her seat. So family, or particularly sons, were off the table.

"And Ser Drocash too. A surprise to see you."

"All the union representatives were invited," barked Sol.

She raised her eyebrows. "There is only one from the Sulwith field. Me."

"Not any longer, Sera Beren," thrust in Drocash. "A few of us weren't happy about the way the union's been handling all this, so we started our own union. The Committee for Sulwith Plant workers."

"They voted you in as their representative?"

"Yes," he said, so belligerently she could only assume he'd appointed himself representative and the rest of his bunch had been too weak-spined to object.

"I trust that your members have all properly resigned from the union. Or are we both here representing the same people? A wasteful duplication."

"If you don't like it, you can always take yourself off again."

For an insane moment, that's exactly what she felt like doing. Her father's words alone stopped her. "When you are duly elected by all the Sulwith plant workers, I will consider it. For now, I have members depending on me to do my job."

She stared him down. When he began to shift uneasily in his seat, she again inclined her head to Sol Winter at the head of the table. "If you would, please set out the reasons for this meeting and explain the consequences of this latest shift in Solaris' staffing plans."

Ser Winter scowled back at her. He must have hoped his lapdog rep would hold the union power at this meeting. People didn't call him the Old Man without cause. He'd been around a long time, and she mustn't forget what kept him there.

He harrumphed and began speaking.

At the end, it was much as she'd expected and as bad as she'd feared.

"If the Federal government steps in and forces you to close the field, what happens to my members? Has Solaris a backup plan, and credit reserves in place to fund it?"

"Solaris doesn't need to wait on any Feds to look after its workers. This is our country, our home region. We look after our own."

So the answer was a big fat No. "You have a plan for how you're going to do that? The union requires the financial forecast for the Sulwith solar plant for both the next quadrant and the following five standard years after that."

"That is commercially sensitive information for the use of Solaris management only," said the dry-voiced accountant seated on the other side of Sol Winter.

"And information that the duly elected representative of your workers—me—is entitled to view under statute 603.592." Sar could almost quote that statute verbatim, she'd used it so often. A statute designed to protect workers by ensuring that companies could not withhold financial information showing the potential viability of a company. If the company got richer, the workers had a right to a share in it. If the company was facing financial strife, the workers had a right to know. When it came to their families' survival, they had a right to know whether it was worthwhile staying to help their employer recover or cut their losses and find new jobs.

It was a statute universally loathed by company management but which none had been able to have removed from the Federal lawbooks in the hundred standard years since its creation.

Sar loved citing that reference. Only today she might as well be grasping at empty air for all the effect it had. She shoved on her fiercest face and stared right back at Sol Winter. He surged up, bringing his hands flat down on the table.

"This company is in good heart. There is nothing for your workers to worry about."

"Show me the books and I'll believe you."

"What's your problem, Sera Beren? Your workers' jobs are safe. Isn't that what you want?"

"I don't like to see my members being conned. You're feeding them short-term hope but long-term you're condemning them to oblivion, along with the town we all call home."

Maxell Drocash leaned forward, directing an oily smile to the Old Man before turning to face her, lips curled up. "The wonderful Sera Beren, so caring she condemns the families of her members to hunger and homelessness. Maybe that's not who you're really fighting for. Where is your good friend, Ser Ethan? You think he can give your members the glowing future he's promised them? The one they will magically discover after the only employer in Sulwith is forced to pull out of town."

"That's enough," growled Sol Winter from the table head. "My son is not part of this discussion."

Sar might have crowed at the sudden dismay on her rival's face, but his words hit home. Ethan Winter had painted a different future for the town in that meeting. One in which she and everyone in that room had glimpsed a spark of hope. Now it was gone, and Sol Winter was right. She'd won everything she'd first set out to fight for.

Time and facts, though, can change any plan.

"I ask you again, Ser Winter. What back-up plan do you have for when the Federal government steps in and forces you to shut the Sulwith solar field? For if you refuse to change, refuse to modernise and downsize to give the habitat there a chance to recover, they will step in."

CHAPTER EIGHTEEN

Hours later, all the talking had gone nowhere. The only gain had been in the intensity of the pain beating at her temples. Maxell Drocash at first stayed mercifully silent after his early routing by Sol Winter but had since begun chipping in again. As long as he kept away from mentioning the Winter family, the Old Man encouraged him. Yet watching closely, Sar picked up a faint sneer of distaste touching the patriarch's mouth. She knew how he felt. Maxell Drocash was an opportunist, interested only in power for himself.

That made it even more important that she keep talking, keep plugging away at the tedious arguments put forward by the rest of the table. Her members needed her to keep doing her job if they were to have any genuine hope for the future.

Except that she had no real arguments to counter the ones marshalled against her. Just a bunch of half-formed ideas from Ethan Winter's meeting with nothing concrete yet to back them. If only they'd had more time. By mid-afternoon, the emptiness of her position was blatantly obvious to everyone at the table, including her. She longed to get up from her chair and run as far and as fast as she could.

A man came in the side door and bent to talk to Sol Winter. The Old Man had taken to lolling back in his chair with a half-smile on his face. Almost as if taunting her to face reality and give in.

She was tempted, oh so tempted.

Then he rose. "That's it for today. I have other appointments. Sera Beren, your members are fully covered by their contracts and these will continue unchanged. I suggest you listen to them before you recommend taking any action to put that at risk. This meeting is now finished."

With that, he walked out, leaving her standing isolated at her end of the table, stranded on a lost argument and wondering what in tragging sands came next.

She was escorted out of the building and declined a polite but firm invitation to take the offered seat in a Solaris flyer back home. Telling the woman she had her own flyer and would definitely not be needing help from Solaris was the only satisfaction she'd got out of the day.

She just wanted to be home. Wanted to let it all rush out to her father's ears and listen to his careful dissection of the words she'd heard.

Listen to him tell her it would all work out.

She walked in her front door, tired, churned up, and hungry for the food of her childhood and found … silence.

"Hello. Where is everyone?"

A thumping on the stairs, a barrelling down of a crowd of bodies, and a grunt from the dining room.

"Sar!"

"You're back."

"Where've you been."

Her two brothers erupted into her waiting arms, small arms squeezing her so hard she had to gasp for breath. Behind them, her sister stood with shoulders slumped and arms crossed.

"What's happened here? I just went to a meeting. I told you that."

She tried detaching her brothers from her, but they clung tighter and her heart began to thump. "Where's Da."

"In here," said a low rumble from the dining room.

She turned, hugging her brothers close as their arms trembled and brought them with her.

Her father sat at the head of the table that had seen so many family celebrations, slumped into his chair and staring at his special bottle. Then he looked up, face ravaged and bitter lines gouged into his mouth. "A good meeting?"

"As expected," she said, suddenly at sea.

A grunt, and his hand reached out to cradle the bottle.

"What's happened here."

He looked up, his gaze tracing the small boys clinging to either side of her and her sister standing behind them. "I've been sacked."

Sar heard a gasp, then realised it came from her. White shock held her in place. "Sacked. But who ... who's going to run the field?"

"Tom Crabster. He understands credit sheets, you see; and he believes in the future of this field as it is."

A cold slap of understanding hit her. "Someone told Sol Winter what you said to Ethan Winter."

A slosh as the liquor hit his glass. "They didn't have to. It was obvious from his report."

He set the glass down on the table and stared into the dregs in front of him.

Sar had no idea what to say. This was wrong, so wrong. Old Man Winter wanted no change to this field, so why sack the man who kept it going? And no point thinking he acted out of ignorance. Not Sol Winter.

Especially if that report included what else had to be there. Sacking her father threatened the continuation of the whole field, but taking Ari and Geordie MacTavie out of the system guaranteed an end to any profit from it at all.

Insanity.

The Old Man must be running scared. Either that, or prison had made him hell bent on running Solaris his way, with profit first and last, to the point where he refused to listen to reason.

A nasty shiver snaked up Sar's back. Neither of those described the man who'd dominated this region since she was a small child. Sol Winter was arrogant, profit-driven and overbearing, but stupid and cowardly he was not.

What in tragging sands was going on here?

Her father reached for the bottle again and sloshed the liquor into his glass, full to the brim, then lifted it and drained it in one draught.

She should stop him.

She'd never thought to have to stop him before. The carefully nursed contents of the special bottle that had held pride of place in his cupboard for so many years had nearly disappeared.

She put out a hand, then stopped as he gripped tight onto the bottle, as if guarding it from her. She pulled back her hand.

"It will work out, Da."

He lifted his face from its study of the brown liquid and the dark wells of his eyes mocked her. "No, it won't."

She stood, unable to face the wreckage of her father any longer. "It will," she said, but whether she spoke to her father or herself, she couldn't say.

Outside the room, her brothers met her with scared, staring eyes. Ari had slumped down on the top step.

Sar stuck her hands on her hips. "Look at you three. You'd think someone had died. No one's hurt, we're all here, all together and nothing beats Berens. Now, what about some dinner? Ari, what's in the prepper. Finn, get the table set. Daff, go tidy up the seating room. We're going to have dinner in front of a vidcast tonight."

For a long moment, they all stared back at her in silence. Then Ari said, "Come on, you two." Her little sister put an arm around each of her brothers and pulled them toward the kitchen.

"Thank you," breathed Sar softly after her. Ari caught it and gave her a short nod back.

One more task awaited her, and for that she needed the privacy of her own room.

"Mama," she said to her com link. Within an instant, the vivid face and figure of her mother materialised. She was in full evening regalia, a gown sweeping down to the floor, hair caught up in a formal curve at the base of her neck and her favourite necklace clasped around her neck: the Suarian crystal Sar's father had given his wife on their wedding day.

"You're on your way out. Sorry, I didn't mean to interrupt—"

Her mother broke in, face suddenly intent. "Who's hurt?"

"No one. At least, not physically."

"Who?"

"It's Da." Her mother's face turned stark white and her fingers clutched out. Sar reached her hands into the holo field and cradled the image of her mother's hands. "He's been sacked, Mama. He's lost his job."

"And…"

"The bottle. The special bottle. It's only a third full."

A sound in the background, and her mother brusquely waved someone away. "I'll arrange a flight immediately. Hold on, Sar, I'm coming home."

Sar fell back, stunned. All her life, she'd been told of the importance of her mother's work. How her mother would love to be home with them all, but too many depended on her and it would be unfair to disappoint them when Sar's father looked after them all so well.

Now, Mama dropped everything to rush home.

Sar didn't know whether to be thrilled or terrified. She returned back to the main room to tell the others and thanked the sands for the relief on her brothers' and sister's faces. Mama had been a staple of their childhood and having her back would make home feel normal again.

Sar had different memories.

That night in bed, she couldn't hide from the questions. Why would a man like Sol Winter put at risk the financial viability of a field like this? The man had been running Solaris as long as any of them remembered, and stupid he was not. Worse, Ethan's security still haunted the streets outside her house. She'd nodded discreetly to the man lolling in a sidewalk diner opposite as she walked up to her door. Their presence could mean only one thing. The threat to Ari remained—to her whole family, she suspected, after her father's abrupt dismissal.

Then the other thought intruded. Where was Ethan Winter?

Early next morning she woke, worn out and bleary, to a voice calling her name. She lifted her head and an unmistakable smile beamed down on her.

"Mama. You're back."

"Yes, chick, I'm home again."

She shouldn't feel so relieved. For years, she'd fought being treated as the support act to her mother's success, but this morning, none of that mattered.

Then came the afternoon.

"It's all arranged," her mother announced. "The freight shuttle arrives at the first quartile tomorrow morning. We'll be home by tomorrow night."

Home? "We are home," she said to the hurricane now ruling their house. Finn and Daff looked shocked, but Ari just stared silently. And her father… Her father said nothing, just watched as Mama began rummaging through their house and set packing modules on the floor, filling them with the accumulated detritus of a lifetime.

"Mama?"

"You have a job here, Sar, but not your father. Not after yesterday, and the boys and Ari will be better off in Urbis where there are schools to properly stretch them. Your father and I have been arguing over this for years. Until now, this place has been safer. It gave them a warm and nurturing environment, and we could use com resources to make up for any schooling deficiencies. But now that this has happened…"

"I went to school here, Mama. Right up to higher entrance."

"Yes, dear, and it worked very well for you, but Ari and Finn need more."

"Ari and Finn are years ahead of any contemporaries, and much of that is because of this community. Ari is an integral part of the Solaris field and everyone calls on Finn when they have com problems. That wouldn't happen in Urbis."

"Ari a part of Solaris? I don't think so."

Sar should have known to give up but refused. Not when her family needed her to keep fighting.

Her mother's maternal instincts, once aroused, proved impossible to fight. The next morning, as scheduled, Sar stood in an empty house as the freight shuttle took all her family back to Urbis. Her quiet, uncomplaining father, her white-faced youngest brother, the too quiet Daff, and Ari with a look of a nieten caught between a predator and a cliff face.

And me, what about me? But she kept silent. Her father stopped before they all walked into the freight shuttle.

"You'll be all right? You can still come with us, Wennie."

She shook her head. She'd worked in Urbis as her mother's gofer after graduating. Not a role she wanted to repeat. "I have my own work here."

"I thought the same."

The new pain on his beloved face had her hugging him tight. "You will again, Da. The industry knows your worth. Something will come up."

A tired smile. Yes, it was a trite saying, the one everyone always said to someone whose job had been yanked from under them … but sometimes it came true.

She pushed him gently toward the transporter. "Go look after Mama and the children. I'll be fine. Sera Carmal has always been a good friend to the family."

She'd taken up the offer of a lodging room with their neighbour down the street, a big-hearted woman with a knack for mothering anyone who came within sniffing distance. Better than staying in a home without her family and safer, given Ethan Winter's warnings and the security staff shadowing her family.

Her father's face brightened. "Yes, Farida Carmal will look after you."

Then they were gone and Sar's capsule of belongings floated beside her. She palmed the lock of the house and set the code for prolonged absence. The only comfort: their Sulwith home was not for sale. Her father had won that concession from her mother. The auto systems would keep it clean and vermin free but not loved, not filled with the noise of a family.

"We will be back," she whispered.

She turned swiftly away and began to walk up the street. A young man strolled up beside her. "'Morning, Sera. Need a hand?"

She recognised the man. She'd seen him before, lolling across the road, and checked for the tell-tale lump on his side. One of Ethan's security plants.

"Thank you. I'm just going up to Sera Carmal's house."

"I'll join you. As it happens, I'm staying there too."

She couldn't hide the small smile. "Of course you are."

He gave a grin back. "The boss sends his compliments," he said, and a sudden warm glow melted inside her. She hadn't been forgotten.

"I thought he'd left Solaris," she couldn't help saying.

"Doesn't change who he is, or the shares he owns."

"My family?"

"Are safe, Sera, and will be kept that way. We're working with the Feds on this one."

She wasn't sure if that made her feel better or worse. "Is that necessary?"

A sudden hint of a grim frown before that practiced grin returned. "The boss thinks so, and so do the Feds."

"Oh." What else could she say?

The young man accompanied her right into her new room. "Just helping the new Sera settle in," he said with the kind of smile no woman, young or old, should be able to resist. Sera Carmal did glance at her first, then beamed when Sar nodded and took the young man's proffered arm.

"So that's the way of it. It's lovely to have you here, Sar. You'll be feeling right at home in no time."

Sar doubted that. Not when that nice young man shut the door firmly on Sera Carmal and began testing every nook and cranny with a scanner she suspected was years ahead of anything she'd used.

"Someone hasn't done this beforehand?"

He grinned. "Routine procedures." He finished and vanished the scanner back somewhere in his tunic. "My room is directly opposite yours. Pass me your com."

She slid it off, wondering if she was an idiot and passed it over. She was relieved when he passed it back and the faint weight of the disc on her wrist returned.

He had that grim look on his face again. "Too trusting, Sera. How do you know that was safe? That I am who I say I am?"

Her mouth dropped and she reached for her com to belatedly start up the protect program.

He flashed her an insignia on a personal band, visible only to her. "In this case, I am. The name's Dan, and I was assigned by Ser Ethan himself, but don't ever hand your com over to a stranger again."

She recognised the logo. Solaris security with Ethan Winter's own seal embossed at the bottom. Her com beeped. New program accepted. Source non-hostile.

She still felt afraid.

"You should be afraid," said the young man.

"Are you scanning my thoughts now?"

"No, just reading a face untrained for this. You're good, but the tell-tale trace is still there. You're safe here, Sera, but keep your wits about you."

"Understood."

"Understood, Dan," he shot back with a grin. "Lock your door after me."

Thoroughly chastened, she said her good nights and set a com lock on her door. He'd no doubt left all kinds of sensors in her room, but she welcomed the illusion of privacy. It had been quite a day.

The next few days were no better. She fixed a false smile to her face every morning and carried on as if the weight of the future didn't hover over her. She got used to the sight of newcomers to the town lolling in doorways, lingering at cafe tables, wandering the same way she went whenever she left her lodgings. The first day, she walked into her room and found her nice young man rifling through the bottles on her dresser and running a scanner over her bed, shock held her dead still, but soon it became routine. One day, a crash and a hail of fine plasglas shards littered her at breakfast. She'd chosen a table to one side of the main window, needing the sight of blue sky but wary of being seen. It saved her that morning, the mini explosive causing no more than a mess and a few scratches on her face. She wasn't surprised when Sera Carmal came to her later that morning.

"Maybe it would be better if you were still in your own home."

Sar plastered on a smile, the one designed to ease another's guilt. "Yes, I think you're right. I do miss having my own walls around me."

The no-longer-so-nice young man materialised beside her, a grim set to his mouth. "I'll be leaving too, Sera. Thank you for your hospitality."

For an instant, a trace of panic ran across Sera Carmal's face. Dan and his fellow team members liked their rooms and ate up large in a healthy addition to her income. Then the woman's face glanced at the dining area, and she promised to send them their final bills too.

So she was back home, with a makeshift bed in a barely furnished and echoing house. It still felt safer. Some of her security team made themselves at home in the basement refuge and strongly suggested she join them. When she refused, they simply set up a rotation roster to stay upstairs.

What the town thought of this team of fit young people living with her, she daren't consider. They kept her safe. And knowing that Ethan Winter's people still held to their security brief gave her a warm glow inside even as it reminded her why she must fix on that false smile and refuse to give in to the cheeriness of the town.

Not that she ever saw any of the team come or go, and hoped the same was true for the rest of Sulwith.

A stack of chips, waiting to tumble down on them all. That's all Sol Winter's bright promises for the town amounted to. It rang too hollow for her: both the Old Man's brash assurance that the field would continue unchanged, despite the realities of a changing world she could no longer ignore, and Ethan Winter's empty glimpses of an alternative future, stolen away by his father as soon as offered.

After another fitful night of tossing and turning, of trying to sleep in a makeshift bed that wasn't hers, in a house where she no longer belonged, she woke to a com alert.

"A union meeting today? I didn't schedule one."

And now you're talking to yourself, and to every sensor rigged in this room.

She stopped talking but couldn't stop thinking. Any union member had the right to call a meeting as long as they could get enough other members to back them. She had no choice but to go, though a big chunk of her wished she could dismiss the whole thing and stay hidden in her room.

A meeting called urgently and in ridiculous haste. By whom?

She studied the link. Nothing unusual about it, nothing to distinguish it from any other meeting notification. A notice properly sent out by Marget on behalf of union management.

Except that, right now, she was the union management in Sulwith, and she knew she hadn't called any meeting.

She pulled out her best working outfit. Her war gear, her father called it. Softly tailored with the tunic subtly styled to magnify her height and give her a sense of gravitas, yet the shape and colours weren't different enough from the daily wear of her members to make her look out of place. The one in charge, that's what this tunic and trews said.

For good measure, she added the necklace her father had given her upon her graduation. A reminder to her members that she belonged here, and a confidence booster of her own. Then she added the ring her mother had given her. She glanced at the holo mirror. She looked like someone wearing protective armour. A frown, then a glance at her timer. It would have to do.

As she left the house, one of Ethan Winter's men slipped into place from wherever he'd secreted himself and strolled casually down the street beside her. No doubt the rest of his team were dotted about the town as well, but none of them could follow her into the meeting room. You had to be a full union member for that, unless Solaris security had succeeded in infiltrating there as well.

Or the Federal police? That was a distinct possibility. Dan had said Solaris was working with the Feds on this one. The thought eased her worry yet left her feeling like a traitor as she walked up to the union hall.

Guards stood on either side of the doorway. Union ones this time, men and women she'd known all her life. None smiled at her today and all of them stared at the newcomers shadowing her.

"A good day to you," she tried brightly.

A short grunt back. "They're waiting inside."

"Oh? Am I late?"

"No, Sera Sar, but the call went out to the other members for earlier."

For an insane moment, she thought of asking who'd decided on that. Then looked at the faces in front of her. Too uncomfortable and not yet fully decided about the side they were on, said the refusal to meet her gaze.

But a good way along toward it. "Thanks for the warning," she said dryly.

Inside the hall, a clatter of voices and movement filled the building. Then she walked through the inner doors and silence crashed down. She marched up the aisle to the front of the room, the silence deepening with every step she took.

This was her union, her members, and she was not giving them up without a fight.

At the front, she headed for her usual position at the centre of the head table. Marget sat to one side and a collection of newer faces clustered on the other.

One other man sat there, in her chair. "Ser Drocash. That is my seat." She moved in, crowding the man to make him stand up and give way.

He spread his feet against the floor and slapped his hands on the table. "Not for long."

Marget coughed awkwardly. "Ser Drocash has called this special meeting to announce his challenge for the position of Sulwith Union Representative."

Sar slowly turned to Marget, inclined her head, then let her gaze travel slowly over the room as she spoke in a voice set to carry clear to the back row. "That is his right. Union rules allow for such a challenge, but until the ballot is held—and if Ser Drocash wins—I am the duly elected union representative here. Ser Drocash, you will remove yourself, or do you no longer respect our rules and constitution?"

The silence in the room felt like a collective holding of breath. She had him, and the man knew it. Slowly, Drocash stood, jostling her as he noisily shoved back the chair and sauntered over to stand in the middle of his mob of supporters. All in-and-outers, and she didn't remember any of them taking up union membership. If only she dared challenge their right to be in the hall.

She took her seat, tapped the 'in session' code into her com, "Marget, please read out the agenda."

Marget rose, coughed and stared at the far wall. "There is only one item: a challenge by Ser Maxell Drocash for the position of union representative for the Sulwith Solar field. If the candidates would stand forward, the ballot links will be activated."

Sar tapped her gavel sensor link again. "You have forgotten a critical part of the required procedure, Marget. Before the ballot, both candidates must address the membership. Ser Drocash, as the challenger, is to go first, with me second as the incumbent. After that, there must be a time for taking questions from the floor."

Marget blushed bright red and a murmur rose from one corner. Sar stared them down. Berens did not give way without a fight, and certainly not to a no-good, bootlicker like Maxell Drocash.

"I have no dispute with that," the man said now. "As you say, it's procedure." A smirk at her, and he stepped forward to speak, standing right in front of Sar and blocking her view of the floor. All it did was show how little he understood the town or the members. She could see all the ones that mattered. Her friends, her union deputies. The workers she'd been there for when they needed it.

She plastered on a smile as Drocash opened his mouth.

"Fellow workers. Today, you are offered a simple choice. Full employment or poverty and homelessness."

It was a devastating opening and Sar had no idea how to counter it. He talked a bit more, announced he'd met personally with Sol Winter and gained a promise that no change would be made to Sulwith. Not while Sol Winter was in charge of Solaris. Which wouldn't be long if the man insisted on staying blind to reality, thought Sar. The rest descended into a mindless ramble of high-flown claims and muddled thinking that meant only one thing. Someone else had written that opening for him.

It made no difference. He'd caught them with it, and made sure to finish with it, stepping back with a smirk and waving Sar forward.

She stood, shifted her shoulders, set them back and shoved her head high, then plastered on the smile she'd been forcing for days. She looked at the faces of the audience again and saw a change. Faces wanting so badly to believe Drocash spoke truth but fearing otherwise, faces she knew well, men and women she'd talked with about family problems, negotiations for a wage extension, credits to cover the latest family emergency, faces of people who had little margin to survive any change. It's why she'd stood on that road the very first morning Ethan Winter arrived.

And now she planned to tell them they'd all been wrong? That Sulwith had to change and their jobs may not survive?

"Ser Drocash is possibly right … but only for today. What happens tomorrow and in your children's tomorrow? What he promises is a false hope. The Sulwith field uses outdated technology and is killing the land around it. The Federal government will not allow that to continue. More importantly, the planet Arcadia cannot continue if nothing changes."

They knew it for truth, squirming and shifting in their seats, but she hadn't won them. Behind her, Drocash's hulking offsiders sidled into place, no doubt staring down the crowd as they looked up at her. She turned around and glared at them.

"Stand back. You have no place here. I have the chair right now and you do not get to stand up here. Get back to the side aisles where you belong."

Strong words, but for too long she didn't think they would work. She'd grown up watching her mother stare down the predators of the Council, and these newcomers were nothing compared to them. Not for one moment did she let her stare falter and finally, finally, they stepped back a pace, glaring defiantly from the back of the stage. Did they really think she'd tolerate that?

"Not up here. Members have to earn their right to stand at the head of a meeting, and not a single one of you ever worked hard enough to earn your daily wages let alone the regard of Sulwith members. Get. Down."

Drocash rose beside her, that oily smile of bravado on his face. "They're with me."

She turned her glare at him. "Ser Drocash. Your speaking time is finished and you do not yet get to decide how a Sulwith meeting is run. These men have no place up here and will stand down. Now."

He tried to stare her down too. Again, it took far too long to beat him but, finally, a half shrug and he tipped his head to the men then sat back down. They dutifully traipsed back around the table to stand at the head of the crowd on his side of the hall. No one could miss them there, no one could avoid their scrutiny, but they were in the body of the crowd and the mood of the room gave her no more grounds to protest.

"Thank you," she said in her harshest voice. She faced forward, trying her hardest to look as if she were blind to the presence of the man sitting beside her, lolling back in his chair and twisting his face into a ridiculous sneer every time she made a point.

"The Sulwith Solar field must change; this town must change. Together, we can make an exciting future here, a future made up of many strands. Not just one string, solely dependent on Solaris. If you want a future, vote for me. Thank you."

She took her seat and the applause had a kind of rebellious heartiness. Not enough to give her faith. Not with Drocash sneering beside her and his thugs glaring out at the room. There were no questions from the floor and, at the end of the ballot, Marget refused to meet her eyes. The final result came as no surprise.

She was jobless, just like her father. Just like Ethan Winter.

An elbow shoved at her and a hand grabbed for the control panel in front of her. "That's mine."

Maxell Drocash shoved her out of her chair and she had to clutch at the table to stop herself falling. Next minute, a rock came flying toward her. It caught her on the cheek, a solid thud and a rocket of pain shot through her bones. A torrent of shouting below, and sudden silence immediately around her.

This was her home, these her people.

Yelling, too much movement, another obstacle flying toward her and this time she ducked.

A pair of arms grabbed her. She shoved at them.

"I'm a Fed. We're getting you out of here."

Maybe she was being an idiot again, but she believed the voice. She'd heard it before, talking to Dan. The man held her as a woman hurried to stand beside them.

"This way," said the woman.

Through the small door at the far side of the hall, down an alley way, twisting and turning at a flying run through streets she'd wandered since she was a baby.

Side streets, narrow passageways. In a doorway, down steps, into the basement.

"No, no. All these underground passages are monitored and controlled."

"Federal security has taken control of them, Sera. This is the safest way."

They grabbed her arms again and dragged her along. With no other choice, she forced her legs to run. Better than being carried blindly.

"Where are we going?" she gasped at one point.

"Urbis. Your gear is waiting for you."

"You took…?"

"Sera Carmal packed for us and your friends in town delivered it to a drop off point. We collected it from there."

"You are safe."

CHAPTER NINETEEN

Flying through the air over the desert west of Sulwith, Sar didn't feel safe. The man who had rescued her sat at the controls, and his woman colleague sat beside him. They'd flashed a set of Federal marshal IDs at her when they boarded the flyer hidden on the outskirts of town, but neither had said a word since. As if she was just cargo, a body to be delivered … somewhere. All the view screens were locked against her com.

She felt no better when they landed and she learned where. Urbis central. She stepped out onto a private landing pad with no marks, but the pattern of towers and discordant apartment blocks surrounding the pad was all too familiar. Nowhere else on Arcadia matched this jumble of buildings.

"Your family has been advised of your arrival," the woman from the Feds said.

"Oh. Thanks."

The woman gave her a kind smile. "We can give you a lift home if you'd like."

Sar wondered what would happen if she refused. Then mentally shrugged. "That's kind of you," she said, keeping up the pretence.

No more talk in the flight across the outer suburbs. She'd been poised for who knew what. How much on edge she'd been, she didn't realise until they landed outside the block housing senior Council officials. Her mother had lived in an apartment here since returning to the capital. Sar hurried gratefully toward the main entrance. Even better, her parents stood side by side in the residents' entrance way, as did a small squad of security staff, quick-marching into place as she approached. Her guides did something with their coms. Handing her over, she guessed bitterly, and the new squad moved to encircle her.

Her father had that tight look on his face.

"The Sera is safe," said her woman guardian to him. "Your family has been added to the Urbis patrol schedule."

What that meant, Sar hated to think. So did her father by the look on his face but he gave the woman a simple thank you.

That wasn't enough for her mother, of course. "Welcome home, Sar," she said with that huge hug of hers when separated from her family too long. Then she turned to the squad leader. "I expect a full report on my desk first thing in the morning, with a complete summary of the risks to my family: sources, level and type of risk. The lot."

"The representative will be forwarded all appropriate material," said the man in a too smooth voice.

"No, all material," said her mother, before sweeping Sar with her along the hallways and in through the door of their apartment, slamming a control lock on the door behind them. "Upstart marshals."

Then her mother stepped back, holding Sar by both arms and scrutinising her. Sar felt like a first schooler again. "I'm fine, Mama. Don't worry about the marshals. If they have any security concerns about me, they can tell me directly."

She needn't have bothered. Her mother listened no more than ever. Sometimes Sar felt like a changeling child, exhausted by the swirl of energy that encompassed everything around her mother. Taller than Sar, rich bronze hair burnished with a tinge of red, and with a face always in motion, her mother was a force to be reckoned with. One Sar had no desire to attempt controlling at the moment.

"Da?"

"Right here, Wennie." Sar swung around in relief and could have cried at the sight of that round face smiling at her. She threw herself at him, burying her tears in her father's welcoming shoulder. "They chucked me out, Da."

When she was reduced to an odd hiccup, her father gave her a last hug, then stepped back and studied her face. "Sit down here and tell us the whole story." A sharp glance at her mother and a raised hand. "No, Catra, you may not interrogate her. Sar is quite capable of telling us all we need to know without you browbeating her."

"I do not browbeat my children, Rhyn Beren."

"No, love. That's what you do to opponents in the House—and this is not the House chamber."

A taut silence, but Sar wasn't surprised when her mother scowled, then put out a hand to touch her cheek. "In your own time, Wenna."

At first the words came hard. The tears hovered too closely. Then the dam burst and a long time later she discovered the dam had emptied and her parents sat either side of her, holding her hands.

"These security troops. They're still with you?" Her father, practical as always.

She nodded. "Outside. They don't talk much."

A grim smile from her mother. "They never do." She lifted her com as an official message alert came through, reading it with a tightening mouth. "Especially not that section."

Her father's hand squeezed hers. "Which one?"

Mama shook her head. "Not for public knowledge, not even to you, Rhyn. Sar is safe, of that you can be sure."

A hammer thumped Sar's heart. "I'm the focus of a top-rated security patrol you can't talk about?"

Mama had a very set frown on her face. "They told me only because it's family and my own security have been looped in on a need-to-know basis." She drew in a deep breath. "What have you been doing down there in Sulwith? Union matters don't usually get this kind of attention."

"And the Winter family's not the kind to let outsiders anywhere near the top of the management tree, yet the Old Man sacked Ethan Winter," said her father.

"There's still the youngest son," her mother pointed out.

Sar shook her head. "I've met him. He's not interested, nor does he love the company. Not like Eth— Ser Ethan." Sar shifted on her seat. A hollow emptiness lay where the tears had been and she had no idea what to put in their place.

"So what now?" said her father, picking up her mood.

Her mother patted her hand. "She'll be coming back to work with me of course. She'll be safe there; the security in the House is second to none." A beaming smile of satisfaction lit her face. Her mother liked nothing so much as solving a problem. "It'll be like old times in the union, but even more fun. You're a first-rate organiser, dear, and my staff will welcome you in."

Sar couldn't think of a single, rational reason to refuse. Lots of emotional ones, but rational? No, not one. She plastered on her trained smile and thanked her mother.

Her father wasn't as easily fooled. "Are you sure that's what you want, Wennie?"

"Mama is right. It's a secure workplace with interesting work." Also, she suddenly realised, a good place to start looking for who was behind all the threats, but that was not for her parents to know.

A deep gouge tracked across her father's brow. She leaned into him. "I'll be fine, Da." She gave a short shake to throw off her worries. "What about you? What have you been up to in this big old monster of a town?"

His hand still held hers but he gave a nod of acceptance, then a flicker of a smile. "Offers are coming in fast, much to my surprise. With Caleb Winter's Survey on top of the list. They seem to think I know something about improving the efficiency of solar fields."

"You're good at what you do," said her mother. "I've always told you that."

"Yes, love, you have." Her father chuckled and reached across Sar to touch his wife's face with the gentle smile he reserved for her alone. "I was happy in Sulwith, and now I'll be happy here. Though maybe not with the Survey," he added in a wry voice. "The Department of Energy wants to see me. They sound a less controversial solution."

"What about Ari and Finn? Are they included in the offers?"

He mother turned sharply. "Why would they be?"

Her father tapped her hand in warning. The family had always played down Ari and Finn's work for Solaris with their mother. "They're both in good schools and working with the Urbis Higher Schools board in areas that interest them."

"And the Winters?" she asked.

"Are making no comment, as usual."

"That family is a law to themselves," huffed her mother, but Sar breathed a sigh of relief.

"Everything sounds like it's working out then," she said. Maybe too brightly, but her father only raised an eyebrow, and her mother smiled in satisfaction. Solve the immediate problem and move on to the next was her mother's way.

"Time for dinner," said Da quickly before she changed her mind.

Sar avoided any talk of the Winter sons all through the evening of shared family laughter. She watched her brothers and sister closely but was relieved to see they appeared to have accepted the sudden change to their lives, telling her all about their new schools and the new friends they were making with only the occasional wistful word of their Sulwith life. Or maybe their father had told them what they could and couldn't talk about before she arrived, in case they upset her. That she would believe. Ari did grump about Sar's failure to bring any messages from all her old schoolmates in Sulwith, but since her sister was still clearly in daily links with all her friends, new and old, Sar refused to feel guilty.

The next few days passed smoothly enough. Her father got the promised job, and Sar moved into her mother's office in the House building, picking up the same tasks she'd done for years when her mother was the union representative. New building, new systems and new chains of influence, but the rules were the same and so was the work. After the first few frantic days, she slipped easily into the groove of it. She could do the job in her sleep.

A job that held too little of her thoughts, gave too little distraction from fear and worry, making it harder each morning to plaster on her work smile. Da would look at her with a crease around his eyes some mornings. Luckily, the rest of the family were too busy racing out the door, and Mama was too filled with joy at having her family back around her and consumed with whatever latest campaign had caught her spirit to notice anything amiss.

The days began to merge into one. She'd come full cycle, back to being an add-on to her mother. Was this to be all her life came to?

She took to walking between appointments. The streets of Urbis echoed with discordant life, but the cacophony of street vendors shouting, shoppers jostling for a supposed bargain, street vendors hustling for sales, and tired workers elbowing for room in the transit cabs gave her a window to normality. None of these people cared for her worries, not one would stop their frantic rush through their own lives to ask what caused the pale bags under her eyes or the gritty tension keeping her shoulders tight.

You lost your job? Join the queue, Sera. Want to buy something to ease the pain, take you out of your troubles? On special, this week only.

One day, after the latest hustler had shoved a promise of nirvana under her nose and tried to get her to buy, buy, Sar stared at the young girl in front of her, and burst out laughing.

"You should be in school."

It stopped the spiel at least. "Should not," said the urchin.

Hair roughly chopped and tied up in a ramshackle braid, clothes that had last been cleaned in some other era, and eyes bright with too much knowledge for a child, the girl thrust her hands on her hips and glared at Sar, sending a bubble of mirth rippling through her jaded nerves.

"How old are you."

"Legal."

Legally old enough to leave school? Sar doubted it but could only grin at the audacious claim. This sprite was too free minded to be locked down by any school system.

"You want to buy or not, Sera."

"Not, sorry little Sera. But let me give you a credit for your lunch."

The girl's chin thrust forward. "I don't need no charity."

"No, I'm sure you don't, but take it anyway," said Sar. The girl grumbled, for show Sar suspected, then grabbed at the credit link offered. Next minute, she disappeared from sight leaving Sar shaking her head in bemusement.

No one would get the better of that one.

Unlike you?

Suddenly the laughter in her head stilled as the truth of it hit her. She'd let them win. Had let them put her right back to childhood. That little sprat of a street vendor had shoved herself into adulthood while Sar was being shrunk backward.

By her Mama, her family, herself. All guilty.

Not as guilty as those behind it all. From manipulating her sister into making the beam that crashed Ethan Winter's flyer through to using Drocash and her own union members to have her replaced. It was all too much of a pattern to be anything other than a concerted campaign of attack.

By whom, and for what purpose?

She suddenly wheeled around and changed direction. Across the street, a glimpse of a body swiftly mirroring her steps. Her latest security tail, as much a part of her life now as all the other idiocies. Trackers watched all her movements by remote sensor. When it got bad, she clung to the knowledge she wasn't alone in this. One other person hunted those set against her. Where was Ethan Winter now, she wondered yet again. The question haunted her days.

A gust of wind and a slurry of rubbish lurched up the street wall. She stepped to one side to avoid a puddle of something odorous, heard shouts and harsh words, a meaningless strand in the babble of humanity surrounding her.

Then she bumped into a large body and smelled a mix of stale drink, worn out furniture and a tantalising hint of something familiar. She looked up.

And up. Into eyes she would never forget.

"Ethan."

"Sarwenna."

His eyes were rimmed red and his hair hung limply around his ears, longer than the carefully groomed style she was used to.

"You're in Urbis," he said.

"Yes." A pause. "You heard?"

"That you lost your job? Yes, I heard."

"You lost yours too."

She flushed, hating this stupid trading of inanities, then took in the rest of him, eyes tracking up from splashed boots to torn leggings, up to a tunic from the best retailers in the city ruined by stains new and old, and up farther to his face and watched in horror as a red tide of embarrassment washed up his neck. From across the streetwalk, a bevy of catcalls ricocheted from a gaggle of rich young men, laughing at Ethan and jeering at her.

She went to step backward and his hand shot out to stop her. She stared down at it and tugged back. "Your friends are waiting for you."

"No... Yes. It's not what it looks like."

"No?"

"No."

He released her and she stepped back.

"Please," said Ethan. "Can we meet? Somewhere private?"

A shake of her head. She was beyond saying the words to refuse him. He looked so different. His clothes still as expensive but skewed and creased. A man who'd spent an evening drinking and gambling away the pleasure hours.

"I need to go."

"Tomorrow morning. In the park. I'll be waiting for you."

She shook her head.

"I'll still be there," he said.

She twisted away, dropping her head, and scurried down the street, desperate to leave, to get away from the wreck of the man she'd once known before she did something stupid like cry or try to save him.

The man she'd thought…

Now, she was truly alone.

Ethan watched her go, watched her running from him, and silently muttered every curse he knew. He had to let her go, had to shrug as if untroubled, and amble back across the walkway to his so-called friends.

He would be at that park tomorrow, and all the days after.

On the first tomorrow, he hurried to the park with hope in his heart. By the fifth, he walked slowly toward the gate then stopped dead to scan the grounds. What had he expected? She'd seen him at his worst and he'd couldn't change that. Not until he'd found out who lay behind the threat to anyone close to him, including Sarwenna Beren and her family.

On the eighth day he met Cumchdach in their usual hideaway after yet another fruitless visit to the park. The dark bar hidden far from the fashionable streets Ethan currently favoured was a place well known for the exchange of illicit drugs and the like. A place where the patrons minded their own business and careless talk came with a high price. A perfect cover for meetings.

The eldest and most sensible of the den Coille brothers leaned close and cupped his hand around his mug of ale, ignoring the grime on the table and the reek etched into every seat cover and bartender's breath.

"Any breakthrough?"

"Nothing," said Ethan, still filled with the disappointment of that empty park. "No news," he hastily amended. "Possible leads, but nothing definite yet. Seolta?"

Cumchdach scowled. The only den Coille brother still talking to him, Cumchdach was as worried about his younger brother as Ethan was about Sarwenna.

"He's involved," said Ethan flatly.

Cumchdach jerked back, then sighed and took a deep draught, placing it carefully on the table before looking up with a brief nod. "He's too angry and too sharp-witted for his own good."

The second of the den Coille brothers had a brain that could twist knots around the most cunning of opponents and had taken prison hard. "He's angry enough, but why target Solaris?" Or me? Ethan and Seolta had never been easy with each other but Ethan hadn't expected he'd stoop to this kind of dangerous game.

"He wouldn't have been involved in any of the attacks on you. Don't ask me to believe that. Someone's conned him into it."

"Seolta?" Ethan raised his brows.

Cumchdach growled. "He's not infallible. Sometimes all his scheming trips up my too-clever-by-half little brother."

"Maybe. Who's he talking to these days?"

"In front of me?"

A stupid question. "All right. Anyone new trying to make deals with Den Coille?" He had a thought. "The old Survey bosses. What are they up to?"

"Serving out their time on the far most islands of the sub-Antarctic chain. Where they've been since their trial."

"And better stay for many years," said Ethan, lifting his mug to toast the defeat of their old enemies. "What about associates? Do you really think they worked alone?"

"Did other corporates actively support them, you mean? Possible. Even likely," agreed Cumchdach. They'd talked about it a few times in prison, but none of their lists of suspects made sense, then or now. "Ask your brother to look at the head office files from the time. I know the legals are all over them, but he's supposed to be a hero there now."

"That's one name for it." Having already got rid of one lot of crooked managers, the current, government-appointed Survey heads tended to treat his brother with a level of care that sickened Ethan. Caleb too, for that matter. The only reason Ethan could treat it as amusing rather than a threat. "I've already asked him to find out what he can. What about the other federal departments? If the Survey heads went bad, what's to stop others?"

"Yeah, wouldn't that be an interesting twist?"

"Wishful thinking?"

Cumchdach gave a grunt. "Better than being someone we went to school with, someone we've traded with or competed against."

Someone like us, he meant. Ethan heard it in the dry voice.

"Turning a profit doesn't make you evil."

Cumchdach gave that deep-chested laugh of his and clapped a hand on Ethan's shoulder. "So you keep telling me. Can't think why you and Seolta are always at odds."

"And why you didn't go into medicine like your mother is beyond me."

"The hours," said Cumchdach with another chuckle. "You try growing up with a mother who thinks working through the night is normal."

It was an old joke between them. Seolta was the true heir to his father's brain, but it was Cumchdach the company people looked to. Strong, staunch, dependable. A man you could trust. A man Ethan trusted.

"Check the lists again. Add my possibles," he reached over to touch his com to Cumchdach's to securely transfer the file, "then sync it with any known contacts of Seolta's."

"You think I haven't tried that already?"

"You're his brother. He's not going to tell you everything he gets up to."

"And he would you?"

"No, but my staff have watched him for years. Ever since your delightful brother filched a prime investment off me. Bought it from right under my agent."

A big mouthed grin momentarily lit up his friend's face. "That's my brother." Then it disappeared. "Watch yourself, Ethan. If they can fool Seolta, they're not stupid, and not worried about whom they hurt."

"I have good security."

"Solaris," scoffed Cumchdach.

"Yes, Winter Solaris, and they've been with me for years. They're loyal and paid by the Winters, not by Solaris."

"Your father's not innocent."

"In this, no, but family comes first with him. It's why he sacked me."

Cumchdach's mouth twisted but he said nothing. Ethan knew his opinion on that, but he also knew his father. Sol Winter had been protecting his family, from others and from themselves, since the day Caleb was born, and Ethan had to believe nothing had changed. If even that were no longer true...

"Send me the final list," said Ethan and got up to go.

Cumchdach was as good as his word. The list arrived the next morning on a circuitous link thread. When he tried, Cumchdach could be as devious as his brother at avoiding surveillance. Ethan scanned the length of it, trying to find any clue, any hint of a common thread.

He recognised too many names. He'd grown up with the children of these families, had stayed nights at their homes and eaten dinners with these men and women. Now, someone on this list could be trying to get rid of him and his attempts to force change on their businesses.

Put aside those feelings. Go with the gut ones that tell you this man, this woman is dirty. This person's power is threatened. Which ones are hard enough, angry enough, arrogant enough to take action?

All of them, was his first reaction. He re-read the list.

At the end, he managed to winnow it down to a small list of potential suspects. Some he knew, the odd one he'd never heard of. He'd leave them until last, concentrating on the bigger corporations. Those with the heft and power to have something Sol Winter feared or wanted and that Seolta den Coille would think capable of successfully thwarting the government.

How to find out?

A few hours of pacing in his slick new apartment gave him no fresh ideas. He picked up a cushion, sat back in the too shiny seating bank, then threw the cushion at a fashionable artwork his interior decorator had told him was by the "the one to be seen owning now."

"Seen by whom," had been his immediate reaction.

The woman had waved her fashionably painted hand in the air. "People, of course."

He hadn't bothered asking which people. He'd already had to endure her stunned stare when he'd suggested the living area wouldn't do for some of his friends. Forget them, had said the curl of her lip. Those kind don't matter.

The small statuette of a man and woman touching cheeks, both immaculately tidy, toppled in place then crashed to the floor. Ethan viewed the mess and decided to leave it as it was. The cleaner bot would clear it up soon enough and, right now, the dusty pile of shattered pretentiousness cheered him no end. He considered hurling another cushion and gazed around the room for a target … then saw himself in the mirror.

Wild-eyed and idiotic, with hair dishevelled, drink in one hand and the new com list shimmering above the other. The kind of good-for-nothing waster he'd been imitating too often lately.

Sarwenna was right when she ran. This wasn't him.

He flung the cushion anyway but this time made sure it landed harmlessly against the far wall, propped askew on the polished tiles like a drunken sot.

No more. He dragged his hands through his hair, making a cursory effort to pull it into something resembling tidy. He failed, so moodily set the cleanser to the quickest cycle then changed into the kind of clothes he actually liked, called up a winter coat for the bitter streets of the town, and slammed out of the apartment.

He hit the upper level walkways, packed with after-work commuters all heading in the same direction or politely moving onto the opposite flow path. Orderly, constrained, clogged tight with well behaved citizens. He grabbed at the next downshaft and floated down to street level. A more honest level, safe from the predations of the upper-levellers he'd been useless at trying to cultivate. Safer from surveillance too.

Slipping in and out of bars and shopfronts, up another walkway, down to street level again, march and repeat, until he came to a destination, thinking furiously all the way.

What to do? What path to take?

He looked up and wasn't surprised at where his feet had brought him. The park where he'd asked Sarwenna Beren to meet him. It was now afternoon, and he'd asked her to meet him in the morning.

Maybe it was a sign. He laughed at his unkillable optimism, squared his shoulders and glared at the park gates.

One more time. Then he'd leave and put all thought of her aside. If he could.

He walked through the gateway and down the path to the dry zone. The part that resembled home. It smelled wrong, the light was wrong and the shape of it not right, but it looked like home. He stopped and put out a hand to the nearest tuft of coarse brown grasses stubbornly thriving in the coarse gritty soil they'd given it.

Yes, that felt right too. A plant as out of place as he was.

What had made him think she would come? After what he'd done to her and to everyone she cared about in Sulwith. He swung around to leave.

"Ethan?"

A voice he would never forget. He turned back as a woman half rose from a nearby bench. He hadn't seen her, not in the shade cast by the bushes behind the bench. Her dark hair, the dull clothes she wore, her silence all merged into the shrubbery.

"Sarwenna," he breathed. "You came."

She sat back and huddled deeper into her overcloak. It was early spring in Urbis but that was colder than mid-winter in her desert home. He started removing his coat.

She put out a hand. "No, please, I'm warm enough. It's not the cold."

"You're not scared of me?" Please don't let that be it.

A short shake of her head and he breathed again. "Not you." Silence. "Everything else? Yes, maybe."

Silence again. He stayed where he was as if fearful of spooking her. Then she inched along the bench toward him. A fraction closer. He sat down before she could change her mind, breathing in the luscious perfume of her.

"How are you?" Bland, stupid, ordinary enough to be inoffensive?

"I'm working with my mother," she said, "but you know that already."

"Yes." No point hiding it. "My people... Are they a problem?"

She shook her head. "More a reminder."

Guilt hit him. "If you hadn't..."

"What, let you take me up to find Geordie that first day? Let you talk to me? I'm the one who stood up in front of our road blockage that day, who wasn't moving until you'd listened to me. Our meeting was unavoidable. And..."

His heart nearly stopped. She looked across, meeting his eyes for the first time.

"And," she said, "I don't regret meeting you."

His heart thumped once, twice, then began beating again. "Thank you."

He drew in a breath and gathered his courage. "I know your mother has Federal security covering her, but please let my team..."

"Her guards know your people are covering me," she broke in. "Do you mind?"

That their security shared information, he meant. The flick of her eyes said she understood and the fleeting smile had him breathing again. "Your Dan and I, we understand each other well enough. They tell Mama's Feds what's needed."

"Your mother?"

"Possibly. Some. What the Feds think she needs to know, is my guess."

"Which is…"

Another quirk of those enticing lips. "No point waking a sleeping whirligig unless you have to, my father used to say of Mama. Her security team thinks the same." She shifted again, moving fractionally closer. "And you? What are you up to here?"

He watched in fascination as a deep breath lifted her chest. A chuckle and she rapped him on the wrist, jerking his head back to meet a pair of sparkling eyes. "Ser Winter!"

"Ethan," he reminded her. "Just Ethan."

A quick dip of her head. "Ethan," she agreed. "You know what I do, where I go, who I see."

"Only what affects your safety," he hastily assured her.

"Yet I know nothing of you, and don't tell me all you're doing in Urbis is partying. That's not you."

For a split moment, he considered keeping her safely in the dark. Then discarded it. She was already in danger; she deserved to know the truth, and look how badly it had worked out last time he'd tried to keep her out of it. "I'm looking for someone," he said.

A frown creased her brow. Then it vanished as she pushed away from him. "You're making yourself bait for the people trying to sabotage the Sulwith field. The ones trying to kill you." Her eyes glared, pinpoint and dark.

She lifted an accusing finger and stabbed it at him. "You came close to being killed in prison. Don't argue. I used Mama's staff clearance and saw the execution orders. Now you want to risk it again."

"They're after you too."

She waved a hand at that. "I don't count, just someone who got in the way. It's you they're after."

"You do count, to me. Always." So much lay between them still, but that she could believe she didn't matter?

Her eyes widened in shock. "No."

"Yes. And I've made you a target as well. They think they can use you against me."

"Are they right?"

He took a deep breath, staring down at his hands twined together. Another breath, and he unlocked his hands and reached for hers. So different. His hands, softened after all the hours at a desk or holding a drink, and hers: small, bluntly cut nails and the sun baked skin of hands that had known real life. The hands of a woman not afraid to stand up to the spoiled son of a rich corporation.

"They are right, and for that I apologise. You shouldn't have to pay for my misguided feelings."

She rasped her hands out of his grasp and hugged herself tight. Now he'd made her hate him too.

"Misguided. You mean how dare a poor sap like me aim for the mighty Ethan Winter?"

He jerked his head up. "No, no." He reached for her hands again but she tucked them under her arms. He touched her arm and let out a breath when she allowed that at least. "That's not what I meant. You are worth so much more than I am." He was making a real mess of this. "I was the misguided one ... to think you would look twice at a man set on destroying your world."

She took another of those deep breaths that rendered him stupid, but this time he fixed his eyes on her face. What would she say?

"So there's no difference between us. You, the heir of Solaris-"

"Not anymore."

She lifted a hand, waving his words aside, then set both hands on her lap. He reached across and she let him rest one hand on hers. "The once and future heir of Solaris," she said firmly. "Your father isn't the kind to allow his company out of family control."

Not so long ago, he would have agreed with her.

"Whereas I? An ordinary union worker from a backlands, no-account town."

"The daughter of Rhyn and Catra Beren can never be ordinary or no-account. Even without your parents, you're not ordinary. You never will be. Not to me."

She blushed, a delightful tinge washing over her cheeks. "Thank you." Her fist clenched under his hand. "It changes nothing. Not to your family or friends."

Now it was his turn to feel the heat burning his cheeks. "Those men, the other day… They're not friends. Not true ones. I just … I need to make them believe they are, for now."

A gasp. "That's why…" Her hand waved over him, taking in the traces of a beard and hastily changed clothes. "You're trying to make them think…"

"That I'm a discarded rich boy sulking in the city? Yes."

"Is it working?"

He grimaced. "Not quickly enough," he heard himself admitting. He could tell this woman things so easily.

She snatched a breath, opened her mouth then shut it again. Then she pulled her hands out from their refuge and clasped them around his. "So what will you do instead?"

He saw the tightness in her face, the lower lip caught in her teeth, as if to stop herself saying something quite different. Something to stop him from his goal. To keep him from danger.

She had gathered her courage and given him her backing. The glow of it warmed the frozen core of him and the words rose easily as he leaned closer to her.

"As I see it, I've got two options. One: use my investments and lure the greedier corporate types in that way."

She opened her mouth again, then closed it with a snap. He had to grin.

"Use my non-Solaris investments, that is. I've dabbled for years. Making money is my hobby and my career. Enough to have them believing I can make them a fortune."

He couldn't believe he'd told her that, but she didn't back away. Maybe because it sounded too outrageous to be true, but her fingers relaxed in his and she gave him that gorgeous grin of hers. The one he hadn't seen for far too long.

"Always knew you loved credits more than people."

"Hey, not all people. Just most."

"Who are the honoured ones."

He grinned back at her. "Family of course, even that stone-headed father of mine. A few friends." She lifted a brow.

"The den Coilles?"

He nodded.

"Anyone else?"

Her head dipped, and he used his hand to gently cup her chin, lifting those dark eyes of hers to meet his. "There might be."

She pulled her chin from his grasp, and gave an exaggerated shrug, as if to say Who cares.

"One sitting not too far from me," he murmured. "One very prickly and stubborn Sera from the edge of the deadlands."

"Oh." That fascinating flush of pink again. Her head dipped and she stared at her hands. "You said you had a second option."

He frowned. One day, she would let him tease her. One day. He had to believe that. He eased away from her and continued in a matter of fact voice. "Keep doing the same as I've done since getting back to Urbis. Reminding the offspring of the corporate families I'm one of them and worm my way into their confidence."

"Make them believe you're no more than a spineless sap drowning in self-pity, you mean? No."

She went to draw back. He had no choice but to open his hands. But she stopped. He shut his hands again before she could change her mind.

"If it's the only way to find out who's after me? After us?" he said.

"It will destroy you. I grew up in a town where following news of your family was a necessity. You're known as the sensible one of the brothers, an upright man who knows business inside out. Not a man to let a temporary setback send you into a downward spiral." Her mouth tightened. "Winters don't give up. Isn't that what they say? You're a Winter through and through."

What could he say? "Stubborn and arrogant, is what our teachers at school use to say. I think it's built into the genes."

She said nothing but the look from her dark eyes said it all for her.

"Can it be you're worried about me?"

She glared but the corners of her mouth tugged upward. "Why would I be?"

"Because I lie wake at night thinking of what could happen to you," he said softly. "You should be safe at home, still fighting for your members, instead of—"

Two circles of red marred her cheeks and her mouth tightened. "What?"

"Forget it."

"My mother's lapdog. That's what you were going to say. It's true."

"You're not happy, and that hurts." He stopped, caught short by the admission. Her arms hugged her body, and that hurt too. He moved closer, pulling her into his side. For an instant she resisted and he held his breath. Then she let out a huff and burrowed into his side.

"You're so much more than your mother's errand girl. That union takeover—the lowlife who replaced you. He must have had something on your members."

"Jobs," she muttered from the depths of his chest. "Jobs and security for their families."

He used his arm to tug her closer. "For how long?"

He couldn't see her face but heard the bitter irony in her voice. "That's what I told them."

"You agree with me now?"

A slight movement of her head. A muffled sound that could have been a Yes. She squirmed against him and he reluctantly let her go. She moved to sit up, so he lifted his hand then settled his arms around her body as she leaned back into him. Letting her go completely was beyond him, and he prayed she wouldn't demand it. When her hip settled against his, he had to stifle a groan of relief and need. Then she turned up a face with a grim twist to her mouth.

"I read your report and did some research of my own. I saw what you saw when you flew over the field, and I listened to my father. The desert is winning. A few more years and it will overwhelm Sulwith."

He nodded agreement. "I came to Sulwith on a fact-finding mission. Caleb's been harping on about the effects of our solar fields for years, trying to get the old man to change. And we could have, years ago. Could have used more modern sheetings and branched out into support business types."

"So why didn't you push it through? You have power in the company."

"My father…" he began. "He taught me the business at his knee from as long ago as I can remember. He's sharp, can tell a profit-maker from a loss-maker within seconds of checking a proposal. And he's my father. He is Solaris."

She sat forward. "No, he's not. You said it yourself once. Solaris is also you and your brothers. It's the men and women I used to represent. It's my father, Geordie and Ari, and all the others who make the company a winner."

"Tell my father that."

"And you, what do you think now?"

How to make her understand? How to tell her what lay at the heart of him? "It's credit patterns, people, industries, technology. All of those. Circles upon circles, interlocking and constantly shifting."

Her mouth dropped open. "This is a business we're talking about."

He shrugged and went to turn away. Only Caleb had ever come close to understanding how he felt about Solaris. Then his brother had betrayed them. Ethan understood why, even came close to agreeing with his reasons, but it had hurt so badly at the time, and the effect of it remained.

A hand caught his chin and pulled his head back to face her. "I wasn't criticising you."

Simple words but they meant so much. Maybe she would understand. "I made a promise to save Solaris. Caleb is right about Arcadia. Business has to change, Solaris and Den Coille in this part of the world in particular, but that doesn't mean Solaris is finished."

"Why such big changes though? What the Council demands will destroy so many lives." She swallowed and looked down at her hands then up again with a frown. "I've read the reports and heard the basics. I understand about the desert expanding because of the killing off of all life under the blanket of the current solar sheets. That's our problem to solve. Yes, there are too many problems elsewhere as well. I get that. But it's up to the locals there to fix those problems." She fell silent, staring at the withering relicts of the desert in the garden surrounding them. Then her chin lifted and she turned back to him, eyes fixed intently on his.

"What I don't understand is what Sulwith's problems have to do with the rest of the plains, or the mountains, or the government way up in Urbis. They've never worried about places like the deadlands margins before."

Caleb had sat him down not long after his rescue from prison and taken him slowly, piece by piece, over the ecology of it all. He'd understood about half of it, but that had been enough to scare him silly. Now he must explain it to her and must get it right.

"As Caleb puts it, Sulwith is just part of a bigger picture. Changes like the increasing dryness and encroachment of the desert around Sulwith is happening all over the plains. At the same time, the den Coilles planted their festia trees all over the mountains. Festia pollen may be a brilliant source of food, but festia only thrive in wet, swampy conditions."

"Yeah, the mountains got cooler and wetter, while the plains got hotter and drier. I've seen the reports."

"When cold air rising over the mountains hits the hot air rising up from the plains, you get trouble: storms of a new magnitude on the western side of the mountains, more droughts, more dust storms and dying vegetation on the plains. Not that it bothered Solaris. Hotter, sunnier conditions only increased our profits."

A fleeting lift of her lips, then they straightened again. "I get that, or sort of get it. I know enough to read a weather report, but the finer details are lost on me. I still don't see what Sulwith has to do with the rest of the planet. The solar field is big, granted, but not planet-wide big."

"It's part of a pattern. At first, I thought it just another of Caleb's over-the-top blatherings. He gets very intense when talking about eco stuff. Then I met him for lunch in the Survey canteen one day. All around us, staff were talking about the latest disaster in their region." He paused, remembering the talk and the fear in that room, so strong you could almost touch it. "We've pushed this world too hard. Overfishing, excessive irrigation, clear-felling in one place and mono-cropping in another. It's destroying the balance of the world."

He glanced down at her. "That's how the den Coille's mother summed it up to Caleb once. And unless we restore the balance—and soon—the Alliance will do it for us."

She gaped. "You believe those stories. This is our home. The Alliance won't just destroy everything Arcadians have built here."

"They can and they will," he said grimly. "It seemed far-fetched when Caleb tried to tell me, but the local Alliance representative made a point of having a word just before I came to Sulwith. They're deadly serious. And they've done it before."

"Evacuated an entire planet? Forcibly moved millions off world?"

"When they broke Alliance rules and abused their worlds, yes. There are plenty of others out there hungry for a home planet like ours, once it's been allowed to recover."

She twisted out of his hold to turn and face him. "You think off-planet interests are behind this? Someone not from Arcadia is manipulating your father and Seolta den Coille?"

Unlikely, he had to admit, but could he discount it?

"You just want a way to exonerate your father."

"Have you met him?" Ethan heard himself asking.

"Yes." Her mouth clamped shut as if trying to gulp back her words. He opened his eyes and urged her to continue. She hitched her shoulders. "Your father thinks he owns the plains."

He had to smile at that. "He does, as far as he's concerned, and he's not about to lose a single grain of dirt to an outsider."

"Agreed, but what about taking a grain of someone else's lands to protect Solaris interests? He'd do it in a heartbeat." There wasn't a trace of a smile on her face.

His gut clenched. That was truth. He could come up with a power of alternatives, but none that rang as true. The widening of her eyes told him Sar thought the same. "Sell out Arcadia to protect his own interests?"

"After what the Survey and Fed troops did to him and his family, my father has precious little loyalty to Arcadia. Solaris and family: that's all he cares about now."

"He sacked you. Took away the one thing that mattered more than anything to you."

"More than my life?"

"You can't believe that. Why would he work with anyone who threatened the life of his son?"

"I haven't been attacked since coming here."

"No need," she said bitterly. "You're doing a good enough job without any help … and it's getting you nowhere."

"How do you know?"

"You'd have told me," she said simply, then shut her mouth in surprise. "Forget I said that."

He chuckled. "You're right though. Looks like it's going to be option one."

"The investment trap? No, too dangerous."

"Probably not as dangerous as option two. This way, I'm offering them the one thing they crave. Credits."

A sharp crease dug into both sides of her mouth. "And when they find out it's a trap? That there are no credits?"

"Ah, but there will be." That worried frown added a final topping to his newfound optimism. He liked plans, liked having a path to follow, and this one felt so tragging right. "Making credits is the one thing I'm good at."

She opened her mouth to protest and he chuckled.

"All right, the thing I'm best at. As for what else I can do…"

She blushed bright scarlet and he couldn't stop himself swooping in for a kiss. It had been so long since he'd tasted her lips, so long since he'd felt those arms of hers cling to him, her mouth open to him. He didn't want to let it end.

Heart-stopping moments later, her mouth lifted from his. "Not the only thing you're good at," she whispered, leaning her forehead on his, then set her mouth on his again.

Afterward, she snuggled into his side, her head tucked onto his chest and a warm glow of satisfaction blanketed him. Then she shattered it.

"What can I do to help?" she asked.

He sat abruptly upright, the terror of it slicing to shreds all his comfortable dreams. "Nothing. Absolutely nothing. You stay away from these bloodsuckers."

Her eyes sparked a warning. "This is my home world too."

"It's not safe."

"You have me well guarded."

"I'll get them to lock you up," he threatened, knowing it for an impossibility and wishing it weren't.

"You need me. Through my mother, I can call up Federal files not even your precious Caleb can access. The kind that record any interactions with off-planet companies and show which ones have been sticking their noses into Alliance affairs here."

"Don't, please."

The stubborn set of her chin put paid to that hope.

His arms tightened around her. "Then keep safe. Please."

A long, fraught moment.

"I'll try, and only if you make the same promise."

The words were hollow, his promise as empty as hers. "I'll try too," he said. When they parted soon after, he couldn't stop himself looking back, and found she'd done the same. Then she turned and disappeared around the curve of the path.

Would he see her again? With a curse, he turned and headed back to the filthy streets and his apartment. He still hadn't told her how he felt about her.

Nor could he, not when she was already intent on running headlong into danger. Tell her he loved her? Bind her to him and put her in even more danger by publicly showing how much she meant to him?

Yeah, not likely.

CHAPTER TWENTY

Sar took the long way home. She had too much to think about. Not least, that last kiss. She'd suspected for some time how she felt about Ethan Winter. There was a rightness in being with him, a feeling of sanctuary.

You don't need that. Not now. Not in the middle of this mess.

She walked most of the way home but slipped onto the transit paths for the last section, stepping into a foot bath first to clean off all signs of the dirt, sand and street level grime from her boots. The daughter of a Councillor did not cavort in lower level streets. Dan was on security duty today and gave her that knowing grin of his. She glared back.

"Not a word to the Feds. Not on this one."

"Got it covered already. Told them you were meeting the boss and it was Winter business only."

"They… You told them? And they stayed away?"

That amused spark lit up his eyes. "'Course not. They're not stupid. Your double is currently leading them on a fine chase and will switch with you next station up. You've been shopping, if you're asked."

She looked down at her clothes. Stained, dusty, and decidedly provincial. She'd been so caught up in surviving this place since her arrival.

"Exactly," said Dan. "Your packets are arriving home about now.

"No, I can't accept…"

"You can. Boss's compliments," a tilt quirked his mouth, "or would be if he wasn't half silly at the thought of scaring you off."

Sar had no idea what to say to that.

Dan chuckled then nudged her. "Station coming up. Take the second tier. Our girl will switch off in the crowd at changeover."

Sar nodded she'd understood. Just before the switch, as she prepared to step off the unit, he leaned forward to murmur in her ear.

"Good luck, Sera. We're all backing you."

He then disappeared into the crowd before she could say anything. He wouldn't go far, she knew. Not when he was on guard duty, and a big part of her wanted to seek him out and give him a piece of her mind. Luckily for him, that would put both of them at too much risk.

She grinned. Half silly was he?

The switch must have worked; she arrived home untroubled by any more attention.

"That you, Wennie?" called her father as she hurried down the hall to her room.

"Yes, just going to get out of these outdoor things," she called back, scurrying into her bedroom before her father could see any stray leaf or smudge of dirt still stuck to her. It made no difference. Her father lifted an eyebrow when she returned to the lounge shortly after and stared at her hair.

She'd used the quick cycle on the hairstyler and knew her hair showed no sign of her visit to the gardens.

"Nice walk?" Her father switched off his com and leaned back, studying her.

"Mm hmm."

He was laughing at her, and with good reason. She tugged at the skirt of her tunic. "Ari's on dinner duty. I've got some files to check for Mama. I'll talk to you later this evening," she said in as prim a voice as she could manage and fled, bundling into her office coat and hurrying out of the house again before her father could say anything.

She nearly escaped but still heard a quiet "keep safe" from her father before she disappeared onto the transit unit.

By the time she reached the main government house where her mother had her offices, she had recovered her poise enough to plaster on a serene gaze as she gave her credentials to the security guards at the door. Her own guards had infiltrated the building already, complete with the required and no-doubt-false credentials, and formed a diffuse shield around her, melding into the crowd of secretaries, hangers on, cleaners and assistants filling up the spacious hallways. She made her way through the famous foyer with its vaulted ceiling, arches and gracious wall murals and headed for the wing holding the Councillors' offices of her mother's party.

Mama's welcome consisted of a brief glance over her shoulder as she scrolled through her latest report. "Sar, you're back. I've got a pile of files to sort out and need you to contact those attending the meeting tomorrow for me."

Sar shoved back her shoulders. "Send me the list."

With relief, she shut the door of her sanctuary, a small room she'd been assigned in her mother's imposing suite of offices. It took about as long as she'd expected to work her way down the list and slot everybody into place for the next day's meetings. It was important, she supposed, though Sar couldn't see why.

Another step on her mother's pathway to power. Don't go there. She gave herself a hard mental shake to dislodge the guilt plummeting down on her. Her mother worked hard for those she supported. She had been voted in for a reason.

Yes, she gave her electorate what it wanted, but they gave her mother the life she craved, set right in the heart of what Mama referred to as "the heart, my darling, the beating heart of this world"—this sprawling and self-contained metropolis that assumed it owned the planet.

She so badly longed to be home again, back with the baking sands and howling winds of the deadlands margins. Right now, though, she'd take any place where the land was powerful enough to cut through human pretensions.

Finished, she sent the link on to her mother and walked quickly through to her office. As expected, her mother hadn't changed position, sitting behind her desk while multiple holo-images of her staff hovered around her.

She turned briefly to Sar then back to her current victim. "Schedule a meeting with the works board. The minor room and basic catering only. No point making them feel important. They'll start thinking we're going to cave in to their demands if we do."

Sar took the seat beside her mother's desk and waited for the spiel to finish. She leaned back in the seat and set her hands in her lap. After a while, as she'd expected, the calm stillness of it got to her mother. Mama snapped off the latest holo-link, closed down the outgoing phases of her com and turned with a frown on her lips.

"You got my list," said Sar.

"Yes, yes. You know that."

"I've checked your schedule for the rest of today. Nothing's top priority, but I did notice a query from the plains' business association. They're wanting to know your position on the bill coming up next week."

"The one about companies needing to file an outcome plan? We've told them the results are confidential. They know there is no risk of a leak. Not from the Council offices."

Sar lifted a shoulder. "Maybe."

"No maybe about it."

Sar uncrossed her palms. "They're nervous after what happened to Solaris and Den Coille."

Mama waved a hand in the air. "An aberration. We're on guard now."

True enough. No department heads would ever be allowed to run free again. Not when it put their Councillors at risk.

"I'd still like to check out why the corporates have become so nervy. Nothing has changed that we're aware of."

An annoyed crease marred Mama's forehead. "You're seeing problems where there aren't any."

"Maybe, but I'd still like to explore it further."

Her mother glanced at her com timer. "Do whatever you want. I've got a meeting coming up."

Sar breathed in relief. "This will only take a day or so. "

"Make sure that's all," said her mother, and switched back to her com links, having lost interest. Sar rose, hiding her inner smile without any difficulty. She'd been doing this for a long time. Then she walked out of the room, quietly closing the door behind her. It didn't stop her hearing Mama grilling another of her staff, passion rising and a decisive snap in her voice. She'd forgotten Sar's quest already.

She released her grin. "I'm heading down to the secured records room," she told her mother's front office assistant. "My mother can access my link but block all other calls to me. I may be a while, so don't worry Mama with my absence." At some point in the afternoon, her mother would realise Sar had gone. Her maternal instincts tended to flare up at inconvenient moments and her assistant was an old hand at running interference for Sar. "Tell her I'll be heading straight home from the records room, and I'll see her there tonight."

The man lifted a hand in acknowledgement. He and Sar had quickly formed a bond, slotting easily together to smooth the passage for her mother. A slight smile of understanding and he turned back to his com screen, leaving Sar to walk sedately out of the office, quelling an urge to add in a skip to her step. Too many vidcams in the hallways around here.

It was worse still in the tightly secured records room. She had to surrender her personal com tab at the entrance. The high security tab they handed her latched onto her wrist with a painful pinch. One size fits all, said the theory. She frowned at the platinum-coloured disc clinging to her inner wrist.

"It's aligned to your skin sensors and DNA," said the woman behind the desk. "You can still use your public com codes. It's linked into the public network on a feed-as-need link."

She didn't bother to ask the obvious. If this com could link in, surely someone outside could link back. Only a newbie would ask such a stupid question. The security on this disc surpassed anything on the planet. The very air in the room felt on guard, seeking out any risk to the priceless files accessed through this bunker room. She passed through one more airlock and into the records room to sit at her assigned station. The issued com automatically linked into the system and brought up a screen, one that reminded her again of the frightening level of tech used in here. So sharp, so vivid with a depth to it that made the data appear as if carved into the creamy stone of her table. She entered her authorisation and search reason, making sure it was generic enough to allow her to roam through the company records. She started slowly, bringing up endless lists of little value and correlations of news items with complaint filings from various corporates.

Hunting for the disaffected, the anxious, the overly fussy.

She left it at that for the first day, filing an analytical request and a broader search request, then walked carefully out of the room before it grew suspiciously late in the day.

It took her three days of precisely timed visits to the records room to get the lists she really wanted and to run the correlations. Another day after that to figure out a plausible cover for exporting the list she wanted to her own com, sending it through the Council-secured channels to her office com, hidden in a batch of other useless lists, then a couple of bounces to district servers and back via a triple loop to her personal com. Traceable if anyone became suspicious, but simple enough that it shouldn't arouse the system security alarm modes. That day, she returned the security disc with a gracious smile and rubbed at the red patch it left behind.

"I do hope the Councillor won't send me down here again soon," she grumbled to the man at the desk. "I hate wearing these high-sec discs."

He gave her a grin. "Regulations, Sera. You wouldn't believe the tech built into these little beauties."

She gave another rub and awarded him a small chuckle. "Thankfully knowing about such stuff is well above my pay grade."

A slight wave of her hand and she walked out, taking care to keep her pace to a weary trudge. More patience tore at her nerve endings as she walked back along the corridor and into her mother's rooms.

"You finished your project?" said Mama's assistant.

"Yes, thankfully. Has Mama asked for me?"

"Nothing I couldn't handle. Did you find what you wanted?"

"Good as I could. It should be enough to show up any trouble spots." She rolled her neck. "I'm off home now. A session in the gym and a long soak afterward. My muscles feel like they've knotted up from lack of use."

"Night, Sera."

Another hand lift and she was out the door, keeping carefully to that same end-of-day plod. Onto the transit paths and into the first unit, bound for her quarter of the City.

Then a switch at the first crowded station, a swivel back, more crossings and downslides to dive into the teeming anonymity of the street level.

She'd lost her security detail two stations back and finally came to a halt in a small sidewalk café, bustling with the hum of the afterwork crowd stopping for a drink and gossip on the way home. Dan must be furious. She tapped her com and lifted the silence mode.

As expected, an angry buzz sounded in her ear. She touched the disc to connect.

"Where are you?" The absolutely furious voice of Ethan Winter. "Dan said you gave him the slip a full half hour ago."

"Nice to hear from you too." She took a deep breath. "We need to meet."

By the look on his face, he was still fuming when he arrived at the deserted playground in a small suburban park. She grinned at the mud-splattered figure of Dan puffing at his heels, face red and glaring at her as angrily as Ethan Winter.

"Don't you ever give your guards the slip again," Ethan said as soon as he reached her. Then he hauled her up and brought his mouth down on hers.

Long moments later, he released her.

"Sands alive. Maybe I should get lost more often."

His hands tightened on her arms. "Don't you dare. Have you any idea the kinds of things I imagined you facing when Dan said he'd lost you."

She went to shrug, then the stark lines on his face made her think better of it. "Sorry. It was the quickest way to get you to meet me. Anything else, and you would have refused, in case you put me at risk," she added, mimicking his deeper voice and smooth top-school accent.

He groaned. "I'm trying to protect you."

"This is my fight too. If I want protection, I'll ask for it."

He growled at that. "I am not standing down your squad, and even if I did, the Feds would still follow you."

"I didn't ask you to. Being followed everywhere may not be much fun, but I do accept it's necessary. And knowing you're in the same boat makes me feel better," she added with a grin.

Luckily, Dan had chosen to merge back into the bushes. No doubt he'd give her his own dressing down later, but right now, she needed privacy. "Tell Dan this meeting is on a need-to-know basis," she said. "He's to keep out of my com feed."

"I tell him that and every Fed agent assigned to the both of us will be scouring your com feeds for weeks to come."

He was probably right. "Can you give me a banded personal link."

A wicked spark lit his eyes. "Give me your wrist and your mouth. Most Feds have to listen to more than their share of lovers talk. They'll do anything to avoid it."

She didn't object. There should be a law against this man's mouth.

A faint groan from the tree cover. She ignored Dan, as she should.

After a while, a soft whisper came through her com links.

"You have me here. What was so urgent," he murmured in a voice designed to make her forget everything.

She lifted her mouth slowly, staring with shocked heat into those startling green eyes. "A list. I have a list for you."

His hand grabbed hers, his mouth close to hers but the pressure of that hand gave the lie to the brush of his lips. "What list? And what did you do to get it?"

"Nothing I couldn't handle," she murmured back as softly, the clench of his hand a sudden drench of reality. "Give me your fingers."

He did, so quickly that she knew he hadn't given up on demanding every detail. She laid them over her com and clasped them close to set them moving in the pattern to activate a link between their coms. Then she set her com on his and sent through the list. A lover's link was said to be unhackable. She hoped it was true and held her breath.

No Dan, no galloping in of Federal agents. Either they couldn't break the link or they'd been fooled by those kisses.

Not surprising. There was nothing false in the movement of Ethan's lips and mouth. Her own still bore the tingle of their touch.

"I think we're safe," she murmured softly. "Check this out, see what you think. There is one small company that doesn't make sense." She had highlighted it in the upload, "Can you check whether it has any unusual connections?"

"Anything for you," he chuckled, a touch louder and leaning his forehead against hers. It was a ploy, a trick to fool the watchers. She didn't care, leaning closer and letting him bring her body to body, chest to chest, arms surrounding each and both. "Be careful. No more searches," he said into her ear.

"Tell me what's on that list. Then I'll consider it."

"You should come with a warning, Sera Sarwenna."

Another touch of those lips, and there was nothing of artifice in it. Slowly, his hands let her go.

"Please don't lose Dan and his colleagues again."

She looked into his eyes, saw the shadow from the fear of those lost moments. "Not unless it's important," she promised. "I need a way to contact you though."

He gave in slowly. Recognising defeat, an amused part of her guessed. A touch wrist to wrist, fleeting and easily missed. "I've input my personal code. It's known only by my parents and brothers."

"And now me."

"Yes, now you. To be used only if you're in trouble. This has to be goodbye, Sarwenna. It's too dangerous for you to be seen with me."

The last parting of hands and arms left her cold and untethered. He meant that goodbye, and she couldn't ignore him. Not if she had any care for him. It had to be this way, yet her body called for a different response.

"Keep safe," he said, and saved her the pain of being the one to walk away by twisting suddenly and marching up the street.

He disappeared from sight. Dan emerged from hiding and drifted past with a touch on her shoulder. "I've set a tracker on you,

Sera," said his voice in her com an instant later. A highly illegal device. An angry chill edged his voice. "Please don't make us use it."

She wished she could promise him that. On the way home, no guards were visible but she received a continuous stream of scoldings from Dan and every other squad member following her.

"It was necessary," she kept telling them. It made no difference. They didn't stop until she stepped inside her own door.

"You're home." Her father met her at the door, lines of relief clear on his face.

"What's happened?"

An enraged Ari erupted into the room. "It's all your fault. Everything's wrong here. All the school kids hate me."

Sar doubted it but knew better than to say any such thing. "Finish your homework then tell me what's the problem."

Ari merely glared at her and stomped out of the room. Next, Finn ran in, his little face tear splotched and red. "I hate Ari. It's all her fault we had to come to this stupid place." He flung himself at Sar. "I want to go back to my old school. They're all mean here."

Above his little head, her father looked on helplessly. "Leave it to me," she mouthed. "Mama?"

"Not home yet," he mouthed back. One blessing then. "but on her way," he added and her one vestige of hope was gone.

She picked Finn up and he curled his head into her shoulder. He was too heavy for her now, but she said nothing, carrying him through to the lounge and letting him curl up on her lap as he had when he was very young.

"Tell Sar all about it," she murmured.

It took a while and came out in pieces between hiccupping sobs and clinging hands.

"Da restored her com access?" prompted Sar to the first, fractured words, "and asked you to put a monitor on her links?"

Of course Ari tried to jump straight back into that banned com room. "The room still had an open invite for her?"

A grabbing of hands and a sobbed, "Yes."

Now that was a worry. Most rooms banned any underage minor following a com-link shut down by their family. Risking a charge of corrupting a minor was too much of a threat.

Why would the room's owners be so keen to hold onto Ari?

"And Ari blamed you when Da pulled her access again?"

"Da told me to do it."

"I know, I know," she said, rubbing his back in long, slow strokes. "And you were right to do it."

After that, she held him until he finally fell asleep. Her arm was numb and she passed him over thankfully to her father.

"He's getting so heavy," she whispered.

"I'm sorry you had to run damage control."

"It's all right, Da. We all forget he's still just a little boy."

"He can beat most students at Higher School when it comes to com programs, but…"

"He misses his friends."

Her father nodded. "Sulwith was small but they'd all grown up with Finn."

"He wasn't a curiosity there."

"No."

A sound at the outer door. Sar shooed her father off. Mama mustn't see her baby's face in the full light of the lounge. Off to bed with him where the lighting was dim.

A strained smile from her father as he carried the sleepy child to bed. Another beep from the entrance door alarm. Mama must have forgotten the door code again. Typical of the day.

She opened the door, and another boy hurled himself at her. Older than Ari, but a boy who should be safe home in bed.

"Geordie, what are you doing here?"

"Man doesn't want me. Patterns. Says I can't look after the patterns."

Sar's heart thumped down hard. "Come on in. We'll com your mother and let her know you're safe with us."

Geordie's face lit up. It took so little to make him happy again, and Sar felt like kicking someone. Starting with plant manager Ser idiot, Tom Crabster.

"She put me on the transit," he said.

That was something then. "And you made it from the station all the way here on your own. Well done."

"Ma told me what to do." Geordie's saving grace. Give him a set of instructions and he would follow them to the letter. His mother had been living with her son's need for independence for years and had long ago mastered the art of giving him the kind of precise blow-by-blow instructions that would make any systems programmer green with envy.

Sar put an arm around the lanky teenager and led him through to the kitchen, sending a quick com message through to her father. "You can choose," she told Geordie, setting the prepper controls in easy reach. His eyes lit up and he quickly dialled up the most disgusting combination of sweet sticky profol breads and a big sized plate of brothero. Rich red sauce over a fat and protein pile of nieten sausage and fried cadbo chips. She eyed his scrawny body and wondered where he put it all.

Her father came back once Finn fell asleep. "Geordie. Nice to see you."

Geordie barely glanced up from his feasting. Her Da was an old and trusted ally. He mouthed a grunt at Daff and Ari when they came down as well. Sar held her breath when Ari walked down the stairs. She shouldn't have worried. Geordie had been an unofficial family member since Ari was a baby.

"Hey Geordie," she said as if his arrival so many hours' flight time away from his home was no different than when he used to land up in their kitchen most afternoons.

A grunt back from Geordie between mouthfuls and Sar breathed a sigh of relief. Ari sent her a raised eyebrow in query with a head tilt at Geordie and Sar mouthed, "Later."

Another good sign. Despite whoever had their claws into Ari, she hadn't lost all sense of family. Hurting Geordie came high up on the Beren list of things never to do.

"Time for bed, Daff," she said, catching her brother's yawn.

"But, Sar. What about home? Geordie…"

"Will be here in the morning and you can ask him all about your Sulwith friends then."

"Aww."

"Enough. Bed. Now."

Daff gave in with a grumble, and she thanked the sands yet again for her normal and steady brother.

"Same to you Geordie," said her Da. "Finish your dinner and we can chat before you head off to bed."

"Sera Beren?" A worried note sharpened Geordie's voice. Their Mama had never understood Geordie's place in the family.

"Working late. You can say your hellos in the morning." Da patted Geordie's shoulder. "Relax. She'll be glad to see you're safe and sound."

Sar wasn't so sure, but Geordie uncurled again and attacked his plate. When he finally finished devouring enough food for a whole family, Da clapped him on the back. "Come on, let's get you settled for the night. The spare room made up, Sar?"

"Of course." She'd learned too many years ago that guests could arrive at any time in their household. She picked up the pack Geordie had carried in and opened it. Then grinned. "His mother packed for him."

"So she did know he was heading here. I sent off a com message to let her know he arrived safely."

Her Da led Geordie off to the family bathroom, chatting about Sulwith and the people they knew all the way. Sar tidied up the dinner things and held on tight to the tension coiling knots in her belly.

The grim frown on her father's face when he returned didn't help a bit.

"He's asleep already. Worn out, poor man."

"Did you find out…"

A fierce twist of Da's mouth, unlike his usual calm. "Oh, yes. I'd like to have Tom Crabster and Maxell Drocash in front of me right now so I could kick their sorry backsides down to the river and back."

"It's bad?"

"I ran the local 'cast channels to back up Geordie's version. We knew Crabster could ruin the field but the partnership with that Drocash creature is worse. Output has plummeted and they're blaming anyone who speaks out. Due to industrial problems, they've cut the pay and conditions down to a level unheard of. The best of the workers have already left. Can't afford to stay in Sulwith, they say. Casualty rates are rising badly too."

Sar gasped at that last bit. "Work conditions?"

"Yes. Increased hours until people are too tired to work safely and ridiculous lengths of exposure to heat and sun."

"Tom Crabster has lived in Sulwith for years. He knows better."

Da said nothing. Everyone knew about Crabster's secret dodges, but up till now the rest of the locals had been able to manage the effects of them. Even Crabster knew how far he could push it, and having the man front the Sulwith plant had saved Da from the bother of administration and higher company politics. Now people they knew, people who had trusted them, were paying for it.

"Solaris showing its true colours." Why Sar felt so betrayed, she couldn't say. She was the one who had abandoned the workers.

Her father slumped down in the seat next to her, shaking his head. "Not like them. Not like the company they used to be anyway."

Sar grunted and sprang up, unable to stay sitting a moment longer. "Things change."

"Maybe." He didn't sound convinced, but his fists still clamped down on his knees. "I'll ask around and see if there's any work for Geordie. He can't go back home. Not yet."

No. Sulwith was no home for Geordie. Not if he was barred from the field that was his reason for being. What else for him?

"Solaris," she spat again. Da had worked for the company for years, but Sar had sat across the desk from management too often. "The only reason they treated their workers well is because the union made them."

A slight tilt of Da's lips. It was an old argument between them. "Maybe."

Sar stalked around the room. "This is all so wrong." Geordie, Da, Ari. The heart of Sulwith solar. "How long has Tom Crabster been waiting to prove he can run the field without help."

"Oh, years I'd say."

"Stupid, pompous, greedy wannabe. Vicious too. What did Geordie ever do to him, or Ari, or Finn. Or you."

"Made him look irrelevant. Few like that," said her father dryly.

"Still no excuse for it." Tonight changed everything. Sar kicked at a seat, then paced across the room before throwing up her hands and coming to a stop in front of her father. "I need to see Ethan Winter."

CHAPTER TWENTY-ONE

"Display financials." Ethan watched his comscreen shimmer into view and frowned as he tracked down the figures. He looked at the man sitting opposite. "Doesn't look like much is happening for you."

"We just need capital."

Ethan had heard those words too often. Eager hopefuls keen to step onto the business ladder but too careless, too quixotic, too tragging entrepreneurial to bother with the hard slog required for a successful start-up.

"You need a lot more than capital," he told the man. "Come back to see me when you've got the groundwork in place. Right now…"

The man opened his mouth. A spiel was coming. Ethan shoved up a hand, plastered on the implacable smile he'd learned at his father's knee and gestured to his assistant to show the man out.

He heard her talking to him as he left. The man was wasting his energy, despite her occasional polite reply. Ethan didn't let junior assistants make business decisions for him. Not for the first time, he regretted the loss of Graffin, supercilious pomposity and all.

You miss Sarwenna, that's your problem.

His inner voice could take a holiday, preferably a permanent one. This was the way it had to be. He leaned back in his chair and swivelled to take in the view from this shiny new office of his. Close to the main river branch, down the slopes from the commerce district and taking in all the bustle, all the beauty and ugliness of this massive city. It was a view most would have envied him.

A pity all he wanted to see was waving grasslands or dry desert hills.

He owned the building too, had done for some time, but that wasn't something he shared. It was a handy place to impress the entrenched elite of Urbis. An apt façade for a man with credits behind him and a goal in front.

Except it wasn't a façade. He really did have those credits and the banks made him welcome in their plushest chambers. His current purpose, though … that, none guessed.

Keep as close to the truth as you can. That's what his father had taught him. Out there, someone thought they could use Solaris for their own ends. Someone so intent on stopping corporate concessions to the changing environment of Arcadia they were prepared to hurt the heir to one of the planet's biggest corporations.

Hurt? No, kill. And he was that heir until his father disowned him.

A bang on his outer door. His next appointment wasn't due yet. He stood, frowning, as his new assistant rushed into the room, ordering the door closed behind her.

"I told her you're not to be disturbed."

Another crash. Then the one woman he must never see again erupted into his shiny new office.

"That will be all, Sera Graciana."

His assistant spluttered something, but he gave her the look and she backed out, looking like a frightened ganda.

Sarwenna stopped just inside the door, head up and teeth clenched, eyes wide and dark, destroying all his well meant controls. He marched over and grabbed her arms, but she put up her hands and wrenched away from him, a bright flush marring her cheeks.

"What's happened. Who's hurt you?"

She crossed her arms over her chest. "You. Solaris. Do you know what your father's doing?"

"Running Solaris his own way, as usual."

"Yes, into the ground, taking my workers with him."

"You don't work for the union anymore," he said automatically.

"They're my people."

Idiot. Sarwenna Beren never gave up on anyone. Except you.

And so she should—if she's to stay safe.

He took a deep breath, wishing he could think of something other than his desperate need to hold her tight and feel her body against his. "Take a seat and explain. I don't work for Solaris now, remember."

"Born a Winter, always a Winter," she shot back, taking the chair across the desk from him.

Too true for him to deny. He couldn't give up on his company any more than she could stop caring for her workers. "What's happened?" he said again, forcing patience into his voice and walking back to his own chair when all he really wanted to do was tear the world apart for her.

"Your father has sacked Geordie MacTavie and any other worker who won't stand for his slashing of their pay and conditions."

"Slashing…? Solaris pays a fair wage." Or it always had. "Who told you this?"

"Geordie. He arrived on our doorstep last night."

"Geordie? The boy's half simple—"

"Is not. He sees things differently, that's all, and Da checked his story with his other contacts."

Ethan grabbed another breath. A mistake. All it brought him was a whisper of her unique perfume, a scent of the desert, of morning chill and the plants of the night. Of her.

She leaned over the desk. "Geordie loves the Sulwith field. It's all he knows, all he wants to know. And that bootlicking manager of yours took it away from him because he thinks he knows so much better how to run a solar plant."

"No, he doesn't." Ethan had met the Sulwith manager's type too often. A man who looked good in the part and said all the right things, but had no substance. Worse, from what Sarwenna had let slip, a man who looked after himself too much. "The Sulwith set-up worked. It's the only reason Crabster kept his job so long. Getting rid of your father was stupid enough."

"Yes, it was." She sat back again, hands clenching the chair arm.

"Tell me the full story."

For too long, he thought she'd refuse. Then she began to speak, scrupulously setting out what Geordie had told them and what they'd learned from their contacts in Sulwith.

The Old Man had taken leave of his senses. "What's production down by?"

"Thirty percent at present."

"And plummeting?

"Will be if he loses any more workers. At least, of the kind who know their jobs. Few enough of them are left and, from the sounds of the ones he's bringing in, other folks will be leaving Sulwith soon."

"Not safe?"

"Exactly."

This wasn't Solaris. His father couldn't know about this. Or if he did, why in all the deadlands let it happen. Sulwith was the biggest field in Solaris' battery. Lose production there and the Solaris credit balance was going to start squealing. He leaned forward, elbows on his slick new desk and chin in hand, thinking hard.

Only one answer came to him. "I'll have to see my father."

"I'm coming with you."

"Into Solaris territory? I don't think so."

"I'm not good enough to be seen with?"

She couldn't believe he'd think that. "Of course not."

"Then I'm coming."

He reached out a hand and took hold of hers. "Please." Begging was all he had left. He just wished it would work. Then he noticed the look in her eyes as his fingers rubbed against hers and hope flared. "What are you thinking?"

"That I wish you didn't look so good." Then she gasped, dragging her hand out of his. "How do you do that to me?"

He had to smile, though the twist of it hurt his heart. "I'd like nothing more than to haul you around this desk and show you exactly how much I've missed you … but you shouldn't have come. Where's your guard?"

"Outside in the streets. I asked them not to forewarn you."

"They didn't," he assured her. "After the last time … I told them to obey any orders from you, as long as they don't put you at risk. Warning me … I guess that came into the non-risk category." A bittersweet look washed over her face, matching the one in his gut.

"And yours?" she said instead.

"One on guard in the outer office. You wouldn't have seen him." he said. "I don't step foot anywhere without full live and electronic surveillance. Orders of my father."

"Aah." A sudden softening of her face. "So you do know how I feel."

"I wish I did," he murmured. "About so many things. But the guards? Yes, I know what it's like to never be alone."

She fell silent, as if waiting. For what, he had no idea.

"It would save Solaris and the Feds a pile of cash if we combined homes," he said with a forced grin. Then could have kicked himself at the flush on her face. He'd meant it as a joke. Or maybe his wayward tongue gave voice to what his body craved. "That was crass. I'm sorry."

She waved a hand aside. "Not at all. Not a bit." Disjointed mutterings that left him feeling more guilty. She clasped her hands together and shoved them into her lap. "This is not the time. We need to find out who's after you."

"Us. Your family are at risk too."

"All right. Us. Whatever. It's time we stopped them."

His heart jolted. "Stay out of it. I'm working on it."

The flush faded and she thrust that tough chin forward. "I was in that flyer with you when it crashed. They shot at me too, that day in the desert. And it's my sister being used, my workers losing their jobs."

"I'm making some good contacts here. Leave it to me," he begged.

"No," she said flatly.

He studied her face. Stiff and unbending. She was stubborn, his Sarwenna, and to reject that was to reject who she was. He grabbed onto what remained of his courage.

"All right."

Her brows flew up. "You agree?"

"Do I want to expose you to the risks that come with helping me? No, of course not. Do I think I can stop you haring off on your own if I refuse? No. You've got me in a corner, my brave Sarwenna."

Her face flushed and that twist of her mouth said she doubted it but she lifted her chin. "Give me all you know and I'll tell you anything you missed," she said, briskly matter-of-fact. "And I want your promise you'll do something about Sulwith."

He thought for a split instant about lying to her … then knew he couldn't, and not only because she'd probably see through him. He just couldn't, not to her. "That list of yours. I'm working down the more interesting contacts. I've forwarded it to Cumchdach den Coille as well."

A shocked gasp and she thrust up from her chair. He reached a hand to her. "Stop. Let me explain."

She subsided but sat on the edge of her seat, like a desert ganda ready to flee.

"The den Coille's are caught up in this too. Someone attacked Manascraoch. Probably because Bram den Coille's more open to change than the Old Man. He's started on the changes the Feds and the Survey demanded."

"Yes, we heard that even out in Sulwith."

"So Den Coille is a target too. Cumchdach had been looking into possible suspects. He's as worried about his family as you are your sister," he said deliberately, and waited.

Only a gasp gave her away. She stayed seated, so rigid she might have been glued to the chair.

"That beam? Has she admitted yet that she made it?" he said gently. I will not hurt you, he hoped his voice said. Not ever.

She perched right on the edge of the chair, hands clamped together as if seeking a lifeline, but made no denial. Nor did she answer directly. "Have you found anything in those lists I sent?" she said instead, staring belligerently back.

He should push it, make her tell him everything she knew, but all that would do was break the fragile link between them. He shook his head. "Nothing concrete. There's a few possibles. The strongest—that small company you highlighted in your list. The ownership of it seems genuine, but something doesn't fit. I need to meet them."

"I'll come with you."

"No." He shouted, fear filling him. "Not if there's any chance they're the ones causing trouble."

That strong jaw of hers thrust forward. "I'm coming."

"We haven't made an appointment with them yet," he tried.

"You don't need one. Why would Solaris or Den Coille chase a small-time outfit for business?"

"I'll make them come to us."

"What, do a credit squeeze on them? Use all the capital of Solaris and Den Coille against them?"

"Not exactly."

"Then what?"

Ethan took a breath. She already balked at the pull between them, already found Solaris an obstacle. Could he tell her the full truth?

Did he have a choice?

"The banks will put the squeeze on if I ask them to."

A flare of eyes and she leaned forward, finger pointing. "Because you're the heir to Solaris?"

"Not quite." Another deep breath. "I've dabbled in other interests for some years now."

"Yes, so you said the other day, but banks want real wealth, not a secondary reserve fund."

She sat rigid, listening, but that wariness was back.

"More than dabbled," he admitted. "Business. Credit patterns. They've always fascinated me. Playing the market is more than work for me. If you do it long enough, it's a game that pays for itself more than adequately."

Her eyes widened. "Are you telling me you don't need Solaris. That you're rich, even without it? And, Ethan Winter, think very carefully about your answer."

He sat up, sweaty hands hidden under the desk. "It's true. My credit balance is of an order… The banks are only too ready to help me."

"Richer than Solaris?"

He felt the ghost of a smile falter on his lips. "Not quite. I'm not about to buy it out and put my family on the streets, if that's what you're asking."

"Your father wouldn't sell," she said flatly.

"No, he wouldn't."

Her arms crept around her body again, hugging tightly, as if she had to hold herself in one piece. "How did I never hear about this? The union and Mama have tracked Solaris affairs for years."

"I run my personal investments through a double blind. It stops them affecting Solaris's credit ratings."

She dropped her head, stared at her boots.

Then sat back and looked up, straight at him. "Is that it? No hidden brothers in the woodwork, no hidden wife anywhere." A twist of her mouth with that last one.

"No wife, no other woman. How can I see another woman with you sitting there in front of me and all I want to do is to shove this desk from between us and everything that comes with it? But I can't do that. Not without risking you and everyone in this world."

Silence. A blank void that he didn't know how to fill. Nor did she, from her shocked face and wide, dark eyes. Then those arms, those bands of iron clinging tightly to her body, sudden released. She stood.

She was leaving him alone.

But no movement, no sudden swivelling to the door. "I have no answer to that," she said. "How I feel about you? I think it may match how you feel, but you kept secrets from me."

"And you haven't done the same? Your sister?"

Her hand reached for the desk, grabbed onto the edge of it. "I've already admitted she could be the one who designed the beam that downed your flyer. Do I have the kind of proof that you can take to the Feds?"

"I wouldn't," he put in swiftly. "She's a child being used by a lowlife traitor."

A swift drawing in of breath. "Thank you. For the record, I never thought you'd use it against her."

A bright wave of heat washed through him. Had he failed some test or just passed it? "She's safe, but there's a reason she is being guarded, and it's not only because she's your sister."

Her other hand reached out to grab hold of the desk as if to stop her from falling. "That ventilation malfunction? That's all it was. It has to be."

"I don't know. Nor does my security. They can't access your house systems."

A brittle laugh. "Finn has them under a shield. It was the first complex program he designed. He was so proud of it."

"One day, the Feds are going to love being told that a child beat them. They'll probably offer him a job, if he hasn't been courted by every systems corporation out there."

She sat down with a thump. "We really are in this together."

Not quite how he'd hoped to join with her. "Yes, my Sarwenna … which doesn't mean that I want you sticking your head into more danger than necessary."

Slowly, her hands let go their hold of his desk edge. "Tough," she said. "You need me. To start with, there's that small company on both our lists. Something doesn't make sense there, and if they're part of the group targeting my family, I have as much right as you to be involved. So, ideas, Ser Ethan."

No chance. He would not expose her to danger, no matter how unfair. He couldn't.

A bustle near the door. Voices in the outer office.

His new assistant: "He's with someone."

"Don't worry, he'll see me," said a deep, male voice he knew too well.

The pair burst into the room and a rare grin erupted on his new visitor's face.

"Brilliant timing as usual, Cumchdach," said Ethan dryly.

All he got back was that mad grin from the supposedly sensible eldest den Coille son along with a perfectly executed mountain bow for Sarwenna.

"Introduce me, Ethan," demanded the man he'd thought a friend.

There was no way out of it. Not after that sharp-eyed look from Sarwenna.

"Sera Sarwenna, let me present Cumchdach den Coille. Cumchdach, Sera Sarwenna Beren."

"Ethan. Proper names please." Another of those precise mountain bows. "Cumchdach mar Bram an Scathach den Coille, at your pleasure, Sera. A gentle day to you."

Sarwenna stood, mouth agape, then hastily shut it and gave an abbreviated nod back. Deadlands folk were not known for their formalities. Ethan felt his own grin form.

"The Sera is here to discuss union business. Solaris business. How about we meet up later. I'm sure your business can wait."

Ethan should have known better than to try. "It can't," said Cumchdach at his bluntest. "And you don't work for Solaris now, nor does Sera Beren for the union from all I hear."

He pulled up a seat, bringing it close to the desk and sitting down, legs sprawled and making himself at home. "This is important."

Ethan tried shaking his head frantically. Sarwenna was too involved already. He didn't need her caught in the den Coille side of the mess as well.

A wave of Cumchdach's hand. "Not that. Far more important." A hand smacked down on the desk. "You haven't replied to your invitation. Are you coming to my wedding or not?"

CHAPTER TWENTY-TWO

Sar stared at the man dominating the other side of the desk. She hadn't met a den Coille before but had heard enough about them. Standing not much above her height, the man sat square on his chair, brown hair, dark eyes and skin clear of the traces of sun and wind that marked those of the plains and desert. He looked to be some years older than Ethan, yet she could see why they had become friends. There was a steadiness about both of them. Staunch, solid. The kind of men who would take responsibility seriously and whose word once given would be inviolate.

Men you could trust.

It didn't mean she was about to risk her family's safety. She shut her mouth firmly and watched Ethan scrabble for an answer.

"You did get the invite?" demanded the den Coille Ser.

"Yes, I think so. It's somewhere in my com log."

"Somewhere… It's in two days' time."

Then the man leaned forward, eyes sharp and mouth grim. "You're not coming."

A sigh from Ethan. A frown and his mouth twisted. "How can I, Cumber? You heard your father."

"A wedding is different. Mountain law prevails, as you well know."

She must have made a sound. Both men whipped their heads around, and she blushed. "Mountain law?" she said to cover the awkward moment and wished she was anywhere but here.

The mountain man glanced at her. "A wedding is family first, business second."

"Not yours," put in Ethan.

A shrug from the older man. "It's good for business, but mountain law still puts family first. Wedding guests and host alike are required to set aside any hostilities. A hangover from the days when marriages were as much political alliances as love matches," he said to her. "A good wedding healed many a dispute. But those days are past. We marry for other reasons now."

"Does Anna know that?" Ethan said.

A sudden frown from the mountain man. "She will, one day. I hope." And Sar had to wonder at the pain in his voice but dared not ask.

"Are you sure about this, Cumber?" said Ethan.

"It's time. We're not getting any younger."

"You could find someone else."

"She's been my best friend since first school. There is no one else, not for me."

Ethan fell silent and Sar eased back in her chair. Thankfully, both men appeared to have forgotten her.

"Please, Eshta. It's important to me. My father has given his word you'll be safe. You know you have mine."

Sar gasped. "Safe?" She'd thought from the way they talked these two were friends. But the den Coilles had been the main rivals to the Winters for financial supremacy on the central part of the continent as long as she could remember. "I thought your families were allies now."

"There was a … misunderstanding last time he visited Manascraoch," Cumchdach den Coille said.

"That's one way of putting it. Your father warned me not to return."

"Nor should you, except for this."

"And your family? Your brothers?" Ethan said.

"Will all welcome you."

Why the sudden tension, wondered Sar. She swung on Ethan. "More secrets?"

He flushed and his friend raised his brows. "It's nothing," said Ethan.

Yeah, nothing. And she'd been stupid enough to think there just might be something between her and Ethan Winter. She thrust up from the chair. Time to get out of here. She swung round to head for the door.

A rush of movement from behind the desk and next moment, a hand caught hold of her elbow. Not hard, but unbreakably firm. She turned around to push him away. "How can I trust you, Ser Winter? Whatever you claim to feel for me, it's a sham." She tugged at his hand, struggled to pull away.

"This secret isn't mine to tell."

"Of course it isn't. There's always a reason." She tugged harder, dug up every far-off memory of self-defence lessons, and twisted back against his arm. Free at last, leaving him gasping from the fist shoved hard into his gut. She refused to feel guilty.

"I'll accept a security detail, but please ask the Feds to take over from your Solaris people." Then slammed her hand against the door controls.

"Sarwenna, wait. Please."

"Ethan," said a warning growl from the mountain man.

She stopped in the open doorway as Ethan turned to the den Coille man.

"I have to tell her, Cumchdach. She has a right to it. Her family has been targeted too."

A scowl from the other man.

Ethan swung back to her. "It's the system governing that teen com room of Ari's. Silas recognised a pattern in the programming."

"Claimed to recognise." The mountain man thrust up too, belligerent and angry.

"Yes, he's tricky as all sands, but every systems designer has a pattern, even him," shot back Ethan.

Sar stared at both in bewilderment.

"You're asking me to trust family safety to a stranger," said the den Coille.

"Would you trust Anna with this?"

"I already have. But she's mountain born."

"And Sarwenna is heart of the plains. Deadlands heart."

Another growl. "All right. On your head. But only if you come to my wedding, and you bring her with you."

"No."

"Yes."

"No," Sar gasped. She'd grown up union. Go as a guest of a Winter to a den Coille dynastic wedding? Not by all the grains of sand in the deadlands.

The two men gave no sign of hearing her.

"She will be safe. You know that."

Ethan turned on the spot, glaring first at the den Coille, then back at her. She had to get out of here, now, before insanity won.

"Please, Sarwenna. Please, just listen."

Something in his voice caught at her. A jagged hitch, a broken and exposed echo below the smooth edge of the corporate accents.

"All right. Talk," she said.

He kept dead still, as if scared of frightening her off. "Silas studied the patterns of that com room of Ari's."

"The one Da banned her from? Yes, I got that. What about it?"

"Something about the design was familiar."

A jolt fizzed through her. "You know the creator?"

"Maybe, maybe not; but it was based on a pattern Silas had seen before."

"Who?" Pain lodged in her chest and the fizzle died out fast. "Another of your friends? Another who thinks ordinary working folk are no more than pieces in a corporate game?"

"No."

A cry from his heart. Could she trust it? "You know the person though?"

A voice behind them spoke. The deep voice of the eldest den Coille son. "My brother Seolta is a man of many talents, Sera. One of them is dabbling in com programming."

A gasp. A sharp tearing of breath. Hers, she suddenly realised. "I have full-time security, thanks to those trying to kill me and my family, and you tell me your brother is part of it."

"May be a part of it," growled the mountain man. "Or may know those who are."

A snort from Ethan. "Seolta was like my father when he was released from prison. Angry as a desert storm and hell-bent on revenge. He hides it better than the Old Man, but it's just as bad."

An unhappy growl from Cumchdach. "It's eating him up."

Sar needed a seat. She glared at Ethan until he retreated to his own side of the desk then she dragged her chair to the farthest corner of her side of the desk and perched on the edge of it. "I want all the details, now. Neither of you leaves here until I get the full story."

"We don't have it. Not yet," said Ethan.

Cumchdach glared back at them both. "My brother would not do this."

A tense triangle: Ethan in his seat, Cumchdach den Coille bristling at one long end of the desk and Sar at the other. The shiny surface reflected faces taut with distrust and desperation.

What could they see on hers?

"Talk," she ordered and shoved her hands deep in her lap so neither could see them shaking.

Slowly it came out. The horrors of prison, the cold fury of the second den Coille brother, Silas Winter's analysis of Ari's com room pattern. She cringed when she learned how quickly the Winter brothers had marked her little sister as a probable creator of that beam.

The patient, subtle digging ever since, by both Ethan and Ser Cumchdach, hiding their search always from Cumchdach's too astute brother, Seolta.

All she knew for sure at the end was that she needed to meet Seolta den Coille. Needed to look in the face of the man who thought nothing of using a volatile young girl for revenge. Then realised there was a critical bit missing.

"What happened in Manascraoch on Ethan's last visit?"

Silence crashed down.

She dug her fingers so hard into her palms, she was sure she'd drawn blood. "Tell me the truth, all of it, or I go out and do my own digging."

"No." The word escaped Ethan. His lips clamped tight together.

"Yes," Sar said. "Tell me what happened, Ser den Coille, or I take everything you've told me to the Feds."

"She wouldn't," said Ethan.

"I will," said Sar, refusing to look at Ethan. "How much danger will Ethan be in if he comes to your wedding."

Now the man looked plain insulted. "None. Not for the duration of the celebrations."

"And after."

A glance of apology at Ethan. "Best he's gone before that."

"And me?"

"Are safe always, Sera. We do not harm guests."

"But you do our companions."

The man jerked up. "Not if you're with him," he said as if she'd given him a deadly insult. She'd heard about the formalities of the mountain people, and something in the man's tone made her believe him.

"So Ethan's safe as long as I'm in Manascraoch?"

"Yes," said the mountain man reluctantly.

"Don't tell her that," said Ethan quickly.

Sar allowed herself a smile of triumph. "Right. Now talk, and make me believe you're telling me everything."

She stared at Cumchdach den Coille until at last he folded. "Ethan came asking about Seolta. We are a family; we protect our own. My father read it as a threat to one of his sons and threw him in prison."

"So much for mountain courtesy. I can see why you wouldn't want it spread around, but it's not enough to cause a scandal. Not given the history of den Coilles and Winters. Is Ethan's life at risk if he returns."

"Not from my family; or not most of them."

"Seolta?"

"He's still angry."

"Your father?"

The den Coilles had thrown Ethan in jail. Not for long, given the short time he'd disappeared from Sulwith, but Ethan's jaw was locked rigid and the waves of tension radiating from him hurt to see.

"What else happened in that jail?"

A choked cry from Cumchdach. He turned to Ethan as if begging for help. Sar waited, hands clenched tightly, eyes locked on Ethan.

His voice when he spoke came out on a strangled breath and he refused to look directly at her. "I have a thing about confined spaces. I made a bit of a fool of myself."

The word Cumchdach uttered was one she'd never heard but must have come from the seediest streets of the mountain cities. "Never, Eshta. My father… If he'd known."

"Known what?"

Cumchdach turned to face her, mouth grim and leaning toward Ethan. As if to protect Ethan, she realised in shock.

Then she heard it, in simple, short words. The horror of those weeks in solitary confinement and the lasting effect on the man behind the desk.

"You dare ask him to return to Manascraoch?" she said angrily at the end.

"It's my wedding, and Eshta is the best man I know to stand with me. We went through a lot together."

"He is not going through this. How can you even ask it?" To think the den Coille claimed to be a friend to Ethan.

A slow smile spread over Ethan's face and she watched, amazed, as the tension in him drained away. "Thank you, Sarwenna mine."

She sagged back in relief. "You're staying then."

"No. Cumchdach has more than earned my presence at his wedding."

The mountain man stood, his big hand reaching over to clasp Ethan's forearm. "Thank you. It means a lot."

Sar gaped. "What about your security?" Silence, and not the comforting kind. "So they're not welcome?"

Cumchdach den Coille coughed, looked down, even squirmed under her glare. "Not Solaris security ... but we couldn't stop the Feds coming. The winds know there's a pile of them sniffing around the city already. Will that reassure you, Sera den Beren?"

"It'll have to," she finally said, "but I'm coming too."

Nothing Ethan said could stop her. Not even his dropped jaw and stunned look. "Didn't you hear what we told you. The den Coilles don't play meaningless games."

"This den Coille has promised we will be safe."

"She's right, Eshta. What happened that last visit was an aberration. You threatened one of my father's children."

"Didn't feel like an aberration. And the Sera stays here. You are not coming, Sarwenna."

"I am," she said sweetly. "Which means that you will be safe as long as I'm there, as long as you do nothing stupid to put us at risk. Me as well as you. So you will just have to be extra careful," she added with a sudden grin. Why hadn't she figured that out quicker, and a warm glow of satisfaction bloomed inside her.

Ethan could only scowl as Cumchdach gave a crack of laughter, and just like that the tension in the room vanished.

Days later, she stood beside Ethan and nervously watched her luggage capsule being deposited in his flyer, thinking of all the new and expensive outfits it held. The ones Ethan had insisted on buying her. She flinched when the loading bot dropped it with a clunk into the baggage hatch.

Maybe this hadn't been such a good idea after all.

She felt it even more when the fabled tree-top city of Manascraoch came into view. Home to the den Coille's and their empire, the city was woven through the enormous baullnia trees unique to these mountain slopes.

"Where are the houses?"

Ethan gave her a quick grin. "Wait."

Next minute, the flyer sank down through the greenery and settled into a typical flyer port hidden under the branches. Typical if flyers usually landed in tight gaps between the living branches of a tree to perch precariously on what looked to be no more than side branches growing scarily high above the ground.

"Are you sure this will take our flyer's weight?"

"Baullnia branches have the tensile strength of the best construction plascrete. You're fine."

It didn't feel it, despite the clunk of restraint clamps echoing through the cabin. Even less so when she stepped out and felt a faint tremor with each footfall as they walked over to the welcoming party. Caleb, his wife Fee, and Cumchdach den Coille, with an unfamiliar woman beside him.

Caleb chuckled at her tentative steps over the platform. "First time in the city, Sera?"

She nodded, unable to think of any reply that wouldn't insult her hosts. His wife gave her a grin that flitted across that ever-mobile face and lit up her eyes. "Your expression is just like Caleb's the first time I took him for a stroll around the city."

"Clambered over branches a killing distance above the ground, you mean," he shot back with that special look in his eyes she'd noticed the last time she'd seen these two together. Cumchdach stepped forward with the quiet woman beside him, her hand resting lightly on his forearm.

"Welcome, Sera Beren, Ethan. May the trees shelter you and keep you safe during your stay." He turned to the woman, subtly bringing her forward. "My wife-to-be, Anna ingh Eolas an Sumhneas den Falasch.'"

The woman gave a slow head bow in greeting then spoke in a low, musical voice strong with the lilt of the mountains. "Welcome at this happy time, Sera Sarwenna ingh Rhyn an Catra den Beren and Ser Ethan mar Sol an Helena den Winter. The city is yours, our home is open."

A formal mountain greeting, guessed Sar, at a loss for how to answer such a mouthful. Ethan gave a small bow and she copied him. Then he laid her hand on his arm, a copy of Cumchdach and his wife-to-be, and drew her forward. "The Sera and I thank you. May the waters of life sustain you always."

No one appeared to expect her to say anything, so Sar plastered on a polite smile and touched cheeks with the woman, then clasped both hands with Cumchdach.

"Please, come this way," said the woman, Anna. "Your rooms have been readied and the rest of the family are eager to meet you when you are recovered from your journey."

Sar felt like a puppet in some kind of weird theatre as they formed a procession: Cumchdach and Anna in the front, she and Ethan wedged in the middle, and Caleb and Fee bringing up the rear, depositing her in her room and leaving her with Ethan to settle in.

Their rooms were beautiful, she supposed. If you liked the constant spring of movement under your feet and a forest of plants sprouting around you.

"I'll grow mouldy in here." She slowly turned, taking in the plants, the beams overhead, the window opening onto more greenery and the soft, misty air wafting in when she opened it. She looked down and hastily pulled her head back in, slamming the window controls to shut it firmly.

Ethan bent over laughing. "This city has been here for hundreds of years. They have climate control the equal of anything in Sulwith."

She glared at the plants. "Doesn't mean I have to like sleeping in a forest."

"There's only three plants. That's a desert to a mountainer."

She stopped beside one that crawled up the wall to tower over her. The thing had grown into the walls.

"I'm in the next-door room," he said with what she guessed was meant to be a reassuring smile, but nothing about a relationship with a Winter promised a happy ending. What she felt for Ethan Winter set off all kinds of warning daggers.

"The link door is behind you," he continued, "and has a lock on both sides. I've coded the one on my side to let you through whenever you need me."

"I'll do the same for the one on my side," she heard herself saying and didn't know where the words came from. Yet she didn't call them back. She needed to know Ethan would come if she called. "This place must be getting to me," she muttered.

Thankfully, he said nothing to that. "I'll leave you to change. We're expected in the family parlour, and that's not a cosy room for a relaxed get together. Not in a mountain home."

With his warning ringing in her ears, he opened the door he'd pointed out to her and disappeared through to the other side. She wasn't sure whether to feel relieved or lost when it clicked behind him. She then gave herself a firm mental shake, slotted her luggage capsule into the wardrobe of the room and waited for it to sort and hang the contents. All that did was expose once again the truly terrifying amount of credit they had cost. He'd even included jewellery and other accessories that looked too real to be the usual synth ones. How she was going to wear them without shrivelling with nerves, she had no idea.

"Since you're coming only because of me, it's the least I can do," he'd said to her protests with that wry half-smile of his. "Think of it as me doing my patriotic duty for the reputation of the plains."

When she walked into the family parlour, she forgot her resentment and breathed a silent thank you for his highhandedness. Bigger than the whole ground floor of her home in Sulwith, the parlour was unlike anything found in a Deadlands home. A high ceiling, supported by large beams, decorated in soft blues, greens and with a myriad of plants in pots or reaching out from the living branches that served as dividers, couch supports and tables. Living tree and human-engineered furniture blended seamlessly in a natural pattern of co-existence.

Then she noticed the people filling the room and her nerves plummeted to a whole new level. She knew the den Coille family was a big one, but surely not all of these were family?

A confusing time later, she discovered that's exactly what they were. Parents, uncles and aunts, the two daughters and four sons of the family and an exhaustive phalanx of cousins, kin by marriage and allies. She took an instant liking to Samhchair, the elder daughter and second in age to Cumchdach. She had the same quiet strength as Cumchdach and Ceart, the largest and least talkative of the brothers. The youngest brother, Aigherach, made her think of Finn as he would be as a young man. The same coltish excitement, dampened in this youth by the taut lines etched into his face and the limp that still dogged him.

"The doctors tell me they can fix it in time," he said with a grimace as he caught her eye on his leg, "and it's a lot better than it was."

"It looks painful," she said gamely.

A sudden smile made the youth look even more like her youngest brother. "Not now, Sera, not like it was, but thank you for the thought."

The boy had the makings of a fine man, she decided. Then she came face to face with Bram den Coille, patriarch of the clan and, beside him, his son Seolta. The slimmest and most whip-like of the brothers, Seolta den Coille would have done well in the casinos of the Sulwith strip. Unreadable dark eyes studied her, a slight smile twisted his mouth, and his lean face was a façade of planes and angles, telling her little.

This was the man responsible for luring her sister into that com room.

"Sera Beren," said the deep voice of the man beside him, and Sar reluctantly turned her attention to Bram den Coille. After the confusing plunge into the family relationships of those in the room, she had become more used to the mountain habit of using a mouthful of names to address anyone instead of the simpler plains ways and managed to remember the full name of the head of Den Coille.

"Greetings, Ser Bram mar Gliocas duine Scathach den Coille," she said with the required slight bow. "Thank you for your hospitality. A blessing on your House at this happy time."

He returned it with the required response and gave her a semi-smile. She'd passed approval, at least.

"You are from the town of Sulwith, we are told."

"Yes, Ser. It's on the edge of the deadlands."

"No trees, then?"

"No, Ser, not like you are used to," she said, "but the desert has its own beauty."

From his polite murmur of agreement, she appeared to have passed another kind of test. She didn't make the mistake of breathing normally, though, and was grateful when the head of the den Coille clan passed her graciously on to his wife.

Something in the open smile of the woman who had given birth to this memorable brood had her trusting Scathach den Coille in a way she would never be able to trust the den Coille father. She was also a doctor, which meant she should listen to reason before making a decision.

The look on her face as she glanced at her children said she did have one thing in common with Sar's own mother. Come what may, she would leap to defend all of her brood of dark hatchlings, and a silent shiver trembled up Sar's spine.

It was late in the evening before she managed to engineer any kind of meeting with the brother she hunted, cornering Seolta den Coille in the short passage between the supper table and the doorway to the ladies' withdrawing room. It was an old and hackneyed ploy, but desperation had her tripping over the back skirt of her overtunic and stumbling against him.

"Excuse me, Ser … Seolta, wasn't it?"

A quick gleam flickered in those shadowy eyes, then he smiled politely as he set her back on her feet. "Yes, Sera Sarwenna mar Rhyn. You have a good memory, given the crowd of us."

"I did my homework before I came," she admitted, and was rewarded with a small easing of the suspicion on the man's face. She'd learned long ago that a dash of honesty got you a long way in a delicate negotiation. "It wasn't much help when I first entered the room, though. My own family is much smaller, and holo-images aren't the same as living faces."

"No."

A familiar and very masculine scent surrounded her and a firm hand settled on her arm. "Are you all right, Sarwenna."

She turned to face Ethan. "Yes. Just a bit of a stumble. Luckily Ser Seolta was here to catch me."

"How fortunate." His hand gripped her tighter and she looked up at him sharply, then across to Seolta. The edge in Ethan's voice matched the glitter in the den Coille's eyes. "Thank you for your assistance, Ser den Coille. I can look after Sera Beren from here."

"As you wish." Seolta den Coille lifted his arms wide, setting his hands clearly away from her. "It's always a pleasure to be of assistance to a beautiful woman. I hadn't known the desert grew such charming flowers. Maybe I should spread my sights wider."

"Don't trouble yourself," snapped Ethan, and jerked at her arm, leading her through the doorway and down the hall. He didn't stop until they were well away from the main room, but Sar could still hear the echo of Seolta's laughter.

Ethan dropped her hand like it was burning him, and she discovered what little amusement she'd found in the encounter shivered into nothing.

"What were you thinking?" he demanded. "Didn't you hear anything of what Cumchdach said?"

She thought about shrugging, then swiftly discarded it and squared her shoulders. "I heard every word you said, but you seem to have forgotten one important point. Ari is my sister."

"And Seolta den Coille is dangerous."

"There's no need to tell me that, but the man has avoided me all night."

"You should be thankful."

Sar glared. "How can I find out whether he's involved without talking to him?"

"Leave that to me and Cumchdach."

"You've been trying to break him open for weeks now."

"And we'll keep trying until we succeed."

"Until my sister is coerced into ruining her life and my town is run into the ground? I don't have forever, Ser Winter. How about you learn to trust that I can help you?"

His mouth opened, then snapped shut. She had him, and wished she didn't feel so small about it.

A hand shoved through his hair. "All right. But please, not on your own. Do not let Seolta get you alone."

That had her mouth gaping open. "You think he would do something here in his family home? To a guest?"

Tricksy, Seolta's brother had dubbed him, and the man's sharp eyes had her believing the title. Would he break the precious hospitality rules of the mountain? A man as angry as Ethan claimed at the outside world?

Ethan's mouth twisted and his hands clenched. "Maybe not," he conceded, "but that tongue and mind of his are first class weapons. He mustn't find out what we suspect."

That she could agree with. She was certainly not going to let down her guard around that particular den Coille. She promised Ethan she would be careful but wasn't surprised when she left the ladies' room some time later to find him waiting for her, just inside the parlour door.

Of Seolta, there was no sign.

Ethan held out his hand. "Had enough of being polite to den Coilles?"

More than enough. Giving herself no time to think, she reached for his hand, to feel it suddenly clench tightly on hers then ease back. "Home, Sera?" he said lightly.

Why did she feel much more lay under the words?

At her door, he reached down and gave her a simple kiss on her cheek. Then released her and deliberately stepped back.

"Goodnight, Sera Sarwenna. You're safe, and I'm next door if you need me. Until tomorrow."

He didn't move, though, waiting for her to open her door. It wasn't until she'd shut it behind her and engaged her personal com lock that she heard his footsteps move off to his own door.

The one right next to hers.

She toed off her shoes and surveyed the room with its alien plants and overwhelming organic life. "Evening mode," she signalled her com and the lighting shifted to a gentle half-light. Warm, restful, sleep-inducing.

It didn't help. She felt none of those things … too keyed up, too full of impressions and questions. She eyed the door. The second door. The one between her room and Ethan's.

No, she couldn't.

She escaped into the cleansing unit, switching it up to full, pummelling massage, then tried the soft waves of the soporific mode when that failed.

At the end, she was scrupulously clean and perfumed with her favourite fragrance carrying a hint of the elusive flowering shockra bush, found only in the heart of the desert. Even that reminder of home didn't help. She was right back where she started, staring at that interconnecting door.

"Stop overthinking it."

All her life, she'd considered consequences, looked out for repercussions, chosen the logical, safe, appropriate path. Now her head was a jumble of imperatives and she needed help to sort them all out.

No, she needed Ethan Winter.

She put out a hand and shoved at the door control.

Ethan stood by the sleeper, one hand slapping closed the seal of his night robe. It was the loose palla of the desert, brithen silk in an emerald sheen that mirrored his eyes. She recognised the fabric's pattern. It was one of Maddie's. He'd bought it in Sulwith.

A frown creased his brow. "Is something wrong?"

"No. Yes. I don't know." Could she sound more stupid? "It's this place. These people. This…" she ended lamely, with a jerky wave of her hand. At what, she couldn't say.

He looked back at her with contained eyes that hid everything. The man could mask his feelings better than anyone she'd come across. Then she looked down and saw his hands, saw the white knuckles tucked close to his side.

She shoved up her head. "I don't want to be alone. Not tonight."

A sharp hiss of breath. A tightening of those wide shoulders. She took a step closer.

"This is not a good idea, Sera," he said in the formal tone he used for business. But she'd heard that hiss, saw the taut rigidity of his body and smelled the clean, fresh scent of him. Warm, dry and free of the clammy dankness of the mountains.

The smell of home.

In the half-light of the single lamp still glowing by his bed, a scent that meant something else entirely. He shifted and the light fell full on his face, on the eyes she'd thought so contained.

Not now. Not with that pinch of mouth and sharp lines as he focussed totally on her. As those eyes studied her, from her barefoot toes peeking under her robe, up the lines of her body under the fall of her palla, her hands clenched in front, her shoulders, the lines of her neck, her mouth, to at last ensnare her eyes.

She stepped forward.

"Be sure, my Sarwenna," he said as she reached him and his hand hovered over her shoulder.

It was too late for that. She shook her head and stretched up to pull his head down with one hand as her other found then released the closing seal of her robe.

A deep chuckle woke her as a hand feathered over her nose. She shook it away, then slowly became aware of sensations. The dim light of early morning. A strange moistness in the air causing her to duck back under the cover, and a man's body holding hers. Warm, safe.

She smiled.

"No regrets, my Sarwenna?" said that laughing voice, and she opened her eyes.

Then smiled again. She had seen many faces of Ethan Winter since his arrival in Sulwith. Full business mode, on edge, tight with suppressed anger and exasperation, a sudden burst of laughter, regret and tenderness ... but never before the lightness shining from his face now.

He looked happy.

"No regrets," she said, "and a good morning to you." She looked at the window. "Although it's barely morning yet."

A hand traced a beguiling pathway over her shoulder and down her back, settling her closer into the curve of his big, warm body. She tucked in and let her eyes drift closed again, breathing in the warm essence of him. A kiss took her deeper, back into the delicious warmth of desire. Another chuckle and his hand became more insistent. "Near enough to morning. You need to be back in your own bed."

She snuggled in and shook her head. "It's warm here."

Another light kiss. "It is," he agreed, "but do you want the entire den Coille family to know about this?"

He had a point. She grimaced and lifted her wrist. "Com, heat my sleeper and room." Then wriggled closer in. "It'll take a few minutes to get to the right temperature."

A delighted chuckle. "Yes, it will. Now, how can we fill those minutes?"

He managed with a joy that rendered her breathless, extravagantly thorough in his attentions and more than skilful. She was laughing still when he deposited her back into her own sleeper. After a lingering kiss, he left her.

Did she regret the night? A smile still lit her face. She wasn't an idiot.

But she ought to. So much still lay between them.

Did she regret it?

No.

She woke again much later, with a misty light washing through her bedroom window and no warm body sharing her bed. The memory of Ethan's last kiss still fluttered inside her, a kiss that had been both thanks and a question. One she was wondering how to answer. Maybe today, in some quiet moment together … and a smile traced her lips. After a night like last night, today must surely be theirs. She'd worry about the rest of it later.

Reality quickly soused her in cold water. It turned out the day before a den Coille wedding was filled with duties and social posturings. The only quiet moment she had with Ethan was a passing glance at breakfast and a murmured good morning. Adding to that, after being so elusive on the previous day, it seemed she couldn't walk a pace in the treetop city without Seolta den Coille dogging her steps. Ethan reacted to his presence in the worst way possible.

The sight of her with a constant guard of a dubiously smiling Seolta on one shoulder and a scowling Ethan on the other no doubt afforded a great deal of amusement to the city's inhabitants, but it left her tense and exhausted by day's end. Worse, it got her nowhere with finding out anything about Seolta den Coille. He was subtle, tenacious and, yes, the day taught her to read the signs of the anger Ethan warned about. A low, deep simmer that he kept well hidden but which coloured all he said and did. An edgy, haunted man.

A man who thought that justified abusing the trust of a young girl caught in the intensity of early teen emotions?

Nor did Ethan join her in her rooms that night.

"Cumchdach has asked me to his baggacrich night," he said apologetically as they walked back to their rooms.

"And Samhchair has asked me to her suite this evening for what she termed a small gathering."

The grin on Ethan's face confirmed her suspicions. "That will be for Anna's bruithen. Good luck."

She quickly learned what he meant. Warned by his grin, she wore one of her most expensive gowns. One look at the faces masked in politeness as she entered Samhchair's rooms had her watching every word she spoke and every thought she uttered. By the end of the evening, she had even more respect for the skills of the eldest den Coille daughter and could only hope she'd let free as little useful information as Samhchair, or as Anna den Falasch.

The next morning brought the day of the wedding, thankfully. She was barely awake when Ethan burst into her room.

"Sarwenna?"

She pulled up the top cover, blearily opening an eye and wishing she could wake up looking as good as he did. Despite tousled hair and clothes, donned quickly by their atypical disorder, he stood tall, his skin shone and his eyes sparked with a dark intensity.

"What's the matter," she managed, tugging uselessly at the spiky mess of her hair.

"You're safe."

"Of course." She peered suspiciously at him. "How did last night go?"

A wave of his hand. "Nothing of note happened. Today is too important for Cumchdach."

"Huh." She settled back, trying to burrow under the cover and hide her sleep-ruffled self from his fierce scrutiny.

"We weren't drinking. Not much,'" he said. Then blushed bright red. "I had a dream."

"Oh? What about?" she asked, at a loss for an intelligent comment.

"Nothing," he muttered defensively, "but I needed to see that you are safe." Then he stepped closer and his hand reached out to her face. "Please, today. Be careful."

A bustle outside and the unmistakable sounds of excited women came through the door. Ethan swung around, a look of horror on his face.

"Samhchair. She promised to include me in the women's party."

"Sands alive. I'm out of here." The laughter came closer. He bent over and, to her surprise, dropped a quick kiss on her lips. "Promise me." He waited only for her bemused agreement, then literally ran out of the room just as her door alarm signalled she had visitors.

She snapped on her com link, "A moment, please," then jumped out of bed, shoving on her robe and dragging ruthless fingers through the errant wisps of hair, and set the door controls to open.

Next moment she was engulfed in a crowd of excited, laughing women with Samhchair the calm centre of the storm. "You're the last," she told Sar. "We're here to help since a mountain wedding is new to you. Come on, ladies."

In the tumult that followed, Sar had little time to think back on that strange episode of the morning. It wasn't until much later, when she had been bathed, groomed, gowned and buffed to within an inch of perfection and the mad party swept on to the bride's chamber that she had a moment to reflect back on it.

A bad dream sparked by the capricious movement of the mountain rooms. That had to be the reason behind the fear in Ethan Winter's eyes. She looked around the table at the happy crowd of women helping themselves to the abundance of mountain treats laid out for the first meal. In the far bathroom, a smaller crowd were intent on lavishing a more elaborate version of her own awakening treatment on the bride, and the rest picked at food and gossiped madly.

Then Anna came out, and Sar's heart leapt into her mouth. Beautiful. That was the only word to describe the elegant mountain woman. This was a bride worthy of the heir to house den Coille.

If only the woman would smile.

Sar caught a hint of trouble on Samhchair's face, a match to the quiver in her own. If it had been her… and Ethan?

She turned to one of the mountain woman beside her gazing entranced at the bride. "Have Sera Anna and Ser Cumchdach known each other long,"

"Oh, yes, forever. Since they were children," the woman assured her. "We've known for years they would marry."

Maybe, but Anna ingh Eolas an Sumhneas den Falasch didn't look like she'd got the memo about her future … or been asked whether she agreed with it. "Children often grow up and change their minds." Although not Cumchdach, by what he'd said of Anna den Falasch that day back in Urbis.

The woman shrugged. "Cumchdach asked her years ago to marry him, and she finally agreed. They've been a couple forever and neither is getting any younger. If they wait much longer, it will be too late for children."

Sar said something inconsequential but couldn't help feeling sorry for Cumchdach if his bride had accepted him for such a reason. She'd come to a grudging liking for the eldest of the den Coille brothers as a man who stood by those he cared for. His bride was getting no empty promises, but Cumchdach…

It's none of your business. How often had Da told her it wasn't her job to fix the problems of everyone she came across. And neither Cumchdach nor Sera den Falasch came across as the type to welcome interference from an unknown plainswoman.

She fixed on a smile and set out to be the perfect guest. Ethan was part of the wedding party, so Samhchair had charged a friend of hers to stay with Sar through the long and complicated ceremony. The great hall of the city of Manascraoch was filled to overflowing with what felt like a huge swathe of the population swelling all tiers of the room and spilling out the doors.

"Come on, we've a place reserved just behind the family's," her guide had yelled, dragging her pell mell through the arriving throng to a seat right in the middle of the front block. Mountain folk sat on either side leaving no escape possible. In the front of the hall, every one of Cumchdach's brothers stood up with him, including Aigherach, doing his best to hide his limp and give the impression of being as fit as ever he'd been before the shot that had shattered his leg bones. None of them compared favourably in her eyes with the tall figure of Ethan standing out among the dark-haired den Coilles like a blazing beacon of strength.

The woman accompanying her slid away at the end of the wedding, leaving Sar fighting off a crowd for a clear exit. She took one look at Ethan muscling through the crowd and leapt for him, grabbing onto his arm.

The feel of his big arm surrounding hers had her leaning against him in relief.

"I'm here. You're safe," he murmured.

And she was, for now.

CHAPTER TWENTY-THREE

Ethan saw the light stir to life in Sar's beautiful face, and the slim flame of hope from that precious gift of a night flickered brighter. One day, if she could overlook who he was…

Unfortunately, he wasn't free of his wedding duties yet. He still claimed the luxury of catching her hand and holding on tight. "I have to do the small-talk thing," he said in apology. "Stay with me, please."

Sarwenna found it hard to refuse a plea for help, he'd discovered, and he was desperate enough to use any stratagem. The feel of her hand in his settled the churning knot inside him, as he plastered on his business smile and talked his way through the celebrations.

Mountain weddings were known for the lavish amounts of food on offer and, by the size of the spreads being set out on the tables that ran the full length of the massive hall, the marriage of the eldest son of the den Coilles had brought out the competitive edge in every chef west of the ranges. The operation was slick, tables and food magically appearing thanks to a veritable train of servers.

"How many are they planning to feed?" said Sar beside him, staring at the continual shuttling of platters.

"The entire city and outlying settlements, by the looks of the crowd." Ethan chuckled at her wide-eyed stare. Cumchdach and Anna sat at the bridal table, being offered the choicest delicacies and the good wishes of a queue of people.

Sar followed his gaze. "Should I join the queue?"

"Later. Much later," said Ethan. "His people have been waiting years for today. They deserve to go first. Meanwhile, there are still some guests I need to talk to."

He didn't know what he'd do if she made her excuses and left him to it. She was in this as deep as he was; the people he wanted to talk to had as much importance for her. But that wasn't why he wanted—no, needed—to have her with him. The skin on the back of his neck was on fire with pinpricks of warning, and he wouldn't feel safe until they had finished this tragging wedding and he'd flown her well out of den Coille airspace.

"Choosing your first victim, Ethan?" The smooth voice of Seolta den Coille broke into the space beside him and Sarwenna.

"Who says I haven't already? What about you? Tallying up the size of the addition to the den Coille books this marriage will bring?"

A smile slithered across the man's face, as deliberate and purposeful as the one Ethan sent back. He tightened his hand on Sar's, needing to remind himself of her presence, and felt her slight stiffening.

"A sensible union," agreed Seolta.

"Does Sera Anna think the same," said Sarwenna.

"Does it matter?" said Seolta. "They've been friends and lovers for years. Marriage is but a further step."

"Some would say marriage is more than that."

"Dreamers," Seolta said with a dismissive wave of his hand. Ethan tugged at Sarwenna's arm, judging it time to leave.

"Time to go hunting," he said in the driest voice he could muster.

A curl of a groomed lip. "Just remember this side of the mountains is den Coille land. We look after our own," said Seolta.

A swift step and the man merged into the crowd, fake smile fixed on his victims.

Sar watched him. "In some ways, you two are alike."

"Not in the ways that count."

"No, he missed out there." She stood beside him, making no effort to hide her study of Seolta's passage across the hall, with a word here, a quick burst of laughter over there, before stopping at a cluster on the far side of the hall.

Ethan's breath caught and Sar glanced up before turning back to watching her prey. "Who's that he's with?"

He kept his eyes on Seolta as he answered her, noting how the den Coille leaned in close to the striking older woman in red. "Sera Malgrave, the deputy attaché to the Alliance representative. The overdressed man beside her is the head of Berings Cooperative."

Her head swung up. "The small outfit on your list?"

"Yes. I wonder what he's doing talking to Seolta den Coille and Deputy Malgrave."

"Let's find out." She took a step toward them.

He tugged at her hand, shaking his head. "Too obvious. Let them have their talk."

A twist of her mouth said what she thought of his strategy.

"This is my territory," he reminded her. "Seolta will shut down quick smart if we barge on up to them." He sent her a grin. "And there are plenty of others around them only too willing to pass on juicy gossip about the second son of the den Coilles and his fascinating companions.

He steered Sar away from the far end of the room, all the while keeping a discreet eye on Seolta.

"He seems to be very friendly with them," said Sar.

"Mmm."

A hand clapped down on his shoulder. "Young Ethan. Slumming it down here in the provinces? I heard you'd abandoned the plains for the delights of the capital."

"Ser, a pleasure to see you again," he said to the owner of the booming voice. "Sarwenna, let me make known to you Representative Joe Gibbs, the Upper House Representative for the plains region."

"No need for that, young man. Sera Beren's mother and I are old sparring partners. Her electorate lies within my region, remember." The big man bent his round face to Sarwenna, giving her a far-too-familiar brush of cheek. "And how are you, young Sar? Still trying to keep that brood of your parents in line?"

Sarwenna laughed. "I gave up on that many years ago, Ser Gibbs. These days, I settle for trying to contain their chaos so it causes the least damage."

A big-bellied laugh accompanied that. "You always did have the best of your parents."

Of course Sarwenna would be known to Joe Gibbs. He just hoped she knew to be wary of the man's jovial appearance. The Representative was as devious as he looked harmless.

"Doing the rounds, young Ethan?" the big man said with a glint in his eye Ethan thoroughly distrusted. "So you should. There's a parcel of interesting folks here tonight. Plains and mountain mingling like this. Never thought I'd see the day."

Nor had Ethan, but being the victims of a common enemy brought people together. "They're not so different from us."

"Hmph. If you believe that, you're not the man I know. Where do you think Solaris will get with thinking like that?"

Ethan felt the blaze of heat on his cheeks and saw Sarwenna stiffen. "Solaris and I aren't... You did hear I've left the company?"

"Got booted out by that half-warped father of yours? Of course I heard. A temporary aberration."

"You think so, Ser Gibbs?" said Sarwenna, and Ethan was startled at the pleading in her voice. As if it mattered to her.

"The boy will be back making a nuisance of himself with his plans for Solaris soon enough. He can't leave it alone, and Solaris needs him."

"Then tell his father that, please, Ser."

"No," said Ethan hastily.

"Don't have to," humphed the representative. "Sol Winter knows it. He'll come round when he's cooled down some and seen sense." The man's eyes wandered. "Talking about those who need to cool down."

Ethan followed the older man's gaze and saw his eyes had locked on Seolta den Coille, across the room laughing with the Alliance woman and the man from Berings. A fourth person had joined them. A man Ethan had never seen before.

"Interesting," muttered the Representative.

"You know the new man?"

Joe Gibbs never took his eyes off the group. "Not personally, no, but I've heard of him and would very much like to know what he's doing sticking his nose into mountain business. So would Bram den Coille by the look of him."

Ethan looked around, startled, and saw what Gibbs meant. Bram den Coille stood a short distance from the group, making a show of listening to the elderly guest beside him, but his eyes never left his son's party, and the tension in his stance was visible even from here.

"Who is he?" he asked softly.

"It's what he is that matters," said the representative as softly and tersely. "An off-worlder from a company infamous throughout the Alliance. They're strippers. They find business assets in trouble, buy them up and strip off anything of value before leaving the leftovers to flounder and die. Scavengers, that's what they are. What in all the deadlands sands is he doing here?"

He turned and fixed those shaggy brows on him. "You have a job tonight, young Ethan. Find out what that man's up to. You're the most subtle of your brothers; time to put every trick you know to the test."

He would like to, but there was no way he was taking Sarwenna any closer to that group. "Not tonight, Ser Gibbs."

Gibbs took one look at him and Sarwenna standing beside him. "Aah, so that's the way of it. If you'll excuse us, young Ethan. Sar and I have a lot to catch up on."

Obviously, Joe didn't know Sarwenna as well as he thought. "I don't think so, Ser Gibbs. I'm here with Ethan," she said.

"Please, Sarwenna. Go with Ser Gibbs."

"While you go sticking your nose into a wernet's nest of trouble? I don't think so."

"I'll be fine," said Ethan.

"Safer on his own, young Sera. Worrying about you will distract him."

Sarwenna looked so torn at that. Was it possible…?

"Only if it really is the best option," she finally said, "and I'll be doing my own snooping."

"Of course you will, my dear," said Ser Gibbs. "Starting with the ladies' room. Your very delectable nose is in need of attention. It's almost glowing."

Ethan had to quell the chuckle when her hand automatically shot to feel her nose. "He's right, you know. You can hear things in there we don't have access to. Splitting your forces is an old and true strategy."

"All right, but only if you promise to be careful. You disappear from sight and I will come looking for you, no matter where it takes me."

She reached up and touched her lips to his. Ethan was too stunned to do more and cursed when she drew back after a too achingly brief moment. "Go do your worst, Ser Winter," she whispered, then laid her arm on the representative's gallantly outstretched arm. Ethan watched until he saw them disappear down the corridor leading to the ladies' room.

Joe Gibbs would keep her safe.

Meanwhile… He turned back and started to make his slow and meandering orbit of the room, moving surreptitiously closer to his goal with each passing chat, each greeting and short farewell.

As he made his way around the room, he came up against the whole gamut of reactions. Luckily, the den Coilles believed in keeping disputes in-house and no one but the close family knew anything of Bram's threat to him. Since the events of the previous year, Ethan had visited the brothers in Manascraoch often enough to be a familiar face to many of the guests.

They'd all heard of his shift to Urbis.

"The big city losing its gloss already, Ser Ethan mar Sol?"

"No, Sera. Just visiting. Wouldn't miss this day for anything."

"They took long enough to get the deed in writing," humphed an elderly man beside them. A second cousin by marriage, Ethan seemed to remember.

"Yes, silly pair thought they could go on as they were forever. Friendship don't make babies."

Ethan turned the conversation and slipped on to the next group.

"Aaah, young den Winter. What's the latest news from the city?"

Ethan gave the man his company smile and slid into the new gossip stream. "A good turn out," he said after a while. "It does honour to Cumchdach mar Bram an Scathach."

"As he deserves," said a sharp-faced man of middle years. "Solid to the core, that boy. His brother, now."

As if triggering an avalanche, all around the speaker ears perked up and eyes gleamed. Ethan shut his mouth and waited.

"Seolta mar Bram an Scathach, you mean?"

"He always was one needing watching, but now…"

"Who are those people with him? I recognise the Alliance Deputy."

"Yes, and why does she need to be here?"

There it was; the smell of fear.

"Those others? Are they Alliance spies too?"

Ethan offered them Joe Gibbs' information on the stranger.

"An off-worlder. What's Seolta mar Bram an Scathach doing with such a one?" was the edgy response.

Another woman came up, listening in for a few moments then butted in with the self-importance of one with news to spread. "It's the doing of the Berings man. He's a distant cousin of the den Coilles, apparently. The off-worlder is visiting him, that's all. A delightful man to talk to."

Yeah, Ethan just bet he was. The rest of the group heaved a proverbial sigh of relief and moved onto a blow by blow analysis of the off-worlder's clothes and manners. Not bad, for a barbarian, they decided after a while. Ethan made his excuses and passed on to another group.

No one could add much more and finally he had to make his way to the source direct.

"Seolta mar Bram an Scathach." He tipped his head in the required formal courtesy and knew a short burst of satisfaction at the flicker of surprise in Seolta's eyes. *I do know the correct mountain forms. Have you forgotten how much time you and your brothers spent teaching them to me?* "A fine ceremony," he added in his best family-friend voice.

Seolta lifted an eyebrow. "Thank you. We poor mountain folk try to keep up with our plains colleagues."

Ethan demurred. "It does honour to my old friend." *What was it about this second den Coille brother that set him on edge so readily?*

The twist of Seolta's mouth said he knew exactly how much he riled Ethan.

"Please," said Ethan, "introduce me to your friends. The Alliance deputy and I are old—acquaintances—but I haven't had the pleasure of meeting the other sers. And in their own usage, I pray you. Mountain address may do honour, Seolta mar Bram an Scathach, but it can be confusing for those not used to it."

"Not at all, Ser Winter," came back the man from the insignificant Berens company, "but thank you on behalf of our off-world guest."

If Ethan suspected Seolta was as irritated by the man's effrontery as he, the mountain man gave no sign of it. The smooth smile slid back and Seolta offered a slight bow to the newcomers. "Of course. Ser Ethan Winter, let me make known to you Ser

Keownmar den Rith, of the Berings company based on Meanuigh Island, and Ser Hilmar a Kevand3."

They both returned the bow in the correct mode, telling Ethan that whatever reason they were here mattered enough to warrant learning the required forms of the region. He half-bowed to the man from the island.

"A long way from home, Ser den Rith." Then turned to the other man and gave the brisk bow to a stranger of undetermined status, head facing forward and eyes open throughout. "An off-worlder?"

Seolta gave that untrustworthy smile of his again. "Ser Hilmar is from the Kevand3 corporation, based on the planet Surned."

Ethan had heard of the world. Any businessman with an eye on his back had. A dead world halfway across the Alliance, populated by corporations that exploited its rich mineral reserves. Corporates that left the predators of Arcadia's business world looking like babes in arms, said the talk around the bank district bars, and if Joe Gibbs was right about this one, he was staring at an alpha predator of that hell world. He set his most affable smile on his face.

"We see few off-worlders on Arcadia. Welcome to our planet. I hope we can make your stay a … pleasant one, Ser."

"Oh, I'm sure it will be," said the man from the dead world, and Ethan felt his skin crawl. "I understand you represent the Solaris company. Even on our humble world, we have heard much of the premier energy company of Arcadia."

"You flatter us, Ser." Ethan dared not look at Seolta, the man who had brought this predator into his family hold. "Are you making a long stay on Arcadia?"

"Not as long as I would like, but I will be back, of a certainty."

Ethan supposed he said the right things after that. The man had told him all he needed to know in those first few words, and Ethan soon had to get away from him before the bile churning his stomach erupted.

"That scuzzbag is after Solaris," he said to Sar as soon as he found her. Her hand reached out and he grabbed it tight, desperately needing an anchor.

"Are you sure, young Winter," said Joe Gibbs, smiling around the room at his congenial best.

Ethan gritted his teeth and tried to copy him but had a feeling he failed miserably. "Did he tell me as much in plain Standard? Of course not … but he did tell me."

"And this Seolta is helping him?" said Sar, turning her back to the room and leaning into his side. He felt the tension quivering through her.

"I don't know. Maybe. He has no love for Solaris or Winters, but to help an off-worlder against us…"

"Tell your father. If he's involved, he deserves to know the truth behind whatever game he's fallen into," said Gibbs.

Ethan agreed. "For my father to be fooled like this…"

"Anger makes fools of the best of us. Humiliation is bitter, and prison brought both to Sol Winter."

"And Seolta den Coille." Ethan knew the rage stirring inside the mountain man. Too much of it stirred deep inside him too, but he'd vowed long ago he wouldn't let it destroy him. Not like it was doing to Seolta. "He's betraying our world. You don't come back from that. Not if you're part of it."

Gibbs turned from his scrutiny of the room and the genial smile vanished. "No, you do not. The Council won't tolerate it."

"You'll take action then?"

Gibbs gave that other smile of his, the real one. Teeth showing and a glitter in his hooded eyes. "We must be careful. He's still his father's closest advisor and a man unlikely to leave a trail of evidence. But we will certainly deal with Ser Seolta den Coille, one way or another."

The tension in Ethan unwound a hitch. "Let me talk to my father first."

"If he's knowingly involved in this…"

"In destroying Solaris? No, it's his lifeblood."

"Maybe," conceded the politician. "I'll alert the Federals watching den Coille and their visitors. That will give you a few days, but no longer."

Ethan gave a brisk nod. "We leave first thing in the morning. One more favour; would you please escort Sera Beren safe home to Urbis?"

Sarwenna's cry of denial shot down that plan. "I'm coming with you, and don't think otherwise."

"Please."

"No."

They had one more night here, and this time he went to her. A night of desperate hope within the greyness, and as precious. Afterward, he wasted the too short hours left trying to get her to change her mind. She finally stopped him by curling into his shoulder and falling asleep. And the sight of her long lashes and mussed hair in the faint light of the mist covered moonlight banished any more thought of wasting time.

Any last hope she might agree to go back to Urbis with Joe Gibbs vanished the next morning. She stood on the flight platform with him, mouth set and a dark glint in her eyes as they watched Joe Gibbs' flyer lift off while her luggage was loaded into Ethan's flyer.

"You're heading straight back to Urbis?" said Caleb, standing beside them.

Ethan opened his mouth.

"Don't try it," said his older brother. "You can't lie to me. Where are you off to?" Caleb had that stubborn look on his face, the one that said he wasn't going to accept a half-baked answer.

"We're calling on the Old Man on our way. I need to have a chat with him about some Solaris business that wasn't fully tied up when I left."

A grim frown marred Caleb's face. "You can do that by com link."

Ethan waited for the rest of the lecture. But Caleb surprised him.

"Just don't do anything too stupid and report in to me tonight. You miss the call and I'll come hunting you. And I won't be happy."

Ethan had to grin. Caleb had come hunting him a few times in his teen years and being not happy was an understatement for his brother's mood when he'd found him. Having a backstop suddenly made him feel a whole lot more optimistic. "Good to hear, brother," he said, and clapped him on the shoulder.

Lifting off, he looked down and saw Caleb at the side of the platform, looking up at their departing flyer. He gave a quick flash of the grounding lights and got a hand lift in reply.

Then they were up through the ever present clouds and his brother had vanished from sight. He turned the nose toward the east. "Time to go home," he said, and wished it was that simple.

Sarwenna sat silently beside him and stared straight ahead at the ragged crest of the ranges. Then sat back and closed her eyes while they lifted over the buffeting air currents. She didn't open them again until he told her they were in clear air above the welcoming waves of the plains. Gloriously golden under the bright sky of the eastern side of the ranges. "Home," she murmured. "Another beautiful day on the plains."

"With no rain, thank the sands."

She lifted her face to the light and gave him that beautiful smile of hers. The one that turned the world right side up. "No rain and a clear sky. I began to feel half-drowned back there," she added with a chuckle.

He grinned back, revelling like her in escape from the eternal mists of Manascraoch. For a few precious hours, it was just him, her and their own plains country below. He settled back and commed the controls to automatic. His father, Arcadia, Seolta den Coille and all his slimy friends could wait.

"What did you think of the rest of the wedding?" he began.

At first, she said little. No matter. He had time and she was important. Slowly, he got her to open up. He took a quick check on their surrounds. All normal, so he rustled up a drink and snack for each of them.

"The first time in Manascraoch can be intimidating," he said.

"The den Coille's are quite a tribe. But … I like them," she said, sounding as if she'd surprised herself. "Well, except for Seolta. Him, I don't trust. But Samhchair…"

He passed her a bun. "Not surprising that you two get on well. You both had a similar childhood. Being the big sister in a lively family isn't always easy."

She chuckled, then gave a pretend huff. "My family are perfect. Nothing like hers."

"If you say so." He grinned as he took another mouthful.

"All right. You have a point. But the boys look sweet when they're asleep." She took a bite of her own bun, and a blissful smile spread over her face. "Sulwith flyers never had food preppers like this."

She leaned back, took another bite and shut her eyes as she chewed, savouring each mouthful. He could have watched her all day.

"Any more where that came from?" she said at the end.

"As many as you like. Always," and meant so much more. One day, he vowed, there would be a moment for telling her everything. When Solaris was sorted, when his family made sense again. When…

There would be a day. She'd come to his room. She might fool herself that it was a moment in time only, but she couldn't deny the truth of what happened between them. Not forever. One day, she would accept it. She must.

He glanced over at her again.

Not today. This trip wasn't over, though, and Ethan set himself to enjoy every moment of it. Only when they began the descent toward Dridust did he bring the talk back to reality. The chuckles and wry quips faded, and both fell silent as they watched the approaching skyline.

"In the Solaris offices … please, let me do the talking. I don't want… Don't put yourself at risk."

The smile had dropped from her face. "My family is threatened by whatever your father's up to. I have a right to be part of stopping him."

"Yes, you have the right, but we don't yet know what we're heading into. Just remember that family comes first for him. Whatever happens, whatever is said, he will keep his sons safe, but you…"

"A deadlands union supporter. Not who he wants for his heir."

Ethan flushed. "I'm not his heir, not anymore."

"You will be, and he won't want me by your side."

In the dregs of bitterness, Ethan suddenly found hope. "And you? You see yourself at my side."

A flush, an endearing pink wash, coloured those sharp edges. "Maybe. Ethan Winter, the man? Yes, maybe. The heir to Solaris…?"

She's considering it. For the first time, she's admitted to considering it. He felt the grin tug his cheeks. "Just be careful in there," he said, less forcefully, and had to concede she'd won this round. He'd just have to be extra vigilant himself.

CHAPTER TWENTY-FOUR

Sar tried not to stare. She'd never seen this part of Solaris headquarters before. The public offices they used for union meetings had nothing of the softness or downright wealth of these corridors. Walls covered with real pictures, hand-made by artists whose work she'd only ever seen in vidcasts. Stuck here on walls as mere furnishings.

She stopped, staring open-mouthed. "That's a Grimard."

Ethan stopped too, halted by the tug of her hand held tightly in his. He barely glanced at the priceless image on the walls. An image made of real tints and fabric, one she remembered from Higher school. Hand-painted over many days and nights by one of Arcadia's most famous classical artists, now the famous face stared down at her in all its regal, condemning magnificence.

"My great-grandmother. My great-grandfather wanted it done," was all he said before tugging at her hand.

He'd grabbed hold of her hand as they left the flyer and been tugging her with him ever since. She'd tried to disengage, but he'd muttered a strangled, "Please," that cut through any defence she still had against him as he pulled her through a high security entrance she didn't know existed. Family section, he'd said in explanation.

Whatever these corridors were, his clearance still held even though he was supposedly sacked from Solaris.

"This…" she tried, waving a hand around at the softly glowing walls, the extraordinary art, the comfortable chairs and furnishings dotted precisely along the way.

He turned back, and her shock must have finally got through to him. "It's just the family part of the building. I have an apartment here; we all do. It's handy for when we're in Dridust. The big house is too far away if you're working late. So over the years, we've made it feel more like a home."

She could say nothing to that. Yes, the halls spoke of comfort, but of a level she'd never been in before. Not even in her years working as her mother's assistant. Few politicians on the worker side of the political divide dared indulge in displays of wealth, and none she knew could have pulled off something like this. Wealth, yes, but also a degree of artistry that could take pieces that should be in a museum and blend them into a gracious whole. Homely, it was not but, that it was a home, yes, that she could see.

She and Ethan Winter had never felt more different. "Maybe you should do this on your own."

He shook his head. "Your family is threatened too."

Yes, but these corridors threatened her more. The place reeked of an ease with power so deeply engrained that none of the Winters noticed it.

He had seemed normal. How, when he'd grown up surrounded by this?

"Please," he said again, body rigid.

She waved a hand at the paintings and walls. "I don't belong here and never will."

At first his face showed incomprehension. Then he followed her hand. "You think this is me?"

"I know it is."

He shook his head. "They're just things. Yes, I grew up here, but I also grew up on the plains. My father had us out chasing stock and tracking over the land as soon as we could sit on a horse."

"You're a businessman. You love business."

"And that makes me less somehow? You live to help people. I help them in different ways. I give them jobs, food on their table, a roof over their head."

She finally got her hand free and stood there, fists clenched by her side. "Not like this, and it's not why you're in business. Not what you love about it."

He flushed at that. "I've always believed in treating fairly anyone who works for us."

Yes, that was true, even though the union sometimes had to remind Solaris management where the fairness line fell. "But…"

A deeper flush. "I like business. Is that a crime?"

This time, she was the one to reach out and grab his hand. "I didn't mean to sound like I'm condemning you, not for who you are. This place, this building, this business, is who you are." Suddenly, she was the one with a hot flush of shame washing over her cheeks. Yes, he was wealthy, to a degree she'd never fully understood until now. Yes, by his own words, he'd used that inherited wealth to make himself even richer. But that wasn't what drove him, no more than the power of being a union boss drove her.

She took a deep breath. "So why me? What do you want with me?"

A gasped laugh, harsh and strangled and his hands lifted to her. "Everything, Sera Sarwenna."

It echoed that chord inside her, the one she fought so hard to deny. "You have enough already," she said, with another lift of her hand to the walls around her.

"Without you…" He took a deep breath and suddenly the walls, the paintings, none of it seemed quite so important as the look in his eyes. He reached out for her hand again. "This is not how I imagined saying this. One day, on the plains or the desert. In the open air." Another deep breath, and he gently tugged her closer, setting his arms around her and pulling her body into his. She let him, stepping closer, to be answered with a twisted smile on his face and eyes open and vulnerable. "What do I want with you? I love you, Sarwenna Beren. Not for your power, not to get the union on side, not to make Solaris bigger or better. I love your laughter, I love the way you look after your family, that core of strength in you, your toughness and your gentleness. When you're angry, your eyes spark, and when you're happy, they glow. None of that can I buy or possess. You're free to leave here, now. Fight my father and his backers your own way. The Feds will still protect you."

Never had she seen Ethan Winter so stripped bare. His face, that bland business face banished completely. Eyes fixed on hers, mouth tight and body stiff.

She had one answer only, she found. "I'm here, and I'm staying. I hadn't understood before. … I didn't know all of you." She broke off, looked down and dredged up her courage. "Who you are. Who Solaris is. It's huge, and right now, it feels overwhelming."

"But…"

She shook her head. "You said I'm tough. I thought I was too. Could you give all this up?"

He opened his mouth, and she put up a hand quickly. "No, I'm not asking you to. Don't promise me that, not ever. We can't build a future on lies. This is who you are." She shook her head, desperately seeking the words to explain it, to him and to herself. "It's not the power, not the prestige. The challenge of it, building something and pitting yourself against the credits, that's who you are. You tried to tell me once, but I didn't understand. Not then; but you've never stopped fighting to protect this company, this family, your world."

A strained chuckle. "Caleb's the hero in the family. One of us is enough, and he's better at the big moments."

No, she couldn't see Ethan Winter leading a march through Urbis like his brother had done. Ethan's way was quieter, tenacious, more painstaking, slowly working to gain his goals.

And she had become one.

She took a breath and gathered up all her courage, all that she'd tried so hard to bury. "I love you, Ethan Winter. I love your courage, your resilience. Most of all, I love the solid core of you. You will always be there for family, for workers, for those who look to you. You work hard and do not ask for reward."

"I'm not poor," he protested.

She touched his arm. "I didn't mean that. I can see you're not." A twisted smile. "You forget, I've seen you ready to sacrifice everything to save me and, later, my town. It's why I took a second look, why I started to question.

"You love me?"

Certainly filled her. "Yes, Ethan Winter. I love you."

She reached up, put her arms around his neck and tugged his head down, pulled his mouth down to meet hers. They emerged long moments later, and Sar knew she had just crossed a bridge. One with no way back. Still holding tightly around his neck, she squared her shoulders. "We have a meeting, Ethan Winter, and we are already late for it."

He burst into laughter, leaning his forehead against hers. "You turn me inside out and you want to talk meetings?"

What could she say? "I love you. Doesn't change any of the rest of it."

He swooped in again, and for long moments she was lost again. Finally, it was he who drew back and rested his forehead on hers, whispering softly. "Yes, it does, my Sarwenna. It changes everything. We have a meeting, a planet to save, and a wedding to plan."

"What? No. Not to me."

A huge grin covered his face. "Yes. You to me, and me to you."

"Your parents will be horrified."

"At being related to Catra Beren, scourge of the corporates? Yes, probably."

"My mother. She'll…"

"…be equally horrified?"

Sar had a sudden picture of her mother's face at being told her daughter was marrying a Winter. This time, it was she who collapsed in giggles. "If we agree to marry—"

"When you agree to marry me."

A flush. "It's not that simple. There's so much…" she flapped her hands at all that lay between them. "If we agree, I will be the one to tell her."

"Yes, dear," said Ethan Winter in a voice so humble she felt like shaking him. Then his normal voice came back. "Now, we have a meeting."

This time, she really could have wiped that grin off his face, except it matched the one beginning to dawn inside her. Maybe, just maybe, together they could do this.

One look at Sol Winter's expression, the glacial stare on his face when he took in her presence, seriously jarred that hope.

"There is no need for Sera Beren's presence," he said.

Ethan ignored him, taking a chair in front of his father's desk and waving for her to take the other. It's just like a union meeting, she told herself. She managed to refrain from perching on the edge like a frightened schoolgirl but couldn't bring herself to sprawl in her seat like Ethan, long legs out front and returning his father's glare with his own brand of displeased hauteur.

"We've just come from Cumchdach mar Bram an Scathach's wedding."

"The den Coille heir. Yes, I heard."

"Where we heard some concerning things," returned Ethan, dropping the insolent sprawl and leaning forward. "Talk to do with Seolta den Coille, the Alliance and a truly irritating off-worlder."

A hint of a flush stole over Sol Winter's face. "What's that got to do with Solaris."

"Nothing, I would hope. Can you promise me that, Father?"

"I don't answer to you," said Sol Winter, and Sar felt the disappointment bite into Ethan. He kept up the illusion of pride, but Sar could see the rigid set of his muscles keeping him upright. His father ploughed on, pointing out to Ethan exactly how he had let down his father, how his ideas had cut into Solaris profit.

"The Sulwith field. What's the profit curve on that like now?" said Ethan in a dry voice that Sar wondered whether his father knew covered the pain inside his son.

"Down a bit, but that's temporary. The output still exceeds any other field."

Sar knew bluster when she heard it. Sol Winter might act the injured party, but he was flat-out lying, and to his own son.

"Not with the men you have there now," she said. Ethan shouldn't be the one to accuse his father. "Any worker capable of managing that field correctly has left or been driven off by your new team."

"This is none of your business, girl."

"You destroy my hometown and sack my family, along with many others I grew up with? It's my business, right enough. Once a unionist, always a unionist, or haven't you heard that one?"

He actually growled at her, and part of her took a secret delight in rattling the almighty head of Solaris.

The company that gave your father the best years of his life and is the heart of the man beside you. Maybe, but it was past time Sol Winter discovered the company was more than him.

"It is my business, Ser Winter, and my affair when the head of Solaris starts playing games with the future of my town. I don't know what your goal is, but you're not taking all those I care about with you."

"What do you know about protecting people, girl You've never sat in prison and listened as corrupt upstarts pronounce a death sentence on every single member of your family?"

"Not Caleb and Si," shoved in Ethan, uselessly trying to jump in between them. Sar could have told him not to bother.

"Didn't they tell you boys that one? They condemned them in absentia, for daring to stand up to their thugs. That will not happen again. Winters stand together." He glared at Ethan. "Winter one, Winter all. Isn't that what you boys said at school?"

Ethan looked as if his father had slapped him. "You think that justifies whatever deal you've made here? Someone is trying to kill me and Sarwenna. That's who you're in partnership with, Pa."

"You were safe in Urbis. Go back there, son, and leave this to me."

Sar kept hoping, but no matter what Ethan said, Sol Winter stuck to his line. Her heart bled for the man beside her, stiff and hurting, as he tried one gambit after another. Business, logic, profitability and reality. None worked on the Old Man of Solaris.

"You'll let Solaris be stolen from Winter hands, and for what?" finally said Ethan, for once letting all the pain show in his voice.

"I know what I'm doing," said his father. "You don't need Solaris funds. Nor does Caleb, nor will Silas. Not with that boy's touch for com systems. Go back to Urbis."

Ethan sat like stone and she reached out a hand. Only then did she feel the fine tremor running through the muscles of his arms. He made no sign of it but his hand took hers, openly and provocatively. Then he stood.

"This company, this planet, our home is not for sale. Not by me. Good day, Father."

Then he clamped down on her hand as if to a life raft and turned and marched out of his father's office.

Not a word did he speak until they were safely back in his flyer, and Sar had no desire to break the silence in those corridors. Not when it felt like the very walls listened to each breath they took. They lifted off and Ethan stared straight ahead. Then, just as he was about to input the coordinates, he turned his head once and stared down at the great block of Solaris headquarters with its distinctive sunburst logo on the roof.

Then he deliberately swivelled his head forward and stabbed at his com. The flyer shot forward with a whoosh that had her slamming into the back of her seat. She couldn't stop the gasp of air, and Ethan muttered an apology. She clamped her mouth down to stop more sounds. Not yet, not yet. Let them get clear first.

He levelled off high above the land, hovering over the one wisp of cloud skittering over the rolling grasslands below. They sat silent and let the vista scroll over the viewing panel in front of them.

"It's so beautiful," he said after a while, and Sar badly wished he hadn't made it sound like a farewell.

"Where to now," she said as brightly as she could force through her lips.

His face turned grimmer. "My mother is at the big house."

It wasn't a long trip. A couple of standard hours only. The silence that filled the flyer made it seem much longer. They headed west, back toward the mountains and deeper into the grasslands of the plains. Golden heads of long waving tussocks, interspersed with shrubby thickets, more Solaris fields and the odd rock-filled bed where water would rampage after the sporadic deluges that made for summer rains here.

Then she saw it. A stand of trees, splashes of colour in stylised garden beds, and set right in the middle, a large and gracious building that could have come straight from a history 'cast. It should have looked out of place, but the plantings around it merged effortlessly from plains to native shrubbery to exotic, never-before-seen tree types surrounding a garden that wouldn't have been out of place in the great parks of Urbis. In the centre stood a house that shouted out a claim to the land as surely as the Winters who called it home.

She gulped. "Is your mother expecting us?"

"No, but the sensors will have told her we're on our way."

"And we're going here why?"

The harsh cast of that usually controlled face should make her feel guilty. She refused to be and turned toward him, waiting for an answer. His eyes were set on the house. His childhood home.

"Your father was lying to you?"

"Oh, yes. Not in so many words, but in spirit, yes. Until the last bit. That was truth."

"And your mother? Is she likely to know what he's up to?"

He kept staring at the rapidly growing homestead. "In the past, I wouldn't think twice. She knew everything. Now…"

"But she will guess," Sar suddenly realised, "and you think she's less able to hide things."

A twisted smile. "My mother grew up prevaricating in front of the best politicians in the land."

"Like you," she said with a smile and was rewarded with a brief easing of the tension in him.

"It's handy sometimes." Then his face sharpened again. "Since prison…"

She didn't prod him further, seeing the pain in his face. Helena Bascombe Winter had a formidable reputation, but no one had ever claimed she didn't love her sons. Merely that she aimed high for them. That tough core in Ethan he hid so well didn't come only from his father.

When she came face to face with the woman, she kept repeating the thought as a litany inside her head, quelling the automatic impulse to curtsy in deference. Helena Winter had that kind of presence. Ethan had led them around the back of the house, to what he called the family entrance, and ushered them into this stunning room. Green patterns lit up the walls and floors in a delicate and soothing pattern that reminded her of the mountain homes. Lighter here, better suited to the open plains, but a cooling refuge after a day under the hot plains sun. In a chair in the centre of the room, a reader in her lap and a steely gaze on her face when she set eyes on Sar, sat the matriarch of the Winter family.

It was the only word that fit.

Then Sera Winter looked back at her son, and her eyes softened. Only to change back again. Sar had just been classified as a threat to her son.

"Mother, let me introduce my good friend, Sarwenna Beren from Sulwith."

The woman gave her a long, slow appraisal. "Yes, the union organiser. I've heard of you, Sera. Welcome to our home."

A big fat lie, as was Sar's own response. She let Ethan do the talking after that and clung to the memory of his words. Especially when the woman brought up her mother. "I take it that Sera Catra Beren has settled herself back into the Urbis bustle again. She will be much happier."

She murmured agreement, wondering when her mother and this woman had fallen out. Not that it was surprising. Her mother had literally nothing in common with Helena Bascombe Winter.

No, that was unfair. Both loved power and she suspected Helena Winter enjoyed pulling the strings in this house every bit as much as her mother loved tweaking the reins of government up in Urbis.

She really didn't like this woman. Then she glanced at Ethan, and saw the crease in his forehead as he watched his mother.

He listened, negotiated and traversed her every word, even the most extreme, all with that frown line carved into his head and a soft-voiced murmur to deter her worst excesses.

It made her look at the woman again, and now she saw the pulse beating in her neck, the darting flutter of lashes.

Helena Bascombe Winter was terrified.

One of her hands strayed from the rigid hold of her body and over to Ethan. Not touching, but near. As if assuring herself he was still there.

"You're heading back up to Urbis next?" said Sera Winter.

"After we call in on Sulwith. Sera Sarwenna needs a few things from her old home." Not that Sar was aware of. "It will be interesting to have a look at how the field's getting on, with all the new changes."

"No, don't." A sharp cry, hastily smothered and Sar watched in fascination as the woman dragged her control around her. "I'm sure the manager is handling everything. You don't need to worry yourself over such trivialities anymore. Not when you have your own businesses up in Urbis. Far better to concentrate on those and let your father worry about Solaris."

"Maybe you're right," said Ethan, and the relief on his mother's face was unmistakable.

They left soon after. Sar held her silence until they had taken off and he'd set his course. Not till the house had disappeared from the rear viewscreen did she turn to Ethan.

"So where are we heading."

"For Sulwith, of course. You left behind some important family keepsakes and I need to have a serious chat with Tom Crabster."

Sar smiled in satisfaction.

At first, Ethan kept his course straight for the gap in the ranges leading to Urbis. They flew high above the grasslands and from time to time she caught him looking down, as if at a familiar haunt. Not till they reached the first of the foothills did he change course for the east, sweeping close to the rough country leading up into the northern ranges. Back to the deadlands and Sulwith.

A good move. The ranges were good at muffling flyer signatures.

"You think someone's trying to track us?"

"It's a possibility," he said. "We're safe enough here, though, and our security are the best outside the Feds at keeping hidden." Their squads had picked them up just after leaving mountain airspace, and Sar had been surprised how relieved she felt at hearing Dan's familiar cracks at his boss.

Ethan unbuckled his webbing. "Want a bite to eat while we have time?" He set the controls to auto and walked over to the prepper, bringing back wraps and a cool drink.

The food helped, although it couldn't banish the shimmer in her guts. She leaned back and shut her eyes, trying to find peace for just one moment.

A blare of light, and a screeching siren split the cabin.

"What in…"

Ethan dropped his wrap back onto the plate and grabbed for the controls. Then cursed, in language she hadn't heard him use before.

Then she saw why. A large, silver-bellied vessel filled the holo-field, bearing down on them from the upper quadrant. A vessel that hadn't been on their viewscreens or sensors only a moment before. Her heart thudded hard.

"It's tracking us?"

"Worse," he said. "It's locked onto us. We're trapped in their field."

"Can you break out."

His fingers flew and she watched as he set the com to direct brain to com connection. Then he shook his head. "They outclass, outpower and outgun us. Buckle down. Their traction beam is pulling us in now, and I doubt they're too concerned about how well we survive the tug."

"Our security will deal with them." Dan had been full of his usual sauce after they left the Winter house with comments that had struck just a little too close for comfort, leaving her red-faced and choking back laughter.

Right now, no laughter touched Ethan's face.

"Tell me," she said.

"My external links are dead. I can't raise them."

"They will follow us."

A grim frown twisted his face. "That ship is shielded and running com-silent. Now that we're locked into its field, we're invisible too. They've lost us."

CHAPTER TWENTY-FIVE

Ethan's fingers played desperate games in the control field. Engine speed, navigation, thrust and stop, an abrupt sideways sheer. Vain orders to a locked-down system. He had to break out of this beam. Not just for himself. After all the previous attacks, their enemy must know the security forces were on high alert and any harm to a Winter would be splashed across all the vidcasts after the scandal of last season's arrests. But Sarwenna? Her mother had told the corporates often enough what she thought of them. Targeting her daughter wouldn't surprise anyone.

He risked a glance at her. Eyes flashed in annoyance, but her hands clutched the sides of her chair and her feet were braced against the floor.

These brakka had frightened her, and that was not acceptable.

"Hold tight," he said. The folds of the hills might help. He tried another sharp drop, then lurched the ship every which way. Tractor beams pulled in one direction only.

Nothing. Still that ominous tug hauling them in, closer and closer to the swelling silver belly above.

Sar leaned forward to peer at the image on the com field. "Any markings or field signature yet?"

"No. They're running quiet, and this ship has the best tech available to Solaris. It can read any but a Fed vessel."

"You think it's one of theirs?"

He wished he could say yes. He shook his head. "I haven't seen anything like it."

"It's from the Alliance, then." Sarwenna's hands fisted on the sides of the chair. "Someone needs to tell them they don't own Arcadia yet."

Maybe, but Ethan doubted telling that to Deputy Malgrave would have any effect on the woman. He tried sending a message on his com, using all the Solaris and Winter codes. He even resorted to the Survey code Caleb had forced him to add to his database. Right now, he'd try anything.

If only he had a hope they were getting through.

The security details knew their last location. They'd be looking for them.

A clunk, and their flyer met the other vessel. Then more grindings, bangs and thumps.

"They've locked on. They'll either breach the hatch next or take us somewhere." His father had put them all through security training. Ethan knew the forced takeover routine by heart. "No matter what they do to me, don't show any sign it affects you. I'll be doing the same."

"Don't give the bad guys a weapon to use against us. Got it," she said dryly. His Sarwenna had courage.

"I'm sorry about this. If we'd never met."

"We did, and what you said at Dridust," she took a breath, "it still holds for me. We will get out of this, and we will make them pay."

He reached out a hand to take hers. She accepted and he breathed again.

"They'll take us somewhere else, I'm guessing," Sarwenna said. "Do you have any kind of nav function?"

He checked the route record. "Basic ship functions are still normal. All except steering."

"Calls for help?"

"I've tried, but best to assume they're not getting out."

She didn't look surprised. This was a woman who'd faced down angry unionists and brangling bosses.

After a while, she asked where they were headed. "It feels like we've turned around."

"Tracking back to the west," he confirmed. She brought up the local holomaps. They were heading back along the ranges to the gap leading to Urbis. Or almost. The line through the holo-field didn't track north enough to make the gap. Wherever they were going, it wasn't to the metropolis.

A long time later, the trace stopped. He listened to the sounds of his flyer. "We're hovering. I'm guessing their base is below somewhere.

Her finger swirled over the holo-field. "North of Winter lands, but across the western ranges from here is the edge of den Coille country."

"You're thinking Seolta is in charge of this." He'd had to consider it a possibility, but even now he found that difficult. He and Seolta had never been friends, not like his other brothers, but to be a party to kidnap or worse? The whole thing was so beyond rational that he had to assume there was little chance they'd get out of this alive. Or at least, of Sarwenna getting out alive. Even now, he found it hard to believe they'd try anything against a Winter.

And prison taught you nothing?

They began to drop. Sarwenna leaned over the holo-field. "There's nothing here."

Ethan glanced over, then a jolt of recognition hit him. "See that shadow in the third gulley from the north?"

Her finger found the dark hollow. "This one?"

"Show subterranean layers to the first depth," he ordered his com.

Sarwenna gasped. "It's an entire system of caverns. How could they know about it?" A quick swivel and her eyes narrowed. "How did you?"

"Ceartas and Seolta showed them to me a few months ago. It's one of the den Coille hideouts, set up after the Survey attacked them. In there are enough infrastructure and supplies to keep an army."

"With monitoring slotted back to den Coille central, no doubt. You think Bram den Coille is a part of this too? Or your friend, Cumchdach?"

"I'm tragging sure they're not; but surveillance can be tampered with. My brother Caleb taught me that."

Her hand disappeared from his grasp. A hollow emptiness invaded him in its place.

"Secure your com. We will get out of this," he said, and wished he believed his own words.

A clank, a swoosh as the ship landed, with his flyer still glued to the side. They were stationary, and the next instant he heard the sounds he'd been waiting for. The grinding and banging of the ship working to access his flyer.

"Head high," he said. Then the hatch blew back and booted feet slammed onto the deck of his flyer. Next minute, uniformed guards filled the door to the cockpit.

Solaris uniforms.

The shock on Sarwenna's face matched his own. "Nice to have known you, Ser Winter," she said, head jerking back, and he would have liked to smash every one of those stony faces surrounding him. But their hands held C49 blasters, and one wrong word could see Sarwenna Beren lying dead at his feet.

"Ser Winter, if you will please join us," said a man wearing the stripes of a senior guard. The wave of his blaster took away all thought of there being a choice. Ethan put out a hand to help Sarwenna rise from her seat. A formal gesture, the kind he'd been taught to automatically offer any woman, but there was nothing automatic in his reason. He needed to touch her.

Then he felt her flinch and cursed their captors. As soon as he was free, these brakkas would pay dearly. If he got free.

"If you would follow us, Ser Winter." The words may be courteous but the two men holding him and the nudge of a blaster in his back gave the lie to them. He could walk, or be carried, said that heavy prod.

He walked.

Had any of his alarm calls got out?

Beside him, two equally thuggish guards held Sarwenna as tightly, and another guard poked a blaster in her back. One wrong move by Ethan and she was dead.

Into the foreign vessel they marched them. They hadn't bothered with the sun-splash design here and the rest of the crew wore nondescript beige ship overalls. Nothing showed their origin, and all hurried past with eyes averted.

Whoever they were, none of them was innocent. The few words spoken by his guards were in Standard with an accent he couldn't place, but that meant little. Many parts of the western continent were unknown to him. They passed through the ship's passages and out the freight entrance, into a cavern ablaze with lights. Nowhere to hide, not here. The guards hurried them across the expanse and into the bowels of the caverns beyond, lights blazing into life as they passed. Sarwenna's captors marched her ahead of him, gripping her hard enough to leave bruises, but her head stayed high.

The corridors branched. He kept looking for signs to identify their captors, all senses alert.

Then he saw Sarwenna's group take the branch opposite his.

"Hey." He dug his heels in, struggling to get free.

"Stop, Ser Winter, if you value your life—or hers."

"Where are you taking her?"

The nearest scum gave him a shove in the back. "Don't worry. She's safe enough, for now."

He had meant to keep his cool, to keep his distance from her, but the sight of an ashen-faced Sarwenna disappearing around a corner destroyed any veneer of control.

"You harm one hair on her head and you'll answer to the Council." And to me.

"We are aware of Sera Beren's connections, Ser Winter."

If only he could believe they meant anything to this man. Another shove and he nearly fell to the ground. Only pride saved him, driving him to scramble his legs under him before they could push him over again. Down a corridor they dragged and thrust him, and with every step the fear of what could be happening to Sarwenna grew.

Finally they stopped at a doorway and he drew himself up straight. The senior guard played a code on the control panel, too fast for him to catch, and then it slid wide.

A boardroom. What he'd expected, he didn't know, but definitely not the kind of room in which he'd spent far too much of his working life. It even had that same chemical odour of recent cleaning. They pushed him into the chair at the near end of the table, locking his legs and arms down with restraint fields, and stripped his com from his wrist. All the while he stared at the dark shadows at the far end, hiding those seated there. An old tactic, one Ethan had always scorned. He sat and waited, striving for calm.

Don't think about her. She's safe. As long as you cooperate, she's safe.

He closed his eyes on the thought, then opened them. Right on cue, the lights came up at the far end of the room. Not bright, but enough to make out the silhouettes in the shadows. His captors clearly favoured the dramatic.

He recognised the three figures seated at the end and wished he'd been more surprised.

"You're playing out of your league, den Rith," he said to the man from the minor company on that hard-to-remember island, recently met at Cumchdach's wedding.

A slight sound from the left-hand figure, quickly stifled. Then the head leaned back and the man tried to loll casually. Did he think Ethan was a novice at this?

"A good day to you, Ser Winter," said the remembered voice. "Our apologies for your discomfort, but this shouldn't take long. A few misunderstandings to clear up, then this minor unpleasantness can be forgotten."

Never, vowed Ethan. "What about Sera Beren? I do trust no unpleasantness will be involved there."

A shift in the shadow as the man lifted a hand. "Temporary only."

You needed a deeper voice than that for an effective threat. The kind Ethan's father had taught all his sons. "You spoke of a misunderstanding?"

The central figure leaned forward. Unlike den Rith, Deputy Malgrave was a master in the use of voice. "The Alliance requires evidence of a united corporate focus if Arcadia is to be maintained in its present ownership. Unfortunately, it appears that you and your father are not in agreement over the future course of Solaris."

He shrugged his shoulders. "Solaris is the largest providers of renewable energy on this continent. Father sees no reason for us to change how we operate."

"And you want to cut back on energy production. An interesting idea, but what replaces the energy Solaris no longer supplies?"

"You've obviously read my internal Solaris reports, so you know I recommended changing the solar collection methods and decentralising energy production. There would be no decrease in output. We move into building and supplying domestic and small scale commercial solar generators instead. You don't need one big commercial entity producing everything."

A snort from the upstart from the island. Ethan had no trouble ignoring him. The Alliance deputy was the one that counted. Her and that other, still quiet figure.

"Ser Hilmar," he said to the silent off-worlder. "Where do you fit into this?"

The shadows remained around the man, but the barely glimpsed figure sank down as if seeking more anonymity. A coward at heart but also a bully had been Ethan's summation when he first met the man, and today proved him right.

"Kevand3 are here as consultants," said den Rith. "They're experts in businesses operating in environmentally marginal conditions."

"Which Arcadia is not yet, and which we are working hard to ensure it does not become. Moreover, I understand that Kevand3 is primarily in the business of acquisition and distribution of assets."

They're blood suckers, den Rith, and you've been well and truly suckered.

"Not in this instance," said the Alliance deputy firmly. "The Ser from Kevand3 is an observer, no more."

He'd thought little could shock him, but the proof of it still stunned him. He'd never trusted her but had never expected an Alliance deputy to be on the take. "Observing what? The destruction of an old and respected business? Or is he more? That flyer that brought us here is like nothing I've seen before. Just like the flyer that ambushed us over the Sulwith solar field."

The lights came up then, and the Alliance deputy sent him that cold smile. The same one she'd given him the first time he met her. The man from Kevand3 crossed his arm and leaned back and Ethan would have dearly loved to swipe the smirk off his face.

Only the man from the islands frowned. "You were never in real danger of being hurt."

"You think so, den Rith? You can't have read the medical reports. Without Sera Beren's local knowledge, you wouldn't have the pleasure of my company here today."

"A pleasure that can be cut short." The man from Kevand3 sat up. "We're wasting our time here. This man isn't going to cooperate with us."

A threat from a bully. Usually he ignored them, but this time, the man could back it up. Those full lights exposing their identity confirmed what Ethan hadn't thought possible till now. His chances of making it out of here weren't good, but Sarwenna hadn't seen their captors yet.

Suddenly, a commotion was heard at the door. Then the last man Ethan expected burst into the room. "What's going on here," said Seolta den Coille, and Ethan's temper threatened to smash his hardy control again.

"Nothing of concern to you," said the Alliance Deputy.

Seolta ignored her, barging around the table and grabbing at Ethan's arms. "Let this man go."

"Don't bother playing the innocent, Seolta." said Ethan. "Go home; go back to ignoring the reality of what's happening on Arcadia."

Seolta tugged at Ethan's hands again, and Ethan had to snarl at him to stop before he pulled his arms from their sockets.

The Alliance deputy stood up. "Ser den Coille, you have no place here. This is outside our arrangements."

"You're supposed to be helping corporates stay powerful, not kidnapping senior executives."

Ethan sneered at Seolta. "What happened to all your vaunted business smarts? They're interested only in their own power and interests, not that of any Arcadian company."

Seolta lifted his hands from Ethan, and stepped back, fists clenched. "We had an agreement."

"One that keeps you rich and hits back at anyone trying to change that. Yeah, I figured that out already. The only thing I can't figure out is what you promised they'd get in return."

A red flush swept over Seolta's lean face. "A share in the stable and growing wealth of this planet, in exchange for keeping the Alliance out."

Ethan turned a head to take in the trio sitting at the top of the table. "You put your trust in a greedy, two-bit player, an asset stripper from a barren wasteland and a crooked Alliance official? Not like you, not without checks."

"The benefits to them should have been enough."

"What, to justify helping them try to kill me, helping them attack your home city? Helping subvert a com room to manipulate a child into doing their work? You did know they used Arianna Beren twice at Sulwith in their attacks against me. The girl may be a certifiable genius, but she's only in her first year of Higher School."

The trio at the top let them talk and Ethan knew he signed his death warrant with every word he spoke, but not Seolta's, not yet. From the look on the den Coille's face, the man had just realised how badly his famous trickery had betrayed him.

"You figured the odds wrong this time, Seolta. Take a look at them. The Alliance deputy is loyal to the Alliance and herself, and the other two are as miserable as you thought them, and twice as greedy. They don't share."

Seolta stepped back as if struck. "You're wrong."

"No, I'm not," said Ethan, barely stopping his fear and tiredness from swamping his voice. "If I am, ask them where they've taken Sera Beren."

Now Seolta swung his head around to the top table. "The Sera? You took her too? You had no reason to do that. She has nothing to do with Solaris, not anymore, and her mother is the kind to make trouble."

Ethan glared at Seolta. The idiot was going to get himself killed. "Bit late to find a conscience, Seolta."

The man's head snapped back, his lean features sharp with fury. "What would you know? The man who wants to sell Solaris down the drain and destroy everything your family spent generations building."

"And I always thought you the clever one of the family. Guess I made a mistake there."

"Enough." The woman from the Alliance stepped in with the voice of one bored with the squabbling of children. "Ser den Coille, this matter is ours to resolve. Our agreement stands. If you want to review our contract, we can make a meeting for tomorrow."

Ethan fought the restraints to appear to loll back in his chair. "Yes, Seolta, why not take a meeting. Check their contract and see what more you can squeeze out of betraying your family and your home world. That's what you do best."

Seolta rounded on him. "Like they did when they threw us all in prison and sentenced us to die? You were there; they tried to execute you too. You think I'm going to let that happen again."

"Criminal thugs did that. Not Arcadia. Believe what you want. Skulking around and listening at the wrong door is your thing."

Seolta took a step forward. "I don't have to listen to this."

"No, you can leave." Ethan tugged at the restraints. "Me, I take my pleasure where I can." He shook his wrist uselessly. "No other choice."

One more push, one more word. Get out of here, Seolta.

"Ser den Coille," the woman from the Alliance began.

"Yes, Ser den Coille," shoved in Ethan. "Such a worthy Ser. Go run to your brothers and tell them how that worthless Winter insulted you. Aigherach idolises you; he'll listen."

Finally, Seolta's fists began to unclench. The fury began to seep from his bones and his eyes widened. Then it was back and he stepped away, with a face visible now to Malgrave and her crew. "That's it. I thought I owed you for Aigherach, but it doesn't cover listening to this kind of muck."

He turned to Ethan's captors, tight-mouthed and eyes glinting. "My apologies, Sers and Sera. I thought I owed a debt of honour to this man. As you've heard, I was mistaken. You have the matter satisfactorily in hand, so I'll leave you. Please be assured that our agreement stands."

With which he swung toward the door and marched out, pausing in the doorway. "Sera Beren? I'm heading up to Urbis from here. I can take her with me. She'll keep quiet about this. Too embarrassing for her if it comes out, and I doubt she's happy with Ser Winter here at the moment. Not after being exposed to both his parents."

Ethan put a snarl on his face. "What's between Sera Beren and me has nothing to do with this."

"Your parents welcomed her with open arms?" Seolta wore the sneer he'd mastered so well. "No, didn't think so. Treated her like a reject from the gutters more like. What did you expect if you take up with the wrong side of the worktable?"

"She'll change her mind." Ethan put all his rage into his voice. "As soon as I get out of here and talk to her."

"Good luck with that. Farewell, Ethan ingh Sol an Helena." Seolta flipped him an obscene gesture, matched by the scowl on his face, and stomped out of the door, slamming the control plate on the other side. The door slid back with a solid crash.

It reverberated through Ethan. Could he trust someone as slippery as Seolta?

He slumped in his chair, abandoning his defiant slouch, then struggled to sit up again. A Winter didn't give up. "What's next on the entertainment schedule? You going to bring my father in too? Show him what happens if he fails to cooperate?"

"Your father fully understands the situation," said the Alliance deputy.

The slime ball from Kevand3 rubbed his hands together. "Very adequately, if not quite accurately."

"You're going to let Solaris run itself into the ground by ensuring they make no effort to change. What else is there to understand? You were behind the sacking of anyone who knew how to run the field and your puppet manager made sure the field stayed with the solar sheeting that turns all the area under it to empty desert. The type the government will not tolerate. When does the

Council step in and seize control of Solaris, selling what's left of it to anyone kind enough to take it off their hands?"

Ethan waited, hardly daring to breathe. The sum of their intent had only just come to him and he was a fool not to have figured it out sooner.

"Shortly, Ser Winter," said the nobody from the islands.

"Then you divide the spoils up. How much have they promised you, den Rith? How much to betray your home world?"

"More than enough," smirked the man.

"Then you're an idiot," said Ethan.

The off-worlder shoved his chair back with an oath. "We're wasting our time here. Ser Winter, the situation is simple. You write a second report rescinding the first and sign over your Solaris shares to us, then Sera Beren is free to go."

"Out of the question. Nor would anyone believe it."

"They will when the reports surface of the nasty break up between you and the sera. How you discovered she'd only been using you to get what the union wanted. You got so mad you renounced your company and home world forever, leaving the planet in a fit of pique."

"A ridiculous story."

Except that the gossip vids would love it, spinning it more and more with each new telling. A stupid, silly story that was just the kind of nonsense their followers would love.

"A badly told version," agreed the cool voice of the Alliance deputy. "Our media bureau is not that inept. Hints of a bigger story will go out first, teaser snippets, followed by ever more juicy morsels. Helped of course by your departure on a luxury passenger service, leaving a suitably aggrieved com message behind for the sera."

Ethan tried tugging at his restraints, flexing his ankles and squirming uselessly around in search of freedom. "My family is not powerless. They routinely squelch stories like that."

"And we routinely deal with the media."

"Any contract giving you my share of Solaris will be thrown out by the courts as soon as it hits the bench. The Fed lawyers will easily expose the whole thing as a sham."

"Not when you confirm it," said the man from Kevand3. "Monitors on," he ordered.

At the side of the room, a vid-screen came to life. On display, a room with Sarwenna sitting on a hard bench seat. Nothing else showed in the room except for a basic amenity cupboard. Her fists lay clenched in her lap and she stared straight ahead, as if well aware she was under surveillance.

"Take a good note of the room, Ser Winter," said the off-worlder, "while you can."

Then the lights dimmed and he saw Sarwenna stiffen. Darker and darker until the room became an inky black well of nothingness. Not a hint of light, nothing.

"A nasty game you're playing," he said, wrestling to control his voice and show nothing of the horror in him. He'd seen an inky blackness like that before. Lived through it, with only the touch of roughened walls and the feel of a dripping tap to prove he still existed.

Then he realised her room held no tap.

No, there was a service cupboard. If only Sarwenna remembered how to find it.

"Turn on the sound," he ordered.

"So you can hear her weep?"

"She won't." Sarwenna Beren wouldn't give them the satisfaction.

"Not yet," agreed the scuzzball off-worlder. "It will be interesting to see how long it takes to break her."

Ethan believed him. The man sounded too eager, too much as if enjoying this. A door opened behind him. Bootfalls stomped in and rough hands grabbed at him. The restraints vanished, but others gripped him, circling around his chest and legs. He could walk in a rough stumble, but that was all. Hands, arms, head, all held tight by the field's grip.

"We will talk to you again, Ser Winter, when you have reconsidered our offer."

"And Sera Beren?" he managed to gasp out.

"Will be released when our business is finished. Until then…"

"Don't worry, Ser Winter," put in the miserable leech from the islands. "You can watch her from your own quarters—for now."

Ethan's heart began pounding. The threat in those words. They couldn't know about his weakness.

Seolta worked with them.

No.

The guards marched him out of the room, out of the corridors with smooth plascrete coverings over the rough stone walls that lay behind them and down a level. Then another, and another. They emerged into a tunnel where nothing hid the raw stone walls and the only light came from glowing panels set into the ceiling.

You're not locked in. There is still an exit.

Then he saw him. The very den Coille he'd hoped was well out of here and on his way for help.

Seolta stood in the middle of the passage, barring their way. "Where are you taking him?"

Ethan cursed inside. "I thought you'd be long gone. Haven't you done enough already."

"This wasn't what I contracted for," said Seolta den Coille in the nearest to an apology Ethan had heard from him. "Where are you taking him?" he said again.

The guards merely pushed him aside and kept dragging Ethan along. A new set of bootsteps told Ethan that Seolta followed. Then they stopped at a door. It opened on a room ominously like the cell he'd seen Sarwenna sitting in. But this room had no service cupboard, nothing except a hard bench. No window at all. His muscles seized.

Seolta shoved up beside the guards. "You can't put him in there. Stop this."

"Get out of here, Seolta. I don't need the likes of you watching this."

"Not in there. Get him another one."

"Don't you ever stop talking?" Ethan had reached the point of desperation. The cell in front of him began to shrink. This room had no way out. Walls collapsing. In another moment, he was going to disgrace himself and he didn't need Seolta watching that. Worse, he would be failing Sarwenna.

Seolta shoved forward again, thrusting in front of the guards. Ethan looked him straight in the eye.

"Get out of here, you scumbag brakka offspring of a nieten. You want to help? Spare me having to do this in front of the likes of you." He carefully worked his mouth, concentrated hard, then shot out a blog of spit, and gave his best leering grin when it landed square on Seolta's face. "Leave me alone."

Seolta's jerked up a hand to swipe away the mess and clenched his fists. "Just remember. I did try to help. But some fratters aren't worth the effort." His face disappeared. Next, Ethan heard the rapid beat of retreating boots, echoing against the long corridors of this place. Not a moment too soon. Despite himself, he felt his heels dig into the ground and the sweat break out on his forehead.

They were going to shut him in.

A quick shove and he fell inside. The field released and he began to pick himself up from the ground, just as the clang of the old-fashioned door slammed behind him, followed by the unmistakable sound of a lock engaging. He struggled to his feet and felt for the bench, swept his eyes quickly around the room, then waited, trying to breathe as slowly as he could, fighting to stave off the panic.

Don't give in. Don't let them win. That's what he'd said to himself, over and over in that cursed Survey prison. It had kept him sane, after a fashion.

A black holo-screen jumped to life on the wall opposite. A screen showing nothing, but he could hear sounds. Hear the harsh breathing of another human, then a quiet curse in a familiar voice and he nearly laughed.

Sarwenna Beren hadn't given in yet, nor would he.

At that exact moment, the lights disappeared and he was wrapped in the same inky blackness.

Shut your eyes, it's not real.

Touch the bench under you, feel the world.

Seolta is leaving. They have to let him go. He will act on this.

Caleb will get your message.

Sarwenna is still fighting.

That last was what saved him, helped him slow his breathing and spread his palms on the reality of stone beneath him.

Feel the chill in the air and listen hard for the sound of her breath.

Then another sound intruded. The voice of the brakka scum from Kevand3. "Welcome to your new home, Ser Winter. I trust you are comfortable. If you would like out, you have only to say the word."

"Which is," he ground out.

"Sign the contract."

"And you'll let me out?"

A slight chuckle. "In a manner of speaking."

Ethan refused to let the chill of that laugh get to him. He'd known they had no intention of letting him go as soon as they'd shown him their faces. But Sarwenna hadn't seen them. Not yet.

"And Sera Beren?"

"Will be released to the care of her family as soon as you agree to our terms."

Then the faint hum of background noise vanished and the communication channel cut off.

So there was a sliver of hope for Sarwenna if he agreed to their terms, and if he could trust them to keep their word.

His best option for now: buy time. Seolta would be free soon. Just maybe the den Coille brother he'd never trusted wasn't yet lost to family and honour. Or maybe his call to Caleb had got through.

There might be a way out of this prison.

There wasn't out of your last prison.

Ethan bit down hard on that last thought, refusing to give in to it. He kept his eyes squeezed shut, desperate to hold off the madness threatening to overwhelm him if he gave in to the reality of this place.

This room had an exit. He couldn't see it because his eyes were shut, but it had a way out.

He held his breath to listen and heard with relief the sound of a woman breathing. Of Sarwenna still breathing. Controlled, harsh but not panicked. Not yet. She still fought their captors and so must he. Time to act.

Quietly, keeping all noise down so he could keep hearing that breath of life from her, the in and out of another human, he stood and toed off his boots. Then softly, ignoring the feel of the rough-cut floor on his feet, he edged along the bench until he reached the far wall. Hands splayed, he made his painstaking way around the room, fingers searching each crack, each knob and change of level. One wall, then the next, until the third rewarded him with the machine-cut edges that told of the doorway. He stopped, leaning his forehead against the door that led out of this room, concentrating hard on the sound of Sarwenna.

A mutter this time, a hint of a whimper. *No, my love, don't give in.* Then a hard curse using words he'd heard in the streets of Dridust, and he could have cheered aloud. These brakka holding them had no idea of the quality of their prisoner.

He squeezed his eyes tight, fighting the urge to open them.

This room has an exit. You just haven't found it yet.

Painstakingly, he traced each side and top of the doorway. Then ran his fingers across the entire surface, forcing himself to keep to a rational pattern. Crossways, from top to bottom, then down the length of it, from one side to another.

At last, a slight dip. Carefully his fingers slid along the shape of it, and he built a picture in his head. Under this panel lay the locking mechanism. He dredged up from childhood images of old-style latches. The archaic type used by the first settlers for their makeshift shelters when energy was still scarce on this new world.

When he explored this place with the den Coille brothers, they'd told him the caverns were one of the first homes of the plains settlers. The Winters had headed south from here, seeking lands like the ones they had left back on earth, but other settlers continued to use this place as a refuge and storage caverns for those early generations. These lower caverns had been abandoned for many years, forgotten by all except the locals and curious den Coilles. Or would Caleb have known of them? It was just the kind of place the Survey would have used in the years they were forced to work undercover to save Arcadia from environmental disaster. Now they worked in the open, but maybe, just maybe, a corner of this complex still lay in their files. Thanks to his wife Fee, Caleb often worked with the mountain Survey teams.

Another sliver of hope to add to the flimsy wall protecting him from madness.

Again and again, his fingers traced the even lines of the depression, pressing and finally pounding in frustration. He had to get through to the mechanism inside that cover plate.

If he just had something to break the lock.

There is an exit.

One more blow, and he wrenched back his hand, sucking knuckles rank with the metallic tang of blood.

This room is old, and these walls are of rock and dust. If you're not careful, those grazes will get infected.

Hah. As if he'd live long enough to worry about infection.

Listen for Sarwenna. He smiled as the sound of a song filled his room. An old union ballad, with a brisk beat and the throb of worker fury driving every line. Thank you, my darling.

Hold on to your courage. I will get you out of here.

Then he made the mistake of letting his eyes open to the inky blackness surrounding him. The walls zoomed in and his heartbeat rocketed. He collapsed on the ground.

No. He squeezed his eyes shut, listened hard for the sound of her voice, and nearly wept when the sounds of a plains lullaby broke through his nightmare. A song he imagined her singing to little Finn and Daff. A song that said all was safe in the world and the grownups were in control. That it was safe for a child to shut his eyes and sleep.

He reached behind him and felt for the wall then crawled over and curled up against it, head on knees, listening intently as the song repeated over and over. Now and again, a slight quiver told of nerves, but then a pause and he waited, heart in mouth. Always it started again, an edge to her voice until the song worked its magic and the notes came out smooth and strong.

Alive, for now. How long that would last, he dreaded to think. Reality had banished the sliver of hope he'd held for her. He'd seen their faces and so must die, and she was a witness to the crime. No hope of using a crashed flyer with his body in it as cover if she lived to say otherwise.

The fear in her voice was the final proof. Their captors must have had heard the rumours going around Sulwith, and he'd stupidly confirmed it for them. Sarwenna's only use to them was as a weapon against him. No matter what he did, no matter how much he cooperated, her life ended as soon as he gave in to their demands.

Followed by his. He had to get them both out of here.

That door. He could open it, if only he had a hammer, or stone. Or his boots.

He breathed in, slowly in and out. Breathed until his mind stopped questioning the lies he told it. This room has an exit. He just had to find it, and keep his eyes shut.

He reached out to the wall behind him and began to inch around the room again. A corner, then the last wall. Now the start of the bench. Fingers, feet, feeling their way back to where he'd started and there were his boots. Best quality from a premiere boot smith in Urbis, with heels and sole designed to withstand the toughest the desert could throw at them. He tucked them under his arms and began to inch his way back to the door.

Slowly, keep your breathing under control, don't let your captors hear you moving.

And when he tried to break down the door? He'd seen no sign of the tell-tale shapes of surveillance sensors in that brief time before the lights vanished, but he had no doubt they were in here. The velvety blackness of the holo-field feed from Sarwenna's room proved the cell came complete with modern technology.

And the door? Who says that doesn't have a sensor on it too?

He needed a cover for the banging.

In this bare room?

You have two boots and a voice. Before he could overthink it, he hurled the first boot right at that holo-field of black.

"Turn it off," he yelled at the top of his voice. "Let me out of here." Then began to whimper, forcing the sound of tears into his voice. Then a gasp, a choking cough.

"I will not let you win. Those Survey scum couldn't break me, nor will you."

He drew deep breaths, in and out, slowly, slowly letting them ease off. Then waited, counting over and over, badly missing the timer on his confiscated com.

Nothing happened. Nothing. He breathed softly again and waited a bit longer.

Then laughed inside, not letting a hint of it show in his breath or voice. He'd just given them what they hoped for.

He repeated the performance at odd intervals twice more, each time crawling slowly around the room then spreading himself across the floor on his belly until he found the spot his boot had landed, then making his way back. The second time, he made it louder, made a show of the mad scramble and curses of a man who'd failed repeatedly then must search for his far flung boots.

He hugged both boots tight to his chest and waited. Longer this time, interspersed with defeated whimpers and wavering cries.

He should have gone into acting.

Except that there was too much truth in his sounds. Panic shimmered beneath the surface, waiting to leap out and take over.

There is an exit. This room has a way out.

Finally, he made his way back to the door, wailing and screaming, banging the boot repeatedly against the doorway. "Let me out, let me out."

A new voice spoke from the holo-field.

"Ser Winter, are you ready to agree to our conditions?"

He didn't have to try hard to force out the gulps and choked breath. "No, no. You can't make me do this." Then clapped his hand over his mouth with a loud slapping sound. "Not yet," he said through muffled hands.

A chuckle. "You need more persuasion, Ser Winter."

And now he heard, horrifyingly, the sound of Sarwenna crying. Torn, frightened, then silence. He could only wait, listen with every part of his body, and nearly cried out loud when he heard her laboured breathing.

"Leave her alone," he called out, then started his banging again, one, two, more. Harder and harder, right over that trace of a hollow on his door panel.

CHAPTER TWENTY-SIX

Sar huddled on the cold bench. Water, fast and cold, surged from the amenity cupboard and glugged across the floor.

Water that had no way out of this closed cell. For one terrifying instant, she broke, and hated her captors for that.

Enough. You can beat them. What did she see before they plunged her into this lightless nightmare? A brief glance, lines only of a bare stone space, a bench and the simple service cupboard almost directly opposite her. She threw herself off the bench, ploughing through the rising water to the cupboard. Banged on every surface, until finally she found the control panel. A smack on the off switch and the ominous flood of water stopped its deadly cascade.

There ought to be a drainage hole in the floor of the unit. Her fingers groped along the base, felt the toilet cavity, tried the basin. All exits blocked, all locked tight with elevated plugs and her scrabbling fingers could find no release tab.

If her captors decided to override the controls in this cell, that water would flow back, keep flowing until it rose right to the ceiling.

Until it displaced all the air and left her to….

No, don't say it. Do not let them win.

Breathe in and out. Sing, curse, do whatever is needed to force back the sounds of terror stuck in her throat. She splashed back to her bench, feet and hands wet, and trousers clinging damply to her legs. Maybe they'd decided to finish her by hypothermia. It would be fitting. Hypothermia was the most common downfall of those lost in the wet and cold mountain wilderness that was home to the traitor Seolta den Coille.

How long had she been shut in here?

At least she wouldn't die of thirst, she mused grimly.

Nor of hunger, it turned out an unknown time later. A rattle from the direction of the door and a small patch of light glowed in the middle of the darkness. Her eyes latched greedily onto it, drinking in proof she still lived. She hadn't been abandoned to her fate. Then a hatch opened and a bowl appeared in a hollow. She leapt off the bench, careless of the splash of cold water, and snatched at the bowl before the hatch and its light could disappear again. Back to her bench, huddle up on the dry shelf, all while clutching the bowl and its precious contents close to her chest.

The smell of the food would normally have done little for her appetite, nor would the texture. A bland porridge of unknown content. Vegetable or other, she couldn't say. It was warm and her nose and tongue said it was food. That was enough.

No spoon, no utensils. Hands and mouth did swift duty instead, gobbling down the mush before someone could come and steal it back from her. Then sanity crept back and she slowed, savouring each mouthful. Taking the time to assure her body the end had not yet come.

Her captors saw fit to feed her. That meant she had a use for them still, that Ethan still lived. Nor was water a problem, though surviving whatever microbes swam in the slosh spreading over the floor might be if she lived long enough.

The handbasin was full. That must be her first supply.

The toilet still worked too. Fortunately, it was a modern vacuum type with no water supply. No worry about overflowing sewage. And don't even think about what's on this floor. She had water to drink, food to eat and a place to relieve herself.

The immediate threat came from the dank chill invading the room. Her captors must need her frightened, to keep believing she might not survive.

If she could face down a room of angry workers and survive the political tempest that was her mother bent on a project, then she could survive this cell. She must.

How to escape? There lay the rub. Did she dare hope someone would come to her rescue?

No, the question was did she believe in Ethan Winter enough to hope for rescue? What were they doing to him?

She'd told him she loved him, and he'd promised the same, but he had known about this complex. She'd seen the flare of recognition in his eyes, and the guards who captured them wore Solaris uniforms.

Is your love so small?

He had promised her his love and she had given him her trust.

If only she had more information. Instead she was stuck here, sloshing around in an ice bucket of a cell, waiting to freeze to death if they didn't drown her first.

Pathetically waiting for her hero to save her. A small flame of anger burst to life inside her.

Someone rattled the door. "You've had enough time. Put the bowl back in the hatch."

"And if I don't," she called back.

"You'll be swimming."

She believed him, trag it, and pushed off the bench, sloshing through water up to her ankles. For a few precious moments, the open hatch granted her a beam of light and she used every bit of it, eyes sweeping round the four corners, memorising everything she could. Then she shoved the bowl back into the hollow and both light and bowl disappeared.

The darkness slammed her back into despair. No, mustn't give in. Don't let them win. She forced her fingers against the doorway, searching for the missing hatch.

Smooth, modern materials met her touch. This doorway had been made in recent times. Not like the rough-finished walls carved out of solid rock. Could this place be a first settlers' refuge? She'd thought they were all mapped and under heritage protection by the Culture Ministry.

Not when den Coille and Winter Solaris kept them secret. Ethan took so much for granted. The right of his family and the den Coille's to own places like this among them. She doubted he even realised it.

She made her way around the walls. Start to prioritise, she ordered her fingers. Find the risks and stop them. Make time for yourself. The disappearance of Ethan Winter will not go unnoticed.

Then there were their security teams. Her team had reacted quickly enough in the past when she'd disappeared. Right now, the Feds must be looking for her.

Your Dan works for Solaris security.

Ethan Winter was in love with her. He would come for her.

She let out a bitter laugh and didn't care who heard her. Let her captors learn what she thought of them and their allies.

The Feds monitored her team. Even Cumchdach den Coille had accepted that the den Coilles couldn't keep the Feds out of

Manascraoch. She had to believe they'd learn of her disappearance and act on it.

She might not be a Winter or anyone of note, but she was the daughter of Catra Beren and a union representative—both newsworthy connections. All she had to do was buy enough time for the Feds to find this place and free her.

First problem, stop the water. She kept following the trail of her fingers, remembering all the details seen in that brief moment of hazy light. Nearly at the cupboard. She had to close off both the tap and cleansing unit outlets.

If only she had a proper sealant. She thought ruefully of her trousers. Wet, no more use to her and designed to withstand desert conditions but not waterproof.

They were all she had. Without more thought, she reached down and grasped the bottom, then tugged up. Nothing. Too tough. Only after repeated tugs and finally using the washbasin tap for leverage did she at last make a rip in the fabric then had to grab the edge of the cleansing unit to stop herself falling back into the water. She could not afford to get any wetter. Her feet might feel like they were dropping off with cold and her hands already clumsy, but the core of her body was still warm enough to keep her alive.

Careful now. Pull slowly down the rip line and hold tight to the rags, ripping them off at knee height. She stuffed the strips hard into the tap opening and the cleansing spray unit, tying the ends off around the tap. The cloth plugs wouldn't stop the water coming in but they would slow it down to give her a bit more time.

Was that all she could do? Make time and wait? There had to be more. She waded slowly around the rest of the room, fingers seeking and touching every surface she came to, searching for any advantage she could find. She wished she could reach the ceiling.

Somewhere there must be a ventilation unit, given that the water refused to escape under the doorway.

She stopped. Don't think that. Taking away air? Could they be that vicious?

You're alive still; they have a use for you. All she had to do was survive.

If only she knew what was happening to Ethan. What were they doing to him? She came back to the bench and clambered back up, tucking her feet under her in a vain attempt to warm them.

She'd heard his cry when they were separated, and if Seolta den Coille was part of this, he must have told their captors she'd gone to the wedding as Ethan's guest. It had to be the reasons she was held. To use against Ethan. A hostage to his cooperation to force him to work for them. They had Den Coille through Seolta, given their presence at the wedding dance and his cosy junction with the off-worlder and the Alliance, and now they wanted Solaris?

Even at a distance, there'd been something about that trio with Seolta that had raised the hairs on her neck. She had no proof they were involved, though. Not yet. No proof of their captors' identity, beyond the Solaris uniforms.

Too easy, too obvious. Uniforms could be stolen. She curled her legs up on the bench, hugged her arms around herself and huddled back against the wall.

Stop reacting and start thinking. Ethan knew of this complex, but so did Ceart and Seolta den Coille. She dismissed Ceart, too quiet and too solid in character. Which left Ethan and Seolta.

Ethan Winter promised he loved her, had done more than make empty promises. He'd saved her life at the risk of his own, back in her desert homeland, whereas Seolta den Coille set off warning signals every time he came near her. And that off-worlder he'd been with at his brother's wedding? A man of a breed she recognised.

The kind of man who abused his workforce and worked them for every last gram. Know a man by his company had always been a rule of thumb that served her well. Which left her trusting Ethan over Seolta den Coille.

Use your mind, not your heart.

She was trying to. She may not know who held her, but both reason and gut rejected Ethan having anything to do with them. Nothing in his past suggested it, nor did he have anything to gain from holding her. She was out of the union. All he had to win from her was herself, and that she had already promised him. Her heart clung to him, desperately clung to the memory of all their time together and that sense of coming home she felt every tragging time she met him. She'd denied the bond between them for so long, but that made it no less real.

Her first guess had to be right. Whoever it was held her, they wanted Solaris, and with both Ethan and Seolta under their control, they could take over the whole region. They would be the prime driver of credit and influence for the central continent.

If Ethan refused them or failed to hold out against them, how long would they give her or Ethan? How long before they got fed up and discarded her as useless? Before killing them both.

The water seeping through the cloth plugs flowed over the floor, rising slowly but inevitably up the walls.

In his cell, Ethan hammered his boot against that lock plate, over and over, all while screaming and wailing at the top of his lungs to mask the sound of it.

"Let me out, let me out."

Jeering laughter was his only answer.

There! The smallest of vibrations and a slight cracking sound. The one his ears had strained for between pummelling the panel and screaming out his panic.

He stopped, forcing out harsh breaths and noisy whimpers as his fingers explored the panel. Yes, the smallest of breaches. A few more blows.

He started again, banging against the door and yelling out his fury. Broken, his voice cracked, the cries of a man with his shame laid bare. Let those brakkas think they'd won.

Stop again, reach for the panel. Repeat the panicked breathing.

Keep your eyes shut.

His fingers tore off the panel and reached for the mechanism. He resumed the banging, less forcefully, but enough to cover the sounds of his fingers tracking along the ancient mechanism within.

This is a trap, said his rational mind. Why would they put him in a cell so easily broken out of?

Because they expected him to panic in this darkened, shut-in hole. Seolta must have told them of his weakness, and his fury roared to life. When he got out of here, he was going to have a reckoning with the second den Coille brother.

A click. He slowly pulled back the latch.

The latch released.

No time to think. The prison must have sensors. They'd be onto him instantly.

She'd never forgive him for this, but she would live.

He flung the door open, heard with satisfaction a thump and the sound of metal meeting human flesh, and the clunk of a man falling.

One guard down.

He thrust through the door at a run, hurling himself against the other two guards standing opposite. Surprise served him for microseconds, long enough to let him barrel into the first and shove him toward the second, then grab at the blaster swinging into the man's hands.

He knew about weapons, and these were Arcadian standard. His fingers found the controls automatically, set them to full stun and poured a full blast at all three guards, including the man trying to rise from behind the door.

First hurdle over. They'd be down for a while, but he was running out of time. Where were they holding Sarwenna?

Thankfully, the passage had lights and an exit at each end, the only things keeping him sane now. He must not panic; her life depended on it.

Up to the next door, view through the hatch. Another cluster of guards, sitting around a control table. Not federal or Solaris troops, not by their careless placing of weapons and scruffy uniforms. Low grade mercenaries, recruited from the criminal gangs that infested the poor sector of any city.

He quietly opened the door, then thrust it back in one shove and shot the blaster through the room. All but one went down in that sweeping blaze. He'd switched the blaster to half stun for the last, aiming the field at the man's lower legs and then jumping forward and ramming him into the far wall.

"Sera Beren. Where is she? Quickly, if you want to live."

The man stuttered, wide eyed. "Up a level. Third corridor, cell at the end."

Ethan began to take his hand away.

"But you're too late." Ethan's hand clamped down again.

"Tell me. Tell it all, now." He set the blaster to sear the wall beside the man, watched as the guard stared in horror at the blistering wall.

"Too late. They set an alarm. You set it off when you broke out. Her cell. Flooded."

Ethan's hand tightened and it was only the choking gurgle of the man that brought him to his senses. He dropped the brakka on the ground and began to run.

Flooded. They had flooded her cell.

She could hold her breath. He could make it in time.

More guards, more thugs lay in his path, and too soon his blaster pack showed signs of depletion. Fists, feet, whatever it took.

A siren blared through the passages and still he raced, seeking uselessly for a way up to the next level.

There. The main upwell. He slammed his hand on the panel just as he heard the downwell door opening and men carrying blasters poured out. He slammed his hand again, then turned to find another way out as a voice yelled at him to stop.

The water lapped halfway up her bench. Sar pulled her feet up, huddled back against the wall. A spasm shook her, the cold already seeping into her body. She'd tried shoving more plugs into the outlets, tearing what was left of her trousers to shreds, tried banging on all the control panels. All she'd gained was to get soaked through.

What would defeat her, the cold or the water?

She looked up, desperate for any sign of a way out. Any sign of light, any crack giving hope.

Nothing. Just the inky black well of her prison. And now the water lapped over the bench, spread across her refuge reaching her feet, then legs, then knees. Ice cold tremors shook her body, and the water kept climbing. She scrabbled backward, leaned into the wall, wishing hard she could see the water level.

The cold called to her, rose up legs and into body and arms. Dangerously seductive, urging her to give in and let the freezing temperatures take her into oblivion.

Don't give in. Don't give in.

Now she was swimming, then she felt a bump on her head. The ceiling closing in on her. She couldn't see a thing, still blind to her room. Above her, nothing but thick stone, a massive weight, solid and unbeatable. It waited, hovering over her, poised to block her in.

Finally, she could hold out no longer. "Help. Help. I'm drowning in here. Turn it off."

She yelled and yelled as the water rose up her chest, up to her chin, faster and faster, no longer slowed by the rags plugging the exits. Now the water gushed into her cell. It wasn't going to stop, not this time. Ethan had failed. Or worse, but that she refused to think about. Something had happened and she no longer mattered to their captors.

She grabbed for a hold on the wall, slipped off and went under in a glug, then pushed up again.

Swim, paddle for your life.

Do not panic.

She tilted her head back, kicked out with her legs, desperate to keep her nose and mouth clear of the gushing water as she pushed up into the dwindling space of precious air at the top of the cell. There must be a way out. A ventilation panel, the circuitry board. Something. Her hands scrabbled over the ceiling, legs kicking against the surging waters and fingers desperately searching. Nothing. Not even a crack in the solid surface.

"Help." A gurgle of water, and she choked on a mouthful. Push up again. One more try.

Then the precious space at the top of the cell disappeared.

A man in a uniform blocked his way, barking out an order.

"Winter, stop."

Ethan ignored it, looking around for an escape route, any pathway out.

"Ethan, it's me," said another voice.

Ethan turned slowly. "Caleb. What are you doing here?" he asked stupidly.

"Looking for you of course."

Ethan could hardly believe it, but the slap of his brother's hand on his shoulders told him it was true. "These troops?"

Then he looked properly at the men surrounding them. The black uniform was unmistakeable. The same uniform worn by the men who had last freed him from a prison cell.

"You're Federal marshals?"

A man stepped forward wearing the three bars of a senior marshal. "Your security detail notified us as soon as you disappeared from the screens. Seolta den Coille gave us the location."

Ethan could barely breathe. Seolta had come through.

"Sera Beren. We have to get to her cell. They're flooding it. This way."

"No, Ser, wrong level."

Ethan had no time to argue. "The guard said she's one level up."

"And the databank said she's on this level, second corridor."

"Split them," said Caleb to the senior marshal. We'll take this level; the others go up."

Who to go with? He looked at his brother, then back at the way he'd come and the guards. "I'm coming with you," he said to Caleb. "This level's quicker, and the local guards are out of commission."

"They all are," said the senior marshal. "This complex is on shutdown. We've immobilised all their troops."

Caleb swung round and began running. Ethan hoped he was right. Thoughts of Sarwenna floating lifeless hammered through his head. He raced on with his brother.

The trooper second-checked his com screen. "Down here."

Then they were banging on a door in a deserted corridor. Nothing on the outside.

The senior waved a trooper forward. "Blow it."

The woman set a charge against the panel, then the rest stood back. Ethan had to be dragged back. "You don't want to get blown up too, Ser."

A loud thump, and the door shot open, water pouring out. In the middle, a body. Still and not moving. He grabbed for her, managed to snag her before the waves took her careering down the passage.

"She's cold."

Another trooper muscled forward, com and medikit at the ready. "Leave her to me, Ser."

Ethan had never felt so useless. Too late. They were too late.

He watched the troop medic lay his com on her chest, watched intently as her chest refused to move. Watched as the medic lay a screen across her face and into her nose and, as he forced air into her body, watched each rise and fall of her chest. Each time the medic paused for her to copy the movement, Ethan held his breath, as if in synthesis with her.

Breathe, Sarwenna. Breath, my darling one.

Too late.

No, a gasp. A shudder. The medic shoved her onto her side, held her back as she spewed up water and bile, as she coughed out the vile liquids that sought to steal her life, then sat her up as she took one gasping breath then another.

The medic passed his scanner over her, then looked up. "Bring the stasis stretcher here. She's barely back and in hypothermia. We need to get her into medcentral hospital urgently."

Ethan sank to his knees in relief. "She will be all right?"

The medic had a look on his face Ethan had seen before. The one medics wore when they couldn't give a family false hope. "With time and luck, Ser Winter."

A hand clamped down on Ethan's shoulder. "She will be," said his brother. "Now, let's get you out of here and into the sunshine."

"Before I freak out, you mean."

Caleb's set mouth said he refused to apologise. "Come on."

Ethan dug his heels in. "Once Sera Beren is on her way."

It was his answer to any protest. He followed her stretcher all the way back to the surface. Up the lift well, along more dark passages. All with exits marked and light wells at the end of each level. Past a huddled mob of guards looking none so brave now. Ethan took great pleasure in seeing the marshals clamp their wrists tight with full-security-level cuffs.

They loaded Sarwenna into a medivac flyer and Ethan had to watch as it lifted off and swung north.

"Where are they taking her?"

"Urbis central. Her parents are waiting for her there, and they have the best facilities."

"It's too far."

The Senior's face softened. "Our medic is good, Ser Winter. If he says it's her best option, then you can count on it. Time to get you back to Dridust central hospital. Your parents are probably on the com to the Council head by now demanding to know what's happening."

"No. I can't. Get my flyer. I'm going to Urbis."

The man looked genuinely apologetic. "Can't do that, Ser. Not yet."

"Caleb?"

"Don't look at me, little brother." Caleb's face wore the same tragging expression as the marshal's. "You're off to Dridust before we have a planetary incident. Mother is in full autocrat mode."

He still tried to make a break for it and felt the punch of a sedative patch slapped onto his shoulder.

"Sorry, Ser Winter," said the marshal, in the instant before the darkness took him again.

CHAPTER TWENTY-SEVEN

Daylight splashed on her face. Sar squinted, opened her mouth, remembered too late and snapped it shut. But no water poured in, no freezing depths held her prisoner. Warmth and a firm bed hugged her body and fresh air filled her room. She carefully opened her eyes and took in her surroundings.

A hospital room. Where? Who kept her here?

She held very still, taking stock of the room. Bed, med cabinet, soft colours and gently diffused light that appeared to be natural. Then a sound of hammering footsteps and her brothers rushed in, leaping up onto the bed and hugging her tight.

"You're awake," crowed Finn. "Ari said you'd never, never wake up again."

She lifted her arms and threw them around her baby brothers. The sound of their voices, followed by the big smile on her father's face and the glow on her mother's coming in behind them was all the proof she needed. She was free. Free and safe.

She struggled to sit up and her father hurried forward.

"Where am I?" she asked.

"Urbis Central Hospital. The medics just told us they were bringing you back to consciousness. You've been under for three days." His hand shot out and grasped the part of her arm not already holding tight to Finn and Daff.

Daff wriggled to free his head. "You got brought here by the marshals. Real life marshals, not the ones in the vids."

Another face appeared behind her mother. Ari, white and scared. Sar opened her arms wider and her sister rushed forward, hugging her tight and crying great buckets.

"It's all my fault. I did this to you." Sar's mouth dropped open. "The marshals told us all about it. How awful it was."

Sar groaned. "They exaggerate."

Her mother huffed loudly. "You were kidnapped, held prisoner, and nearly murdered by drowning. How do you exaggerate that?"

Luckily, her father took hold of her mother, hugging her tight and putting another arm around Ari. "Sar is fine, but the doctors said not to worry her."

Her mother stiffened then glanced at her husband. "Of course. You're right," she said. "Come on children. You've seen Sar is fine but she needs to sleep now."

All she'd done was sleep. Then she looked at her sister's tear-swollen face and gulped back her protests. Braving another explosion of teenage guilt was beyond her today, she discovered.

Her father herded the family toward the door. Then came back, his hand reaching out to touch her shoulder.

"You will be all right, Wennie?"

She returned his clasp. "I'm fine," she said, and breathed a sigh of relief when he let the lie stand. He stood to leave, but she had to ask. "Ethan. Ser Winter. Is he…?"

A twisted smile on her father's face. "Fine too, as far as I know. They took him to Dridust Central first, then sent him up here once his doctors and family gave the Feds the all clear for travel. They've got him recuperating in a top-level, private suite with security even worse than yours."

"And the rest?" Her captors, she meant, but couldn't bring herself to say it. Not yet.

The twisted smile on her father's face flattened and turned grim. "The marshals have it in hand. That's all they're saying."

"But?"

He shook his head. "Get some sleep while you can. A Federal team is waiting at the door. As soon as the doctors clear you for more than close family visits, they'll be in here asking questions."

"Oh."

After another pat on the shoulder from her father, he left her to the silence of her room, unbroken except for the medical beeps that said she lived. She leaned back and stared at the ceiling. It was all like a bad dream, one she could barely believe. Worse, she had so many questions buzzing in her head. Had Ethan Winter really said those things to her, told her he loved her? Then the black horror of the cell returned. He'd told her he loved her, but their captors had tried to kill her.

Which meant that Ethan Winter had given them what they wanted.

Didn't he know the price she would pay?

She took a deep breath. She needed this all to end, and the start of that waited outside her room. She pinged her com channel. A nurse bustled in soon after, morbidly cheerful and full of solicitations.

"What can I do for you, Sera Beren."

"Tell the marshals I'm ready to see them."

Despite wearing the triple stripe of a Senior Marshal, the woman leading the marshals in looked and sounded like her great aunt, the one they'd visited each summer as children, who kept a treat jar full for small children and a home stuffed with the favourite toys of her own children. Her great aunt had been a cheerful lover of gossip with a ready laugh as she told over the latest quirks of all her neighbours.

The marshal gave her that same cheery smile as she walked in the door. "Thank you for seeing us, Sera, when you're still recovering from your ordeal. We won't keep you long. Just a few details to clear up."

Sar went on immediate high alert. This woman wasn't her great aunt and would want a great deal more than a few details.

She was right. When the nurse marched into the room a long while later and ordered the marshals out, Sar could have cried in relief. The nurse tapped her foot. "You should have rung for me earlier. Now, lie back before you fall asleep where you sit."

Sar had felt her eyelids drooping for some time but hadn't dared give in to the weariness sapping her energy. The marshal's chatty talk had dug out far too many forgotten details of her capture. Small things she'd didn't realise she'd noticed. What was true and what false? She didn't have enough facts to decide and wasn't sure the marshal did either. Or if she trusted her. The women's overly friendly manner hid too much.

Her mother might be a Councillor, but Ethan Winter's family was an economic powerhouse.

She lay back and stared at the ceiling, feeling an unwelcome urge to burst into tears.

You're just tired and recovering from a terrifying experience.

Recovering alone. While Ethan Winter lay in an executive suite being pampered back into acceptance. A man like him wouldn't have to deal with Federal investigators.

He was a man from the other side of the industrial divide. She was union; he was a boss. Remember that. Sulwith needed her, the union needed her, and the workers needed her. Someone had to find a way for her town to survive the coming changes.

She frowned. When had that happened? She'd considered it, toyed with the idea, fought against it for so long but, somewhere, acceptance that Sulwith must change had snuck in. Why?

Because you've seen the truth of it yourself. You've seen the changes in your home country. You felt the excitement in that room in Tollic as Ethan Winter challenged her town to find new work and new ways to thrive. For a brief moment in time, she'd glimpsed a future bright with promise.

A glimpse brutally destroyed as soon as offered.

She needed so many answers.

And that other future? Ethan Winter and her. That terrifyingly enchanting future.

She'd been a fool to ever believe it possible. A man did not buy freedom with the life of the woman he loved.

Ethan glared at the doctor holding the scanner. "I'm fit, healthy and ready to go." He'd earlier tried marching out of the room, whatever the medic claimed about his condition. He'd got as far as the door, only to find a full squad of Federal marshals and Solaris house troops barring his way and sending him back into the room.

"You had a very traumatic experience, Ser Winter."

Ethan scowled at the man. "You think I'm going to fall into another cataleptic fit. I got through my capture. I managed it, and nothing physical happened to me."

"Then explain the bruising."

"Fight bruising. No worse than you'd get from a weekend brawl after a night out in Urbis."

Since gutter crawling and brawling in the streets had never been a vice of Ethan's, it didn't surprise him when the man cocked an eyebrow and kept on with his scanning.

A tap at the door, a man entered and Ethan had hope again. "Marshal an Fallon, it's so good to see you. Get me out of here."

"Not so fast, young Winter. I stage rescues from criminal traitors, not highly qualified medical staff trying to do their job."

Ethan swung his legs off the bed. "They've scanned, poked and prodded me for days, and your people have been in here grilling me anytime the medics gave me a moment's peace, but not one of them will tell me anything."

He reached for his clothes and the medic put out a hand to stop him. The marshal coughed politely. "You know your duties better than I, doctor, but I have reason to know that Ser Winter is tougher than he looks. Are you sure it's in his best interests to keep him here?"

Ethan's jaw dropped, but he sensibly said nothing while Marshal an Fallon managed the doctor, the security squads and every other over-concerned well wisher keeping him shut up in this room. He even sympathised with Ethan's mother's fears and turned every one of them around, until his mother almost pushed him out of the building.

"It's enclosed spaces without exits that affect me, not well lit and comfortable hospitals with plenty of windows and doors," Ethan said to her anxious look.

The marshal's face stayed as severe and unrevealing as ever once they were safely out of the building and up at the flyer roof pad. Ethan tried thanking him, to be firmly rejected.

"You have business to attend to. No time to hang around in bed for no good cause."

"Yes, business. Starting with Sarwenna Beren."

"Not a good idea."

A sharp pain stabbed his gut. "Has something happened to her. She was breathing when I last saw her, but no one will tell me anything."

At a tic in the marshal's jaw, Ethan's panic rocketed up.

"She's fine," said an Fallon hastily. "They kept her in a coma for some days, but she has now woken and is recovering satisfactorily."

"Where?"

The marshal's town skimmer stopped in front of them and the hatch opened. Ethan balked. "Take me to see Sera Sarwenna or leave me here."

"Both are out of the question, and you should realise that."

Ethan had been through too much to be put off. "You can and will take me. Or I go to the nearest vidcaster and tell them everything." So far, the vids had been suspiciously quiet. Somehow the authorities had kept the whole sordid affair secret. The marshal gave him that cool military stare, and Ethan stared right back.

"You'd do it," said Marshal an Fallon finally.

Ethan stepped back, ready to run and aware of the troops standing between him and freedom. None of them would injure a Winter son, whereas he had no compunction in landing any kind of blow needed to get him free to find Sarwenna.

The tic was back on the marshal's face. "I'll take you to her."

"A promise, on your honour as a loyal servant of Arcadia."

An angry glitter crossed an Fallon's eyes. "My word on it," he said tersely.

Ethan breathed and stepped into the skimmer. Marshal an Fallon's word was famous. The marshal didn't follow him. "You don't need a skimmer. She's here."

Ethan banged his head on the hatch. "She's been in the same building as me all this time?"

The marshal nodded. "But you may want to reconsider trying to see her."

Ethan refused to listen to him. "Take me to her, now." He needed so badly to see for himself that she was safe. To know she lived.

His anger grew as he followed the marshal. "These are the public wards. For ordinary, low-priority patients."

"Sera Beren does not come from a wealthy family, nor would she or her parents approve of being held in a private wing."

Ethan could have hit someone. "I do, and she's not ordinary."

The marshal carried on punching his codes into the control panel of the entry door.

Ethan stood closer, forcing the man to look at him. "Maintaining security is a nightmare in this section. Do you have everyone who attacked us locked up?"

Ethan knew he didn't, but an Fallon merely gave him a short, "Not yet."

"Once we've seen Sera Beren, you owe me a full breakdown on the state of play with this whole situation."

Thankfully for his temper, they passed through three security screens before getting anywhere near her room. At last he came to it, a single room at the end of a shielded corridor, with a second escape exit also shielded.

Ethan felt the tingle of the shield scanner probing him. "Federal grade shield and guards?" Their uniforms said that but Ethan took nothing at first sight now.

"From my personal section," confirmed an Fallon.

She was safe enough, then, or should be. He waited impatiently as the last screen scanned retina, fingerprints, odour and DNA, then slammed a hand on the panel of her door and had to wait yet again as the panel scanner confirmed his identity.

The door released and he thrust through. He could have cried in relief at the sight of Sarwenna sitting up in bed, mouth dropped open at his sudden entrance.

Except that look of surprise was quickly replaced by a shuttered withdrawal, her beautiful mouth tightening to a straight line and her eyes flashing with suspicion.

"Ser Winter. You survived."

What right do you have to expect any better? You nearly got her killed. He gathered his pride about him. "Thanks to the Feds. And you? You're safe and well?"

"Yes, thank you. You didn't need to come. I have all I need and the authorities are looking after me perfectly adequately."

"Unlike me?"

Her mouth pursed and her eyes narrowed. She pulled herself up on the bed and he hurried to help her. A flinch, one that cut through to his heart.

"What have I done? What did those wernets say to you?"

"They told me nothing. They didn't have to. It was abundantly clear my only value as a prisoner was as hostage for your behaviour. I was safe as long as you did nothing."

She pulled her knees up in front of her, clasping her hands around them. "So what did you do, Ser Winter? I nearly drowned in that cell."

"I escaped," he admitted, and her eyes blanked in shock. "I had to. That cell was going to break me, and then we'd both be dead. Our only chance lay in escape."

"And of course they locked you in a cell that was so easy to escape."

He thought of all his banging, and the stubborn, archaic lock. "They didn't need top security on my cell." He took a breath and dredged up his courage. "Not when they knew I'd go mad in that space. I told you I don't handle confined spaces."

Her arms still hugged her body. "You survived that one though."

"Just," he admitted. "They piped in a live audio feed of your cell. I guess they thought the sound of your screams would make me buckle more quickly."

"But they didn't."

He shook his head. "Not as long as I could hear you breathing. Could hear I wasn't alone. I knew they'd stop you breathing if I gave in."

How to make her believe him? He took a step forward, but she huddled back against the headboard, arms tightening around her. "So you broke out. And someone found me."

"The marshals. Seolta got out and raised the alarm. They took over the complex and broke into the data banks. That's how we found you."

He probably shouldn't have used Seolta's name. Her chin lifted at the name and her eyes grew even colder.

"Nice to know you had an ally in there."

"You think I plotted with Seolta? Connived at crashing my own flyer? Near killed my own brother with that gas attack in Sulwith and got thrown out of the company to which I've given my whole life?"

"I only have your word you were ever in danger."

"No, you don't. You have the word of the marshals and every doctor who treated me. And my word is good. If I promise you something, I mean it."

"No matter what?"

Ethan reached for the nearest chair and fell into it. Then shot up again, pacing from one side of the room to the other as all the disappointment, the betrayals, the loss of every dream he'd ever had tumbled around him. "I love you, Sarwenna Beren. That hasn't changed. But all you can see is the Winter name, not the man, and you've spent your whole life fighting Winters."

"With good reason."

"Why? We pay fair wages."

"Ones that ensure you make a profit."

He swivelled at the end of the room. Even with the haggard lines on her face and the dark hurt in her eyes, she looked so beautiful. "Profit that keeps your workers in jobs."

She sat bolt upright, hands thrust hard against the bed. "Jobs that last only until Solaris—until you say they're gone. Isn't that why you came to Sulwith? To shut down the Sulwith field? To get rid of an annoying glitch in your wonderful new plans for Solaris?"

He stopped dead. "I came to assess the situation at Sulwith and to modernise the solar array. Change it to a kind that the Federal government would tolerate. The kind that would keep Solaris in business and workers in jobs."

"Some in jobs. You always knew you'd have to make redundancies. What about the ones who lost their job? What plan did you have for them?"

He thought back to the man who had arrived in Sulwith that day. Redundancy packages and soothing words did little for the lost. He'd known that, but ignored it, focussed on keeping Solaris alive. He dragged a hand through his hair, unable to meet her eyes, and saw her slump back again.

"Maybe I could have forgiven the man you were, but you had to turn around and give us hope. That meeting in Tollic. You were right. There is so much Sulwith folk can do. You showed us a new kind of future then you disappeared."

"I had no choice," he said lamely. A man always had a choice and he had chosen defeat and retreat.

"In Urbis, you tried to fight back."

"Not hard enough."

She looked up and the pain in her eyes slashed him to the core. "I believed you were," she said, "and I believed the words you said to me that day in Dridust. When you told me you loved me."

"I meant every single word," he said desperately.

"They why did you leave me to die?"

How to answer? He wanted so badly to touch her. "I thought I could get to you in time. My arrogance nearly killed you."

He stared at the floor, unable to look at her and see the contempt in her eyes. "I'm sorry. It's not much, against what you suffered and I don't expect you to forgive me." He lifted his hands in despair. "I couldn't see any other way out for us. I'd seen their faces and you were a witness. They couldn't let either of us live."

The room began to feel like that Survey prison cell, the one that had broken him. The walls caving in and threatening to destroy him. "I'll leave you in peace, but please, know that if ever you need help, it's yours. I won't intrude on you. You can get a message to me through the marshals' office."

He backed toward the door, then swung around. "Goodbye."

It's all he could bring himself to say. Any more would be one more burden laid on her. He carefully shut the door panel and hurried out, thrusting through the guard and marching down the corridor.

Behind him, he heard a sharp pounding of boot heels and a familiar voice called his name.

"Marshal, whatever you have to say to me can wait. Not now."

"Yes, now, Ser Winter," said an Fallon, curt as ever. "Or does saving your life twice count for nothing."

Ethan marched on, around the next corner and down a corridor, with those boot heels pursuing him. Not fast, but unrelenting. Around one more corner, finally safe from any sight of her door, he stopped, heaving in deep breaths.

"Say what you have to, then leave me alone."

"And the rest of your family? The fate of your company? These mean nothing to you?"

Ethan battled for control. He'd lost her. There was no way back from what he'd done. "Talk to me tomorrow."

"You think we can wait that long? Or don't you care whether the people who tried to kill her get away with it. We've already lost the Alliance Representative and a Kevand3, they've left the planet, but the others haven't. We need your testimony to nail them."

"You've already questioned me for hours. I've told you everything I know."

"You have, but recorded reports have scant power compared to that of a living accuser. Your name and your record mean you get a hearing. What you say in person counts."

The horror of it struck him. "You want me to stand up in front of the vidcasters, of the whole planet, and tell them all how I nearly killed Sera Beren?"

"I want you to stand up and tell the whole planet how outsiders and opportunists sought to destroy you and our world, purely to enrich themselves. Or does your home world mean nothing to you, Ser Winter? Was it only ever credits that mattered?"

An Fallon had him. How could Ethan deny him, in the face of such an accusation? He bowed his head, feeling the blows of the day hammering down on him. He reached for the wall behind him, leaned back against it and thrust upward. Back rigidly straight and head up, he looked an Fallon straight in the eye. "Tell me the whole."

"You'll testify?"

"What other choice do I have?" he said. "Tell me what you've got so far. Den Rith, Kevand3, Deputy Malgrave: they were the ringleaders?"

"They're the face of the conspiracy, but how deep it goes? That we don't know. Nor how many corporates are involved."

"My father, you mean?" said Ethan bitterly. "You want me to betray my own father? He may be angry at what happened, but that doesn't turn him into the kind of man who'd try to kill his own son."

"No, but it does make him the kind who learned about those plots and took steps to remove his son from danger. What exactly did he say to you the day he fired you?"

Ethan's hands clung to the wall behind him to keep upright. "You go too far, an Fallon. I've no doubt the marshals' surveillance covers all the Solaris offices, including the Old Man's."

An Fallon didn't deny it.

"So you know everything that was said and can guess well enough what lay behind it. You don't need me to corroborate. I'm not about to help you to put my own father or Seolta den Coille back in a cell."

"Even if it keeps Sera Beren safe?"

Ethan stared stubbornly back, and the man's mouth twisted, as if satisfied at what he'd learned. "As it happens, that's not what I'm asking you to do. Your father isn't likely to be the only corporate head involved."

Now Ethan was the angry one. "What, you planning on throwing a whole bunch of corporate heads into prison as a warning to the rest of us?" He pushed off from the wall. "You'll crash Arcadia's economy and leave the Alliance laughing. Their work done for them by our own government."

A hint of a twitch stirred that contained face. He'd been right. The Fed was leading him down his own tortured pathway. He shoved past the man, ready to walk away.

"When did you last check the Solaris accounts, Ser Winter?" said an Fallon.

Ethan stopped dead.

"I don't have access. My father blocked me from every account except my personal funds. Nor do you need to tell me the Sulwith field is losing money. Of course it is, but even my father has to see reason one day and fix it."

"And if he won't? Or can't?"

Ethan drew in a deep breath and studied the man before him. Hair greying at the temples, a gaunt face that too often resembled a mask, the body still lean and fit, Marco an Fallon had a hard-earned reputation as honest and reliable.

And the man had freed him from illegal capture twice now.

"Take me to somewhere unmonitored," Ethan said.

The marshal lifted a brow and led him down a series of corridors to a Federal flyer. Soon after, they landed in the courtyard of the Feds' head office and Ethan followed the man through darkened doors and into floodlit, stark white hallways. All his senses twitched and he had to batten down his nerves.

This place has an exit.

Finally into a large meeting room, one with a whole bank of windows opening onto the main plaza and a second door at the other end, Ethan saw with relief. A meeting room with three people sitting at the far end.

He knew two of them personally, but the third only from her images on the news casts. On the left sat his banker, who also happened to be head of the financial oversight committee, and on the right, the head of the audit office. A man Ethan had made a point of cultivating early in his excursions into independent investments. In the middle sat the Chief Judge of the Paramount Court, the highest judicial body on Arcadia.

He gathered up every vestige of pride he still possessed and gave a formal bow to the trio. "Sers, Sera, I'm honoured.

Many hours later, he wasn't so sure about that. "These figures are real?"

"Taken directly from the tax surveillance records. You are cleared for limited time access if you want to check them."

Ethan very much did and put out his hand with a grim sense of foreboding. A few moments later, his com lit up with the seal of the Revenue audit section then came alive with scrolling records he viewed in dismay. They matched exactly the scenario laid out by the trio at the head of the table. The one he'd been refusing to believe ever since they started talking. The figures had to be true. The revenue service had access to all corporate accounts and had never been hacked. Given the seniority of the officials granting him access, he had to give in to the reality facing him.

"Are you telling me my father is deliberately driving Solaris into the ground?"

"No, but he has made some injudicious investments." The banker lit up the transactions in question and Ethan scowled at the names: den Rith and the off-worlder corporation Kevand3.

Had his father taken leave of his senses? Sol Winter checked his company's performance too often for Ethan to think he could have missed this nightmare. Losses in every branch of the business, with too many of their credit lines on the point of being withdrawn. "We'll be bankrupt in days unless this is stopped."

How could the fortunes of a company like Solaris go downhill so quickly? The Sulwith field was in trouble thanks to the staff losses and refusal to upgrade, but that wasn't enough to cause this.

"Solaris funds were solid when I last saw them a few months ago. This shouldn't be possible."

He stared at the damning figures, hands swiping away graph after graph, all showing signs of a sudden and fatal slump.

"My father can run Solaris in his sleep. Yes, it can be more profitable if he updates the solar tech, and I've been telling him for years we need to diversify into manufacture, but that was a long-term development. Solaris should still make more than enough profit without changing anything. What aren't you telling me? What could make the Old Man do something like this?"

"We are aware he's not a friend to the current government policies," said the judge.

"He was angry when he got out of prison, but that just made him twice as determined to keep Solaris safe."

The woman raised an eyebrow. "Angry enough to join forces with those promising him revenge?"

Ethan's heart sank. More than enough. But not like this.

"And if he accepted contracts that promised independence, only to find that they contained unseen consequences?" said the auditor coldly.

"He never signs a contract without having our lawyers go over it in triplicate." Then it hit him. "He didn't have these ones reviewed," he said quietly. There was only one reason the Old Man would keep a contract away from Solaris lawyers. "The sands know he's played close to the line a few times, but never crossed it. Not before this. What laws…" He was too scared to go on.

"No action has been taken against Solaris. Not yet," said the chief judge.

"Thank you, Sera." His fingers jabbed at the figures again, trying to make them change. "Not that you'll have to. It looks like Solaris will save you the trouble."

The banker frowned. "You know as well as we do how many people are employed directly by Solaris. You think we want a crash in employment levels of that magnitude?"

"It will affect only the plains." How badly, Ethan hated to consider. Solaris was the biggest employer in the region and many other enterprises were dependent on his family's company.

The head auditor leaned forward. "Don't be obtuse, Ser Winter. The failure of a company the size of Solaris will send the Urbis markets into the kind of panic that will have us fighting a recession. This planet has quite enough problems already. A recession will destroy any hope we have of meeting the Alliance timelines. Or is that what you want? Are you part of this conspiracy too?"

Ethan drove up from his seat. "Take that back."

An Fallon's hand fell on his shoulder, shoving him back down. Ethan tried to rise again and discovered the difference between a businessman who sat at a desk and exercised for leisure and one who fought for a living. It didn't stop him trying to force his way up again.

"Sit down, Ser," hissed an Fallon, his hand biting into Ethan's shoulder as he turned his head toward the trio at the tabletop. "The Ser has cooperated fully with the marshals' office and my section vouches for his innocence in this. He came here to help, not to be insulted."

The Auditor frowned. "How? By buying out his own company and running it in compliance with Federal aims? Solaris needs someone loyal to this planet at the helm, not a family bent on their own enrichment at the expense of the rest of us."

He was being played. The words came too easily from the auditor's mouth. It didn't stop the surge of anger and his automatic response. "Winters run Solaris. No stranger gets my company."

"You were fired. It's not yours anymore, young man. All of society witnessed your reaction to that in Urbis." The judge looked down the length of the table at him, nose pinched as if smelling something unpleasant.

Ethan leaned forward. "I was hunting, Sera. Someone tried to kill me and Sera Beren. That, I will not tolerate."

"But you do tolerate your father's mismanagement of Solaris."

"There is a world of difference between mismanagement and deliberate sabotage of our world."

The banker folded his hands over his substantial stomach and stared back, unimpressed. Had he pushed it too far? The financial oversight committee was tasked with regulating corporate governance and was answerable only to the Council. If the committee decided the current management of Solaris posed a risk to the financial stability of Arcadia, they had the power to put Solaris under direct Federal control. It would destroy his parents and damage any chance Solaris had of riding out the current threats. Bitterly, he recognised the trap. They'd left him only one option.

"An Fallon can vouch for my loyalty to Arcadia. Would you accept a change of majority shareholder in Solaris?"

"Such as?"

Ethan took a deep breath, praying he was right in his guesses. "I have independent funds unrelated to Solaris. I'm willing to use them to buy out my father's share and take over control of Solaris if the committee, the audit office and the court accept. In return, I would expect that my family is exempt from any charges relating to the current conspiracy."

He waited, wondering for long moments if he'd misjudged it. Finally the judge addressed an Fallon. "Do the marshals agree to immunity for Ser Sol and Sera Helena Winter for any possible part in this conspiracy?"

An Fallon set his fingers together, tenting them. "On condition that they cooperate fully with the marshals' office in all investigations related to this matter."

How in sands Ethan was supposed to guarantee that, he had no idea but nor did he have a choice. "They will," he promised.

Hours later, Ethan sat in another board room with an Fallon behind him again. A sound at the door and his father marched in.

"Ethan. What's going on? You're supposed to be up in Urbis."

Ethan might have bristled if he hadn't seen the flash of fear in his father's eyes and the quick flick of a glance at an Fallon. He waved to his father to take a seat, then sat himself. An Fallon retreated to the wall, out of sight but certainly not forgotten.

"The audit office, the financial committee, and the Chief Judge called me in for a word today. They showed me some figures."

They hadn't let him bring the full data set from the Revenue service records but he had enough to prove his point. He opened his com and set them to scroll in the middle of the table. "Are you deliberately sabotaging Solaris or is it someone else?"

A bluster and a red flush. For one of the few times Ethan could remember, his father looked vulnerable. Ethan pulled up the transactions with den Rith and Kevand3. "What have these two-bit outfits got on you? Solaris doesn't work with dirt dealers like these."

Another attempt at bluster, one of the Old Man's fingers repeatedly tapping on the tabletop. Suddenly, his father looked old. "Times change. Or have you forgotten being thrown into a jail cell and threatened with execution?"

"No. Nor do I forget who did that to us. Criminal thugs manipulating the proper process of government for their own enrichment. Just like the two sewer crawlers you're trying to defend."

"You don't understand. They promised…" and suddenly his father shut his mouth. An Fallon moved back to the light and took a seat beside Ethan.

"What did they promise, Ser Winter?"

His father shoved his head up and glared back. It had no effect on an Fallon, although Ethan wished himself anywhere but here.

An Fallon had on his work face, flat-eyed and grim-mouthed. "The Federal government has no desire to collapse the financial systems of our world. Because of that only, the Chief Judge has advised that immunity is available in return for full cooperation. First, though, those threatening the continued sovereignty and survival of this world need to be identified and dealt with. Because whatever they told you, that is what they intend."

"It's not like that. This government is well on the way to wrecking our economy. Who benefits from all this change you're forcing on us? Not my company, or any other company I know of."

Ethan groaned inwardly. He'd heard his father say this too many times. Time to bring it to an end.

"If we don't change, Solaris is dead. You didn't believe me the first time I told you that, Pa, and I don't expect you to believe it now." He braced himself, hoping he looked more convincing than he felt. Then he remembered what his father's games had cost Sarwenna. "You leave me no choice. I'm sending notice to our bank of my intention to buy out sufficient of your share in Solaris to give me a majority holding, and that I will be taking over the managerial operations of Solaris, effective immediately."

His father shot up from his chair, bellowing. An Fallon ordered him to sit down. The Old Man ignored him.

"Solaris is my company. It'll be yours when I'm dead in the ground, son, and not before."

An Fallon gestured him down again. "What did they promise you, Ser Winter?"

His father raised his hands. For help, to stop him, he didn't know. Finding out was an Fallon's job.

Ethan stood up and walked out.

CHAPTER TWENTY-EIGHT

Sar heard a ping on her entrance pad. She was sure she'd set it to 'No Entry' but it opened for the visitor. A man entered, and her heart lurched.

"You've got a nerve coming here."

"Without my help, you'd be dead, Sera Beren, so we're even," said Seolta den Coille. He strode in, ignoring her angry gasp, and took a seat on the chair beside her bed. "The doctors tell me you're nearly ready to leave hospital."

"My medical condition is none of your business."

"So you're fit to face hard facts," he continued as if she hadn't spoken.

She hauled herself higher up the bed, refusing to look up at him while he attacked her. "What facts, or rather whose dirt are you spreading now?"

"Just watch this." He held out a com sliver. The kind you used when two parties wanted to avoid com sharing for fear of contamination. This one was stamped with the badge of the Federal Marshals office.

"It's safe?" she asked none the less.

"Why ask me when you refuse to believe anything I'd say? I served time with Ethan Winter. I saw him when he came out of that isolation unit in prison. We may clash, but he's a man whose word I will always accept, and he doesn't deserve what you're doing to him."

Sar's mouth dropped open. This was about Ethan Winter.

Seolta den Coille gave her no chance to argue. A twist of that untrustworthy mouth and he turned and walked out of her room, leaving her with too many questions and a churning in her gut that had a nurse hurrying in moments later. Her fist closed about the sliver, keeping it hidden as the nurse checked her parameters then frowned at her.

"You need to rest, Sera. You had a nasty experience and you're not yet fully recovered."

Sar dutifully slid back down the bed, waiting impatiently for the woman to leave. The door snicked shut and Sar made sure that this time she hit the lock then dialled up full privacy.

She placed the sliver on the bed and held her com over it, running a full scan first then cautiously linking into the contents. So far, so good. Or so she thought, before the holovid began and plunged her right back into that hell of a prison. The filthy thing was a feed from her cell. No, she realised with a thud as a man cried in agony. From Ethan Winter's cell.

His voice cut right through to her heart. He was on the edge of breaking. She remembered every word Cumchdach had told her of what happened to him in the Survey prison. Now she saw the truth of what it had done to him.

Was it real? She checked the feed data for any signs of tampering. The Feds were good but every fake feed had something about it that just felt wrong. This one? Her com said it was genuine and so did her gut. The com also verified the recording was from both an audio and visual feed, yet the cell was inky black. All she could hear or see was Ethan's voice and his breathing.

No, her breathing. It had to be. Her own mutterings broke up the harsh gaspings. Ethan had said they'd fed the stream from her cell into his. That the sound of her breathing had stopped him breaking.

Only this audio denied that. Those screams and yells came from a man close to insanity and desperate.

But not yet broken.

Another voice came on, frustrated and bored, with a strange accent she'd briefly caught once before. It was the off-worlder from Cumchdach's wedding. "Are you sure of your information on this one, Ser den Rith. You said the man would crumble after a few hours in a closed cell."

"Listen to him. He's nearly there. Just a bit longer and you'll have all you need."

A third voice, one she'd never heard before. Cold and clinical. "The subject may sound at breaking point, but his physiological readings are not there yet. We need to increase the negative stimuli."

A few moments later, she heard her own voice crying out and the gurgle of water. The flooding of her cell, she realised.

"You'd better stop," said den Rith's voice with a nervous quiver. "She's no good to us dead. Not yet."

The cold voice came back. "We've got enough recordings to loop them back if she dies. All that matters is that Winter believes she's still alive."

Grimly, Sar listened through to the end. Back to the hellish time in that wet, dark cell, back to the black waters greedily claiming her, right up to the point when Ethan Winter's door crashed open and she heard his voice threatening a guard.

Demanding the location of her cell.

He had been nearly too late. The marshals had told her she was alive only because Seolta den Coille had broken with the conspirators and showed them the way into the caverns, then gave them a code to splice into the complex's plans. The guard had told Ethan the wrong cell. This vid confirmed it.

He had tried to save her.

She slapped off the file and carefully stowed the sliver in her personal pack. Then lay back and stared at the ceiling.

Weeks later, she stood on the edge of the landing pad at Sulwith. She'd been here before. Stood here with the same ominous sense of fate laughing at her.

Did Ethan Winter know who waited for him?

He must know of the clean-out of those who had been involved in the plot against them. Tom Crabster had kept his nominal position as manager of the solar array here, but Maxell Drocash's dirty tricks had been well and truly exposed by the Federal marshals. After his arrest, his family had left town with their com access controlled by the Feds, and the union had unanimously voted for her reinstatement.

So something good had come of those dark days, she supposed. She glanced back to the public area and got a thumbs up from Ari and a cheery wave from Finn, Daff and Geordie, all perching high on the barricade keeping the locals well away from their powerful visitor. No one in town wanted a repeat of the last few months. Beside her, Tom Crabster glared in warning. He couldn't do anything else. Solaris had specifically requested to meet with both the company and union heads.

It didn't stop Tom Crabster trying to hustle her into a back row, no doubt hoping she would go unnoticed there and couldn't cause trouble. She elbowed him off and held onto her place at the front.

"I'm only here because he asked me to be and because I owe it to my members. So wipe that sour look off your face, Ser Crabster."

A slight twitch touched her father's face from his position on the other side of Tom, but a shout from the top of the field put a stop to any more jostling for position.

"They're coming."

Then a huff of dirt, a blast of hot air, and his flyer settled onto the landing pad below. Not long after, the occupants emerged.

He looked the same as on that day so long ago. Brown hair immaculately cut, his clothes a touch more expensive, as if wanting to impress the locals, that tall, lean body walking ahead of his staff. She even recognised the smile on his face. His business smile. A mask assumed to disarm his opponent, as he'd once admitted when she called him out on it.

Back when they'd felt free to tease each other.

She shifted from one foot to the other, then caught herself. A union representative did not show any sign of nerves in front of the bosses. That was the first lesson her mother had taught her.

His voice hadn't changed either. That educated accent overlaying the easy tones of the plains. She'd heard him modulate it to suit his audience and now the slight clip of vowels said politeness didn't come easy today. She doubted Tom Crabster realised, although the man's overly eager clasp of Ethan's outstretched hand said the manager knew exactly how precarious his position was and who he needed to impress to keep his job. Luckily for him, Sar's father had already refused the manager's job, preferring to keep running the place quietly from his workshop like he'd always done.

"Speeches and hand clasping aren't my thing," he'd said to Sar. "Tom Crabster can do the front of house stuff. He's good at it and now knows not to interfere with the back room stuff. Ser Winter assured me he'd made that plain when he asked me to come back."

Sar had heard a lot of what Ser Winter had promised people since she'd returned to head the union. She'd see about that. Her job was to make sure bosses carried through on promises. Solaris hadn't been a bad company under Sol Winter, but the Old Man ranked making money before giving handouts to workers. He'd outright said so during one memorable meeting when her mother was the union boss.

Now the talk claimed Ethan Winter ran the whole show. Sol Winter still had the title of Chief Executive, but her Da and too many locals reported that Ethan had taken over the day to day running of the company. Others, including Marshal an Fallon, said the same, and he'd have no reason to lie to her. The marshal had also helped save her life, which gave a decided force to anything he said.

As had Ethan Winter, according to the marshal. With the help of Seolta den Coille.

"Sera Beren. A good day to you," said a never-to-be-forgotten voice.

Sar swallowed. He'd finished with the others and moved on to her while she'd been cloud gathering. "A good day to you too, Ser Winter." Her voice came out as stupidly stilted as his, but he was a better actor. Except that his eyes studied her and a faint flush washed his face as she met his gaze. She shoved back her shoulders. "The union requests a formal meeting as soon as you have finished with your site tour, to discuss the proposed changes to this field."

He hadn't offered his hand, and she made no attempt to touch him. A formal bow of the head was all she received. Nor did he thrust onto her the smooth geniality he'd shown the company management. She wasn't sure whether she was insulted or grateful to be spared the shallowness of it.

Then he moved off toward the field where workmen had already begun dismantling the old solar sheets and laying struts for the new. Struts that covered a fraction of the old field area and were spread much farther apart. Struts that carried rotating filaments that needed far fewer checks or maintenance. Struts that cost twice as much as the old ones. Ethan Winter must have a big war chest to fund all the changes.

Sar's best guess was that the new field would need only a quarter of the old work force though, according to her father, it would generate twenty percent more output.

She didn't follow Ethan on his company tour. Truth to tell, she didn't trust herself. Why did the man have to look so good? Duty alone kept her by the main office instead of hurrying away to hide somewhere in the town.

She sat in the Solaris office, scrolling through irrelevant reports sent by the union reps at other Solaris sites. She'd read them all before, reports on changes being instituted. Reports heavily cloaked in fear and distrust. Reports heavy with warnings of job losses and pay cuts, but light on what to do about them.

After a while, she switched off her com in disgust and traced dust patterns in the air, tapping her foot in time with the beat of the air recycler unit. Ethan Winter should have finished his tour long ago. He'd been here before; his name was fixed to every order that came through this office and he could recheck any square of the field through holo-images. He didn't need to trawl all over it in person.

Had he decided to avoid her and already escaped town?

No sooner did the thought strike her than she stood and hurried out, racing toward the landing field. Only to round a corner and career right into a hard body. Big strong hands set her back and held her safe from falling. Hands she remembered all too well.

"Sarw…Sera Beren. Are you all right?"

She took a deep breath to recover. Only that was a mistake, the warm scent of him filling her head. "Yes, thank you, Ser Winter." She extricated herself awkwardly and he dropped his hands as soon as she began to struggle. "My apologies. I thought I'd missed you. I do need to talk to you."

Then she noticed the crowd surrounding him and felt the heat rise up her neck. Of course he wouldn't be allowed to walk alone.

Ethan glanced at them, as if at unimportant specks, then back at her. "If I remember, your office lies a short distance along here. Maybe we can talk there." He turned back to the crowd. Including security guards, she realised. Her own had disappeared once their captors had been caught and the plot exposed, but Ethan Winter would always be a target. "I will meet with the union representative in private. Ser Crabster, thank you for your time. I'll let you get back to your duties now."

A minor huffing and a dark look from Tom Crabster, but he had no choice. Her father stayed regardless.

"The Sera is safe with me," Ethan said gently to her father. "The union has a right to hear Solaris' plans for the field."

Her father held his gaze and Sar wondered if she imagined the message passing between the two men before her father swung back toward his workshop.

Ethan lifted an arm in the direction of her office. "Sera?"

Her members counted on her. She turned and walked back up the street with Ethan Winter walking silently beside her and a small squad of guards surrounding them both. At her office door, the guards surged in front and put out a hand to stop Ethan. Two went in to check it out before their esteemed employer was allowed to enter.

Ethan cursed the necessity of the security check but he'd promised his mother and an Fallon. "A routine precaution," he said to the woman at his side, trying to ignore the jolt that hit him every time he looked at her. She'd lost weight, but the strength in that face and long body hadn't changed. Nor had his want for her, and he knew himself well enough to know it never would.

He had hurt her badly. He'd let her down and lost her trust. Today, he was only the company boss she must deal with.

His security head gave him the thumbs up and the all clear signal on his private link.

"Thank you for your tolerance, Sera Beren." He put out a hand, gesturing her to lead the way into her office.

Inside, his guards lined the walls. Sarwenna took the chair behind her battered desk, looking like a queen in residence, and he took the other one.

"You may wait outside," he com-signalled to his guards. A horrified chorus of objections pounded the airwaves and the nearest he'd ever seen to a trace of emotion cracked their leader's face. He put on his sternest expression, hoping it would work. "You've cleared the room. I'm safe enough with you outside. This meeting is private."

The leader stared back, and Ethan held his eyes, refusing to back down. Finally, the guardsman gave a brusque gesture to the others. "Our com alerts are on full, Ser," signalled the man privately. "Anything happens, you signal immediately." With unhappy faces, they filed out. Sarwenna—his beautiful Sarwenna—lifted an eyebrow and followed their departure, turning back to him as the door closed, leaving them alone.

"I thought you would prefer a private meeting," he said. Not in a million years, said the flare of her eyes. "To discuss the union's concerns," he hurriedly added and felt like dying inside.

He'd known this meeting would be hard, but not how hard, how thoroughly he'd destroyed any hope of her trusting him again.

She's alive because of what you did.

"The changes you're making," she began. "The union has received the formal notice but not the attached conditions."

He touched his com. "I was waiting to discuss them in person. I'm forwarding you the document now. We don't need to finalise the details today but if you could read through it, we can go over the sections one by one."

He reached his wrist out, touching his com to hers. Almost touching her skin, so fine and soft on the underside of her wrist, and a sizzle shot through his body, leaving him sitting uncomfortably. Thank the sands for the desk between them.

"The summary list is at the front. It includes re-training of those retained, redundancy packages, further education and re-location costs for those who leave, and access to finance for any wanting to stay and start up a business in Sulwith. We can add any other details you think of as we go through."

He watched her throat muscles work as she swallowed, watched her fingers trace through the document, wishing she would meet his gaze so he could see what her eyes said. A pause in her scrolling, a flat question and plain comment from him in reply.

So it went on, with question and answer followed by her noting the point down as agreed or to be discussed. Nothing personal, nothing that told him how she was, how she felt, was there any hope for him.

Finally he could take no more. "And you? How are you," he had to ask. She looked up, eyes wide with shock, as if he'd asked her to expose her most secret, most personal desires. His hand shot out automatically, reached for hers and covered it. She pulled it from his hold with a gasp and thrust back her chair.

"I'm fine. Thank you for asking, Ser Winter." A pulse beat in her throat and her gaze shifted to focus on some point over his shoulder. "I think we've covered everything necessary. You will receive the union's full reply in due course. Thank you for your time." She stood and turned to walk out. To leave him.

"Sarwenna, wait. Please."

All that did was make her pause for an instant, before scurrying madly for the door. He was losing her again. He stood and reached for her, not to hold her, just to touch her, to ask her to stop. His hand curled around her arm and she froze.

Sar couldn't believe it. One touch from him and a jolt of awareness pulsed through her body, every nerve attuned to that one hand clasping her arm. He wasn't holding her hard. She could easily break away and carry on out of the room. That's what she ought to do.

Her feet refused. Instead they slowly turned her back to face him, to see his face, clear of all masks and stark with need. "You left me to die."

"I'm sorry. I didn't mean to. I thought…"

"I was surety for your behaviour. You did something and water filled my cell."

She put up a hand to ward him off, to stop his other hand reaching for her other arm. One was bad enough. One touch already had her aching to give in, to come home. Two would destroy any chance of refusing him. Yet she owed him one truth.

"Seolta den Coille showed me the surveillance record. You broke out and came straight to my rescue. Thank you for that."

His hands tightened. "I had the wrong room. If it weren't for the Feds, you would truly be dead."

A weird gust of laughter cut through the room. From her, she suddenly realised, and hoped it didn't sound as manic as she felt, as torn in two. "I tried to find a way out of my room. Nothing. They even blocked off the ventilation panel.

She knew it sounded accusing. She couldn't help it. Anger and love mixed too closely in her veins at that moment. Not when dealing with Ethan Winter, the man she'd come to know and love over so many months. The new head of Solaris. A man who had mattered to their captors. Unlike her. "I was disposable. Nothing more than an asset to control you."

His hand tightened on her arm. "Never that. Do not let gutter dwellers make you think otherwise. Because of you, I had to look twice at Sulwith. Because of you, Sulwith has a future."

"What future? You're firing people, changing the sole support of this place." The words came out as an accusation, but she desperately needed him to deny it.

He lifted his hand from her arm and she breathed a bit easier. But then his fingers traced her face and trailed through the wildfire strands of her hair. "I don't know what the future holds for Sulwith, but neither do you. That day in Tollic proved that. So many ideas, so many new pathways. All they need is people to bring them to life. People like you—and me, if you will let me." His voice dropped on the last words, slow, deep, and unsure, and his eyes sought hers.

Her breath stopped somewhere in her belly and her body leaned toward his, breathing in the warm musky scent of him. That clean masculinity and scent of dried grasses. Why a man who lived in offices should smell of the outdoors, she had never understood, but with her nose full of him and her body begging for his, she had no choice. Not when he set aside all power and handed it over to her. She lifted her hands and he stepped back immediately, his hands hovering as if impatient to touch but fearful of rejection. She raised her arms and circled his neck, then pulled his mouth down to hers and his body closer. Then showed him with her mouth and hands and body how badly she had missed him.

Much later, clothes strewn in a wild frenzy about the room, she lay twined in Ethan's arms on the hard floor of her office and felt better than if lying on the finest sleeper in an Urbis hotel. Had the unplanned and tumultuous moments solved everything? Of course not, but together, the two of them would. His arm holding tight about her and her leg crossed firmly over his promised that. She reached up a hand to slowly trace the line of his face, his mouth and up to the line of his hair. "Your guards will be worrying."

A snort of laughter as he lifted his head for another kiss and his fingers trailed in exploration over her bottom. "Wondering whether you've murdered me? Or worse, wrung concessions for the union that will enrage the shareholders?"

"They will? I understand you're now the majority shareholder."

A slight grimace and his hand locked tight as if still unsure of her. "An Fallon gave me no choice. Nor did my father."

She might have thought it an apology when she first met him. Now she knew that wasn't his way. A statement of fact, pure and simple, one he must live with. She tickled his ribs, then traced her hand down and over those firm muscles and lower still. A groan and another snort of laughter.

Later still, it was Ethan who opened his arms and pulled her to her feet. "My guard will be breaking down the door soon, and no one but me sees you like this." A rueful twist of his mouth, another quick kiss, and he determinedly stepped back and looked around for his discarded clothes. "I don't suppose you've got a cleansing unit attached to this office?"

She did and pointed it out, but the look on his face when he looked inside had her doubling over with laughter.

"It will have to do," he said in a pained voice.

She'd seen his office and had to agree. The only advantage, she supposed, was that the confined space made no more games possible, and she should not regret that so badly.

Soon, they finished and sat primly down again with the desk firmly separating them. Sar set the door to unlock and his senior guard almost tumbled into the room, stopping at the sight of both of them sitting as they'd left them and clearly unharmed.

"Sorry, Ser. You didn't answer your com."

Ethan looked at the man with that smooth business smile back on his face. "We were busy with negotiations."

"Have they been concluded satisfactorily, Sir."

"Oh, yes." He glanced at her. "Most satisfactorily for now. Sera, would you accompany me to dinner at my hotel to celebrate."

She bowed her head in acceptance, quelling the giggle inside her, and feeling like a soapcast queen.

"Afterward," he said, "I'll take you home. We have things to discuss with your family."

He met her look, eyes wide open, and the room felt at once too small and eternally expanding. She put out a hand, ignoring the guards' keen scrutiny. "Yes, I will come with you, to your dinner and to my home. I will," she added softly.

There was much more to work out, of course, but none of it truly mattered, she discovered in the next few months of chaos. They had made a promise to each other that day, and words would only set the seal on it. In the meantime, both of them had much to organise and set in place. Together, they called back the core members of that long ago meeting in Tollic and formed a new enterprise group in Sulwith. Soon the fear of redundancies had been replaced by a growing curiosity and excitement, thanks in no small part to the graduated process Ethan adopted of downsizing and retraining, matching each worker's pathway to their particular skills and needs. Even Geordie scarcely mourned the loss of his precious sheets, to the enormous relief of his mother and Sar's family. His skills were in heavy demand by the engineers setting the new field arrays and Geordie grinned with delight each time one of them asked him to read the sky for them, dancing around and turning his face up to the warm rays of the sun before telling the engineer precisely how to align the strut. Ethan spent most of his time in Dridust, but every moment he could, he escaped back to her. She couldn't leave Sulwith, not yet, but soon she would have to. Would have to leave both home and union to make a new life for herself. Solaris and Sulwith needed Ethan in charge too much for him to be the one to make the sacrifice.

Not that he asked it of her, and for that she loved him even more. But they needed a home together.

Then came the day she stood before him, their families, and the most senior judges on Arcadia to make her promises to him and hear his back again. That night, Sulwith partied as it hadn't for years.

Moline Granth, the plant safety officer, had agreed to take on the union job, much to Sar's relief. Moline would steer them on a steady course through any headwinds to come. She could feel the collective settling of nerves through the town when they stood together in the hall a few days later and asked for votes to confirm Moline in the position.

Sar found Ethan outside afterward, standing discreetly in a patch of shadow on the street corner waiting for her. He had refused to come to the hall meeting. It was the union's business, he'd pronounced, not Solaris management.

"Everything satisfactory?" he said now.

She grinned. "A unanimous vote. Moline almost looked shocked."

"Told you."

"They've asked me to head the Tollic group taskforce instead."

"Thought they would," he said with an insufferable grin on his face. He was going to pay for it later that night, she decided, and that had her grinning too as they walked down the street, wickedly inventive ideas swirling in her head and blood stirring to heady life.

A month after that, Sar and Ethan stood hand in hand in the planetary space terminal to farewell a man she still couldn't forgive and wasn't sure if she ever would. Ethan had wanted to be here but knew better than to intrude into a family hurting like this, so they waited back from the crowd.

With Seolta den Coille had come every den Coille, silent and drawn-faced, standing for their brother and son as he waited to board the ship taking him far from Arcadia. In the middle of the crowd, with his mother silently weeping, his father's face drawn and his brothers all taut-faced and on the edge of rebellion, Seolta stood alone. That clever face listened to his elder sister's instructions and his eldest brother's exhortations with no sign of hearing any of them.

The man had saved her life. She had to remember that, when everything inside her said his departure left her safer. He stared out at the ship readying for lift off, machines scurrying around the base carrying out the last minute checks before the passengers were called to board.

Sar had never been off planet, never wanted to.

Nor did Seolta den Coille. That too contained look of distance on his face and his tightly pinched mouth spoke for him. His sister Samhchair might remind him it was only temporary, but Seolta den

Coille understood politics too well for that. Exile: that's what the government had decreed, and whether he ever returned depended entirely on the will of the government. When he'd proved himself safe, when the climate here changed enough to welcome him back. When there remained no chance of his actions becoming public. That's when he might return.

A part of her, a mean, scared part of her hoped it would be never.

Ethan felt the tension in Sarwenna and understood it fully, torn as he was. She was alive because of Seolta but had also nearly died because of him. The man had believed too much in his own cleverness and allowed an unscrupulous group to manipulate him. Ethan was both furious at the second den Coille brother and forever grateful. The rest of the den Coille brothers were still the men with whom he'd survived that prison hell, the men who had stood by him when all the world turned against them. He owed them an eternal debt and would count them friends always.

The brothers were hurting badly today. He recognised the fury in the rigid backs, the frustrated rage bringing back everything they had endured before. That vicious helplessness. All the den Coilles had pled their brother's case to anyone who would listen or could help, though Seolta had asked them not to.

"I did this. You tried to tell me I was wrong, Cumchdach, but I wouldn't listen."

Ethan had watched as Cumchdach put his arm around his brother's head in a mock tackle, knocking lightly on his skull. "You stubborn, wooden-headed idiot. You think we don't understand you were blind with anger?"

Now the brothers stood silently as Samhchair pleaded with Seolta to be careful. "I know the feds have asked you to find out how deep this plot goes in the Alliance and amongst off-worlders but you're no spy, Seolta mar Bram an Scathach."

The government hadn't asked Seolta, they'd ordered him, but Ethan knew better than to tell Samhchair that. Not when the usually staunch den Coille sister looked about to shatter.

Seolta put an arm around her and hugged her briefly. "It's my business acumen they've asked me to use, not any secret spy tricks."

"Just you remember that, son," said Bram den Coille, holding tight to his wife and reaching out an arm to grasp Seolta's. Even Seolta's preternatural calm looked about to break at that. Thank the sands the siren sounded just then, the signal for all passengers to board, and the whole disaster must come to an end. One more heart-breaking round of farewell hugs and the den Coille son must turn toward the departure gates.

No, not the end. Seolta lifted his head to Ethan and Sarwenna standing at one side and walked up to them. He bowed first to Sarwenna. "My apologies for all you suffered, Sera. One day, I hope, you can understand." Then he put out a hand to Ethan. "I will find those who threatened you and bring them to justice. You have my word on it."

Ethan put out his hand, returning the clasp brother to brother. "I'll hold you to that. See you in the usual, next time you're in town."

A sudden lop-sided twist of Seolta's face. "You can count on it. Good fortune with your dealings, Ethan Winter."

"And to you, Seolta mar Bram an Scathach den Coille."

The man lifted a hand in one last farewell to his family, then marched head high through the doors of the departure lounge to where two Federal marshals waited. With a silent swoosh that echoed in hollow mockery, the doors closed and they disappeared from sight.

Ethan had never been so glad of Sarwenna's presence. His wife knew when to keep silent, he discovered, clinging tightly to his hand as they walked to the back of the viewing lounge. Not a single den Coille moved, all of them staring out the large windows and tracking the movement of the passengers along the corridor to appear one last time as they entered the shuttle to take them out to the spaceship: young Aigherach, Cumchdach, Ceart, Samhchair, Fee clinging to Caleb's arm, Bram and Scathach den Coille, all stared intently at that distant cluster of specks as the passengers boarded. One paused at the ship door, then he moved inside and a sigh fractured the lounge.

The man had nearly caused their deaths, but Ethan remembered his fiery courage in prison, the ruthless anger that had refused to back down from their captors. Did Seolta deliberately try to have him and Sarwenna killed? No, but did he realise the risk of it?

Ethan didn't want to know.

In a roar of rocketry, the ship began to lift. The den Coilles stayed where they were but Ethan gave his brother Caleb a taut smile, then turned back to his wife.

"Time to go home, boss man," said the woman who had come to be Ethan's life. "You've still got a company to save and I've got a taskforce demanding answers."

Yes, they did.

Together, they walked out of the building.

Thank you for reading TAKEN. I hope you enjoyed Ethan's story as much as I enjoyed creating it. Please consider posting a review on your favourite ebook site. I appreciate all honest reviews.

Look out for EXILE, the next story in the Arcadia series. Seolta den Coille let anger rule him and lost everything because of it. He's been given one chance to make amends: go into exile and track down the off-world interests who tried to use Arcadia's problems to steal control of its most powerful assets. If he succeeds, maybe he just might be allowed to return home one day.

For advance notice of new releases, including Seolta's story, and special subscriber extras, sign up for my newsletter at:

www.marybrockjones.com

ACKNOWLEDGEMENTS

With thanks to all those who have helped me bring "Torn" to reality. Firstly to my amazing and hugely knowledgeable editor, Laura Daniel—any remaining errors are due to my stubbornness—and to Louise for her very helpful insights. To Amygdala Designs for my lovely cover. To Victoria who first set me on the right path to formatting. And to my fellow writers at SpecFicNZ, RWNZ and RWA, particularly the Auckland specficers and RWNZers: thank you for your generosity, your never-ending support, the laughter and the mutual moans, but most of all for helping me to believe I can do this!

Biggest thanks of all go to my family. To my parents, for raising me in a house full of books, taking us to libraries and taking it for granted that we would all get an education and be able to think for ourselves; to my sons who are always proud of what I do even when it seems weird to them; and most of all to my husband who is always there for me, even though I'm far away in my own world more often than not. Thank you all for your acceptance, for everything you've taught me over the years, and for the smiles on your faces when I really need them.